Three Women in Paradise

Other works by Victoria Avilan:

The Art of Peeling an Orange

A Small Country about to Vanish

My Delicious Life

Three Women in Paradise

a novel

Victoria Avilan

Shaggy Dog Stories

For Tracey who walks by my side

Pleasure and Pain 13

Inferno   139

Purgatory 229

The author gratefully acknowledges the following people for their support in the writing of this book: Tracey Dodd, T.T.Thomas, Gena Ratcliff, editor Beth Hill, Salem West, Ann McMan, Suzie Carr, Melissa Walker, Elizabeth Hodge and my dear mother Miryam Levy for *soul-baring*, the cover image.

There is a theory which states that if ever anyone discovers exactly what the Universe is for and why it is here, it will instantly disappear and be replaced by something even more bizarre and inexplicable. There is another theory which states that this has already happened.—Douglas Adams

Pleasure and Pain

…the closer a thing comes to its perfection,
more keen will be its pleasure or its pain.

The Divine Comedy, Dante Alighieri

i. Virgil

"She's a breathing, living talent," said Virgil, forever fifty years of age and dead before Christ took his first breath. "She's the one."

Beatrice Portinari, twenty-five years old and dead 730 years, sipped her energy drink like she enjoyed it. Her slick midnight hair gave off the minty sweet scent of patchouli when it slipped from its bun and covered her sculpted shoulders. "Can she see you?"

"And hear."

"Even the dead can hear those." She pointed at his Roman sandals and chuckled at her own quip. "Get yourself a pair of sneakers and some jeans. Maybe then more of them will want to see you."

"It's just as well they don't."

He and Beatrice moved among the living, keeping to their own space between the worlds, seeing everything, yet perceived by very few.

A new mission always loomed on the horizon and they constantly searched for the next living candidate.

"I hope you're right about her being *the one*. We don't want another fiasco." Beatrice raised one shapely eyebrow. "Why are you so sure?"

"I feel it in my old Roman bones."

"You felt it in your bones once, long ago in the Colosseum, but *she* turned out to be the hysterical type and dumber than a rock."

He found it funny to hear a woman born so long ago, and dead for an eternity, spouting such a recent cliché. Funny, but not surprising. Beatrice adapted easily.

"Does your wunderkind have a name?"

"Elektra Brooke, but most call her Ellie," he said. "You'll see, the kid is different. She's bright and her memory is solid."

Beatrice shrugged one shoulder. "Okay. So I go check her out now. What then?"

"Don't make a spectacle of yourself," he said. "If you agree with me, we let her learn a few more things, meet the right people. We wait."

"Yes." Her red lips smiled, but her serious dark eyes were all business. "Got to go. Yoga starts in five and they lock the doors."

He raised his cup of coffee in salute. "Here we are, parting again at the Gates of Paradise."

"This hot, sweaty place?" She pushed the glamorous sunglasses up her nose and that simple motion had so much grace. "Inferno, more like."

Virgil stood up and finished his last sip. "Where do you get the stamina?"

"Seven hundred years of daily yoga and this." She drank down her revolting green Energy Boost.

Under the WildWest Hot Yoga sign, she turned back. "I do hope you're right," she said in the sweet voice that had so captured Dante Alighieri more than seven centuries ago.

Virgil stretched his ancient limbs and headed east on Wilshire Boulevard, his sandals clicking on the pavement and his white toga billowing in the evening breeze.

Unlike him, Beatrice thrived on attention. She lived on the edge of being discovered and everything about her said *look at me*. With her shiny hair and her graceful figure in the cropped tank top and the tight yoga pants, she could easily pass for a contemporary fashionista. Dante's beloved resented not being noticed by more admirers as she remained young, vain and obsessed with various fads through the centuries. Despite Virgil's warnings against closeness to the living, the beautiful Beatrice tried her best to form friendships. When people came too near and asked probing questions, she navigated the truth without revealing too much of it.

Where are you from? Florence. *Who are your parents?* They're both dead. *Are you married?* My husband died. *How old are you?* Twenty-five.

She'd never age beyond twenty-five.

What year were you born? Oops, got to go, she'd say, suddenly in a hurry to make a yoga class or a business meeting.

Virgil didn't have to worry about answering questions because no one rushed to befriend a man who wore a dried-up laurel wreath and a white toga. Well, except for Ellie. Ellie was different.

2. The Portrait

On a hot night, I stopped for coffee at the UCLA cafeteria, dripping sweat from my yoga class. A psychedelic ad on the bulletin board caught my attention.

If you like adventure and you want to share my digs, I have a special deal for you. Call Sophie.

Below the ad, a phone number was repeated on paper slivers, some already torn off, the rest dangling like loose upper teeth in a chinless face. I planned to move out of my mother's house and find my own place with rent that would leave me enough money for an occasional hot meal. As I was broke on my ass, I found the *special deal* intriguing, but as a budding sci-fi/fantasy author, I was captured by my weakness—that mention of adventure.

As I pinched off one of the slivers, a hand came from behind my ear and pinched the one next to it. I turned around. My just as sweaty competition smiled her white teeth, annoying me with her perfect figure and that noxious combination of sweat and patchouli.

"Hi, Ellie," she said. How did she know my name? She added, "Ten minutes ago? WildWest Yoga? I heard your name enough times when the teacher kept correcting your pose."

"Right," I said, recognizing her. The teacher hadn't corrected her even once.

"Bea." She offered one hand for a shake while dialing with the other, eyes on her keypad.

I swiftly beat her to it.

"This is Sophie," a perky voice said on my phone.

"My name is Ellie Brooke," I said. "I saw your ad."

"Come up now," she said. "I'm in the high-rise on Wilshire and Gayley, apartment 801."

I headed over right away, but not before giving Bea a *gotcha* smile. She just stood there, looking gorgeous.

A rickety elevator crawled slowly to the eighth floor, so slow, it made me regret any deal before even making one. To my left, I found apartment 801 and tentatively pressed a green eyeball I imagined to be the doorbell. I recoiled at the haunted sound reverberating down the hallway.

A pretty California blonde towered over me at the open door, wearing a wide smile and a man's muscle shirt streaked with blue and yellow paint. Her baggy shorts showcased shapely legs that reached from here to way up there. Her bare feet were splashed with more yellow and some green.

"Halloween is four months away." I pointed at the green eyeball.

"The doorbell's a gift from one of my sitters," she said in a lilting voice. She stretched her arm out as if for a handshake, but instead, her fingertips brushed my long hair. "Oh my God, your hair is perfect Titian red." She let the door slam behind us. "Is Ellie short for anything?"

I hesitated. "Elektra."

"No shit." Her adorable smile was slightly asymmetrical. "What gives?"

"You want an elevator pitch or a synopsis?" I asked.

"Make it short and sweet for now," she said.

"Well, my absent father was into dreadful Strauss operas and my mother was too stoned to give a shit when he named me. Then he fucked off, leaving me with a pretentious name and a lazy mother who does nothing but grow and smoke pot." So used to explaining my name, I recited my curriculum vitae in a single breath.

Sophie whistled. "Awesome. Elektra is deliciously romantic, but you prefer Ellie?"

"Unless you want me to fetch something. My mother soured me on the chore thing." I took a deep breath and mimicked Mama, saying, *"Elektra, mix us some cocktails. Elektra, get me the towel. Ele . . . lektra, what's for dinner?"* In my own voice, I added, "She might as well have named me Cinderella."

I was surprised at my ease of spilling out my great embarrassment to a perfect stranger, but Sophie's relaxed manner was disarming. Like a shot of tequila, she stripped me of my defenses.

She laughed. "Here we fetch our own shit, so Ellie then." She grabbed my hand and pulled me in, measuring me so openly, I felt uncomfortable. "You're incredible," she gushed. "You have it all, great legs, great skin and this mane . . . Do you ever cut it?"

"Never." My face burned.

My red hair had never seen a stylist. Other than the occasional trimming of split ends, I'd let it grow until it reached below my knees. It kept getting caught under me when I sat down and its weight gave me headaches, but vanity ruled. It was my best feature and my trademark. I'd once read somewhere that pins and various doodads could damage the shaft, so I'd mostly wear it in a long braid, knotted a few times at the back of my neck, or simply tied with a soft scarf. For special occasions, I'd become a cliché and let my hair down. Red cascades would stream around my shoulders and down my back. I'd imagine myself as a heroine from my own rich fantasy life, riding the back of a dragon—sometimes a broom—in flowing silk dresses of bottle green or sky blue. In real life, I'd wear green or blue T-shirts to play up the color of my hair.

The sliding doors of the balcony opened to breathtaking views of the 405, currently crawling in both directions in the dying daylight. To the right of the freeway, the spread of the UCLA campus, with its majestic old buildings and green lawns, and farther ahead, the white Getty Center nestled in its cradle of dark mountains.

Floor-to-ceiling charcoal sketches of nude bodies overwhelmed the living room walls.

"Is this your art?" I asked.

"Mostly studies from my life drawing class, but I still have a lot to learn."

It wasn't a calm space. The chaos of an artist's studio had its charms, but as I grew up in chaos, I was hoping for serenity in my new place.

"Turn around," she said. I did. "Wow, those beautiful long legs, your dancer's walk... You're really perfect."

Sophie's gushing embarrassed me. I decided to stay the polite course, then get out and never come back. The place was wrong for my needs—too cluttered, really one big mess—and she probably expected me to pay a staggering rent for those city views.

"What am I perfect for?" I asked.

"For the special deal. Isn't that what you're here for?"

"You actually hooked me with *adventure*."

Sophie examined me from all directions, like a sculptor checking her own creation.

"You wow me. I'll do anything to have you sit for me."

"*Whoa*, I'm here for the roommate thing," I said.

"Of course you are."

She roared with healthy laughter. Raw energy burst from her dirty blond hair to the bottom of the bare feet stomping the hardwood. I pitied the neighbors below.

I picked up one of the sketches from the floor. It was a back view of a standing male nude. Another sketch featured the front of the same male. Both drawings contained disturbing distortions.

"Studies for a religious piece called *The Staff of Moses,*" she explained.

I lifted an eyebrow in question.

"This very talented model did much more than sit for me. Let me show you something."

I followed Sophie to her just-as-messy bedroom. A large canvas, angled to catch the bright light from a bare window, portrayed a male nude—backlit by rays from heaven—striding down a mountain, his towering erection leading the way. Sophie's proportions weren't great, but she had a good sense of perspective, depth and color.

"Your ample use of pinks and angelic blues gives it an optimistic quality," I said, a smile curving my lips.

Sophie cocked her head sideways to assess her work. "The painting was commissioned by a gay couple in the Hollywood Hills for a disgusting amount."

"Who commissions a nude religious painting?"

"I don't judge. I give them what they want and take the money." Sophie picked up a paintbrush loaded with blue and corrected the skyline behind her Moses. "I need a new male model for his ass."

"You're showing the front," I said.

"Good point, but I do need an ass model."

Sophie took Moses off the easel and underneath, resting on the same easel, already dry, was a portrait of a woman who bore an uncanny resemblance to Ms. Angie. She was the first woman I'd ever loved and lost in a way that had scarred me for good.

"How did you...*Where* did you?" My voice was muffled in my ears and the air was suddenly stuffy. Heavy. "How do you know this woman?"

"Beautiful, isn't she?" Sophie asked. "I doodle my classmates and teachers and this one came out so good, I expanded it to canvas and—what's wrong?"

"That resemblance . . . Some air, please . . . " I needed to breathe. Sophie rushed to the window and opened it. I said, "I thought she was...well, dead."

"Gina Caldwell is very much alive and still teaching medieval poetry." Wearing a tragic face, Sophie recited in a gravelly voice, "The double grief of a lost bliss is to recall its happy hour in pain." And even that voice...

"*Inferno*, canto five," I said, my vision clearing up. My breathing eased, but not my mind. My mind was racing.

Angie Mead, alive and teaching?

"Wow," Sophie said, impressed. She hopped to the kitchen and returned with a bottle of cold water. "How do you know Dante so well?"

"I read the book and I have so many questions." About this *Gina Caldwell*, not the *Inferno*.

I couldn't take my eyes off the painting. Ms. Angie's image had been imprinted on my heart, and here she was in full color—the short golden hair, the warm eyes following me, the full red lips about to smile.

Back in the living room, Sophie gestured to the couch. "Make yourself comfortable."

I scanned the cluttered living room but couldn't find a clear horizontal surface.

"Ah, sorry." She swiped her arm on the drab couch, and a stack of drawing papers with more nude charcoals flew to the carpet, piling on top of more piles. She asked, "How do you like it here?"

"I like it." I hesitated. How do you tell someone they're too messy for you? "But I shouldn't be wasting your time. I can't afford such a nice place—"

"Sit for me and I'll lower your rent by a lot."

"Is this the adventure you promised?"

"And the deal. My Aunt Lisa owns this place and she charges me half the going rent for the area."

Her aunt probably wasn't aware of what Sophie had done with the place, but then, maybe the mess was an improvement on Aunt Lisa.

My mind kept going back to the portrait in the bedroom. I had to know if Angie Mead was alive. I just had to know. I'd add that class to my summer quarter list first thing tomorrow morning.

I said, "Tell me more about yourself."

"I'm an art student." Sophie futzed about in the open kitchen. "I paint shit that sells and lowbrow sweet nothings I call Nouveau Kitsch. I sell my work to people who consider art any *superficious* object that makes them happy. That helps pay the rent and my tuition."

"Superficial," I corrected.

"What?" she called from the kitchen.

"The word you want is *superficial.*"

"Thanks. I always mess up the big words." She dropped a spoon on the floor and cursed. "I paint in my bedroom, but when I have a sitter or work a particularly large canvas, I spill into the living room, where I get the best light. You may come home to a naked man or woman posing on the couch—"

I jumped up and eyed the couch, looking for telltale stains.

Sophie half scoffed, half laughed at my reaction. "No worries. I cover it with rich brocade or shiny fabrics before they pose. Also, I love to fuck and I'm very loud."

"Now *you* wow *me.*" It was my turn to laugh. "That wasn't in your ad."

Over the noise of the ice-crushing blender, Sophie yelled, "I also eat a lot and I don't gain weight. It's hereditary."

"Now I hate you," I yelled back. I had my weight battles, although I was never fat.

From my seat in the living room, I could see the kitchen's ceiling. It had been sprayed red and pink. "Do you paint in the kitchen?"

"What?"

I pointed when she turned to me.

"Ah, the blender's cover doesn't seal well." Sophie fumbled inside a cabinet. "I barely clean, but this morning I did, and I improvise fairly good meals and cocktails any time, day or night. Can I offer you a bowl of chili con carne?"

"Sure," I said. "You're starting to grow on me."

She stomped into the living room in her booming bare feet, carrying two frosted glasses filled with pink slush and decorated with tiny green umbrellas. I promised myself to ignore lipstick smudges.

"I may not be the poster-child roommate, but I mix the meanest margaritas from any frozen fruit, including oranges and grapes."

"Is this your defense for not being the poster child?"

"This is the pineapple of my creation."

"Mmm." The heavenly slush gave me an immediate ice-cream headache, but I was compelled to correct that word. "Pinnacle."

"What?" she asked.

"The *pinnacle* of my creation."

"Thanks again." She kept touching her left forearm, where four angry red scars in the shape of fingernails marred the otherwise smooth skin.

"Did you have a fight with your last roomie?" I asked. That was probably something I needed to know.

"Yes. She died," Sophie said quietly, and I feared that she was telling the truth.

"What happened?"

Sophie's forehead creased. "Long story." Immediately she smiled. "Relax, I didn't kill her."

I was far from relaxed. To ease my strong discomfort, I said, "Well, I'm not exactly a great prize. I listen to opera when I work."

"I don't mind opera," Sophie said. "I love Bocelli and Il Divo and did you hear that little girl on *American Idol*—"

"Nothing so popular," I said. "I have an old gramophone. I play old recordings of famous and not-so-famous singers."

Sophie seemed interested, so I kept on about my passion longer than I should have. "Dead sopranos like Callas, Schwarzkopf, Anna Moffo and Rosa Ponselle..."

When her eyes finally glazed over, I switched subjects. "I study creative writing. A few of my short stories were published in magazines, but I make ends meet by editing and formatting manuscripts for my friends and their friends. When I have enough material, I'll write a novel."

"Oh, baby, I can supply you with material," she said. Then she pointed with her thumb toward her bedroom, where the portrait rested on its easel. "Sign up for her night classes. We can walk together and you'll tell me your story. There's a story here, right?"

"Maybe I will," I said. If I chose to tell the story of Angie Mead to anyone, it would be easy to tell Sophie.

"Be my roommate and we'll help each other."

My part of the rent was a steal, but what swayed my decision to an emphatic *yes* was the spectacular city view from my bedroom window, the wraparound recessed bookshelves and a full en suite bathroom. I needed my own shower, if only for the lengthy ceremony of washing my high-maintenance hair the way some laundered their delicate lingerie.

I agreed to sit for Sophie. Two bowls of mean chili and a second round of cocktails sealed the deal between us. We became roommates.

3. The Prophet's Ass

"Last round." I leaned against the shaky elevator wall, wiped the sweat off my forehead and smiled up at George. It was the end of moving day, mid-June and the hottest week of the year in Westwood, California.

George had a bushy caveman beard, a saintly calm temper and a big black pickup he used to help his friends move. We had dated for a while before I'd discovered that women were more fun.

"Still the best legs west of the Hollywood sign." He winked. "I'd take you back in a heartbeat."

"Thank you for that," I said, meaning it. George always made me feel beautiful and noticed.

Colorful book covers peeked from the gap in the hastily packed box between us. We were tired and hungry from a long day of schlepping stuff from my mother's house into his truck, then up the elevator to the eighth floor and into my new shared digs with the city views and the private bathroom. I might have agreed to a few dollars more in rent just for that bathroom. And it was far enough out of the way that Sophie's models and guests weren't likely to wander in.

A whistle of appreciation came from the living room as we stepped into the apartment, carrying the last boxes. Sophie was home.

"You'll be the prophet's ass!" She circled George, measuring him up and down and sideways, the way she had the first time she saw me. "I need you," she said.

His bushy eyebrows lifted toward his hairline. "What, no hello, no introduction?"

"She means that literally you can be her prophet's ass." I rolled my eyes and added, "That's Sophie's way of asking you to be her nude model."

"Can I shower first and have some lunch?" he asked.

While Sophie ordered Thai food and George inaugurated my shower, I found a wall socket for my surge protector and immediately plugged in my phone, iPad and laptop. My compulsion to always have my gadgets fully charged was born out of a long-ago night that I'd reserved for study. A power outage and depleted devices left me unprepared for the next day's finals.

I gently dusted my old gramophone and stroked its copper horn and the famous *His Master's Voice* insignia. The thing wasn't worth much, but it still played the best sound. I found a place for it on the lowest shelf and, next to it, I stacked my carefully collected LP treasures, including Callas in her 1952 *Norma* and the Ponselle sisters in their incredible 1932 *Gioconda*.

As I unpacked bed linens with a small floral design, I caught a glimpse of the messy living room through the open door. Here, away from my mother's house, the mess didn't matter, because it wasn't mine to clean up.

My mother completely relied on me to care for her, not due to a disability, but because she wouldn't lift a finger to do anything for herself. Camille had a driver's license and a car, yet she refused to drive. She had a computer, but she wouldn't learn how to use it. My healthy fifty-year-old mother could thrive, yet she'd sit all day with her just-as-useless and stoned friends, her feet up on the coffee table, a cocktail in one hand and a joint in the other.

Out of necessity, I could fix anything, including the car and simple plumbing issues. As I juggled schoolwork, writing, car maintenance and household chores, I tired of her helplessness. I cringed at the sound of that voice, old before its time, calling me by my often garbled full name and demanding that I get her this or that or both.

Rather than argue, I'd stop whatever I was doing to run her errands. I figured that if I moved out, Camille would have no choice but to sober up and take care of herself. My dreams for the future did not include cleaning my mother's toilet. This new room with the fabulous cityscapes would become my sanctuary, and I'd finally write at least that one novel I knew I had in me.

"What will I do without you?" an anxious Camille had asked when I told her I was moving out.

"I'm only a few streets and a phone call away," I'd said.

I straightened up my books on the shelves, and even as I envisioned hysterical calls waking me at night, my phone rang with Wagner's "Ride of the Valkyrie"—Camille needing to know how to turn on the stove. My excitement at having found a new apartment cooled. Would she be okay?

In the shower, George whistled the Wagner to himself.

I pulled the next box close. Books. An avid sci-fi/fantasy geek, I kept my books for good. I took my time opening the box, smelling each well-loved paperback by Asimov, Le Guin and Zelazny, then arranging them on the shelves in alphabetical order. My sweetest dream was to one day add my own novel somewhere between Ray Bradbury and Orson Scott Card.

The Divine Comedy by Dante Alighieri came out of the box, battered and dog-eared with my multiple yellow highlights.

I caressed the cover of my prized possession, a first edition of Virginia Woolf's *A Letter to a Young Poet*. I bought it online for thirty bucks from someone who didn't appreciate its value. The yellowing cover had a round coffee stain in the middle of

Vanessa Bell's illustration. The stain was probably made by the boor who used the book as a coaster, but I preferred to imagine it had been made by Woolf's first cup of coffee on the morning she started *Orlando*.

George stepped out of the steamy shower wrapped in the big blue towel I'd left for him.

"If it isn't the Birth of Venus," I said.

"What's with your new roommate?" he whispered. "Does she really want me as a model, or does she want to fuck?"

"Beats me." I shrugged. "She asked me to sit for her, so clue me in."

When the food arrived, we quickly ate and then I resumed unpacking. While arranging my folded underwear, my old friend and my new friend discussed couch positions like college buddies from long ago.

I was madly in love with my new bedroom: the built-in shelves, the hardwood floor, the city and mountain views. I was home.

By the end of June, Sophie's affair with George—yes, their few modeling sessions ended with a quick roll in the hay—was history, and I felt like I'd known her my entire life.

Sophie was loud. Her barefooted thuds shook the floor, her cocktail blender was the noisy kind, and when she made love, I could hear her across two walls. But she'd kiss and tell, which was a gold mine for a wannabe novelist who was a sucker for stories.

She would brag about her left handedness. "Like Leonardo da Vinci. I learned *chiaroscuro* from his work. See how I achieve light and shade, contrast and volume, by hatching from top left to bottom right? And see how…"

I didn't always listen when she prattled on about technique, but I enjoyed her endearing lopsided smile and the excited glint in her eyes.

"…and Leonardo wrote in his mirror script that all boundaries should be blurred in painting like in nature. See how I did it? The details blur as the objects recede. That's what he called *sfumato*, which means a smoke effect, and see how colors are more brilliant as they get closer to the eye..."

We both had fixations. My scratchy recordings of dead opera divas surely made her head spin, but she never complained or asked me to take it down a notch. Once, when I played a certain aria from *La Gioconda,* Sophie stood by my side, a loaded paintbrush between her teeth dripping red paint, like blood, on my arm.

"Sorry, sorry." She wiped it off, making it worse by smearing it on my white shirt. "That last low note is incredible," she said, tears in her eyes.

So I let her talk about technique.

Although her life drawing was no da Vinci, she had an excellent sense of color and a special feel for *chiaroscuro* and *sfumato.* She'd mix me a noisy cocktail and had me pose for a long time, yet I didn't get bored as she regaled me with saucy tales.

"Did I say something funny?" She stopped her movement, paintbrush paused over her canvas.

"I'm digging up my inner *Mona Lisa,*" I said, keeping still for her.

"I hope this one doesn't take four years," she said. "I need to pay the bills."

"Four years?" I asked, amazed. "He took *four years* to paint the *Mona Lisa?*"

"Maybe twelve years and four years just to paint her lips." Sophie winced, unsure. "She practically killed him."

Sophie would accompany me to my mother's when I got a call—always at night—about a beeping smoke alarm or a rat Camille thought she saw in the kitchen. When I asked about her family, Sophie changed the subject. I knew not to pry.

Every now and then, when Sophie wasn't home, I'd sneak into her bedroom to steal a glance at the portrait, stalk it as I had once stalked the woman whose image it represented, touch it as I had once wanted to touch *her*. I would soon sit in her classroom again, a whole different classroom, grown up but with my memories of her still alive and breathing.

The first week of the summer quarter arrived, another heat wave and nighttime poetry of the Middle Ages.

On the third Monday in September, Dr. Gina Caldwell stepped her black stilettos into a packed auditorium. "I'm happy to see so many young faces willing to sacrifice two evenings a week for a trip to the afterlife," she said, her fingers brushing back her golden hair as she surveyed her crowd.

That voice.

Yanked back years, I seized my seat's armrests. That heart-shaped face. That tight black suit, too small to confine her splendor. Those long legs...

"As predicted by one of the scholars," Dr. Caldwell continued in that raspy voice, "when we arrived at the twenty-first century, Dante was waiting for us."

Right. Angie Mead was alive, speaking and breathing, while I was gasping for air.

"What's wrong?" Sophie whispered.

I couldn't answer with the vomit filling my mouth. I bolted down the auditorium, the concerned stares of my fellow students on me. In the ladies room, I doubled over a bleached white toilet bowl and puked everything I'd eaten since the day *she* had disappeared, leaving me heartbroken and alone.

4. The Mythological Teacher

I was eleven when I fell desperately in love with Ms. Angie Mead, my English teacher. I'd never before met anyone like her, kind when she corrected us, always warm and sunny. She made us read our essays out loud and when someone proved particularly clever, their reward was one of the spontaneous hugs she gave freely, like candy on Halloween. Her genuine joy at our childish humor played like music with her hearty laughter.

Her business suits were too tight and the top button of her white blouse was always open, allowing a glimpse of magnificence. Her too short skirts exposed the full length of her strong legs and her feet clicked away in high heels.

A clear vase of fresh aromatic roses decorated her desk. As she lived in a high-rise with no space for a garden, Ms. Angie lent her green thumbs to the school. With the help of a hired team, she turned an abandoned field of dry brush between two buildings from an eyesore into a heavenly rose garden, complete with dramatic arches and white trellises on which grew climbing vines of hybrid tea varieties. Narrow pathways, lined with colorful roses, led nowhere and into each other.

When the gardening team was done planting, one man remained with the school, an eccentric named Virgil, who carried out various odd jobs, worked the rose garden and mostly sat on his favorite bench and smoked the pot he grew in one of the flowerbeds.

"Weed and roses love each other," he once told me in that strange accent I couldn't place and was too embarrassed to ask about.

Summer or winter, he wore a Roman toga and a dry laurel wreath on his thick curls. His approach echoed loudly and involved the metal clicking of his hobnailed sandals.

"They're called *caligae*," he'd brag. "Still perfectly comfortable after two thousand years."

I was convinced he played up his own eccentricity for some reason. We became fast friends. On my lunch breaks, I'd sit next to him on the bench, and surrounded by roses, we'd discuss ancient poetry. When he recited lines from the *Aeneid* or from Dante's *Inferno*, I told him he should be teaching us English instead of working odd jobs.

"There are no odd jobs," he said. "Any job done right is poetry."

Except for the yellow Donald Duck watch that kept rolling around his thin wrist, he managed a good imitation of the ancient Roman poet. One time, when I reached for it, he recoiled.

"Okay," I said, thinking I understood.

"Nothing personal," he explained.

"On the spectrum?" I asked. Some kids in the special class freaked out when you touched them.

"Something like that," he said. "Show me what she's got you working on today."

While he read my page, I glued my gaze to his yellow watch. The hands were going backwards.

"Good, Ellie. You definitely have the stuff."

That comment from him meant so much to me. I kept reminding myself of it for years whenever I had doubts.

Together, Virgil and Ms. Angie took care of the roses, allowing them the room to grow wild, like spoiled children. Heads of roses invaded the classroom through the window and their potent fragrance sweetened the air.

The garden became the school's pride and joy. The bushes provided protection, hiding you well when you needed that heart to heart with your best friend or a decent solitary cry. Older students returned after school to make out on the ornamental benches.

On sunny days, Ms. Angie conducted her classes out in the fresh air as a special treat. She'd change her high heels for black galoshes—still managing high style—and we'd all wear thick gloves. Hers were mouth-puckering lime green. We helped her weed and deadhead while she gave funny gardening tips such as "plant green side up" and "be careful not to hurt the faeries." We'd make up *roses are red, violets are blue* jokes. Some were pretty raunchy.

She'd point at one of us and say, "Tell a story and make it good." She didn't limit the subject or the word choice, as long as we used the correct grammar. "Our language includes all vocabulary. There are no bad words, only bad people."

"Ms. Angie is a princess," said a girl who loved Disney films.

"She's a mythological teacher," piped in an enamored boy named Pete.

"She's a wild rose," Michael said.

We loved her.

As we sat on the benches, I was fascinated by the quick movements of her hands in those lime-green gardening gloves.

"The right word could save a life," she said. "That same word in the wrong context could destroy entire civilizations. Look what happened to the dinosaurs."

She leaned forward and we followed suit, eager to know what single word had wiped the great dinosaurs off the face of the earth.

"Busted!" she said, following her *gotcha* with that lively laugh that gave me goose bumps. She spread her arms, inviting us to surround her in a group cuddle. Clinging to her like a climbing vine, I breathed in her divine scent and imagined that her DNA was linked with the roses.

She rested a hand on my head and said, "Your hair is pretty."

Done for, doomed, mortally in love, I closed my eyes and pretended none of my classmates were there and this most divine creature was mine alone. In her arms, I was highly aware of a new and pleasant longing I couldn't yet understand. Then and there, I'd decided to never cut my hair and to let it grow long and lush, just for her eyes.

As I was starved for affection, I depended on Ms. Angie's attention the way others depended on school lunches.

I became infatuated with the woman who was the complete opposite of my skinny, stoned and indifferent mother. I envied Lucy, her adopted daughter who had Down Syndrome. She wasn't perfect, but she had after-hours access to warm and kind Ms. Angie, who, unlike my mother, would never taunt her. I was sure Ms. Angie never said, "I'll give you a real reason to cry if you don't stop right now."

My classmate, Corinne, wasn't very interesting, but when I found out she lived in a high rise next door to Ms. Angie, I was on her like pink on roses. I asked Corrine to help me with my math homework and she was happy to do so. I started spending every afternoon until late evening in her apartment for a chance to stalk my beloved. I once heard Corinne's mother whispering, "Doesn't this girl have a home?" I didn't care.

At my insistence, Corinne and I did our homework out on the balcony. It was catty-cornered to Ms. Angie's balcony, giving me a direct view into her apartment.

I'd balance on the thin railing of the sixth floor, leaning as far back as possible without toppling over. I longed to watch her eating dinner, enjoying TV with her family or engaged in another benign activity. Mostly, I wanted to become a fly on the ceiling above her bed and watch her sleep.

I kept my infatuation a secret, certain I'd die of shame if anyone found out about it.

Once, as I sat on the railing, straining to see the forbidden, the curtain blew into Ms. Angie's living room and there she was in a sloppy house dress, as if having just woken up from a nap.

I froze on my perch, and from sheer surprise, was nearly knocked six stories down to my death. At the sound of my yelp, she turned in my direction. Had she seen me? When I regained my balance, she was gone.

"Hey, be careful," an oblivious Corrine said, face buried in her homework. "Here, solve this one for me."

The next day, in class, Ms. Angie approached me. "Come and see me after class," she said in a stern voice. "I need to talk to you."

My breathing quickened. What did she want?

When I followed her to the garden, the sky was light blue. I'll never forget the powerful fragrance of those roses as Ms. Angie, dressed in white and framed by a white arch of some pink hardy variety, towered over me in splendor.

She cupped one perfect bud between two long fingers, then looked at me, her eyes austere. "I can see you peeking through my windows, Elektra. This can't go on."

The trees turned a murky shade of green, and around me, rosebuds seemed to wilt on their stems as my world faded to gray. I'd been found out. She saw me, and now my life was over because my beloved hated me. I'd be scolded, shamed and hung out to dry before the whole school. I'd be in the papers, like that crazed Hollywood fan who was arrested for breaking into the bedroom of her adored movie star and sleeping in his bed.

Ms. Angie continued in her low, gravelly voice. "What you're doing is dangerous. What if you fell?"

Then I'd die for you, I thought.

"This is just between us, Elektra, but if your behavior doesn't stop, I'll have to involve the principal and your mother."

At eleven, I didn't know enough to apologize or to make up some lie.

"Do you understand?" she asked, unaware of my internal destruction.

When I nodded, she left me sitting there. Then I noticed Virgil on the other end of the bench, smoking away, obviously having been there the whole time. He put his finger to his lips, either promising not to spill my secrets or asking me not to betray his little pot garden to Ms. Angie.

I shared the conversation only with my diary, writing it as a form of confession to a living, breathing friend. It was comforting to pretend someone would read my words without judging.

Poor Corinne didn't understand why I stopped coming over when I needed help with math more than ever. It was all or nothing, and I made sure to stay as far as possible from Ms. Angie. Where before I'd run to greet her in the hallway, I now turned and walked in the opposite direction or sneaked into the nearest open door to avoid her.

My love for her grew more complex, branching out like a fern in the darkness of my injured soul. My desire for closeness flamed bright in shades of pink, baby blues and milky white. I was a lost little girl, carrying alone the secret of forbidden love.

One day, instead of heading home after school, I sat on the hidden bench in the garden, and there she was in black rubber boots, clipping roses for her desk.

She noticed me and froze, strangely tragic in the black she wore that day and with those lime-green gloves.

She studied me with a tilt of her head. "Are you unwell, Elektra?"

I should have told her the truth of my desperate love, but I was struck dumb, rendered mute by the sacred vision of her devastating beauty.

"Elektra." Her eyes were sad. "What you feel for me…"

Thunder boomed. A zigzag of rich red lightning painted the sky the exact shade of the perfect rosebud she held in front of her chest. A crimson sky? I reached one hand up, for what looked like thick silk that hung in swirls and made the air heavy.

But, what was she going to say next?

The heavens ripped open and fierce rain drenched me like ocean waves from above and below and from inside my soul. Untouched by it all, Ms. Angie remained very still. Then she turned fuzzy around the edges, lost her depth, and washed into the soil like a mural drawn in chalk.

5. Red Sky

"Where are you?" I whispered in great fear. Nothing was left of her.

I looked down, to where the cut roses had started to wash away. I revolved in a circle, I even looked up, but in the frantic storm, I couldn't see past my nose. I ran my hand on the ground at the spot that had swallowed her, but nothing remained. My throat choked. Ms. Angie was gone.

Somehow I found my bike, and with my heart beating wildly, rode home. My mother and her rowdy friends were getting high and trashing the living room. For once, I was happy that she barely ever noticed me, only this time she did.

"Better put a smile on it, Ele... lektra." Not for the first time, she garbled my name. "Crying gives you ugly blotches and a streak on your upper lip."

"I don't give a shit, mo... mother," I mocked. A devilish new force prompted me to add, "You're not worth her little finger."

"What d'you say?" She tried to stand up and impose her authority but, unsteady on her feet, fell back to the couch.

"Not one tiny shit," I repeated, tears pouring like the rain down my hot cheeks.

One of her friends said, "Hey, Camille, don't be mean to the kid." As I locked my bedroom door, I heard them laughing that drunk laugh I so hated.

A big towel tight around me, I tried to explain to my diary what had just happened, but I knew no explanation. How could a full-grown person wash like dust into the earth?

Such things didn't happen, did they?

Eyes dripping tears, I fell asleep to the sound of cackling laughter and clinking glasses. The last moment before sleep took over, a crazy thought popped into my head. I was seeing people washing into the earth, because my mother and her friends polluted the air with their smoke and I was inhaling it second-hand.

The next morning the sky was blue again. Back in school, my classmates talked about the red rain. Then I was shocked—horrified—to find a field of dry yellow shrubs where thriving roses had blossomed. It was as if the powerful storm had wiped out all traces of Ms. Angie's magical garden, and in its place, sowed dandelions and weeds.

"Did the red rain destroy it all?" I asked no one in particular.

"Destroy what?" Dana asked.

"The roses," I squeaky whispered. "Where are Ms. Angie's roses?"

My classmates gawked like I'd lost my mind.

"Ms. Angie's rose garden is gone," I repeated. "What happened?"

Dana laughed. "Do you think this is the White House, Mrs. President?"

"Who's Ms. Angie?" Pete asked.

"The mythological teacher, asshole. That's what you called her." I was in tears.

They turned away from me—probably because of the ugly blotches and that one streak on my upper lip. I wanted to run home and never come back to that ungrateful place, but home wasn't a comforting option. I couldn't face my mother and her hangover morning.

In the girls' bathroom, I splashed cold water on my face and waited for the blotches to fade. I felt so lonely, so confused.

An excited Corrine met me in the hallway, her feathery hair windswept, just like models on magazine covers. "Did you see the color of the sky last night?" she asked. "And that rain was awesome—"

"What's with you, Corrine?" I lost my patience. "Yes, the sky was red and the rain was awesome. I saw that."

"In the news they called it biblical blood rain," she said, "but the rain itself wasn't red, was it?"

"No. But what happened to Ms. Angie's rose garden?"

"Ms. Angie who?" she asked.

"Stop being stupid," I cried.

Two girls coming out of the stalls hurried around me and out the door.

"Our teacher," I whispered. "Your neighbor, Ms. Angie."

"I don't know anyone by that name, and what do you mean by a rose garden in this dump of a school? Are you kidding me? They won't even let us have a playground."

What the hell is going on here? I thought, then said, "Did you all decide to mess with me this morning?"

Corrine said, "Come on, we're late."

She linked her arm with mine and dragged me into the classroom.

I sat unmoving among my classmates, expecting the clicking of Ms. Angie's high heels at the door, but when it finally opened, a man I'd never before seen marched in. Without an explanation, he started teaching what I assumed to be English grammar, but I couldn't understand a word he was saying.

I watched my classmates. *No one* seemed upset at Ms. Angie's replacement.

While the new teacher droned on, videos of the previous night played in my head. I had a crazy feeling that Ms. Angie's disappearance was somehow connected to the red rain.

In my mental replay of those moments, I didn't hop on my bike, but instead searched for and found her. There in the storm, I bravely disclosed my unnatural love for her, my hopes, my fantasies. She lowered her eyebrows in disgust and said I was a revolting little shit and to get away from her. She told my mother, the principal, the school psychologist, but her anger kept her in my world.

Little Lucy was now motherless because of my cowardice.

I ran out of the classroom and slid to the floor, my back against the wall. Bare legs in colorful sneakers walked back and forth, but I searched for one pair only, long white legs in elegant heels...

I hid my face between my knees. Then the tears started again because I knew deep in my heart that she'd never be back. She once said we were defined by the words we used and the sentences we phrased. If that was true, she'd by now become the subatomic particles of phrases, words and letters, broken down and washed into the soil, and there was no coming back from that.

In my head, I heard my mother's slurred voice say, *Put a smile on it*, but my smiles dried up. I'd never stop crying, and I couldn't go home because crying wasn't allowed in my world, and tears kept filling my eyes and overflowing and blotching my cheeks red and ugly.

Corrine sat next to me. "Get a grip, Ellie."

I gagged on a whiff of her armpit when she half-assed hugged my shoulders. More than ever, I wanted Angie's pleasant fragrance and both her arms pressing me to her warmth and softness.

"I don't know why you're all so mean and playing tricks on me and making me ugly cry."

"You're always beautiful—"

"Where is she?" My voice cracked. "Where's her garden? I don't get it. Am I going nuts?"

"I have no idea what you're talking about, so maybe you are," Corrine said. "Like Sally that time when she kept talking to her imaginary friend and her mom and dad sent her to the doc. Remember?"

"Ms. Angie is real," I said. "And that doc made Sally totally cray-cray."

"True," Corrine said. "Forget the doctors, but seriously, no garden. The weeds were there yesterday same as today and the week before that. There's no Angie anywhere in the school. Let's go look at the poster."

I got up because I didn't want to smell the old dried up sweat of her armpit anymore. A poster of teachers' heads—safely behind glass—decorated the hallway. Before the red storm, Angie's face had been at the center of the display. Now, she was missing from the poster altogether.

"Angie Mead used to be right here." I pointed at the spot between Ms. Madden and Mr. Norris and the desolation of her nonexistence shot from my fingertip straight to the hole in my heart.

"Okay... Hey, my mom's making your favorite chocolate cake. Come over for homework."

"Sure," I said, hoping to get a chance to check on Ms. Angie's apartment from Corrine's balcony. I didn't care if Angie saw me, and I rather hoped she would.

We had to get through the rest of the day first, and the day kept hurling puzzling disasters at me and one calamity after another.

When I couldn't find my set of colorful pens, those Ms. Angie made us use for special projects, I turned to Corrine. "Can I borrow your yellow felt tip pen?"

"What the hell is felt tip?" Corrine asked.

I stopped prodding for answers because the whole class was obviously playing dirty tricks on me. They'd somehow found out about my stalking love for Ms. Angie. Later they were going to get together at the gym and make fun of me. I wasn't going to give them the satisfaction of falling for it any further. I kept sneaking glances out the open window, expecting a wild rose to peek in.

On the railings of Corrine's balcony, I strained to see into Ms. Angie's place. A man's laughter rose up from inside the cracked-open glass doors, followed by a woman's shrill voice that sounded nothing like Angie's.

It seemed she meant nothing even to her husband, who had some girlfriend on the side to keep him happy. His wife was gone only a day and he wasn't even out looking for her. Did he pay someone to make her disappear, like in those mob movies Mama and her friends liked to watch?

I never again mentioned Angie Mead, not to my friends, not to my mother. I was angry with my classmates for acting as if she'd never been our teacher. I blamed myself and mostly I was insulted on her behalf. It was ironic how I—the one she hated—was the only one left to remember her. In a way, it was fitting because I'd learned the word *irony* from her, which was even more confusing.

But Virgil also remembered. He continued to perform various jobs for the school—cleaning floors and windows, changing light bulbs and being ignored by everyone but me. While carrying out his duties, he moved about in his own world, living his separate life. His knowing looks told me that he alone understood my sorrow.

One day, months later, Corrine and I walked our bikes in the street, licking vanilla ice cream cones because my favorite blackberry flavor also went missing from the world. Nobody remembered *it* either. I was pretty sure I couldn't have imagined something that tasted as sweet and yummy as blackberry ice cream, so I didn't try to figure out how I remembered— how I could taste—something that no one else had ever heard of. Anyway, we spotted Peter, Angie's husband, with little Lucy and another woman. Lucy called her Mommy.

"Who's she?" I asked.

"You know her," Corrine said. "Lucy from the slow class lives next door to me."

"I know Lucy, but who's the woman who replaced Ms. Angie?"

"These are Lucy's adoptive mom and dad . . ." Corrine frowned at me, both hands on her red bike. "Why, why are you going on about some Angie again?"

"Why don't you know her?" I yelled in my frustration. "How come no one remembers her and her beautiful roses?"

Corrine's hair blew in the wind. "What's this new obsession of yours about roses and blackberry ice cream and about those pens and—"

"It's *with*, not *about*," I said in anger. This thing I learned from Ms. Angie about pointing out the correct word became my way of dealing with stupid people. Corrine seemed puzzled when I explained, "Obsession *with* not *about* roses."

"Maybe you should see a doctor about that movie in your head that stars some woman that doesn't exist *and* your sudden need to correct people when they speak."

I raised my arms in surrender. "I have to go."

"What about our homework?"

"Forget homework."

Distraught, I rode to the field of thorns and dandelions within the school. I sat on a big rock among tall weeds in the approximate spot I'd last seen her wearing black, a sad smile and those lime-green gardening gloves.

Elektra, what you're feeling . . .

She had spoken her last words to me, yet what else was she going to say? I searched the ground for the roses she had cut—they'd be wilted and dried up by now. Then Virgil approached, his steps echoing in my ears as if coming from inside an invisible metal tube.

"You miss her," he said.

"So much." My eyes started dripping. "The sky turned red and she was gone, and she took the roses with her and felt tip pens and blackberry ice cream. Her students and her family forgot her, everyone but you and me, and I don't even have a photo to remember her by."

"You'll never forget her." He nodded with understanding. "You are *the one*."

"*The one* what?"

"The one who'll never forget."

"You know," I said. "When I need guidance, I ask myself *what would Angie Mead do?*"

"Yes," he said, and even though he agreed with me, I thought he meant something else altogether.

I sniffed. "You don't think I'm crazy?"

"Not at all." Then *sotto voce*, he recited, "*Out of the tear-drenched land the wind arose which blasted forth into a reddish light, knocking my senses out of me completely.*"

"Why always poetry?" My voice was tear drenched, like the ground in the poem.

"Dante also grieved for his one and only love."

"Will she ever be back?" I asked the universe more than him.

"Give this a try." He rested a paperback on the rock, as always careful not to touch me. "Notice the parts about me."

At his pride I lost my temper.

"I don't give two shits about Dante," I lashed out. Then I leafed through the book, searching for ammunition to attack him with, yet the feel and whisper of the pages somehow calmed me. I knew I was lost, because I had to draw solace from the words of a man who wore a bedraggled laurel wreath and genuinely believed himself to be the poet of *The Aeneid*.

When I looked up he was gone, and I found myself doubting the existence of the two most important people in my life, Virgil and Angie Mead.

Back home and in my room, I gave the *Inferno* a quick look-see. I didn't know the people mentioned in it and I had to skip the bits too gory for my budding literary taste.

Afterwards I wrote a poem, imitating Dante's verse form, about how I hated my classmates for their goldfish memories, for failing to remember the laughs, the group hugs, the boobs and legs, the funny stories in the now nonexistent garden.

Occasionally, before bed, I'd open *The Divine Comedy* somewhere in the middle and give one canto or another a deeper read. The poem's rhythm comforted me. On Google, I found out that Dante considered astronomy to be the noblest of sciences, and therefore, each canticle ended with the word *stars*.

I wanted to have a special word that meant so much to me, it wouldn't matter if no one else noticed that I ended each poem with it. Then I decided mine would be two words. *Angie Mead.*

My grief and loneliness made me aloof. The greatest sadness may be for a loss we aren't allowed to mourn. I wasn't supposed to mourn a teacher like one would a mother or a sister, but I didn't have a sister, and my mother, who lived her life in a smoky haze of weed, had given up on me long ago.

I searched for explanations in articles about disappearances and strange events. I read sci-fi and fantasy novels, experimental fiction and everything weird and unexplained that crossed my way. Later, when I wrote stories, I resigned myself to the idea that Angie Mead had been my mind's creation: my first fictional character.

Most children are raised by their parents. I was raised by a fantasy. Ms. Angie remained my role model, my true star, burning bright in my mind, adored and worshipped even more in her absence.

6. Red Herring

Exhausted from throwing up, I crumpled to the ice cold floor of the ladies room and tried to catch my breath. Ice cold, like Dante's *Inferno*. That had to be it. I'd crashed into a devilish inferno. I staggered out of the stall and washed my sweaty face, then filled my belly with metallic-tasting tap water and leaned on the sink, waiting for my stomach to settle and for my legs to stop trembling.

My hair framed my pale reflection in the scratched mirror. What an ugly crier I was, with those red blotches as bright as neon on my pale cheeks and that one red streak decorating my upper lip. Again, I was a heartbroken eleven-year-old, mourning the loss of the very woman who was at the moment, across the hall, talking Dante to a full auditorium.

For years after her disappearance, I recreated her in my fantasies and in short stories. I trained myself to believe that she'd been too flawless to actually exist. That she'd been a figment of my imagination, alive only in my mind, living for me and because of me, as my ideal of female perfection.

"What the shitting fuck am I supposed to do?" I asked the death mask in the scratched mirror.

"Go back there and pay attention," said a voice.

A woman suddenly stood behind my reflection. I knew her.

"WildWest Yoga, Westwood," she said in a sweet voice, balancing behind me with one leg high in the air. "Ring a bell?"

Of all the people I didn't want to talk to...

I turned around. "Hey, Bea. Look—"

"Are you coming back in?" she asked.

"I'm dropping the class."

"You can't." She leaned on the wall, arms folded.

"What's it to you?" I asked, annoyed by her intrusion. Something was very, very wrong with me or with the world. I needed to figure out what was going on.

"I'll pay your tuition," she said, "on top of paying you to edit a historical novel I'm writing from the point of view of Dante's beloved Beatrice. You have a lot to learn if you want to help me write that book."

"Save yourself the trouble," I said, splashing more cold water on my hot face. "It's impossible to generate three hundred pages about a woman who was a mere fantasy. Dante's love made her real, but that love never had life."

"And yet she inspired two major works of literature." She planted herself firmly in front of me, arms akimbo, as if personally insulted by my hard take. "He loved her as much as Romeo loved his Juliet, and like Juliet, Beatrice lived about ten minutes. Dante's love for her didn't know earthly life, but the profound power of it never faded for him."

"Unlike Juliet, Beatrice was peripheral to the story," I argued, not forgetting for a moment the woman lecturing across the hall. Maybe dealing with Bea would kick my brain into gear. I was doing a hell of a lot more feeling than thinking, and I desperately craved a few rational thoughts. "She was a red herring, a mere plot device in Dante's life story—"

"Is that what she means to you, a red herring?" Bea gestured with her thumb toward the auditorium. "What would Angie Mead do?"

"What?" My mind exploded. I blinked. Froze.

The door creaked open and Sophie walked in. "Your mouth's wide open," she said.

I turned back to give Bea a piece of my mind and ask her what she meant and how and what else she knew, but she was gone. Managed to creep out on me as swiftly as she'd crept in.

"Come back," Sophie said. "You're missing a totally cool lecture."

"Where is she?" I asked.

"Who?"

"Yoga Bea."

From her post by the door, Sophie quickly checked out the room. "You're alone," she said. "What happened?"

"Something I ate didn't agree with me," I lied. I wasn't ready to share that a woman I loved and probably imagined in my childhood had just broken out of my imagination and tumbled into my very real adult life.

Bea knew something I'd shared only with Virgil, whom I hadn't seen for ten or so years. How? Her delicate patchouli scent still permeated the air—sweet and minty, but also wet, like a cold, dark basement—yet Sophie didn't see her. I thought of my yoga classes. None of the instructors ever corrected Bea's pose or praised her, not even Liz, the pickiest teacher who missed nothing and knew each student by first and last name. Was Bea, like Virgil and Angie Mead, visible only to me? What did that mean?

"She was here." I bent low to search for feet in each stall. Foolish, I knew, but I was feeling pretty desperate.

"What's with you?" Sophie stomped in impatience. "Let's go back already."

What would Ms. Angie Mead do?

She'd go back, pay attention and explore further.

In the auditorium, Dr. Caldwell eyed me with concern.

"Are you okay?" she asked.

I nodded, unable to utter a word.

As she cocked her head in question, my eyes extrapolated the rest of the picture, adding a perfect red rosebud held in a lime-green glove and a trellis of climbing vines.

7. Fuckability

D r. Caldwell turned from me and continued speaking about Dante's *Inferno* while heaven and hell struggled for control inside me. Using slides, she told of Dante's love for a woman promised to another. *La Vita Nuova* recounted his love for Beatrice, beginning at first sight, when they were children until her death at the age of twenty-five. Dante immortalized Beatrice as his guide in *The Divine Comedy*.

"Boy meets girl," Dr. Caldwell said in her gritty voice. "Boy loses girl, girl dies, boy is exiled." She clicked another slide. "Dante lived in the world of Romeo and Juliet. He even mentions the influential and real Montecchi and Cappelletti in a few mysterious verses in his *Purgatorio*."

Someone in the row behind mine tapped my shoulder. "Told you," a gum-chewing Bea mouthed when I looked back, shattering my admiring focus on Dr. Caldwell.

"Stop breathing down my neck," I snapped in a loud whisper.

"Who're you yelling at?" Sophie asked.

"Bea," I said. "I'm sick of her standing, or sitting, or working out behind me."

I glanced back. Bea was gone, and a bearded man sat in her place. How did she manage to sneak out so swiftly again, like a ghost? I couldn't understand, and I refused to kneel in my seat and peer at the feet of the row behind me.

Then Dr. Caldwell mesmerized me again. When she spoke, hundreds of years unfolded before me as full scenes. I imagined myself clad in red robes, strolling the pebbled streets of medieval Florence among the feuding factions of Guelphs and Ghibellines, my head adorned with Dante's laurel wreath and Dr. Caldwell on my arm in a flowing dress.

By the end of that first lecture I was hooked on Dante, on Italy, on Dr. Caldwell's voice, her face, the rest of her.

Sophie filled notebook pages with profiles of our classmates. "You'll have to tell me the whole story and soon," she whispered. "You're totally growing a girl crush on this broad."

"Not growing." My face burned. "I'm actually imagining her in a tight-to-bursting white tailored suit as my bride."

Sophie jutted out her lower lip. "I wouldn't think she'd be your type."

I shrugged. "Who says I've a type?"

"There's this thing called the Fuckability Index," Sophie explained, doodling away in her notebook. "In your case I'd expect you to go for your complete opposite—skinny, boyish girls with tiny boobies."

"I know about your F-Index. She's brilliant and beautiful, and look at those long fingers brushing her hair back."

I was enchanted by Gina, but not so enchanted that I stopped wondering how any of this could be possible. Since Ms. Angie disappeared, I'd googled her numerous times, and over the years, found three people bearing her name, but none fit the profile. One Angie Mead was a retired psychologist in her late eighties. The second was a New York interior designer. The last Ms. Angie Mead, a Beyoncé impersonating drag Queen, performed at a Chicago nightclub. This time the name was different, but the woman was identical in every way.

If Gina was Ms. Angie, how was it that she hadn't aged at all in ten whole years? And if she wasn't her, why did she look and sound the same? I kept scribbling in my notebook in various fonts and sizes and, since I used one of those four color retractable ball point pens, in four different colors. *Same hair*, I wrote in red. *Same boobs*, I wrote in green. *Same legs and wardrobe, same voice and gestures*, I wrote in black, then green, then red again.

Sophie whispered, "I'd want her to sit for my Buxom Venus."

"Keep your paws off her," I warned.

"Let me leave you tonight with Dante's last words," Dr. Caldwell said. In her sultry voice, she recited:

"Here my powers rest from their high fantasy,
but already I could feel my being turned —
instinct and intellect balanced equally
as in a wheel whose motion nothing jars —
by the love that moves the sun and the other stars."

I turned to Sophie. "And how does that score on your F-Index?"

Sophie nodded in appreciation. "I see your point."

My mind went crazy with millions of questions. Was she Angie's twin? A reincarnation? Angie herself with a new identity meant to ward off the mob? My favorite scenario was that Angie had divorced the cheating Mr. Mead and taken back her maiden name. Her husband-less, relaxed life had kept her from aging.

Instead of dangling from a top floor balcony, I now cyber-stalked her from the safety of my room. That night I sat in bed, back against the wall, googling away. Angie Mead — *my* Angie — as I'd found out online on many previous searches, did not exist, dead or alive. I typed *Dr. Gina Caldwell*. I held my breath at the photo of her face, smiling while accepting an instructor of the year award at UCLA. The awkward shot didn't do justice to her beauty, but she was definitely Angie Mead, or her dead ringer.

Her full name was Angelina Rose Caldwell. *Aha* — Angie and Gina were both derivatives of Angelina. It was possible that in her past, she had shortened her name to Angie. At this time, for whatever reason, she was using Gina. That conclusion made sense.

Born in Los Angeles, a PhD in medieval poetry, presently teaches at UCLA ... Awards were mentioned, also a published translation of Dante's *La Vita Nuova*.

And there was my prize.

Dr. Caldwell had taught English and language arts in a local elementary school. I didn't make her up after all.

"Yes!" I exclaimed in a tone that brought Sophie straight into my room, as usual, without knocking. "I knew it." I pointed at the screen. "It's her."

"Her who?" Sophie asked.

"I have a weird story for you."

"Do we need cocktails?"

"Double the tequila for me," I said.

Sophie was the perfect audience, when, over a blended mango margarita, I told her of the mythological teacher and of my great and lonely loss.

"Tonight she waltzes into my life as Gina Caldwell, talking *Inferno*, looking and sounding like Angie Mead, as if she hadn't washed down into the wet soil ten years ago."

"Could Gina be Angie's twin?" Sophie asked.

"She's her."

"Okay, so are you gonna ask her?"

"Are you kidding? I was the creep dangling from that balcony hoping to catch a glimpse of her."

"Come on, I'll go with you," Sophie said, excited. "She'll laugh it off, you'll see. You were a little girl who desperately needed a best friend like me to love you and guide you."

"I stalked her and she stopped existing." I started crying. "They said I invented her and you probably don't believe me either."

"Whether she existed or not, she *should* have," Sophie said gently. "Come on, I saw the foggy specimen posing as your mother. So you used your imagination."

"See? You *don't* believe me," I said, upset, disappointed.

"You truly believed in her," Sophie said. "That's enough for me."

"Thank you," I said. "I wish I had you then. They made me feel so stupid."

"Don't move," Sophie said. "Don't change your expression."

She sat down across from me with her drawing pad. "Your face in this light is so sad but also hopeful. You're my new Madonna."

She sketched quickly, turning page after page, and the sound of chalk on rough paper gave me goose bumps.

"As for Dr. Caldwell, if I were you, I'd take her out for a drink. I'd wine her, dine her, then fuck her brains out to get her out of my system."

"This isn't about sex."

"Sure it is."

"I start trembling at the sight of her and—"

"The quarter is three months." Sophie slammed shut the drawing pad. "That's how long you have to plan a move."

Three months? Waiting for next week was too long for me. How would I find out if indeed she was *my* Angie? I couldn't exactly ask if she remembered me as the stupid little girl who used to stalk her from a sixth floor balcony, could I?

8. Busted

L ike Ms. Angie's before her, Dr. Caldwell's ample beauty celebrated too much of everything. Her tailored suits were too stiff and tight, her long legs too white, her stiletto heels too thin. Her too intimate voice was a caressing hand up and down my back.

Gina Caldwell, I said silently behind closed lips, the way I had long ago whispered *Angie Mead*.

The whole intoxicating package was a tightly wrapped gift I longed to rip open to discover the secret pleasures within. Maybe Sophie was right, and my obsession was about sex.

Dr. Caldwell kept wandering around the auditorium, not restlessly, but unable to contain her extra energy. While listening, I floated on waves of fantasy featuring Juliet balconies in the world of the Montagues and the Capulets. I was totally captivated until my reverie was interrupted by a new chirpy voice from well behind me.

"Why do we study Dante anyway? What's so relevant about such an overrated and misogynistic work?"

A stirring arose from multiple corners of the auditorium.

"Bitch," Bea whispered when I swiveled around, her eyes two slits of indignation. "What a dumbass question."

I smiled. She had to justify and defend her hopeless historical novel.

"Now, now, everyone." Dr. Caldwell cocked her head, as if jiggling a recollection out of some memory bank. "Overrated?"

She tossed her lecture notes into a wastepaper basket and gazed up the auditorium. I expected her to be annoyed, assuming that Dante's long poem was her passion and obsession, but her eyes lit up.

"Overrated work," she echoed. "What's your name?"

"Lilly," said the tiny woman, whose face had reddened. I guessed she probably regretted her question.

"Right, Lilly. You can't approach a work from the fourteenth century with your contemporary views. Besides, Dante's female figures tower over the narrative, especially Beatrice, who is the reason for his journey."

"Right on," Bea said, adding a few solid claps.

Dr. Caldwell passed me on her way up the stairs, bringing with her the delicate fragrance of a rose garden. Every pair of eyes shifted to follow her progress.

She stared down at Lilly from her upright posture. "What you're calling overrated and outdated,"—as she counted on her fingers, I noticed the short fingernails of someone who probably spent her days at the keyboard—"and irrelevant, is the reason you and I are here at all."

"What do you mean?" Lilly asked, her back stiff.

Dr. Caldwell picked up a small coffee cup from Lilly's chair flap and raised it high over her head. "Who likes their espresso strong?"

Excited murmurs came from around the room. She put the cup down. "The first prototype of the espresso machine was invented in Turino, Italy, in 1884 by a dude named Angelo Moriondo. That first machine was improved in 1945 by another Italian named Achille Gaggia, who invented the piston-driven model."

Sophie stopped doodling and narrowed her eyes at me. "Where's she going with this?"

I bit my lip. "Can't wait to get there."

Dr. Caldwell asked Lilly for her glasses and held them up.

"Eyeglasses," she announced. "Invented in the thirteenth century by an unidentified Venetian glassmaker, around the time of Dante Alighieri. Please, stay with me." She returned the glasses with a smile. "Now, who attacks a carton of Rocky Road to cure a heartbreak?"

Laughter. Arms were raised.

"Good. Gelato was invented roughly a hundred years after Dante by Cosimo Ruggieri, not the same one appearing in the *Inferno*, but rather a Renaissance alchemist who had created *fior di latte* at the Medici court in Florence." She spoke passionately, electrifying the air with her expressive hands. "In 1903, Marchioni produced the gelato cone, and since then, gelato, in one form or another, has satisfied our taste buds."

I couldn't tell what she wanted to express in this history lecture, yet I was fascinated by her enthusiasm and by the light and shade playing on the planes of her face as she paced the auditorium in her deadly stilettos.

"*Chiaroscuro*," I whispered, and Sophie nodded, already shading her drawing from left to right, like Leonardo.

"Italic typeface, anyone?" Hands were raised. "Designed in the early sixteenth century by book printer Francesco Griffo. Italian again. You see the pattern?"

She pointed up at the recessed lights. "In the nineteenth century, Alessandro Cruto's filament greatly improved the durability of the light bulb. Microscope? Galileo Galilei. Medical thermometer? Sanctorius, early seventeenth century. The acoustic piano was invented by Bartolomeo Cristofori in 1709."

She pantomimed running out of breath, although she didn't sound breathless. "The oldest violin in existence was crafted by Andre Amati around 1565. Opera—should I list the composers? Last night, did anyone munch on pizza while watching Italy kick Argentina's ass in soccer?"

Boos, cheers, laughter came from various directions.

"The first pizzeria was established in 1738. Later, in 1830, one opened in Naples. You wouldn't have pizza or soccer without Italy.

All those things—including modern medicine, astronomy, Renaissance humanism, math—would not have existed in their present form without Italy, and the man who united her as one nation was Dante Alighieri."

I smiled to myself at the way she brought the argument full circle with her long answer to a question that shouldn't have been asked in the first place. *Why do we study Dante anyway?*

Dr. Caldwell stopped for effect. "Any questions so far?"

Waves of reaction sounded around me.

Hands were raised. "Please elaborate on that uniting thing."

"Dante, Petrarch, and Boccaccio stirred up the Italian Renaissance," she said. "In Europe of the Middle Ages, only Latin was considered suitable for literary works, which left literature and philosophy inaccessible to most of the population. Dante was the first to write poetry in the Tuscan language, borrowing common expressions from the vernacular of other regions. The success of his *Divine Comedy* encouraged Petrarch and Boccaccio to do the same a hundred years later. During the Renaissance, the language of Dante was established as the official language of Italy."

She paused to survey the room, lingering on the enthralled faces, including mine. "As we know, a common language helps to develop a national consciousness. Some claim that Dante is the first reason Italy became one nation; therefore, we have the High Renaissance, ice cream, pizza and fascism. Don't forget fascism."

Boos and hisses again.

"Fascism, people, may not have existed without the rise of far-right Benito Mussolini in the early twentieth century, and without the atrocities of fascism, would the state of Israel have existed? I don't know."

"Hey, my father was born there," an offended Lilly cried out.

"And my mother," Gina acknowledged with a wide smile. "As I said, Lilly, if it weren't for Dante, neither of us would be sitting here in our present form."

That impromptu answer to whiny Lilly Green moved me to the core and may have been when I abandoned the memory of Angie Mead to fall deeply in love with Gina Caldwell, for herself alone.

Next to me, Sophie drew a red heart with a black arrow through it, and in its center, *Gina and Ellie* in a fat gang-graffiti font.

"How juvenile," I said in a loud whisper, drawing all attention to me, including Dr. Caldwell's. She turned to us, her eyes slightly unfocussed, as though she's just glanced up from a book she was reading.

"Ms. Brooke, do you have a question?" she asked.

I was burning inside. "Actually, yes. It makes sense that some of the world's history would be different, and this extrapolation of yours into what could have happened if Dante hadn't lived is fascinating. But ice cream, espresso, the microscope, pizza... Isn't it likely that someone else would have invented those things? I mean, inventions tend to come from multiple sources."

"Absolutely." Her smile melted me.

Again, she came up the stairs, and to my horror, took hold of Sophie's notebook. She examined the last doodle, the tip of her tongue sticking out of her kissable lips.

"Graffiti." Her gaze hopped from Sophie's face to mine. "If it weren't for Italy and frescoes, we wouldn't have graffiti."

"You totally made that one up," I said.

"Busted," she said, her eyes boring into mine.

Was she playing with me? I held my breath. The same word, the same slight tilt of a gorgeous head, the same delicate scent of wildflowers . . . As I struggled not to black out, she seemed to be fading away before my eyes, the way she had ten years earlier.

9. Perspective

"What's upsetting you?" Dr. Caldwell's concerned face cleared up with my vision.

"That's what you said back then." My voice was squeaky. "You said. *Busted.*"

"Back when?" She squinted, puzzled. "What do you mean? *Busted* is just something silly people say when they get you."

I couldn't fill my lungs with air.

Suddenly her face was so close to mine, I noticed her widening pupils. She whispered, "Come and see me after class. I need to talk to you."

She was definitely fucking with me.

Sophie seized me by the elbow. "Let's leave." And to Dr. Caldwell, "I'm taking her home. She isn't well."

Dr. Caldwell took too long to move aside, and on the way out, my arm brushed against hers. How soft she was... Then I was out in the blessed fresh air.

"She's totally that Angie broad, isn't she?" Sophie asked when we made our way home across the dark campus, surrounded by the scent of night-blooming jasmine.

"She recognized me, Sophie." I put her hand on my chest. "Here, feel."

"Your heart is racing," Sophie said.

"That way she said, *Busted* and *Come and see me after class I need to talk to you.* That's exactly what she said back then...

and that face she made... she was so *her*..." I tried not to hyperventilate. "It's like she's paying me back for my childhood offense."

"*Imagined* offense." Sophie linked her arm with mine. "What you did as a child was a non-event for her and it shouldn't count against you. She wanted to talk to you, so do it."

"What should I say?"

"Ask her if she used to be your teacher. If she's her and she remembers, take it from there."

"I can't. I'll pass out or puke. I'm not even sure I didn't make her up because how can a person wash into the earth like this?"

"We live an illusion." Sophie made a big gesture in the air. "It's like in painting: all perspective."

"A person disappearing from existence is perspective to you?" I asked.

"Look, you're a big girl over the age of consent." Sophie pivoted and walked backwards, grinning. "Tell her she's a ten on the F-Index and you want to stick your face between her boobs."

Laughing, I chased her across the street.

We were both breathless when the rickety elevator made its slow upward crawl.

"I'll ask yoga Bea if she knows what's going on," I said.

"Who?" Sophie asked.

"That woman who sits behind me. She asked me to work on a novel she's writing about Dante's Beatrice, *and* she knows about Angie Mead, a story no one knows but you and Virgil. Scared me with what she knew—"

"Okay, you're rambling." Sophie started one of her cocktails. "Introduce me to your yoga friend next time. I'm not sure who you're talking about."

"I will," I said.

I never got the chance, because Bea stopped coming to classes, yoga, and Dante. The entire summer quarter passed, and I didn't see her in any of our study groups. Was she hard at work on her historical novel? I was curious to see if she was talented enough to pull off such a hopeless project.

Dr. Gina Caldwell never repeated her request to see me after class, but she kept surprising me with her uncanny similarities to Ms. Angie. Her wardrobe, her gestures, her voice were identical. She even finger-brushed her hair back in that same motion that started the butterflies in my stomach.

Once, her gaze lingered on me and her eyes narrowed, as if about to point a finger and say, *It's you.* I started dressing for her: a sexy top, a tight skirt. Once, I wore my only pair of high heels and made sure to sashay by her on my way out of class. She noticed.

"She digs you," Sophie encouraged. "Talk to her already, for my sake."

What the hell would Angie Mead herself do in my situation? I didn't know anymore. Although I never forgot what had happened in my childhood, Ms. Angie Mead already faded away, replaced in my heart with Dr. Gina Caldwell.

Still, I couldn't gather the courage to simply go and ask her if she was ever called Angie Mead.

One morning in October, I woke to a monster's face leaning over me and munching hungrily on a cracked-open skull. I choked a scream.

"Effective, isn't it?" Sophie turned on my bedside light. "Our *Inferno*-inspired Halloween costume."

"*Our*?" I asked. "I see only Ugolino."

Count Ugolino, a sinner from Dante's lowest circle of hell, was trapped in ice for eternity and sentenced to munch on the skull of Archbishop Ruggieri, who, in life, had starved him and his family to death.

"You'd be Ruggieri's skull." Sophie held up a motorcycle helmet painted to resemble a partially eaten brain with bite marks. She tried to put it on my sleepy head.

I fought her off. "You nut."

"Here's canto thirty-two." She waved a paperback at me before reading. *"I saw two souls together in a single hole and so pinched in by the ice that one head made a helmet for the other."* She pointed. "See? That's where I got the idea." She kept reading. *"As a famished man chews crusts—so the other sinner sank his teeth into the other's nape at the base of the skull, gnawing his loathsome dinner."*

"Careful. I have an overactive gag reflex." Already I felt the nausea.

On Halloween, she managed to squeeze the bulk of my hair into the painted helmet. A borrowed black graduation gown gave my body the suggestion of nonexistence. At the school's bash, we won first place for the most repulsive ensemble. Dr. Caldwell, robed in red as Dante Alighieri, handed us a just-as-disgusting trophy.

It was a cardboard headstone engraved on the spot with both our names. *Here lie Sophie Sanders and Elektra Brooke, gone before their time.*

Sophie held the trophy for barely one minute, then threw up on it. "I wanna go home," she said. Another heave brought up the rest of the candy she'd gorged on.

The next morning, instead of starting her day with loud and excited chatter, she remained silent and gloomy.

"Did you have a nightmare?" I asked.

She shivered, her face pale. Her mouth was marred with smeared remnants of fake blood from our hideous costume.

When she showered, steam escaped from the bathroom's open door like white smoke from a live fire. Worried, I ran in to see more steam billowing from around the white curtain. I touched the water and shrieked. "It's boiling!"

"I'm still cold," she said in a monotone.

The long scars on her left forearm were inflamed.

"Why are those marks so bright red?"

Her voice chilled me to the bone. "She's angry."

"Who's angry?" I shivered.

"I shouldn't talk about her," she said.

On our way to school, we stopped as usual at Java Jolt on Wilshire, where Sophie typically got herself a cappuccino with tons of whipped cream and a giant burrito she'd devour in five bites. I hoped breakfast would cheer her up, but she stunned me by ordering only black coffee.

"What's with you, Sophie? Was it last night? Did anything upset you at the party?"

"Last night was nothing," she said.

"Did I say something that upset you? Please tell me."

She hurried forward, leaving me behind.

The next evening, Dr. Caldwell surveyed the rows of her attentive students. When her gaze fell on us, she said, "I hope you're feeling better, Sophie. Great costume, you two."

Not even praise for her creation cheered Sophie up. Her dreary silence remained. During the next hour, she kept doodling bizarre images of skulls sprouting thick thorns and snakes.

Dr. Caldwell spoke of Dante's ascent to Purgatory, and I drank in her words, imagining her as my Beatrice, leading me into Paradise.

Sophie said, "He should have stayed in hell."

A chill passed through me. Frightened faces with big eyes turned to look at us from the rows in front.

"Would you care to elaborate?" Dr. Caldwell asked.

I whispered, "You want to tell me what the actual fuck?"

Sophie fled the auditorium, leaving her belongings scattered over the floor and across several seats.

An hour later, when I got home, dark funereal choral music ushered me from the elevator to our apartment. Sophie was at her easel, working an incredible painting of a blue angel and a red demon in mirror images, perfectly proportioned. Each had one *en pointe* leg and the other lifted high behind.

"Is this a commission," I asked.

Her answer was laconic. "Arabesque."

I turned down the music.

"Put it back the way it was."

Her haunted eyes were unnaturally wide. I wondered if she was high, or sick.

"Do you need a doctor?"

"An exorcist." She dipped her left hand in blue and used it as a paintbrush.

The image of her being dragged away by men in white coats was unbearable, but I was ready to dial 911.

I placed a sandwich in front of her. "From Mabel's," I said.

"I can't." She pushed the paper plate away. This was serious. Mabel's Kosher Deli was her favorite.

"What's frightening you, Sophie?" She looked haunted, hunted, afraid.

"She is…"

"She is what?" I asked, but I couldn't get another word out of her. She kept working, possessed.

The next day, she hadn't regained her natural joy or her sense of humor. She kept working at diabolical speed, her music blasting through my earplugs.

So far, she mass produced whimsical canvases in spring pastels. Those pieces paid the bills.

This new style was different. Spine-chilling demons floated above murky surrealistic landscapes of jagged cliffs and stormy waters. Each painting included a blue angel facing a red demon, both in arabesque.

Her dark paintings were superior to her bill-paying happy stuff. Still, her regulars wanted art that brightened their homes and offices. Not this.

Two weeks passed, and she remained in the same mood. Our study group dispersed and classmates who used to hang out with us stopped visiting. They wanted the sunny version of Sophie, her laughter and her cocktails. So did I.

I spent more time working and studying in the library, keeping myself awake with vending machine coffee until I fell asleep at my desk. Anything—even my mother's calls for small repairs—was better than evenings in my once paradise, turned hell. As my mother became more independent, my roommate stopped caring for herself and showing up for classes. Again, I became the caretaker, pushing Sophie to eat, sleep, shower.

"You need help," I said one morning, shoving her in front of the mirror.

Sophie touched the mirror with stained blue fingers. "I can't see my reflection."

"Something wrong with your eyes?"

"Hell's inside me."

When I suggested a therapist, Sophie refused. She increased her already frenzied pace, producing incredible works, intense, and dark in color and mood. The music blasted and more grisly scenes dried around our apartment.

She played her loud music night and day. When I asked, she'd lower the volume, but she'd slip back into playing it loudly. The light was never bright enough or the music loud enough for her.

I once went through her phone and her purse—the cardinal sin against another woman—but couldn't find anything about her family. I'd never heard her speak of her parents, and I had no idea how to reach them, or the aunt who owned our apartment. I was frightened for Sophie and helpless.

Dirty brushes and paint tubes were strewn everywhere, including my room and throughout the kitchen. On the night I mistook a tube of mustard yellow for real mustard and squeezed it onto my hotdog, I made up my mind to get Sophie professional help. Then I escaped to study in the library.

10. Botticelli's Madonna

I n the death-like silent library, I rested my head on my arms for a catnap and recited quietly, "...*as in a wheel whose motion nothing jars—by the Love that moves the Sun and the other stars.*"

"That translator is faithful to the gorgeous *terza rima* verse form," a calm voice said. The grind of a dragging chair followed.

I lifted my sleepy gaze. Dr. Caldwell cocked her head to one side in that charming way, and the diamond stud in her ear stole a ray of light from the air and made her glow like a saint.

"A deadly, *sexy*, mysterious Strauss heroine who represents grace and power," she said, extending the word *sexy* into three syllables. She then hummed the Final Jeopardy tune and answered with a question, "Who is Elektra?"

"Shit." I sat up straight and wiped my laptop keyboard clean of my drool with my T-shirt. "Am I in big trouble?"

"Huge." She was so adorable in her jeans and tight white T-shirt. "What are you doing here so late?"

"Looking at the so-far-unknown *Madonna in Blue Jeans* by Botticelli." Her intoxicating fragrance stirred in me an old longing for a childhood idol who had faded away in a red thunderstorm. "Oh God, did I think about Botticelli or actually say it?"

She smiled. "It's late."

"Why are *you* still here?" I asked.

"You go first," she said in that husky voice.

"I can't go home because…" The truth just spilled out of me. "Well, my roomie is possessed with the ghost of Hieronymus Bosch. She's playing scary Halloween music and painting green demons with fluffy edges." I demonstrated horns with my fingers and crossed my eyes.

She lifted an eyebrow. "By *roomie* do you mean Sophie, who dressed up as Count Ugolino and thought Dante should have remained in hell?"

"She still does." My heart thumped. "What's your story?"

She said, "My perfect prick of a boyfriend is being more of a prick than usual. In fact, at my request, he's moving out at this blessed moment, and I'm giving him space." She sighed. "I'm not a fan of moving parties."

"Category, alliteration," I retorted, Jeopardy-style. "Clue, Dr. Caldwell's boyfriend. Answer, what is a perfect prick?"

"Please, call me Gina." She smiled, and I decided I'd definitely feel that one uneven tooth with my tongue if I leaned across and kissed her.

Get real. She's straight now, and she was straight before, in that other life.

"Let me buy you coffee," I said, immediately giving her a way out. "That is, if you don't have ethical issues fraternizing with your students."

My offer was miles more sedate than Sophie's suggestion— *Tell her you want to stick your face between her boobs.* Still, I couldn't believe how casually I was treating the woman who had been my idea of paradise way before I learned of Dante's journey through Hell. What would we talk about, rose bushes?

"Tequila is more my thing this time of night," she said.

I suppressed my yelp of glee. "Sophie hides the real expensive stuff in a secret drawer of our messy kitchen."

She gestured toward the exit. "Let's go check out those paintings."

"You'll like them." I stuffed my laptop into my backpack. "If you're into torture art."

"Into it?" she asked as we inched toward the exit. "Who's teaching you Dante?"

"A visit from our most admired teacher may shake her out of her craze," I said. "But I apologize in advance if she asks you to pose for her in the nude."

"Is she any good?" she asked.

"Lately she's excellent," I said.

"I may agree. Wait, you guys adore me?"

"That is not correct, I'm sorry," I said. "The word was *admire*, but the board is yours. Pick again."

She threw her head back in laughter. The double door slid open, and we were out in the cold October night. On Wilshire, she hopped into a mini-market and emerged carrying a rustling paper bag.

"Tortilla chips and limes for that tequila," she explained.

"What's in the bag?" I asked, then worried I might be overdoing her little game. She grinned and saluted, so I relaxed.

Hip-hop blasted my eardrums when we exited the elevator. Inside the apartment, the fumes of turpentine and stale air made me sneeze, and the bright lights burned my eyes. Paintings in various stages of drying leaned against the wall, concealing each other like unresolved childhood trauma. The beautiful hardwood floor was streaked with oil paint and strewn with squeezed tubes and dirty paintbrushes.

Once I adjusted to the overstimulation, I saw the place anew from Dr. Caldwell's eyes, the eyes I wanted to impress.

A skeletal Sophie was feverishly working behind her easel, her dirty hair in unwashed clumps. Her forehead was smeared with green, and her stained UCLA sweatshirt slid off one bony shoulder. A belt held her jeans in place. Slim in good times, now she was wasting away.

"We have a visitor," I announced, turning down the music.

She glanced up at me with the sinking eyes of starvation one sees in photographs of world hunger. A shadow of a smile appeared on her gaunt face. "Dr. Caldwell," she whispered in reverence.

"Call me Gina, please, both of you."

The canvas Sophie worked featured piled up bodies in assorted positions of torture on the shore of an island mountain.

Gina held her breath, and a flicker of awe lit her eyes. Not a big reaction, only a flutter of her heavy eyelids. The painting moved her.

"*Mount Purgatorio*," she said.

Cheers came in through the balcony's sliding door and livened up the night. For once, the loud music came, not from our place, but from a student party in the high-rise across the street.

Our teacher produced her checkbook, scribbled a number and added a flaring signature. "If this amount is okay with you, *Mount Purgatorio* is mine when it's done."

"It just needs a protective glaze." Sophie stared down at the check in disbelief. "Are you shitting me?"

Such ungratefulness. A sale was a sale, and if Dr. Caldwell wanted to buy a painting, Sophie should have gifted it to her.

"I'm sorry I can't pay you more." Gina kept her eyes on the painting with that adorable tilt of her head that made me weak at the knees. "I just bought my ex's share of the house, so this is all I can afford, but one day you'd be paid ten times this."

"Five hundred saves my ass." Sophie's eyes glistened. "I haven't..." She stopped herself from saying more, but I knew how long it had been since she'd sold a painting.

"If you don't mind, I'd like to use this image in my lectures."

"Mind?" Sophie perked up. "I'm so beyond flattered, I need libation."

"Get the good tequila," I said.

"You bet."

Sophie was already rummaging in the kitchen cabinets, in hostess mode because we had a guest or because the money in her pocket made her light on those dirty feet. My real Sophie was re-emerging, her gloom lifting like the corner of a heavy tablecloth.

ii. In Death

"**N**ot those." Sophie cracked open the bottle while I gave three shot glasses a long scrub. She poked around in an upper cupboard, producing her aunt's antique shot glasses meant for special occasions. Gina had joined us in the kitchen, bringing along that exquisite scent that took me back years.

"You're wearing wildflowers," I said, sniffing the air.

"That's right." She sliced limes into wedges and arranged them on a white plate that also got a good scrub from me. "The fragrance is called Wild Rose."

Angie's roses. Images from my childhood flashed before my eyes.

We carried the drinks and the munchies to the balcony, where the air was clear and cool and the laughter of party girls emerged from the street. Our little party—with Sophie ascending from hell, and Gina Caldwell descending from academia—was about to become more interesting than the one across the way.

Sophie wrapped a blanket around herself, as if gathering courage. "You're sort of an authority on the afterlife, right, Dr. Caldwell?"

"Gina, please." She crunched a tortilla chip. "Medieval poetry doesn't make one an expert on the afterlife, but I have my theories."

"Do you believe the dead visit us?" Sophie laughed in embarrassment. "I mean, who in their right mind believes that *superstitial* shit, right?"

Superstitious, my inner Ms. Angie was tempted to correct, but our thoughtful teacher chose to use another word altogether. "Nothing irrational about it. The dead walk among us, invisible." Gina let her gaze travel from Sophie's face to mine and back, as if checking out her audience before beginning a lecture. "Did you ever shudder and use the expression *somebody is walking over my grave?*" Her husky voice was no louder than a whisper.

A sudden gust of wind swept the balcony and made me shiver. I unknotted my hair and let it fall like a protective blanket around my shoulders.

Ms. Angie. What would she do or say now?

"I don't believe in ghosts," I said.

"Me neither." Gina measured me, serious. "Those white booing things are a simplistic image of death. The dead are actually with us here and now."

"Here, now?" My voice sounded hollow in my ears.

The crackling water bottle in Gina's hands startled me.

"Don't give me that face, Elektra," she said. "Some dead walk among the living because the living can't let them go. They're around us, roaming the earth as spirits in their favorite places—their homes, workplaces, gardens—but they can't interact with us. Some people claim to see them." She slowly blinked her heavy eyelids. "Do you?"

"I don't know," I said.

Haven't I always seen more people than anyone else? Virgil came to mind, Angie Mead, yoga Bea. They were living people. Weren't they?

"I don't know," I repeated. Even Gina seemed unreal in the half-light of the balcony. Were there more of them?

I turned around, expecting something to jump at me. I turned back. Gina's gaze bore into me, my own horror reflected in her face. Was she suddenly remembering the troubled little girl who had risked her life to stalk her? I was trembling and not because of the ghosts. She'd soon say, *It's you*, twist her face with revulsion and leave us in a huff.

That would be the end of my life. I'd surely die of heartbreak, the way I died back then, years ago, by the blooming roses.

She turned to Sophie. "Why did you ask that?"

"I sometimes . . ." Sophie cleared her throat. "I sometimes feel like a ghost walking among the living."

Shrill laughter erupted like hot lava from the neighboring party, followed by cheers and louder music. The three of us turned to watch the packed-to-the-gills apartment across the street. Blue disco lights flashed through the dancers' skulls and skeletons, so many of them, the cantilevered balcony didn't seem strong enough to support the weight of humanity in *danse macabre*.

"I shouldn't be alive." Sophie pulled her dirty feet up and pressed her knees to her chest under the blanket. "I imagine the world as a better place without me."

Gina pointed toward the living room, where the horrifying painting slowly dried against its easel. "Without you, we would have lost a great artist and—"

"*Mount Purgatorio* isn't my work," Sophie said.

"What?" I jumped up. "We both saw you painting it. Your real talent shines through this work."

"Not mine." Sophie grimaced.

Gina's eyes met mine as if agreeing that yes, my roomie had lost her mind. Yet Sophie seemed sane and even thoughtful when she fidgeted with the ripped hem of her dirty T-shirt and repeated, "*Mount Purgatorio* isn't my work."

Gina leaned against the balcony's railing and slowly sipped her drink. "Tell me about the painting that just emptied my bank account. If it isn't yours, whose is it?"

"Peggy's," she said. "My twin sister was switched with me."

"At birth?" Gina asked.

"No." Sophie hid her face in her bent knees. "In death."

12. Twins

Wow. Gina and I sat down, silent, both of us speechless and Sophie's words reverberating in the air. "Tell us," I said.

"We completed each other's sentences, fell asleep holding hands, and woke up from the same dreams. I didn't know where I ended and she began. We were like the two halves of a peach. I'm a lefty and Peggy was a righty. Even our smiles and frowns"—she grinned like a Jack-o'-lantern—"mine twists to the left and hers to the right. People couldn't tell us apart, not even our parents, so Mom dressed me in blue and Peggy in red, but we often switched colors to mess with people."

"If you're a lefty and she's a righty, isn't that something that parents would notice?" Gina asked.

"They were totally clueless." Sophie shivered under her blanket. "When we switched, I'd end up screwed, because Peggy would pretend to be me and become vicious to the funny-looking kids. She'd limp around like poor Cindy, that kind of thing. I became known as the mean one."

"Little bitch," I said at the same time Gina muttered, "What a little bully."

Sophie nodded. "You have no idea. She'd pull the wings off insects and kick stray cats. We couldn't have pets because of her. When I showed promise as a swimmer, Peggy got jealous. Once, no one looked and she pushed my face under water and held me down until I nearly blacked out. I'll never forget her evil little smile when she let me up. I quit that day, which was her intention. Then she got herself banned from the pool for nearly drowning a younger boy, but that's another story.

"We also played a lot. We'd each paint separately, then we'd switch easels. I'd add light to her darkness and she'd paint darkness into mine and fix my proportions. I'd sign on the left and she on the right. Above her signature, she always painted two girls in arabesque. You know, that ballet pose."

She gestured with her stained hands, and I imagined her as a little girl, sticking her tongue out in concentration painting away.

"Our styles . . . You could see the difference even in those drawings of stick figures Mom pinned on the fridge with the cookie magnet. Peggy's colors were winter cold and mine were spring happy. Anyway, the year we turned twelve we both got the flu. We even got sick together. I mean, we got it bad. Mom and Dad fed me hot chicken soup and the air whooshed in and out of my throat and I was afraid I'd suffocate. One night Peggy called my name in a choked cry, then she scratched my left arm with her fingernails. She clawed at me and wheezed and when I woke up she wasn't there."

Sophie nursed her tequila, then sat up, her eyes shining. "I'm starving. Can we order pizza?"

"I'm on it." Gina was immediately on her phone, clicking away. "This place delivers all night and pronto. Everything on top okay?"

When Sophie and I nodded, she finalized the order. The sight of my idol ordering pizza like any mortal was surreal.

"Go on, Sophie," Gina said in that low raspy voice. "You said Peggy wasn't there."

"Yes. My bed was empty and I was in her bed, wearing her red pajamas and the color was bleeding out of the red pajamas I was wearing, but it wasn't the color. My arm was bleeding where she scratched me. Look."

Sophie pulled up her left sleeve and showed us what I'd already seen, a forearm patterned with red fingernail scars. "The wounds became infected, so the doctor gave me antibiotics, but my arm never completely healed." She ran her fingers up and down the scars. "Well, when she wasn't there, I cried out and my dad came rushing in. His eyes were puffy from crying and he said…"

Sophie pulled down her sleeve and rubbed her arm again through the material.

"What did he say?" I asked.

"Daddy said that I'd been really sick and that they already buried Sophie."

Gina and I gasped a perfect *pas de deux*.

"*Peggy*," I corrected. "You mean they buried *Peggy*."

She shook her head. "We'd switched beds and colors and they thought she was me."

"No way." A chill ran down my spine at Sophie's horror. "Your parents thought they buried you?"

"I said, *Daddy, I'm Sophie* and he hugged me and said, *Sophie's dead*." Her voice dropped to a whisper. "She was only twelve and they buried…buried her without waiting for me."

"How awful." Gina leaned forward and stroked Sophie's arm.

The three of us were silent, half listening to the wild party across the street.

"Dad said I was too young to go to the cemetery. But my sister, wasn't she too young to be abandoned there?"

Impatient, I asked. "So how long before they figured out you were Sophie, and Peggy was the one they'd buried?"

"I kept telling them I was Sophie, but they didn't believe me. Mom stayed in her bed, locked in the fetal position and so very, very quiet, for a long time. She couldn't even look at me. I was devastated not only because my strong and mean Peggy was dead, but because everyone kept calling me by her name.

The anonymity of her death was an insult." She tightened her arms around her knees. "So was the snubbing of my life."

"What about school?" Gina asked.

Sophie dropped her chin to her knees. "Mrs. Smith assumed I was losing my mind from grief and suggested a therapist. The therapist was convinced I took on my sister's identity because of survivor's guilt or some other bullshit. I was lost without Peggy, like I was cut in half. She always knew what to do."

"That's crazy," Gina whispered.

"Totally fucked, right?" Sophie's gaze was on the mountain range far in the west. "They mourned me and I stood right in front of them. Called me Peggy. So I avoided them. They lived inside their grief and I was left outside, to deal with mine."

I was a year younger when I lost Ms. Angie.

I peeked at Gina, wondering if she'd also lost someone dear to her. She fumbled in the breast pocket of her jean jacket, then pulled out a rolled-up cigarette. She held her lighter with shaky hands and eyed me, then Sophie, one brow raised. We nodded our approval, although I had to shove away the brief, unwelcome mental image of my mother sitting idle and smoking all day. Gina wasn't my mother. Gina wasn't an idler.

She took a long draw, then passed the joint to me.

I inhaled and thought, Gina's lips were here first. How certifiably pathetic I was, swooning over my very straight teacher who had just broken up with her absolute-asshole-but-just-as-straight asshat of a boyfriend.

Sophie took a hit. "I was Peggy to everyone. In her death, my sister stole my identity like she had in life. No one said my name anymore. No *Sophie, I love you*s. No *Sophie, honey*s. I became dead to the world, wide awake and alive only in my mind."

"But how could they not tell the difference?" Gina finger-brushed her hair back. "What about your painting styles?"

"They couldn't tell the difference. My parents are simple folk," Sophie said. "We analyze art, or movies, or music, but they either liked something, or didn't."

"Idiots," I said. "Sorry, but they were asking for it by color coding their kids in the first place."

"Right." Sophie nodded. "They never really knew us."

Gina said, "You must have had at least one friend who wasn't fooled."

A burst of delightful laughter from across the street startled us.

"Peggy and I were like conjoined twins," Sophie said. "Who'd be your friend when you're attached to such toxicity? Now she was gone, they pretty much stayed away from me. I stopped correcting people, because I had no desire for extra sessions with that shrink who didn't know shit from shit. Paint and music were my only friends."

She gazed far below to the 405, where bright headlights and red taillights glimmered against the dark silhouette of the Santa Monica Mountains. Two ever-undulating snakes were slithering home.

"I stayed up at night, painting and letting strange ideas take root in my head. The whole world believed I was Peggy and so did Mom and Dad. If my parents could make such a mistake, why couldn't Death?"

13. Haunting

"Oh, Sophie." I took her hand in mine. "You let me go on and on about some imaginary loss, and you carry this real, abysmal sadness."

Sophie shrugged. "I didn't want to spend time with my parents, who were too blind to see *me*, so my only happy place was my room, where I could pretend Peggy had only gone out. I was afraid to sleep, because I couldn't dream without her. I'd put music in my ears and paint all night."

"How lonely for you," Gina said.

"I wanted to believe my sister was in a beautiful place. One night I painted a serene landscape with spring flowers, faeries and butterflies. Then I finally relaxed enough to fall asleep. When I woke up, the painting had been reworked with dark touches, details like rain clouds and demons lurking behind an icy hill. It was Peggy, working the canvas from the beyond and communicating with me. Is that crazy?"

I saw in Sophie's face the need for our reassurance and clarity. *Am I crazy?* she wanted to know.

"You just imagined she'd made the changes because she had done it so many times before, right?" I asked with hope. "You were the one who added the dark touches to honor her memory."

"No, it was Peggy. She signed at the bottom right and above the signature she painted that emblem of two women in arabesque with their hands almost touching in midair. She also corrected the proportions of my faeries with razor-edged sharp lines. Peggy was more talented. She could draw hands and feet. I couldn't."

She stretched her paint-smudged fingers and slowly rotated her hand. "A well-drawn hand, like a face, should express a personality. It's the hardest body part to get right. I still can't do it for shit, but Peggy mastered hands and feet as a child."

As Sophie spoke, I repeatedly peeked at Gina, and once, I caught her doing the same, peeking at me with dreamy eyes. I had an urge to give drawing a whirl and sketch the expressive hands she now held in prayer position against her heart. I wanted to hear her story and have her all to myself, with Sophie far away.

"From that night on things changed," Sophie continued. "When I stayed up those long and lonely nights, Peggy was in me, using my right hand to paint her dark scenes."

Gina picked up the joint, and Sophie reached for the cigarette lighter and held it for her. Gina blew smoke toward the black sky in a long sigh. Disco lights from across the street blinked in brilliant colors and animated the calm planes of her profile and neckline. That controlled elegance somehow balanced Sophie's wild tale.

On the freeway, red lights crept north toward the San Fernando Valley, and white lights crawled south toward the beach cities. Some come, some go, I thought for no reason. And Gina Caldwell is here, in my apartment, smoking dope, drinking tequila, and listening with me to Sophie's harrowing story. Now that Sophie had hogged the evening, if I told Gina about Ms. Angie, she'd think Sophie and me the strangest roommates in LA.

"The younger you are, the longer time stretches, so imagine those long years," Sophie said. "I lived at home until my high school graduation, then I came to UCLA. My generous aunt had a vacant apartment, then you, Ellie, saw my ad and you know the rest."

"Why didn't you tell me about it?" I asked.

"I don't want to talk about her." Sophie trembled. "Even now, just telling you this, I feel her muttering and whispering inside me. I barely visit my hometown or my parents, because when someone calls me by her name it starts. I feel that black pit and hear her voice, like I have schizophrenia."

"You mean, everybody still thinks you're Peggy?" Gina asked. "Even your parents?"

"Even them."

"You should straighten out the records," I said, incensed. "You're a grown up now. Stop letting them abuse you."

"I can't deal with this," Sophie said. "It brings her back."

"What brought her back this last time?" Gina asked.

Gina was so matter-of-fact about the dead Peggy coming back and using Sophie's hands to paint. Sophie had believed my crazy story, why was it so hard for me to believe hers?

Sophie closed her eyes. "When we won that award, seeing my name on the fake headstone made me physically ill."

"I told them not to use that stupid trophy," Gina said, annoyed. "*Your* name is on the actual headstone, not Peggy's."

"You should go to the cemetery," I said.

"I'm not ready," Sophie said. "I can't, no way."

"Not ready? Why?" Leaning forward too far, I fell off the wicker chair and landed on the cement floor, where I remained sitting cross-legged. "What's the worst that could happen?"

Sophie yanked up her left sleeve. "Look how these scars inflame when I simply talk about her. Ellie, you don't know her."

"But she'd been dead for so long," I said.

"That means nothing to her, Ellie. Nothing. She used to switch us all the time and get me in trouble and she'd come out smelling like a rose."

Gina's phone vibrated with a message. "Pizza's here," she said. "Paid, including a tip."

Before I got to ask more probing questions, Sophie jumped up and ran to the door, clearly relieved at the interruption. Back on the balcony, she attacked the first slice, then sandwiched together two more and made a pig of herself by devouring those too. Gina and I grazed on one slice each while sneaking peeks at each other.

Sophie, oblivious to anything but the food, pointed at the remaining slice, her mouth full.

"Go ahead," I said.

I was disgusted by the way she made the last slice disappear and then licked the box clean of crumbs. She wiped her mouth, leaned back and rubbed her belly.

"That was the best pizza ever." Sophie burped loudly.

We burst out laughing, carrying on for at least five minutes. At the sight of melted mozzarella dangling from Sophie's giggling chin, I lost it completely. She was definitely back to being my happy, funny friend.

"I'm parched," Gina said. "You got some ice water?"

Sophie flew to the kitchen and returned, hugging a bunch of small icy bottles. She let them fall and roll among shot glasses and crumbly tortilla chips.

"So how'd you resolve everything?" Gina asked. "How'd it end?

"It never ends." Sophie drank an entire bottle of water without pause. "It still takes as little as a certain memory, or someone calling me by her name to bring her back. She'll stay with me until she's painted tons of work out of me and I'm half dead from exhaustion."

"What do you do with those dark paintings?" Gina asked.

"Eventually I paint over them. Erase them."

"Show them," Gina said. "They're brilliant."

"No way." Sophie's eyebrows formed a V in her disgust. "I can't even look at those when I feel well."

A screech of a car followed by squeals made us peer down through the railing. People were shouting in the street below, because of a fender bender involving a limousine. A police cruiser slowed to a stop. A group of drunk girls bubbled up and out of the limo's sunroof like a freshly poured glass of champagne.

A woman in a short bridal veil leaned against the cruiser's window and begged in drunken loudness, "Don't ruin our party, officer. I'm going to be a bride."

"A normal night in Westwood," Gina said.

The lights on the freeway dwindled to a trickle. The party across the street got wilder. Here on our balcony, the cold wind made me shiver.

We were but a cluster of pathetic beings speeding toward a certain demise, frightened by ghost stories, excited by a drink, a joint, or fresh pizza. The mundane moved us, and not much would be left of our bodies when we died. My teeth, my bones and the hair now covering my shoulders would survive long after me, but not my daily routines, not the pleasure I got from art or music or a beautiful face. Gina's face.

Dead Peggy kept coming back to haunt her sister. If *I* could choose a time and place to haunt with my immortal soul, it would be this moment, this spot, eight floors above Wilshire Boulevard, with the woman who came back into my life after years of dreams and fantasies.

Gina turned to look at me, as Ms. Angie had, long ago in that blooming garden gone to weeds. Her eyes burned at me in the dark, and she wasn't the impossible Angie Mead of my childhood. Gina Caldwell was my equal, newly open to love.

She smiled with uncertainty and tenderness. When she reached out and stroked a strand of my hair, I thanked the darkness for hiding my blush.

"Elektra," she whispered, and her sultry voice spread magical warmth through my bones and blood. Suddenly, I didn't care a hoot about hell, paradise, or even Sophie, who leaned back and closed her eyes, relaxing for the first time in days. All I cared about was Gina.

A sigh escaped my mouth. "Oh, Ms. Caldwell."

"Gina, please."

"*Ms. Caldwell* is much hotter," I said.

We could both light up the street with sparks of electricity. I wanted to know if her lips were soft. Our faces closed the small gap and I discovered the answer.

14. The River of Fire

"Hey, you two, don't fucking mind me," Sophie said.

"Your turn to clean up." I took Gina's hand and lead her to the only tidy section of the apartment, my room, where the bed was clean and inviting. Some of our clothes came off and some stayed on as we tore into each other like a pair of wild beasts.

I cried out when Gina uttered, "The love that moves the sun and the other stars."

Yes, that's exactly what Gina Caldwell, PhD, said when she came, taking my breath away for more than one reason.

"The love what the fuck?" I asked.

"Pretentious, I know." She buried her face in my neck, laughing. "Sorry, Elektra. This coming announcement started as a joke and I could never shake it. You know, famous last words."

"*Coming announcement?*" I straddled her. "That's what I get for making love to a brainiac."

"I'm sure you have your weird secrets too."

"I have a boob fetish," I said. "I've been dreaming about yours for, let's see, more than ten years."

"You've only known me a few months," she said.

"That's a whole 'nother story." Her bra was still on. I removed it, looked her straight in the eye and kissed each hardened nipple until she moaned. "It involves a trellis of hanging tea roses, black rubber boots and lime-green gardening gloves."

"Sounds painful," she said, a catch in her voice.

"You have no idea."

I decided to tell her everything there and then, and ask if her name used to be Angie Mead and if she remembered me, but she had a few creative suggestions that sent my imagination soaring. In one, she wanted me to sit on her face.

"Can you recite Dante?" A glint was in her eyes.

"Some," I said.

She grasped my ass. "Make it dirty."

"Yes, Ms. Caldwell," I said, obediently straddling her. "Let's see... *I came on top of you from those holiest waters new, remade, reborn, like a sun-wakened tree...*" Her tongue ran circles in the right places as I stuck to the text. *"...that spreads my legs like new foliage to the Spring dew..."* I climaxed in long waves. *"In sweetest coochie, hot, perfect, pure and ready for a fuck."* I screamed the last word.

"That's it," she said. "You're expelled and I'm dropping *The Purgatorio* from the curriculum. How can I ever teach it again with the word *coochie* on my mind?"

I looked down at her face in the moonlight and smoothed her hair back. "Tell me again what would happen if we didn't have *The Divine Comedy.*"

"I guess you'd have to recite *Romeo and Juliet* on top of me."

I inhaled the Wild Rose between her incredible breasts. "Since Dante's Verona inspired Shakespeare's Verona, we wouldn't have *Romeo and Juliet.*"

"Now who's the damned brainiac?" She spoke in her low whisper. "No pizza." Kiss. "No ice cream." Kiss. "No espresso. No medical innovations, no fascism, no football and don't forget lightbulbs. Changing a lightbulb would take three people."

"Now the truth," I said. "You totally made up that bit about the eyeglasses."

"That whole hour was speculative," she said. "But not a waste of time, because I never want to hear ignorant questions such as *why do we study Dante?*"

We slept until daylight, entangled in each other's arms. Then we ventured into the shower and let hot water sluice over our bodies. Gina wanted to shampoo my hair and, for the first time, I let someone do it for me. We remained in the shower until the water ran cold.

I found Sophie at her easel in the sunlit living room, headset on, dancing to the music in her ears and working a saccharine-pink Madonna and Child on a powder-blue background. Seeing me, she pulled off the headset.

"Well, hallelujah." She raised a hand to her temple in salute. "I fuck the world, but *you* dig class."

"And you are finally using your earphones," I said.

"To block your poetry-fucking each other," she said. "I get enough Dante in the classroom."

A smiling Gina strolled out of my room, adorable hair messed up and a towel wrapped around her. When she took me in her arms, both our towels unraveled and fell to our feet.

"Stay right there, you two." Sophie stuffed a paint-laden brush between her teeth and swiftly replaced the canvas on her easel with a fresh one. "Don't move an inch."

Gina separated her swollen lips from mine only long enough to say, "We aren't moving. Ever."

Paper crackled under my feet, one of Sophie's discarded sketches. We remained in our naked embrace while she quickly painted and whistled a happy tune. She was my Sophie again, back to the way she was before her breakdown. I so hoped that after telling us her story, she'd stay okay.

"I'll make you coffee and breakfast," Sophie said. "But don't you guys dare looky-loo until this is done."

Back in bed after breakfast, we made love into the late afternoon, and each announcement of *the love that moves the sun and the other stars* gave me a new fit of giggles.

I held Gina tightly, taking it in, happy. What would she make of the story about Angie Mead? And how exactly do you ask the woman you're crazy about, to whom you've just made love, if she is someone else you crushed on in your childhood? What if Gina, like Sophie, had a secret twin she preferred not to talk about? If I told her, she might leave in a huff and never see me again.

"I googled you," I finally said.

Her hand moved to my belly and lower, starting me again. "I've heard *diddled* and *screwed*. Never *googled*."

"You used to teach elementary school."

"Briefly, in another life," she said.

I grew lightheaded. "Another life?"

"Events made me change directions. One evening I simply couldn't go home to piles of student papers in my lonely apartment, so I dumped myself onto a park bench and turned to pondering my unfinished doctoral thesis. It was called, let's see . . ." She leaned on one elbow and gazed up at the ceiling. "Morals and Philosophy in Dante's *Purgatorio*. Yes, it's a mouthful. You aren't going to believe this,"—she scooted around until her back was against the headboard and she could see my eyes—"but while I sat there, a storm exploded over me out of nowhere, with strange red zigzags cracking the sky."

The old buzzing started in my ears.

I said, "The red sky was heavy, like strips of torn silk, then it opened wide and poured down wave after wave of rain from above, like unrelenting ocean swells."

"What?" Gina's eyes went round and wide. "Did you see it?"

"My story later." I was still unsure what to tell her and what to withhold.

"Okay," Gina whispered. "It was shocking, frightening, but that storm cleared my mind and opened my eyes to what I loved most: the study of Dante's work. The way I was jolted into action was like being born into a new world. The next day I quit my job, then I finished my thesis. I also translated his first work." Her eyes bore into mine.

"At least your new world was an improvement," I said.

"That red storm brought me only misery."

"Tell me."

"If I tell, you may not want to have anything to do with me."

She kissed both my hands. "Try me."

"Okay. Here you go." Then I told her about the first person who treated me with kindness and who made me love her, only to vanish into a void. I also told her about eccentric Virgil, who was my only solace.

When I concluded, the room was in shadows. "After all that, she didn't exist for anyone but me and Virgil." I shook my head. Years later, I was still trying to make sense of the irrational. "That was my first heartbreak, but the heartbreak was mixed with what I took as cruelty from my classmates and maybe..." I was finally going to say it out loud. "I mean, nobody but one strange old guy remembered Ms. Angie, and I'd had conversations with her. I'd seen her with other kids, with her daughter, working in the rose garden..."

"Oh, honey."

"I'm okay, but for so long I didn't know what to think. What to feel." I blinked tears away, hoping they wouldn't fall. "I still don't understand."

She smoothed my hair. "We're like moths, Elektra, attracted to the flame that could burn us. Angie was out of reach, but you and I came back for each other."

"How so?" I asked, intrigued at how naturally she accepted my story. "You not only don't mind being compared with someone else, you almost encourage it."

Gina's gaze bore into my soul. "You never stop loving those you loved before. If Ms. Angie was the reason you're attracted to me, I welcome your memories, your fantasies, everything you are. Look, Elektra, I've watched you now for weeks—"

"Have you?" I asked.

"It isn't only the way you see me. I also see you." Gina played with a strand of my hair. "And here we are."

The fears for my sanity, those terrifying doubts were gone, and I felt free.

"The pain of my childhood was worth this," I said. "This now, this one moment, whether it lasts or not."

"It can last." She held me at arm's length. "With one condition."

She'd want me to quit her class or something else terribly ethical. "Want me to sign an NDA?" I asked.

She stuck her tongue in her cheek in that delightful and naughty Ms. Angie way. "No deal between us could ever include gardening."

She looked so delicious, I started kissing her. "Do I have to recite dirty poetry to be allowed re-entry?" I asked, hand between her legs.

"You just have to dip in the river of fire."

And we became a tangle of arms and legs and whispers.

She pulled me close, her soft lips at my ear. "*At this point power failed high fantasy but, like a wheel in perfect balance turning, I felt my will and my desire impelled by the love that moves the sun and the other stars.*"

"That sounds different," I said.

"This translation contains the words *perfect* and *desire* and this is what you are to me, Elektra." She kissed me.

I was safe. Her words held the promise of forever, like Dante's words that had already lived more than seven hundred years and would continue to live as long as people could read, and maybe beyond that.

15. A Faerie Tale in Seven Time Jumps

Tsundoku

Alone scarlet poinsettia decorated Gina's door, on a street twinkling with Christmas lights. She stood at her gate, statuesque and delicious in my favorite black tailored suit and her long legs in impossibly high heels.

"Oh, you centerfold, you," I said, wild with desire.

A little grin curving her pink lips, she drew her hands from behind her back and wiggled her fingers. Fingers encased in lime-green gardening gloves.

I gasped. "Only last week and already—"

"I take notes," she said in a husky tone.

I was ready to take her, right there, under the sky on the lush lawn, only... there was no lawn or lushness anywhere. The ground was covered with thorns, yellow dandelions and tall weeds. A blooming purple Jacaranda relieved the dry ugliness.

The edges of her image fuzzed up as my vision dimmed. I was again a little girl, lost on a stormy night.

"Don't disappear on me," I whispered in great fear.

"I won't, Elektra." Still wearing those gloves, she took my hand. Then she was warm and fragrant in my arms. Even as I held on to her and she was so real, the memory of losing her flooded me with the visions of a bloody sky.

"What's happening to you?" she cried out, holding my face between her yellow-gloved hands, looking at me with fear-torn eyes. "I'm not her."

Her frightened voice brought me back to the now. I swallowed my fear, although it still laced my soul.

"I'm sorry." She tossed the gloves aside. "This was a bad, bad idea."

"No, it was great. I dig it, really," I said, unsure I did, but appreciating her little joke just the same. I painted a smile on my face, shook off the weirdness, and asked in my normal voice, "What's with the weeds and thorns?"

Gina scanned her front yard, her free hand pressed to her hip. "I told you, I'm no gardener."

"And this tree." I frowned up at the Jacaranda. "Isn't it too late in the year for it to be in such great bloom?"

"This tree never stops blooming."

"Strange." I gazed up at the stunning flowers dripping purple from above. I trembled. Could this ever-blooming canopy protect us from the next blood rain when it comes?

It won't come. I had to change this mood. *It won't come.*

I gave the thorny yard a once over. "A week together may be too early to ask this, but can I have my way with the place?"

"Not before I have my sweet way with you."

Gina pulled me in through a door that needed a coat of paint, then through a small kitchen with scratched cabinets, and a living room with a blazing red brick fireplace. Her bedroom was a mad library, with towers of books tilting in corners and loose books strewn across the floor and the fluffy futon.

She ripped my clothes off as I stood in awe of the mess.

"I forgot to warn you—I suffer from a mild case of bibliomania. The Japanese call it *tsundoku.*"

"I love when you lecture-fuck me, Dr. Caldwell," I said, planting kisses all over her face and neck.

We rolled on white sheets among piles of books.

"I'm a mess," Gina said.

"With tits like yours, who cares?" I asked.

Projects

The toilet was a whole new experience.

"Why does it sway?" I asked, sitting on it for the first time.

"Brian wasn't a fix-it kind of guy," Gina said from the bedroom, "so whatever breaks here remains broken."

"This one's an easy fix." I tied my hair back with a scarf and went to work, tightening the toilet to the floor with tools I kept in my Jeep.

"You turn me on," she said huskily.

Already on my knees, I worshipped her on the spot.

After the first night—sleepless for me because of the screeching garden gate—I replaced the rusted hinges while Gina leaned against the ivy-draped wall and watched me, fascinated. I was excited to impress my new girlfriend with skills I'd perfected over the years.

"I love projects," I said.

"Then you came to the right place," she said. "Make this your home."

"Are you asking me to move in with you?"

"Yes, please," she said.

On a rainy day in January, George helped me pack his pickup and my Jeep with boxes of books and old recordings of dead opera divas.

"Does your hot new girlfriend need an ass model?" he asked.

"This one wants only me," I said, tingling with happiness.

Bliss

As the old house needed TLC, I poured my love into it. The walls needed paint, the kitchen cabinets needed new knobs, the garden was wild. I took my time with the projects, in the process, falling in love with my new home. Mine and Gina's. The interior gleamed with fresh white paint, and when I replaced the weeds with flowers and installed a fire pit, the garden was transformed into a living space, where we enjoyed occasional lunches and nightly dinners in the shade of the ever-blooming magical Jacaranda.

Gina kept teaching Dante at UCLA and, two years later, when I graduated with a bachelor in English, my business grew and I earned a decent living editing and formatting manuscripts. My bills and Gina's became *our* bills, and together we managed a good living with a little left for fun.

Time flew as we built a happy home and a shared life, long rich days punctuated by holidays to San Francisco and New York and once to San Antonio, Texas. Gina looked adorable in a cowboy hat, and when I bought myself a pair of black boots, she suggested that I buy a similar pair in brown for Sophie.

As I shaped other people's books into future published works, I dreamed of one day doing the same for myself. I was scratching at an outline for a novel, yet nothing was anywhere near finished.

Occasionally, Gina regaled me with a Dante recitation before I fell asleep, and when we made love, she'd always announce *the love that moves the sun and the other stars*. The words didn't make me laugh anymore.

Trivia

In our second year together, we decided to lay bamboo floors. It wasn't as easy as it first seemed, but we managed it with the help of dance music and pitchers of margaritas. When Gina looked delicious in a tank top and short shorts, I seduced her on a freshly stuck patch in the kitchen. One of the planks by the stove came off, and we could never make it match the rest. That floor board cupped and creaked and remained imperfect. It became our sacred spot, forever reminding us of another happy day.

One night, maybe a month after my graduation, we were watching Jeopardy! as usual and dazzling each other with our knowledge of useless trivia.

Gina knew the arts, history, and who won an Academy Award for some long-forgotten film, including the artists who designed the costumes. I got politics, science, music, plumbing, and car mechanics. Together we would have made the *Tournament of Champions*, that is, *if* we were allowed lengthy, feverish, and frenzied discussions.

The final category was *famous last words*. To our delight, the clue was *the love that moves the sun and the other stars*.

Both Gina and I yelled the answer, me screaming *"Paradiso,"* while Gina used the correct question form and said, "What is *Dante's Paradiso?"*

A wild-eyed disc jockey named Elviva Geronimo was the only one of the three contestants who answered correctly. That night, pleased with herself for winning, Gina had her way with me on the living room couch. Instead of her usual orgasmic cry of triumph, she cried out "Elviva Geronimo!"

Too bad her coming announcements were a private joke we couldn't share even with Sophie. She would have died laughing over that one.

Sophie

Done with school a quarter before me, Sophie had rented a studio apartment not far from us on the canals. As soon as she moved in, her apartment exploded with paintings in progress and art supplies.

Her place was too cramped for socializing, so we mostly ended up hanging out on Rose Avenue, eating by the fire pit, or watching *Young Frankenstein*, *The Princess Bride*, or *Galaxy Quest* for the umpteenth time.

We remained inseparable; an extended family who stuck by each other and did everything together—theater, movies, dinners, holidays.

One night, Sophie found a golden cocker spaniel roaming, lost in the street. When no one claimed him, Gina and I named him Max and made him ours.

Whenever Gina was too busy to join me on an evening out, Sophie jumped at the chance to fill in as my date. She did the same for Gina when I was buried in work up to my neck. Our friends called her *the mistress*, and we laughed it off. Gina and I were too secure in our relationship to let the jokes sting, and Sophie was too easygoing to let anything bother her.

Anything but her demons.

She mostly painted chocolate-box oil pieces of faeries with apple cheeks and transparent wings, too sweet for my taste, seen one, seen them all. Her buyers had collections of her works, mostly religious paintings such as *Blue Jesus on the Hill* and *Madonna in Purples*, all nudes, painted by number. She paid the rent from her clients' low expectations and deep pockets, selling her mass-produced "shit art that makes them so happy they spit up green." Yet her career never took off the way she wanted. She never landed a single show in a real gallery.

She preferred to work and sleep in the same space, surrounded by canvases and hip-hop music. Among those works-in-progress, she had sex with her models. Men and women; she liked them all.

If paintings could talk...

Paintings didn't, but Sophie did. She was unapologetic about objectifying her lovers.

"Seducing the already naked saves precious time," she'd say.

Over many a meal she prepared and devoured in our kitchen, she'd tell her stories.

"Your life is a faerie tale," I told her when she recounted one particularly hot tryst in intimate detail. "I've been documenting your stories since that day I moved into your aunt's place, and there's enough material for a hot erotic novel. I'll help you write it."

"I'm no scribbling monster like you," she said.

"Come on," I said. "Sex sells."

She raised her arms in surrender. "I don't even like reading, but go for it. I'm too busy fucking my way through life. Feel free to ad-lib, novelize, amplify, dramatize or whatever you writers call fictionalizing."

Sophie was alternately happy and possessed. Every visit to her parents' house started a dark episode that lasted weeks. When it was over, she'd cover her frightful images with white primer and paint over them. As she didn't allow me to photograph those painting, they were lost forever.

In no time, she'd be back to her usual pinks and blues that set my teeth on edge but made her clients cough up those greens. Her models returned, and with them, the sex she'd later describe in detail. And those stories, like Sophie, kept coming.

"I've a new one for your book," she'd say before each yarn, and I would take her newest story as fresh permission to go on novelizing her life.

I shaped her stories into a picaresque novel whose Sophie-like roguish protagonist lived for sex and by her wits.

This was my plot in a nutshell: An artist afraid of commitment goes into her still-wet paintings and has quickie sex with her painted images. She has to leave before the paint dries, or she'd become trapped in ridiculous situations and positions. She often did get trapped.

I was writing the novel for myself, but also for Sophie. I meant to make her realize her own importance and to help her shake off her dead sister's power. I wished I could infuse Sophie with my abundant happiness. As it was, she lived an occasional private hell, and when she did, artistic brilliance sprouted from her mind like vibrant tendrils slithering through the ruins of an abandoned mansion.

First Draft

On nights Gina taught her classes, I packed my laptop and wrote in a small local coffeeshop, where the espresso was divine. One night in March, deep in edits, the familiar metal-tube clicking of hobnails echoed in my ears. I raised my gaze and there he stood with a smile on his face and that same bedraggled laurel wreath on his head of curls. His flowing toga gleamed white in the darkness.

I opened my arms for a hug, but his hand signaled me to keep my distance. Right. He hated contact.

"What are you up to, Virgil? Where do you live?"

"Here and there," he said.

Was he homeless? I didn't know how to ask that.

"Are you still working for the school system?"

"I'm between jobs," he said. "I move around, watching the world and recording history."

I knew it. Jobless and homeless. I was again fascinated by the rhythm of his speech, the length of time he held certain vowels had nothing to do with normal English pronunciation. His voice was the same as I remembered from my childhood, soft and calming.

"Years ago I meant to ask you about your accent. What is it?"

"Latin is my first language," he said. "What today they call Classical Latin."

"Are you serious? Who uses Latin other than priests and certain professionals?"

"No more than a million people." He dragged a chair close and sat. "In my day it was the main spoken language. What you hear in my voice is a mix of my humble background and good education."

Yes, delusional, but still a true friend. As such, he was quickly done with the small talk.

"What are you working on?" he asked.

"The second draft of a novel. Want to read the first?"

He wiggled *gimme* with his fingers.

I gave him the pages. He started reading right there, moving the pages aside very quickly. He chuckled to himself as he read, and at one point, laughed out loud.

"I could take a look at your poetry," I said, "if you have it with you."

"Anyone can look at my work," he said matter-of-factly. "The *Bucolics*, the *Georgics*, and all 9,896 lines of the *Aeneid* in dactylic hexameter. That final one took the last five years of my life and practically killed me."

Exactly what Sophie said about the *Mona Lisa* and Leonardo. *She practically killed him.* Would anything I wrote be intense or good enough to kill me?

He pointed a finger at the page, eyes rapidly reading. "This is good."

Who was he really? The bright white of his clean toga didn't fit with my image of homelessness. Here was a man who couldn't get his shit together enough to hold a job or keep a roof over his head—or so I assumed—mad enough to believe himself to be the actual author of the *Aeneid*, yet he calmly turned my pages.

Gina's theory about the dead came to mind.

That night she first came to our Wilshire apartment, Sophie had asked, "Do you believe the dead visit us?" and Gina had replied, "They are all around us, but very few people can see them."

Dead or alive, was he actually there? What would it mean about my own sanity if some guy pretending to be Virgil was only in my imagination? The small coffeeshop wasn't packed at night. As we weren't disturbed by the few who came in, I didn't get a chance to observe who else could see him.

He was so immersed in reading, I didn't want to disturb him with questions. I waited for a chance to tell him that Gina and I decided to get married.

Finally he raised his head. "Your book is structured as a frame story. It reminds me of *Arabian Nights* or the later *Decameron*."

"You know that one by heart too?" I asked.

"Not too well." He lit up a joint. "Boccaccio came almost fourteen hundred years after me."

I laughed. "What are you smoking there?"

"Try it." He passed me the burning joint. "I call this hybrid *Sfumato*."

"Haze? Clever." I took a hit.

"Do you have a title?" he asked.

"Not yet. Suggestions?"

"Use a saucy phrase your friend used; the one who tells the dirty stories. A good title makes or breaks you. You think my *Aeneid* would have turned into a classic if I gave it a boring name such as *The Fall of Troy*?"

"Come to my wedding," I said, then I had an idea. "Walk me down the aisle and give me away to Gina. It'll be so cool. She knows all about you."

"I'm honored," he said. "but I can't do that."

Touching was the problem, I decided. Walking me down the aisle would involve touching my arm and that, he could not do.

"I'll be there for you," he promised, glancing down at his yellow watch. "Got to run."

"If you let me tighten the strap, it won't keep rolling around your wrist."

"I like it loose," he said. "Like time itself."

"Does it still run counterclockwise?" I asked.

"That's the nature of a countdown watch," he said.

"Countdown to what?"

"When you're ready, you'll know," he said.

Such cryptic answers.

Before we said goodnight, I asked if he had enough money for dinner and he nodded, but I sneaked a few bucks into his hand anyway. "Consultation fee," I said.

The Wedding

When my planted spring flowers turned our garden into a Japanese painting, Gina and I got married under the ever-blooming Jacaranda. We were surrounded by family and close friends, and Max in a dog tux was our best man. My hair, decorated with a garland made of Jacaranda blossoms, free flowed around my shoulders and lower, below the hem of the white jacket I used as a dress.

Gina wore a new white suit I wanted to rip off of her even as we spoke our vows, our bare feet on a natural carpet of purple-violet flowers. Her beauty glowed against the magnificent blooms, as I held her slender hands in mine and declared, "Nothing would ever be perfect, not even heaven, and for most of us, paradise is purgatory at best, yet my paradise is the love that moves the sun and the other stars."

From the corner of my eye I glimpsed billowing white beyond the front gate. Virgil had kept his promise to be there for me, and his presence brought me comfort and a tearful smile. In my all white and with that floral wreath around my forehead, the two of us were closer than ever.

Sophie, our unwitting matchmaker, presented us with *Love in Titian Red*, an incredible painting in happy pastels of the two of us nude, my hair blurring into red veils in the background. We hung *Titian* on the living room wall, where it constantly reminded me of my perfect first night with Gina.

Yet, perfection isn't a natural state and complete bliss has twisted ways of turning into a nightmare.

Opposite *Love in Titian Red*, above our fireplace, we hung a second piece. *Mount Purgatorio* was one of Sophie's best works, and its realism scared me to the red marrow of my white bones.

As for my happiness, each time we were caught in the rain, I expected Gina to wash down, soak in, and disappear into the soil like Angie Mead.

16. Fucking My Way Through Life

An ABBA golden oldie blasted the paint off our living room ceiling. I sipped a margarita and locked my gaze on Gina from across a swaying sea of our dancing friends. Three years together, and she still made those butterflies flutter in my stomach.

You did it, she mouthed.

Encouraged by Gina, Sophie and my elusive friend Virgil, I now had a published novel titled *Fucking My Way Through Life*. Like a new mother who watched her newborn baby from every angle, I couldn't get enough of my creation. I secretly tucked one copy under my pillow and would smell its fresh pages before falling asleep.

"Elektra has lists of the lists she makes," Gina would joke about my obsessive nature. With the publication of this book, my list of wishes had been fulfilled—a loving wife, a published novel that paid off all our bills, and a roomful of friends who celebrated with me.

Sophie twirled to the music, her slim figure swaying with the beat. I had everything, and she still had nothing.

My gaze kept drifting to *Mount Purgatorio*. Gina had paid Sophie a small fortune for it when both of them were broke, and it played a major part in our beginning, but the disquieting piece was out of place in this happy room. As I looked at it, a creeping darkness threatened to wake me from my beautiful dream.

A fake eyelash fell into my eye. Damn those things Sophie had talked me into.

"You should get duded up for your big week," she'd said a few days earlier when we barbecued chicken in the garden.

"You deserve it," Gina had echoed. "You worked so hard to get here, you should look your best."

A hundred bucks later, Sophie said, "Wow, those lashes pop your eyes out," which made me picture eyeballs popping out of their sockets in Dante's hell.

My attention slid from Sophie's horror-filled masterpiece down to a stack of books on the floor, copies of the novel loosely based on her life. The cover art—an artist in the ecstasy of creation—was Sophie's design. Even the title was hers.

Sophie was the inadvertent owner of my life, from the moment she'd given me her low rent deal, until now. I was grateful to her for granting me the permission to tell her stories in my own way.

The book's dedication read, *For Gina and Sophie, my pillars of strength, who were the reason I could write in the first place. And to Virgil.*

Sophie was now hopping about to the money song. She ruled every aspect and corner of our house. Her paintings, my published book, my dog, even Gina's love—all those perfections were mine because of my dear friend Sophie. How could I help her overcome the bleakness that often darkened her soul?

I stepped into the garden, where some of my guests sat drinking by the fire pit.

Hobnailed sandals echoed from the street, then a ghostly figure emerged from the night. I opened the gate wide, but he refused to come in. "I avoid crowds, Ellie."

His bright toga billowed like smoke in the ocean breeze. "I knew you could do it. Congratulations." The brown paper bag he handed me contained a few cigars emptied of tobacco and tightly repacked with marijuana.

"*Dream Queen* variety," he said. "Your title will catch fire," he promised, and that was reassuring to hear, but his next words summed up my fears. "I'm here with a warning. Stay home for the next few days."

"Why? What do you mean by *stay home?*"

"This is what I can tell you," he said. "Remember that red rain and the first time everything changed for you? Please stay under your roof and keep your loved ones with you. All of them."

"I can't." I was compelled to argue my case, although fearful hints from the past appeared like video clips in my mind. "Gina and I made plans to live it up in Santa Barbara for the weekend. It'll be my first ever reading event—"

"It's almost time." He pointed at his sagging watch.

"Your watch moves counterclockwise," I reminded him.

"Countdown, remember?" He tapped the watch face. "Please bury a copy of your book under your magical tree."

"Bury it? Why?"

"For posterity," he said. "What if everything was lost? *Fucking My Way* is greater than the *Aeneid* and *The Divine Comedy*. Greater than both of us."

And that declaration confirmed without a doubt, that he was more cuckoo than the cuckoo bird up the tree. Yes, I got paid nicely for my work, but it was lighthearted fantasy and no greater than any person or any book of classic literature. Virgil's madness was so complete, he came out the other end of the crazy tunnel sounding totally sane.

"The book is published," I said. "It is widely available."

"Do it now." His clear enunciation wiped out his strange accent. "Write an inscription in one of those copies and sign your name. Then double bag it and bury it within the tree's roots."

"What should I write?"

"Make it fundamentally yours," Virgil said.

I pointed through the open gate at a group of my friends who were roasting marshmallows in the fire pit. Most were published with my help and way before me. "I can't imagine any of them burying copies of their books. What would they think of me?"

"You're a storyteller," he said. "Make up something."

"Come meet everyone," I said. "You and Gina would get along well."

"I told you, no one gets me the way you do."

"What does that mean?" I asked.

"It means you have to do as I say, bury the book and shelter in at home. You'll have the rest of your life to celebrate."

I knew not to argue with someone who lived in his own world and believed himself to be a poet who died two thousand years ago. Of course I had no intention of burying anything anywhere, now or ever.

"I'll get you some tacos," I said.

When I returned to the gate, he was gone, and the always hungry Sophie grabbed the stacked plate from my hands and started devouring the food. I lit one of the cigars.

She watched in amazement. "Where'd you get it?"

"Virgil's gift."

"Your imaginary friend," she said between chews.

"Why do you call him imaginary?" I was suddenly irritated. Sophie had no reason to call him that.

"If he's real and he's your friend," Sophie said between bites, "then why isn't he here? Why didn't you invite him to your wedding?"

"I did, but he couldn't come because . . . oh, what's the point?" I waved my pot cigar and glowing embers flew from it. "And how could someone imaginary hand me something real?" I took a hit. A damn good something too.

Sophie stopped eating long enough to say, "Good point." She took her own hit. As she blew out the smoke, for a moment, her face became a skeletal mask.

I gasped. "Sophie!"

"What's wrong now?" She was perfectly fine again. "Best shit I ever smoked. Is it *Cinderella 99*?"

"*Dream Queen*," I managed, before the food I'd eaten started rising up my throat. I barely made it to the bathroom, where I puked it all into the toilet. In the mirror, my reflection was ghostly pale.

Bury the book. Shelter in place. Was I losing my mind? Better than the *Aeneid* or *The Divine Comedy* . . . Or was it better than Shakespeare? Virgil was crazy, and I didn't believe a word he said.

I ran to our bedroom. Where was the copy I kept under my pillow? I tore through the bedding, searching frantically, muttering to myself the whole time.

I found the book on the floor, its corner chewed up by Max.

Everything's okay, I told myself. No need to worry.

Where was a pen, and what should I write that was significant enough for posterity?

The music changed to a slow dance while I eyed the title page. *Fucking My Way Through Life* by Elektra Brooke.

Without further hesitation, I scribbled my wedding vows.

Nothing would ever be perfect, not even heaven, and for most of us, paradise is purgatory at best. Yet my paradise is the love that moves the sun and the other stars. Elektra Brooke via Dante Alighieri.

I picked up my favorite photo from the nightstand—a group shot of Gina, me, Sophie, and Max with *Love in Titian Red* behind us. I could almost hear our giggles and Max barking at the selfie stick.

After sliding the photo from its frame, I slipped it between two pages, sealed the book in two Ziplocs, as Virgil instructed, and headed out to the garden, where my friends still roasted marshmallows and told their stories. They cheered and raised their glasses in salute. "The author, the author!"

I laughed. "Hey, would you guys help me bury this?" My friends fell silent. "An old family tradition on my mother's side," I explained, "meant to grow my inspiration for the next one."

My mother, who could have debunked my claim of tradition, was drinking the night away. She didn't hear my announcement or see my enthusiastic guests picking up various garden implements to help me dig a hole in the soft earth.

As I covered the package with dirt, Virgil's warning echoed in my head and I felt the cold chill down to my toes. *Stay home and keep your loved ones under your roof.*

17. Queen of the Night

Gina's sleepy head fell on my shoulder. We were both exhausted from the previous night and the party that lasted until the morning. It took us hours to clean up—I counted fifty-one empty beer bottles on top of the garden wall alone. Max rested his chin in my lap. How I loved them both and our home. No one could be as happy as I was. As fulfilled. I had everything I wanted. I kissed Gina's forehead and rubbed Max's ear. The crush of waves, an owl singing its calming tune, and gentle raindrops on the window were the reassuring sounds that another day was on its way. Here, I felt safe. Nothing could hurt me.

If only I could add this moment of bliss to that time capsule under the tree.

Keep your loved ones under your roof.

Max raised his head and growled. The wooden gate screeched open and shut. A tap on the window.

Gina was wide awake. "Here comes our bedtime story."

I stumbled to the door. "Damn, Sophie, it's past midnight."

Her smiling face was splashed with blue paint. "You have some of those tacos from last night? I'm starving."

"Help yourself," I said.

She picked up Max, who sniffed the breast pocket where she kept his treats. His Auntie Sophie, his rescuer, was the love of his life.

Gina pointed. "Something blue exploded on you."

"Aphrodite." She flung her heavily lived-in black leather jacket on the couch and headed for the kitchen. There she stuck her face in the packed fridge.

"You won't believe this shit." She stuffed her face with cold tacos.

"We never do." I yawned next to Gina, who poured tequila into three shot glasses. "That's why your stories made a novel, not a biography."

Sophie stuck her tongue out at me and crossed her eyes. "I was painting my new sitter, Aphrodite—swear to God that is her real name—and she's one of the most beautiful women I've ever seen. I mean, perfect face, hair cut short and very close to the head. The boobs..."

She gestured big breasts. "I was painting her as the goddess of love being born from the waves. This one's on commission and it already made me a bundle. I call it *Venus of Venice*. Cool, right?" She noticed my raised eyebrow. "Promise, I'll pay you guys back every penny."

"Use the money for your rent," Gina said.

I sipped my tequila. "You've already paid me with stories."

"So my brush was loaded with blue paint when she was on top of me with her hand between my legs. Next we're rolling on the hardwood floor and she did things to me with her tongue... It was perverse, dudes." Sophie downed her tequila. "Sort of hit three or four spots at the same time... Anyway, I literally died and best thing, when I came to, she was gone."

"What's the point of all the spots if you don't get to return the favor?" Gina poured Sophie another shot.

"Not yet." Sophie lifted an index finger. "Tonight my love goddess will pose again. I can't wait to try her own trick on her."

"Two dates in a row makes it official," I said. "You should settle down with that tongue artist."

"Why ruin a perfect relationship?" Done eating, Sophie was already washing her dishes. "You can put Aphrodite in your sequel."

"I'm on it," I said, although I was already deep at work on a speculative novel with Gina about a world in which Dante did not exist.

It was almost 2 a.m. when Sophie slipped into her leather jacket with one swift move. When she opened the door, a cold gust blew winter into the warm house.

She closed the door. "I can't take it anymore," she said with a shiver, dropping to the couch.

Gina and I surrounded her. Were her demons back?

"Ellie and Gina sandwich." She smiled despite the tears rolling down her face, then she sagged in on herself like a wilting marigold. A fringe of hair fell into her eyes. "The darkness seeps into me like watercolors into absorbent paper."

"Okay," I said. "Now translate. Tell us about the darkness."

"I can never figure out my finances. I always borrow money and you guys never ask for it back and—"

"Look at the book you helped me write," I said.

"You have no idea what this means to me." Sophie picked up *Fucking My Way*. "I know it's fiction, but you made me look important."

"You are important," I said.

Sophie's sultry stories had set Gina and me up for life. My large advance had paid off the balance on our mortgage. It paid for Gina's new dream car, a lime-green MINI Cooper she named BoomBoom, and for Sophie's shiny black Ford Explorer she needed for transferring huge paintings to her clients' homes and to shows.

"I'm so jealous of you guys." She stared down at the red palms of her industrious hands. The tiny cracks lining her fingers were veined with blue and green pigment from the current painting she needed to finish up because she'd already been paid for it. "I'm jealous of your love, your stability, your steady jobs. No matter what happens during the day, you sleep at night in each other's arms."

"Not really," I said. "I get too hot for that."

Sophie laughed, then quickly sobered.

"You'll meet the right person," Gina said.

"I'll never have your kind of relationship. Lovers come and go and ... I really loved someone last year, but I can't settle with one person, because I'm like a werewolf." She bit her lower lip. "What should I do?" At that, she turned to Gina, the teacher who was supposed to have the answers.

"The truth?" Gina asked. "We both get jealous of your freedom."

I nodded. "True."

"I'm about to visit my parents. They'll call me Peggy and she's already muttering in my ears and giving me nightmares and ..." Her voice had dropped to a whisper. "I'm going to die."

Sophie shivered. Max climbed into her lap and she buried her face in his golden fur. "When I found him in the street I wanted to keep him, but I couldn't. Because of Peggy, a dog would never be safe with me, so you guys got him."

"And we're grateful," I said. "But why give your dead sister such control over you?"

The only sounds for a while, were those of the crashing waves and Max's snoring.

"When someone calls me by her name, she starts moving and growing inside me like a monster." She rubbed her left arm, where fingernails had left those deep scars. "My arm burns and she takes over and adds her dark touches to my paintings, just like she did in life. Instead of finishing the pieces that help pay the rent, I work only for her. You know, I can't eat or sleep or fuck or even see my reflection in the mirror and you know how much I love doing those things. It's like I don't exist anymore."

"You could probably make it big with those dark pieces," Gina said, "if you market them to people like me who like depressive art."

"I don't have the know-how or the energy." Sophie wiped away a tear. "Death didn't make her less of a bully. She's costing me my health, my friends and my clients—none of them want to buy that dark shit and you guys always accept me ... I mean, I can't talk about it to just anyone and you love me anyway and what if she costs me even you, my besties?"

"Never," Gina said, and I nodded my agreement. "You're our family even in bad times."

"I told you what we should do." I nudged her side. "I started to say it when you first told us about Peggy, then pizza arrived and you devoured the entire box."

"Actually, you two jumped each other's bones and left the cleanup to me. And in the morning I made you pose nude, which was totally fucking hot."

Gina gestured upward at *Love in Titian Red*. "How do you explain this happy one?"

"A hybrid created when I was still under her influence but right after she released her death grip. My pastels sneak back into her mastery and beautiful happy pieces come out of me. What gave this one its unusual perfection is the merging of her expertise and my syrupy sweetness."

Max purred when Sophie stroked his ear. "She drags me deeper each time and takes more of me away and I'm stuck like a Mack truck in a pile of garbage. If I get any sleep, the nightmares find me." She gestured toward *Mount Purgatorio*. "So I stay up and paint."

She played with the edge of a bandage covering her left index finger. "Ellie, remember *The Magic Flute* at the LA Opera? After that performance my sister appeared in a dream, wearing the grotesque makeup of the Queen of the Night and she sang in German: *You are the one who's supposed to be dead. If I take your place no one will know the difference.*"

We sat motionless, the sound of those terrifying words crushing in and out along with the sound of the waves against the beach.

"What about therapy?" Gina asked, not for the first time.

"My demon-sister holds me hostage. If I said that to a therapist, I'd find myself locked up and painting fruit and flowers, because it's hard to get nude models in the looney bin. I need an exorcist."

"What happens when she's gone?" I asked.

"I come and raid your fridge," she said, which made us roar with nervous laughter.

"We're going to the cemetery," I said.

"I can't." A restless Sophie paced the room. "I'll freak out if I see my name on the headstone."

Gina ran fingers through her hair as if saying, How could I forget? "Right, you haven't seen it."

"Never." Sophie said. "Never."

I said, "Friday we'll stop at the cemetery on the way to Santa Barbara."

Behind Sophie, Gina signaled a cut throat, eyebrows raised in warning.

On Friday night, I had a scheduled reading. Sophie was excluded because Gina and I had planned a much needed romantic weekend to celebrate my success. Gina would teach her morning class, then drive up to Santa Barbara, wearing her sexy black suit with the mean stilettos. She'd stand in line for an autograph, pull on a pair of lime-green gardening gloves and pretend to be a flirty stranger who just happened to talk dirty Dante. Afterwards she'd take me back to the Ritz for champagne and wild sex.

Sophie shook her head. "I don't want to get in the way of your sexy plans."

"You'll visit the cemetery," I said. "Then you'll go to your parents', talk to them and have them change the name on the headstone to Peggy's."

"They're getting old," she said. "My dad's ill. Springing the truth on them will kill them."

"Or make you all closer," I said.

"I can't tell them."

"Then do it yourself," I said.

"Do what?" Sophie looked from me to Gina and back to me.

I asked, "You still have those sculpting supplies?"

"I do," Sophie said.

She had taken a sculpting class at UCLA, and we both hated it. Sophie, because she preferred two-dimensional art, and me, because she made me sit motionless for hours. And the mess... Yet, I had a new idea.

"We'll find the headstone," I said, "and alter the name."

The light was back in Sophie's eyes. "I can do that."

"You'll get arrested for vandalism," Gina warned.

"Only if we get caught," I said, excited for a possible adventure. "We leave Friday early. We'll visit the cemetery, then your parents, and you'll come clean with them once and for all."

18. Foreboding

As I never recovered from the childhood trauma of losing a whole person and her entire world—and being left alone to deal with it—I kept expecting someone else dear to me to vanish. Every time we were caught in the rain, I'd look at Gina, or Sophie, or Max and hold my breath in fear, expecting them to be absorbed by the earth like a chalk drawing.

Thursday, on a barefoot beach stroll at sunset, Gina and I let Max off the leash to bark at the crashing waves while we spoke excitedly of the fun awaiting us up north in Santa Barbara. Max started one of his zoomies, and I joined him, windmilling my arms and turning in circles like a puppy burning off pent-up energy.

I blinked, then rubbed my eyes and blinked again. What the hell?

My nightmare was coming true.

I was alone in the dark, and the sky above me blazed with red zigzags. A frothy wave covered my feet. When it receded, my left foot was crisscrossed with ugly scars.

"Gina," I cried out. "Where are you?"

"Right here, Elektra." She caught me in her arms. "What's wrong, darling?"

I blinked. A beautiful orange sunset with purple edges brightened the sky again, Max was running his mad circles, and all was well. The frightening moment passed, but not its effects. I shivered, cold and sweaty at once. I squeezed Gina to me.

"Did you see the sky?" I was breathing like a heavy smoker forced to march up a hill. "The sky was black and red, you and Max were gone, and something horrible happened to my foot."

"Your feet are fine," Gina said. "The sky is fine. We're here with you."

My bare feet were intact, without as much as a scratch on the blue nail polish.

Virgil's warning buzzed in my mind all day. *Stay home and keep your loved ones under your roof.*

"We're not going anywhere, Gina. We're staying home and locking the door—"

"What's come over you?" She gripped my shoulders and held me at arm's length.

"We should stay home tomorrow. Don't ask me why."

"Why?"

"Remember Virgil, the homeless guy I told you about?"

"Sure. The crazy guy you knew as a kid who gave you a copy of the *Commedia* and showed up again in Venice."

"Well, he came to my pub party—"

"I didn't see anyone in a toga," she said.

"You wouldn't have. He refused to cross the gate. Gina, he was full of dark prophecies. He—"

"What? How dare he ruin your night?"

I stood ankle deep in sand. "It wasn't like that. He told me to stay home because some change was coming to take everything away. He told me to bury a copy of my book in case all is lost."

"That's insane. Why would you believe him?"

"I don't know. I wonder if he's like Angie Mead. If..." I was really going to say it. "If I invented him. It's like his warning came from inside me and I'm losing my mind."

Gina took my face in her hands. "You're expecting the worst because this weekend will be your best yet. You're afraid your good fortune will evaporate, but your time has come. I've seen your struggle and I'm so happy for you, for us." She whispered, "Please enjoy what life has given us."

On our walk home, we stopped at Franco's for burgers and Max devoured his on the spot. As I munched on mine, I let Gina's words soothe me. She knew me well, and Virgil . . . he was insane enough to believe my work was greater than the classics.

When I later stepped out of the shower, I smiled at my reflection in the bathroom mirror, quite pleased with myself. The corner of our bed showed in the mirror behind me. Gina was leaning against the headboard, reading a new translation of *The Divine Comedy* in preparation for her morning lecture. She was reading a stanza out loud, learning it by heart, meaning to dazzle her students with one of her sultry recitations, the way she could still dazzle me.

I watched the bedroom, my happy space, with Gina reading and the sleeping dog curled up on the bedcover. Early tomorrow, I'd drive north with Sophie, Max would go to his sitter, and Gina would teach a class, then come to seduce me in Santa Barbara. At this same time tomorrow, the house would be empty.

And just like that, in the middle of my happiness, the familiar heaviness descended again. What if I was seeing this room with my loved ones in it for the last time?

"Come to bed, Elektra." Gina startled me back from my thoughts of doom.

"Give me a sec." I couldn't breathe.

"This new translation is like reading the *Commedia* for the first time," she said. "Listen to this line: *The more a thing is perfect, the more it feels of pleasure and of pain*," she recited in the husky voice that melted me. "Remember our other version?"

"*The closer a thing comes to its perfection,*" I said, "*more keen will be its pleasure or its pain.* Hell, Gina, I can't do the reading. My voice is too high. It'll be better if you read for me, like you read for Dante."

"Don't be silly." She closed the book. "Unlike Dante, you're warm and alive and you have the right to read your words in your own voice, as imperfect as you think it is. You'll be brilliant and I'll be so proud of you."

Her words and the look in her eyes—and yes, the way she whipped off her T-shirt—had me racing for the bed. Still unsettled, I made love to her with unusual urgency.

"One day, Elektra," she muttered, half asleep, her nose in my neck, "someone will steal your hair to make a wig for the diva who performs that role."

"People are way too lazy to steal hair *or* use my full name," I said.

She fell asleep right away, but I remained wide awake contemplating her strange words. A terrible fear that this might be our very last time together kept me checking her, making sure she hadn't disappeared.

Sleep eventually claimed me. In my dream, a high-strung diva sung Elektra's role, wearing my hair, as I plowed my way through a dark wood, unable to catch up with Gina and Max. Virgil materialized from the blackness and pulled me away from everything that made my life worth living.

When I opened my eyes, the bedroom was peaceful, their breathing familiar and a hint of Gina's Wild Rose was in the air. The mini-blinds were open, and horizontal lines of light moved on the wall with a passing car's headlights, outlining each object in the bedroom—a wicker chair, books on the shelves, the sleeping forms of Gina and Max.

I downed my double espresso like a shot, still experiencing that strange wish to engrave in my memory every familiar scent, sound, sight. That certain floor plank by the stove creaked when I stepped on it and made me smile. Our sacred spot. Sunshine winked through the purple ever-blooms of the Jacaranda, whose extensive roots concealed a copy of my first novel for posterity, whatever that meant.

The day would be filled with firsts. Sophie would soon see her sister's burial place for the first time. She'd tell her parents the truth for the first time as an adult. And later tonight, I'd read excerpts from my first published book to an audience for the first time.

By the end of that reading, it wouldn't matter whether three people showed up or three hundred, whether or not my voice faltered, whether or not my evening was successful. Safely together in our hotel room, Gina and I would celebrate my success.

So why was I more worried now than even in the deep dark of the night?

I sat down on the bed, craving one more precious moment with my little family. I kissed Max on the furry spot between his sleeping eyes, then I touched my lips to Gina's.

She said, "Don't vanish like the happy dream you are, Elektra." Then she fell asleep again, leaving me puzzled. Why would *I* vanish?

At the bedroom door, I glanced back, tears blurring my vision. As I tried to imprint in my memory their treasured images, Gina and Max faded away, the bed was gone, replaced by empty floor. The thin shafts of light from the open blinds shifted position and pointed at me like a set of sharp kitchen knives.

I gasped, but when I blinked, all was well again. The bed, Gina, and Max were back where they belonged. Shivering, I jumped back under the blanket, boots on.

Gina opened her sleepy eyes. "What happened, darling?"

"I should stay home and protect you two."

"Protect us?" she asked, even as Max squeezed between us and licked the worry off my face. "I have a lecture and you have a big day."

"You don't get it." I gave both of them an all inclusive hug. "We should both stay home and not even take Max for a walk. We should close the door and let no one in."

Gina gave me her best older and wiser smile. "Go. Enjoy what's coming your way. Sophie is waiting." She kissed me tenderly. "I can't wait to see how brilliant you'll be."

As always, she put my mind at rest and I could step out of the house. Still, her waking words stayed with me. *Don't vanish like the happy dream you are, Elektra.*

19. Mistakes

I yawned wide and long as I packed a box of my published books into BoomBoom's back seat. Gina wanted to drive my Jeep, so we'd agreed to swap for the day. Sophie arrived, pale and gaunt, lugging an overnight bag.

"Do you mind if I sit in the back?" she asked.

The passenger seat made her carsick. Of course I didn't mind. Rolling out of the driveway, I braced for the bumpy cracks in the concrete caused by tree roots. I admired the rearview-mirror reflection of the purple blooms covering the roof of the house and spilling around its pink tiles.

Would this be the last time I saw this beauty? No. That was a crazy thought, and Virgil was a crazy guy who played a prophet of doom in some movie only I could see.

I was just about to make the turn from Rose onto the heavy traffic of Lincoln Boulevard, when white clouded my field of vision. I slammed on my breaks, stopping in a screech of tires inches away from Virgil.

"What the hell!" I cried out. "I almost ran you over."

His olive complexion was grayish and his face sullen. "Turn around," he said. "Stay home, where a roof and walls can protect you, and close the blinds to lock out the red storm."

"We don't have blinds on all the windows."

"Trust your instincts," he said.

"My instincts tell me that you're becoming a pain in my ass."

"Who, me?" Sophie asked from the back seat.

"I'm talking to Virgil," I said, irritated.

"Not him again," she said.

He pointed at his yellow watch. "There's still time. A new transition will soon take place, and you should be home if you want to keep it."

Obviously, he was having some kind of crisis. "You smoke too much," I said.

"Let's go home," Sophie begged.

I turned to her. "Not you too—"

"Listen to your friend," Virgil said.

"I'm ruled by my fear of success," I parroted a version of Gina's words. Then I drove around him and made a left onto Lincoln.

"Who were you talking to?" Sophie asked.

"He was out there, blocking my way."

"But your window is rolled up," Sophie said.

She was right. I never actually rolled down my window. This was the first time Virgil and I spoke through a pane of glass, and still, I heard his voice loud and clear within me. I'd never considered it strange, but now...

Sophie said, "We should turn around."

"You're not getting out of it," I said. "Not this time." Then I gave her a quick glance. "You *really* couldn't see him?"

"See who?" she asked.

"Virgil."

"Your imagination is wild from writing fantasy," she said.

Again, I pushed back the nagging suspicion that I was seeing ghosts.

Before Sophie had asked for help, my plan was to arrive early at the Ritz and enjoy my morning at the spa with a relaxing massage, manicure and pedicure, then take a beauty nap.

My new plan was to stop at the cemetery, where Sophie would visit her sister. She'd use her art supplies to fill in her own name on the headstone and carve her sister's name instead. Then I'd drop her off at her parents' place, stay for a short, polite visit—I'd never met them and I was curious—and leave her there for the weekend. Sophie promised to talk to them, in the name of healing and self-renewal and explain truths she should have cleared up long ago. Sunday morning on our way back to Venice, I'd pick her up. She'd collect her old paintings from her childhood room and we'd study them together.

Once we got on the freeway, I called the Ritz to cancel my scheduled massage. I was so looking forward to blasting my eardrums on the long drive with a newly remastered recording of Callas singing *La Traviata*. Sophie didn't mind my divas, but as soon as the overture started, she said, "I have tinnitus. Do you mind if we don't listen to music?"

"Sure," I said. I could still listen to some of that old performance once I'd dropped her off with her parents.

When the silence stretched for uneventful miles, I tried small talk. "This weekend is my dream come true, and your stories so inspired me."

"I don't remember what I told you," she muttered from the back seat. "It happened to someone else. Someone alive."

I shuddered. Virgil's concerned face flashed in my mind, his finger pointing at his yellow watch. *There's still time.*

I expected some fear today, but it was good fear, mixed with anticipation for my big evening. I didn't expect a huge audience—I'd be lucky to get a crowd of twenty readers, most of them my friends—but the night would be mine. Gina would smile at me from the first row and later tell me how sexy I looked with my face glowing and framed with shiny red hair. In our luxurious hotel, we'd open a bottle of bubbly and make love with renewed passion. Maybe she'd surprise me with a fresh coming announcement.

This new fear darkened my vision, lurked behind me, and made me shiver in a cold sweat. I was afraid for Sophie and a little afraid *of* her. Her words were a betrayal. *It happened to someone else. Someone alive.* What did I say to that?

Next, even the weather turned on me. The day had started off sunny and warm, but the sky was suddenly cloudy, and a treacherous drizzle dripped trails of dirt down my freshly washed windshield.

Hoping to settle my nerves and to calm Sophie, I changed the subject of my small talk. "Were your parents excited to know you'd be staying the weekend?"

No answer.

"Did you call them?" A touch of hysteria sneaked into my question.

"Not yet," she said.

I hit the brakes. "You had all night. What are you waiting for?"

What if her parents were away? Would she agree to take a separate hotel room or insist on sleeping in ours on a foldout sofa?

"Call them now," I said, anxiety dripping sweat down my back.

"I can't go there." Her voice trembled. "They'll call me Peggy. I can't...I want to be with you and Gina."

"But we planned my big weekend for so long," I said. "Let's stick with our decision."

"*Your* decision," she said, her tone lifeless. "It's always what *you* decide."

"I'm doing this for you." I summoned my most calming tone. "Don't you see, this depression has to stop and the only way we can take care of it—"

"How dare you tell me what to do?" she asked in that strange voice.

I shifted to see her better in the rearview mirror. As my life turned into a horror film, I expected to see the gleam of a sharp knife.

"This is *my* dead sister and *my* parents . . . I can't deal with it now."

Gina claimed that my tendency to make decisions for others was a weakness. When I tell her about this, she'd do her best not to say *I told you so.*

What I knew about Sophie's parents was precious little and disturbing. They could be just as possessed as she was. After all, they'd given a funeral to the wrong daughter. Planning to drop her off with them was my first mistake. Still, we were almost there. I tightened my jaw and drove on.

Shit, now what? The steering wheel was stuck. I sat upright, my hands white-knuckling the unresponsive wheel. Why was it *stuck?* Then a monster force gained command of my hands and—"No, no, *noooo!*" The car went out of my control and spun into a dangerous U-turn.

I slammed on the brakes again and stopped dead in the middle of the road. Whatever mysterious force seized my hands, wanted me to stop or go the other way. Luckily, the road was clear.

Sophie moaned. "I'm gonna be sick," and immediately started retching.

Dread drowned me. I was losing it when I needed every bit of my wits. I rested my face on my arms, heart racing. What was happening? I'd never risk such a stomach-churning U-turn on a two-lane highway and never at such a speed.

Instead of having the time of my life, I was driving on a wet highway, possessed by forces beyond me, and accompanied by Sophie-gone-mad, who was puking on my freshly printed books in the back seat of Gina's clean car.

Once I could pull in a deep breath again, I slow-crawled the car to the right shoulder. Sophie shot out and continued heaving on the side of the road.

I checked the box which—mistake number two—I'd left open next to her. Bits of scrambled egg and mucus dripped from the top layer of the paperbacks onto the layer below, and the shiny covers were curling from both the vomit and the moisture in the air. Yuck, yuck and more yuck.

Mistake number three—and I kept counting—this was the last time I'd choose a glossy cover over matte.

"Shit!" I screamed, my anger boiling over.

I gathered the ruined books in my arms and flung them, one at a time, as far as I could into the cornfield—mistake number four. The books were easily launched, but the puke remained suspended in the air and now drips of slime stained my blinding-white T-shirt. Yes, that was actually the name of the color.

"Shit, shit, shit!" I narrowed my eyes at Sophie and imagined squeezing her neck.

She eyed me with equal loathing. "I let you bully me into this trip. You want to leave me alone with ghosts and have fun with Gina," she said in the bone-chilling whisper that felt even colder out in the open air, with cornfields stretching far in all directions and clouds gathering in the formerly blue sky.

"I'm sorry." I gnashed my teeth and said, "Please get in. I'm taking you back home."

"Not before I tell you this," she whispered in that scary voice I didn't recognize, her strange glare on me. Who was she suddenly? "Everyone calls me the *mistress*. I'm nothing but the *mistress*. That's what I am to you and her. You turned me into a joke."

"I didn't know it bothered you—"

"It's always Gina and you, your life, your happiness, your book with the stories you *stole* from me. How dare you?"

I had to hold back, so I didn't fling *her* into the cornfield after my books. "*Stole* from you? I offered to help you write it, but you wanted me to do it, said you were too busy—"

"*Fucking My Way Through Life.*" She sneered at me. "You stole even those words from me. Think yourself so generous for buying me the car, but you took my stories and made this money and what about other people? What about me?"

"Do you think writing a novel is a breeze, just because someone told you a story?" The wind loosened my hair and now it covered my face. "If you gave me canvases and oil paint and put your models in front of me, could I paint like you?" I made a tight fist in my lap. "I don't understand. I'm here to help—"

"Because it makes you feel better than me." She used her sleeve to dry her tears. "Damn you with your *per*tentious name, *Elektra*. And your *per*tentious hair."

"I thought you loved it." I coiled my hair into a thick knot at the nape of my neck, protecting it and myself from her insults. "You love having me pose for you—"

"I paint a lot of crazy things, but people talk about your stupid long hair and say you should cut it off. Even Gina—"

"Shut up about Gina," I said. "And the word is *pre*tentious."

"I'm sick of you correcting me," she screamed like a demon.

Any remaining joy was draining away with my hot tears. Gina was right. My flaw was making decisions for others. From now on, I wouldn't make any more for Sophie. I'd leave her on the side of the road and keep driving north. She could call a cab to take her to her parents, to her Venice apartment, or straight to hell.

My teary gaze dropped to my boots, then to Sophie's. I bought those for her on that trip to San Antonio. Mine were black, hers were the same style in brown, and she never took them off. Why was my best friend turning on me?

I lifted my chin, and again, was surprised to see her trembling, her eyes big and shiny. She looked lost.

"I'm so sorry, Ellie. I'm not worth the effort. Just leave me here to die."

"What the fuck, Sophie?"

"I'm sorry," she repeated in her normal voice. "Forgive me and don't hate me. It's her, not me. You should recognize her by now. I'd never treat you this way."

"You can go on blaming your dead sister, Sophie, but those words came out of your mouth. Now make up your mind and stick with it."

"I'm an ass. I love you *and* your hair and of course I asked you to write my story. Let's do what you said."

Her hug smelled of puke and I'd already had enough of her. I pushed her away, but she clung to me like those semi-digested bits of scrambled egg. She sobbed and hung on my neck, turning flattened drips of stinky vomit into appliqué designs on my T-shirt.

"Here, clean yourself up." I handed her a bottle of water and a box of tissues. "Then let's do the cemetery, and if you don't want to see your parents, I'll get you a cab to take you home."

"Can I sit with you in the front?" she asked.

"Of course. Get in."

A sheepish Sophie did as she was told. "I love you, Ellie," she said when I carefully turned the car around and again drove toward the cemetery. "I'm so sorry for ruining your books."

Her apologies were just as odious and pathetic as the venom for which she had to apologize. I didn't feel like listening.

"That U-turn was my fault," I said. "Don't blame yourself, just please, do me a personal favor and see a therapist."

"I promise." She sobbed. "I ruined your day and your books and Gina's car."

Despite my anger, I was still trying desperately to be a good friend. "You only hit a few books, the rest are fine." I added an empty promise, "You'll feel better on Sunday."

"I'll never feel better. I ruined your life."

Then she was silent, which I found easier than whiny apologies. My energy was drained.

The endless road stretched for a few more miles.

When the sign announcing Oxnard appeared, Sophie said, "I'm going to freak out now."

"That ship has sailed." I glanced her way. Her eyes were round with fear.

"Look, it's already ten," she said. "You'll be late for your shindig. Let's forget the cemetery and you can take me with you to Santa Barbara."

"I need to get laid tonight, so the answer is no. I'm dropping you off at your mom and dad's."

Sophie said, "You're bossing me again."

"I'll boss and bully and force you and we'll take care of this shit once and for all."

My mother's similar behavior came to mind. I had to drag her like a stubborn child to doctors' appointments. She hated sitting in the dentist's chair, so I'd go with her. Now Sophie kicked, screamed, and mostly whined, but I wasn't going to let her off the hook. She would go to the cemetery, if I had to drag her there by the ear.

20. The Headstone

I stepped on the gas, a grumbling but docile Sophie in the passenger seat. A flash of white billowed against the road. I swerved and stood on the brakes with both feet. Virgil pointed at his yellow watch, then disappeared.

"What's going on with him?" I yelled in anger.

"Your imaginary friend again?" Sophie asked.

"His weed was real enough for you," I said. "But you don't see him, do you?"

"I don't," she said. "Why do *you* see him?"

"No idea." I held my breath.

Lightning painted the cloudy sky crimson, thunder cracked, and more raindrops thudded on my windshield. My nerves were frayed.

Remember that red rain and the first time everything changed for you.

"Do you see the red sky?" I asked.

"That, I see," she said. "What does it mean?"

"He... My friend has been warning me, trying to make me turn around because of some ... some *coming transition*. And no, I don't know what the hell that means."

"I do think you're seeing things. I don't know what the red sky has to do with imaginary guys talking about transitions, but let's do what he says," Sophie begged, visibly trembling. "Let's turn around."

I didn't like the threat of blood rain in the red sky, but we were almost there. If the rain started, we'd quickly run into the car and be under its roof. With the windows and doors closed and locked, we'd be well protected from whatever it was. I wasn't giving up on her. Not when we were so close.

"You won't get out of it." I said. "We'll find the headstone, light the candles, do the thing together, then be out of there. Wham, bam—"

"Thank you, ma'am," Sophie completed the rhyme. "You have sex on the brain."

I relaxed a little. "I didn't, but now..." No, I still didn't. I was too worried about red skies and Virgil. As we rolled forward, I leaned toward the windscreen, searching the road for popping white apparitions.

We arrived at the open gate by eleven. The rain kept falling and the sky remained reddish-dark. Now the fog was rolling in. With renewed confidence I couldn't explain, Sophie took charge and stomped up the road leading to the small white chapel.

This chapel could be a great place to hide, I thought.

She hopped up three steps and called for an attendant. A frowning young man handed her a map, on which we easily found the name.

I gasped. "*Sophie Sanders.*"

"Creepy, right?" Her laugh was nervous.

"We'll take care of it," I said.

"Then I won't be the mess I am anymore," she said.

At the flower shop, we bought a bunch of red roses from a smiling nun with a lazy eye. As real candles wouldn't stay lit in the rain, Sophie bought a set of twenty electric tea lights, batteries included.

The pop, snap, crackle of gravel beneath the tires felt like rocks in my mouth. Suddenly, I was deathly tired. Sophie took calm command and navigated while I steered BoomBoom along a path stretching between lush green lawns and into the heart of the cemetery.

"Here," she said. "It's here."

Since we were alone, I didn't see the point of taking my purse with me. I stuck the key in the back pocket of my jeans and my cellphone in the inner pocket of my jacket. Within seconds, my hair was wet from the rain and growing heavy in its knot.

We found the tombstone with relative ease.

The engraving announced *Here rests, Sophie Sanders our little angel gone too soon.*

The weirdness of Sophie's name on the mossy headstone was a bad omen, as was the incorrectly placed comma. The parents who buried the wrong daughter also killed punctuation, and that was some feat.

The wrong word could wipe out entire civilizations, Ms. Angie Mead had said when she wore black galoshes and lime green gloves. I didn't want to imagine what an errant comma could do. I trembled. In this place of solemnity and grief, each of today's tiny wrongs assumed the power and size of a dark monster.

Sophie ripped the packaging apart to get the tea lights out and counted twelve—one for each year of Peggy's life. She arranged them in a circle on the flat part of the headstone.

Fear, anxiety, overwhelming doom slammed into me with all the warnings of the last day and night: the terrifying moments on the beach walk and at the house, Virgil begging me *repeatedly* to stay put, the crushing certainty that every action I was taking would be for the last time…

I had to stem the panic.

"How are you?" I asked. Talking helped.

"Cool and collected, like dog shit on grass." Sophie showed me all her teeth in a forced smile. My friend was back, full set of spikes intact. Frowning, she turned in a circle, looking for something. "Damn, I forgot...Ellie, can you fetch my sculpting cement from the back seat?"

"Sure thing." I dragged my feet back toward the car, exhausted from a sleepless night, from the drive, the madness, the drama.

"Ellie," Sophie called from behind me.

I turned my head as I walked.

"I love you," she said. "You're the best BFF friend ever."

"That was triple redundancy." I held up three fingers.

"And fuck you too," she said.

Lightheaded, I blew her a backwards kiss over the top of my head.

Another flash of lightning painted the sky red and charged the air with a strange viscosity that made walking difficult. The bright lime-green BoomBoom seemed to draw farther away with every step. My legs had turned to jelly and I could barely breathe.

I turned slowly, treading air as I would water. Sophie was rearranging her tea lights. Then she was face down on the gravestone, sobbing out her heartbreak. Thick fog rolled in through the dense foliage and billowed between us like thousands of Roman togas. It enveloped Sophie. More red lightning struck, sharp through the fog. Distant thunder rolled. I couldn't see her anymore, but her broken words and her sobs morphed into a salad of sounds.

"...sorry..." and, "I was supposed to be the one..." and, "I should have protected you," and, "They didn't..."

At the grave of a loved one, all words are prayer. If self-blame was her prayer, once we did what we came to do, she'd still feel better.

I swayed. She'd sent me to get something from the car, but the car was still too far away and getting smaller. What was I supposed to get? She needed something...to change...

I slid to the grass for a moment's rest, a teensy beauty sleep that would wipe out my fatigue and make me feel new for the coming evening. My wet hair came undone, dragging at me. I ran my fingers through it. Headache.

I closed my eyes…rest my eyelashes for just a sec…long eyelashes she made me get for a hundred bucks…Sophie. So…phie. She'd soon rise from her self-flogging and do the thing she was supposed to do. That thing…I put my hands together, a pillow for my head. Sigh. Hair not so heavy now. She'd feel better. I'd drop her off, then I'd be on my way. Not even a quick hello to the two people who'd ended civilization with their mangled grammar and wrong burials.

My calming mantra ran through my mind, lines of poetry recited in Gina's gravelly voice. *My will and my desire impelled by the love that moves the sun and the other stars.*

"Elviva Geronimo," I muttered to myself. "Where are you, sexy, sexy Gina and your coming announcements?"

When I peeked through heavy eyes, red zigzag brushstrokes colored the sky and burgundy scarves obscured the stars.

Inferno

Midway along the journey of our life
I woke to find myself in a dark wood,
for I had wandered off from the straight path.

The Divine Comedy, Dante Alighieri

21. All the Wrongs

Thunder woke me. The air smelled strongly of cut grass, night-blooming jasmine, fresh earth. My head was lead heavy. I sat up with difficulty, each movement taking me longer than usual. The sky hovered above me like a black shroud embroidered with red-lightning thunderbolts.

A harsh rasp came from my throat. My cheeks felt funny, tingly. I touched my face. Sunken. I ran trembling hands across my bony chest, my ribcage, down to a stomach concave between two rising crests of bone.

"What the fucking fuck?" I grabbed my throat. That croak was not my voice.

Had someone carved hollows in my body while I slept, or was I hallucinating? Skies aren't red and I wasn't a skeleton.

My jeans were loose over prominent hip bones and cinched with a belt I did not own. I was emaciated, yet I felt too heavy to stand up.

Where was I? What happened to me?

It all came back in a flash. While Sophie was visiting with her sister, I must have fallen into a catnap that lasted a thousand years.

Loud thunder rumbled. A thick water drop fell on my scalp, streamed down my forehead and into my eyes. Shit and hell, my hair would frizz up like barbed wire, and what about my book event?

"Let's go, Sophie," I said in that alien voice.

I took my cellphone out of the inner pocket of my jacket. "Four thirty."

I'd slept for more than *five* hours. Now we barely had time to slip through the gate before the cemetery closed for the night. My shindig would start in an hour. If I didn't hurry, I'd miss it altogether. I had no choice but to take Sophie with me —her wish all along. I ran my hands down my skeletal body constantly, dreading. Where was that donut of fat I could never lose? What happened to me, why was I so different, and why did I move so slowly? Was I even alive, or a corpse who crawled out of one of these graves?

"Fuck, fuck, fuck, Sophie, let's move."

The electric candles still glittered on the headstone, but Sophie was nowhere in sight.

I took a step toward the grave and immediately crumpled and rolled on the wet ground. Shit! My left foot was screaming and then I was. Why was I in such excruciating pain?

"Sophie! Help! We need to get out of this creepy place before they lock us in, but something's wrong with me."

Why would she leave me sleeping on the grass? There was no sign of the MINI Cooper. I reached for my keys, but the back pocket of my jeans was empty. I stood. Had we been attacked? Robbed? Was Sophie abducted? I limped toward the grave.

I wanted to smooth my headache away. When my fingers touched the buzz of a recent shave, I screamed, "Where's my hair?" in this strange, croaky voice I didn't recognize.

"Sophie!" I was terrified. "Come on, Sophie. What the fucking fuck?"

This had to be her doing. Her venomous diatribe by the cornfields resonated in my frightened mind. *Damn you with your pertentious long hair. Why don't you cut it and be done with it?* And with more venom, *You stole my stories from under me and made all this money and what about other people?*

She must've taken off. And while that explained what happened to her, what happened to my body? Each movement toward the glittering lights sharpened my headache. Each hobbling step cut like needles into the muscles of my left foot. Winded, I collapsed on the grass in front of the headstone. Through tears and more rain I read again the grammatically disturbing inscription.

Here rests, Sophie Sanders our little angel gone too soon.

Sophie's name on the headstone still horrified me.

There I was, kneeling at the grave of a girl I didn't know, who had died at twelve, whose sister was my best friend. My jeans were soaked from the grass, my foot throbbed, my head exploded with questions and with the agony Sophie would call a ten-tequila headache.

Where was she?

"What's happening?" I cried out, overwhelmed by fear. "What's going on? Where's my hair? Where are you?"

She hadn't changed the name on the headstone to her sister's name as planned. Either she'd been abducted, or she'd hit me over the head and broke my foot, then shaved off my hair before stealing the keys from my pocket and leaving me for dead. Had she always hated me, or was she dealing with one of her dead sister delusions?

Around me, helium balloons bounced and bumped against each other in a devilish dance. Headstones jutted from the dark earth like white teeth in a grotesque black mouth, laughing as I shivered with the chill of death.

22. New Sophie

I had to do something and quickly. Sophie might soon show up and kiss my ass with annoying apologies for a practical joke gone too far. Yet Sophie was never mean or inappropriate, just funny. Why would she choose this time and place to test my sense of humor? Why would she leave me alone in a storm and drive away?

Thin red tendrils occasionally lit up patches in the dark sky, but the rain had stopped. Within a circle of flickering candles and wilting red roses, the strange inscription on the cold stone glared at me, complete with the wrong name and the wrongly placed comma.

I reached into the inner pocket of my leather jacket for my cellphone. My battery was charged ninety percent and I had full reception—a positive sign. Gina teased me about my strange obsession to plug in the phone when the battery fell below eighty. That obsession served me now.

I had to call Gina and let her know where I was, then let the bookstore know I'd be late or possibly not make it at all. Wait. All my programmed numbers were scrambled. The phone must have had one of those useless automatic updates.

With trembling fingers, I went to my comfort zone and dialed home, my first memorized number. Realizing no one would be there—not even Max, who was spending the weekend with his dog sitter—I was about to hang up when a sleepy male voice answered.

"Venice house of pleasures, this is Brian. Our girls are clean. Would you like me to book you a hot date?"

Did I call the wrong number? "How dare you answer the phone this way? Who are you anyway?"

"You called me," he said, annoyed.

"Where's Gina?"

"How should I know and who the hell are *you?*"

"I'm Ellie and I live there." Before I could stop myself, I said, "You must be Brainless Brian."

"Is that what she calls me?" he snapped.

A dog barked.

"Are you watching Max over the weekend?" I asked, hoping for a simple explanation. The dog sitter must have bailed on us at the last moment.

"Look, crazy lady, I don't know who you are and Gina hasn't lived here since forever, so why don't you call the looney bin and check yourself in?" He hung up.

The wind whistled, rain drenched the seat of my jeans, and a natural canopy of tall trees was free-spinning above my head like a carousel.

If I didn't know my wife well, I would have said she lied about having to give a lecture and then fucked her ex-boyfriend in my bed. Why did she suddenly have to teach a morning class when her classes were at night? Was she lying all along, and even though she'd kicked him out and called him Brainless, was he now sleeping in our bed, his greasy head on *my* pillow? No, I was spouting nonsense. She hated him, didn't she?

Absolute Asshole, Brainless Brian, Complete Cock, Dumb Dick. Gina and I, naked and entangled under the covers, had great fun running through the entire alphabet. Sometimes we started our Brian bashing from the end, with Zombie Zitface, and by the time we got halfway through our backward alphabet, we'd be making passionate love. Maybe talking about him secretly turned her on. That's it. Gina was protesting too much when she found it necessary to talk about him at all.

I called her cell next.

"Hey there, Ellie," said the husky voice I'd loved my entire life. That gravelly voice meant home and safety, a blazing fireplace, cuddling on the couch with a warm dog on a rainy night, screaming Jeopardy trivia.

"Where are you?" I asked in relief.

"In the car. Where else would I be?"

Of course she'd be in the car, on the way to meet me and seduce me in the book line.

"Right. Right, honey. You won't believe what happened."

"What's wrong, Ellie?" She sounded concerned, although she didn't call me *darling* or the usual *Elektra*.

"Everything's wrong. She threw up on my books then she freaked out and cut off my hair and left me alone in the cemetery and I can hardly walk and I have a terrible headache." I was sobbing. "And now I'm late and I'm so scared. Come get me..."

Good thing I wasn't talking to a stranger, because I sounded insane.

"No worries, Ellie. We're already here."

We. Was my mother with her?

The whooshing wind and the soft hooting of an owl were my favorite calming sounds. Here and now, those noises filled me with dread.

"Please keep talking to me," I begged in a small voice. "I've never been so scared in my life."

"What do you want me to talk about?"

Her question was strange, her tone aloof, disinterested. It should have been obvious that I wanted, needed, to hear how much she loved me and how brilliant I'd be. That she was looking forward to our romantic weekend. That soon everything would fall into place—my hair, my head, my foot, even Sophie's mystery. I wanted Gina to soothe my frightened soul.

"Do that bit of Dante I like, please," I said, a no-brainer for her. "That version you prefer with the words *perfect* and *desire*.

"What do you mean by *bit of Dante?*" Gina asked, as if she hadn't recited the last line from *Paradiso* countless times like a lullaby when I couldn't sleep.

"The stanza that starts with *I yearned to know how could our image fit.*"

"I have no idea what you're talking about," she said in that tone of finality she'd use on a spam call. Why joke when she heard my fear?

"What the fuck, Gina? You know Dante Alighieri and—"

A tap on my shoulder made me squeal. Sophie. She wore an odd smile, like she hadn't just about destroyed me.

"She's here, Gina," I said into the phone. "I'll see you after I kill her."

Sophie's long hair was a wig, and her white poodle coat glowed in the dark. White boots with fuzzy edges grazed a crotch-revealing white skirt.

"Why'd you shave my head? Was it one of your episodes? Look at me!" I pointed at my head. "And you made me late."

"You're late for nothing, honey."

Sophie never called me or anyone else *honey*. Anyway, this one wasn't the nice *honey* of a friend but the pitying *honey* of a nurse before she strapped you into a straitjacket and shot you with a horse dose of sedatives.

That smile. What was wrong with her smile?

"Let's go." She grabbed me by the arm.

"I could kill you." I started toward the car. "Why'd you leave me alone and where's my hair?" I burst into tears. My hair was me and now it was gone!

She pushed me in front of her as we made our way among white gravestones and bouncing ghostly balloons.

"Stop pushing me." I turned and pointed at her. Those clothes . . . "What poodle did you murder for this coat and what's with the ABBA style, like it's Stockholm 1972?"

"I keep a certain public image."

"For your parents?" She was definitely off.

I didn't know whether to push for answers or first deal with my greater problems.

The visit to her sister's grave had indeed transformed her mood, if not cured her tendency for dumb jokes, and this one was so unfunny, I strangled her in my mind, not for the first time today.

My head throbbed with each step. I could barely put weight on my left foot. I looked around for the MINI. The injured foot was my left, which meant I could still drive.

"Where's BoomBoom?"

"What's a BoomBoom?"

"Gina's car," I said. "You're—"

"Come on," she urged. "They'll close the place on us."

"I'm so fucking angry," I said. "I feel like leaving you here, the way you totally fucked me over."

"I don't like it when you use bad words," Sophie said in a well-controlled voice.

"Right." I laughed despite my anger. "That's rich from the reigning queen of foul language who calls it poetry. There was a reason we came here before tonight's event."

"Of course there was."

Our boots made disgusting squishes in the wet earth.

"I go every year on the anniversary of my sister's death, but this year you wanted to come with me. You had some whatever to tell her before the shindig, and you wanted privacy."

"Of course, the shindig." I slowly limped forward.

I never knew Peggy. Why would I want to talk to her? Sophie was the one who needed to visit her, because she was starting to slip into her madness. That was serious stuff, so why the lies? And why was she treating me like a McDonald's bag on its way to the trash can?

I was furious and in such grief over the loss of my hair. I touched my head again—it was hard not to—desperately searching for my absent hair and hoping to soon wake up from this nightmare. Thick fog seeped into my brain, my foot ached and my eyes filled with tears of anger and despair.

She nudged me with her finger. "Keep moving."

I turned around and poked my own finger in her face. "Don't push me, you idiot. Don't you dare touch me after what you've done."

"Okay, okay." She raised her hands in surrender. "Come. Gina's waiting."

Right. The mention of my beloved kept me moving forward. Her presence would fix everything. Then Gina would give Sophie hell for what she'd done, especially for cutting off my hair.

We arrived at the parking lot, where a lone SUV was parked by the white chapel. It was banged up, a vehicular dried-up prune with rough stories to tell.

"What happened to your car?" I cried out. "And where's the MINI?" My head exploded with questions.

Sophie opened the back door and ordered, "Get in."

"No way." I dug in my heels. "What's going on?"

The washing-machine *whoosh* of blood filled my head. I fought as she pushed me inside, strapped me into the back seat, and closed the door. Through blurred vision, I recognized a stack of covered canvases on the seat next to me. Paintings.

"What's this? I don't understand." My voice crumbled, like my insides, in dread for my very sanity.

"You okay, Ellie?" asked a familiar husky voice from the front passenger seat.

Only my head bumping into the ceiling kept me from standing. "What the fuck, Gina?"

G ina's eyes narrowed. "What's the matter, Ellie?"
"Look at me." I pointed at my head, thinking
she'd flip at the sight of my buzz cut. She didn't
even flinch. Didn't she care? "What are you doing here and
where's your MINI? I drove it here, but now there's this
wreck." I looked back at Sophie, who was futzing in the trunk
of the SUV. "She's such a bitch. You *know* how I tried to help
her. Even this thing was planned for her, now look what she
did to me."

Instead of looking back at me, Gina turned to face the
front.

I said, "Things are all wrong, and—"

"Everything's fine, Ellie."

Ellie again rather than *Elektra* or *darling,* and she looked
very different.

"Your face . . ." I gestured roundness with my hand. "And
your hair . . ." It was really long. "*Why are you wearing a wig?*"
I touched the top of my head. "And what did you guys do with
my hair?"

"Calm down," Gina said. "Do you need a white pill?"

"I don't need a pill," I said from between clenched teeth.
"I need an explanation. In fact, a lot of explanations. For in-
stance, why are you here when you're supposed to meet me in
Santa Barbara?" She remained silent, so I piled on redundant

information to prod a response from her. "We booked the Ritz for a romantic weekend."

"Oh, Ellie." Gina sighed. "I hate when you say such things."

How could she? I massaged my temples, unable to make sense of anything.

"Since when do you hate what things?" I again ran my hand along my scalp, and my surprised fingers met the round and empty landscape of a hostile planet. "What the fuck happened to my hair?"

"Shush," Gina said. "You know how she gets around foul language."

"Is my cussing really the big issue here?" I screamed in frustration. "Because I see greater problems." My throat tightened, and my head throbbed in anger and fear.

Gina had apparently lost her ability to speak in full sentences, so I let my mouth run. "Come on, stop this game. You two had your fun with me, now you're really freaking me out. Am I in a nightmare?"

When Sophie started the car, the yellow interior light shone for a moment on both their heads. They wore similar red wigs.

"Gina," I whispered. "What's this cruel game?"

When Sophie made an angry U-turn, I almost hurled on her canvases the way she'd earlier hurled on my books. We crossed the gate of the cemetery and approached Highway 101.

Endless questions raced through my mind, but the most obvious discrepancy was hair. Mine was gone. Theirs was long and Titian red. At least as far as I could tell in the color distortion of the passing streetlights.

Both Gina and Sophie, each in her own way, were obsessed with my hair. Gina loved to run her hands through it when we made love, and she'd once jested that someone would steal it to make a wig for an opera soprano. Sophie often made me sit for her when she needed that exact shade of red. Earlier on the side of the road, with cornfields spreading around us endlessly,

Sophie had lost her shit, screaming, *Why don't you cut it off?* It was so out of the blue, so suspicious and out of character.

Had they both . . . My mouth gained independence and blurted out the accusation before I could stop it. "Hey, did you two knock me out then cut my hair to make wigs for yourselves?"

Gina's neck cracked when she completed a rapid one-eighty. "Ellie, you know that's not the way it happened. Calm down."

"You can keep telling me to calm down," I said, "but how can I?"

Of course they didn't make wigs from my shorn hair. That took time, that idea was totally paranoid and hysterical, and yet . . . Those things had to be wigs, or how could hair grow so long overnight? Other oddities that should have taken time, happened in the last five hours. I ran my hands over my prominent ribcage. Only hours ago, I'd been padded with a stubborn layer of fat.

"Why is she driving?" My voice hit a crescendo. "I brought us here in the MINI, and now I'm taken away like a hostage in a banged-up SUV."

Sophie ignored me, and Gina asked her, "Do you have her pills ready?"

"What pills?" I was full pelt ugly crying tears that would blotch my face. "Tell me, please someone tell me, where my hair is and why you left me alone. Why is my foot hurting like a son of a bitch, where's my fucking life?"

"I want you to eminently stop the bad language," Sophie said in that infuriating new prissy voice I hated.

Now she got *my* goat. "It's *imminently*, Your Eminence. And don't call my language bad when you use a split infinitive and a malapropism in the same sentence."

"Shut it," Sophie barked.

Gina turned and gestured that cut-throat *don't* that I mostly liked but which now only puzzled me.

"What? I always correct your grammar and it makes you laugh."

What happened to accepting or dismissing me with a loving *fuck you*? This new and strange Sophie impersonator had discarded her good nature and sense of humor, along with her brown leather boots and saucy expressions.

I suppressed the terror threatening to howl out from the depths of my belly. Even in my bewilderment, I knew that a howl of madness was no more than a howl of madness and no one hears the words.

I was scared stiff. The bloody sky did it, I was sure, although I hadn't lost anyone this time, and I wanted to be happy about it, but they were so different, such shits…I blinked a few times to clear the fog. What if I was imagining things?

"Okay, guys." I reined in the begging quiver in my voice. "Can one of you please, please, explain what's going on? Tell me only the truth. No lies."

"We already told you a million times," Sophie said.

"Then you've had good practice," I said. "Tell me again and make it slow and simple. Start with day, time, destination."

"Come on," Sophie said, annoyed. "You know it's Friday, and we're on our way from Venice Beach to Santa Barbara."

Gina rested a calming hand on Sophie's arm and turned to me. "What do you want to know, honey?"

Again, that pitying *honey*. I pictured Angie Mead shaking her elegant head disapprovingly at the ongoing improper use of *honey*: the single word that would end civilization.

"She hates driving, so why is she at the wheel when either one of us could drive?" I was getting angry again; exactly what I wanted to avoid. "Why am I sitting in the back of this banged-up jalopy when I came up here driving the MINI?" I swallowed my tears. "And, Gina, why are you sitting next to her?"

"I don't know where to start," Gina said.

"I keep asking questions and you don't answer, so please tell the big picture, then get into the details." I leaned forward, but the seat belt snapped and held me in place. "Why is her new Explorer so banged up?"

"A few mishaps," Gina said. "We don't like to talk about it. Ask me something else."

"Why, so you won't answer those questions either?" I tried to calm down, but my tense voice betrayed me. "Why do I have a ten-tequila headache, and why does my foot hurt? And my hair? Am I losing my mind, or are you two mad?"

Gina sighed. "You don't remember the injury at all, do you?"

More tears spilled out of my eyes. "I don't remember an injury. How could I end up like this after only a few hours?"

"We should of left her at home, like Camille told us," Sophie mutilated the language in that mean and clipped tone she'd never before used. "Now the weekend is ruined."

Indeed it was. This weekend was supposed to belong to Gina and me.

"What does my mother have to do with anything?"

24. Honey

Gina turned to fully face me. "I'll tell you everything again if you promise to settle." Rather than being the voice of a loving wife, hers was the exasperated voice of an impatient babysitter to a nagging child. "Can you take a deep breath like the doctor told you?"

"I don't have a doctor. Here, I'm breathing. Tell me, please, and make it good, because I've had it with you two."

"Exactly a year ago you suffered a serious injury, and now you forget stuff. The surgeon had to shave your head to drain the blood from your brain. We asked your permission and you didn't mind, so we made wigs from your hair." She shook her head to show me. "See?"

"Are you going to perform *Elektra*?" I asked. Snarky, sure, but what else could I say when my wife makes up a whopper about a brain surgery?

"What?" Gina either forgot her own words, or was playing dumb. Why? She was obsessed with my hair and so was Sophie. When working on her Smoky Pink Madonna—commissioned by the gay and lesbian Unitarian church—Sophie had me pose on green brocade wearing nothing but my cascading long hair.

"You're lying, because if I was injured last year, I'd have year-long hair by now." And she was lying, because *I'd never been injured*.

"You preferred to keep it short," Gina said.

"And you don't mind? You love my long hair."

She hesitated. "It never grew back the same texture and color, so you just kept it short. I think it suits you."

I shot another question at her. "Where's BoomBoom, your lime-green MINI?"

"My MINI is blue."

"You wanted lime green," I said. "Like the gardening gloves you sometimes wear when we have sex."

Sophie shot her a glance. "What?"

"No clue what she's talking about," Gina said. Turning back to me, she explained, "Brian asked to borrow the MINI for the weekend."

"Yes, that." I leaned forward, but the seat belt again snapped and kept me in place. "What's he doing in our house?"

"What do you mean *our* house?" Gina asked.

"I thought he was taking care of Max for the weekend, but the creep said he lived there. Can you believe he wanted to know who I was? Brainless Brian indeed."

"Ellie, you can't harass my tenants." Gina's voice was a frightened whisper. "That's going too far."

"Why would we have tenants? I'm talking about our home. The one I just paid off."

"Brian's been living on Rose with his wife and kid, and the rent pays the mortgage. You live with your mother—"

I was furious. "You lie. I'd rather live in the street."

A call came in. "How is she?" asked my mother's voice, only she sounded different, mature.

"Mama, what's wrong?" I asked.

"Honey, are you okay?" she asked with a warmth that gave me chills, like that scene in *Terminator 2* when John Connor calls his foster mom, and her sudden kindness is a red flag.

"We're cool, Camille," Sophie's impostor said with forced cheer. "Not to worry, we're taking good care of her."

"Thank you for everything," she said. "Does she take her pills?"

Pills again. "What pills?" I cried out.

"She sounds like she needs the white one," said the Terminator posing as my mother.

"She'll take it as soon as we get to the hotel," Sophie said. "How's your drive?"

"We're almost in Sedona. So far, so good." I listened for a metallic hint in her voice when she added, "Ellie, honey, enjoy the night." She hung up.

Why would my mother call and ask about pills? And why would she call someone else's phone? If indeed they were messing with me, why? My world had changed in the blink of an eye, and nothing made sense anymore. My best friend was a total bitch, my wife was distant and lying, my mother was definitely possessed.

"This joke has gone too far," I cried out. "My mother doesn't drive or do anything else for that matter. She never calls unless she needs me to fix something or take her to an appointment. She doesn't call even when I'm sick, yet now she actually sounded concerned. When did you know her to give a shit about anything but getting stoned?"

"That isn't fair," Gina said. "Your mom takes good care of you."

"I don't know what world you live in," I said, and I didn't. Everything outside was the same, I was me, but the people...

Sophie added, "Your mom is the most admirable and capable woman I know and you gave her nothing but trouble even before the acci—well, your injury."

Why did she stop herself from saying *accident*?

"I wouldn't let her take care of a pet lizard," I said.

Sophie nearly slammed into a white Honda, but hit the brakes in time.

Gina said, "Honey, if you don't slow down you'll cause another—" She too stopped herself. *That* was the *honey* meant for a lover.

Bang! Sophie hit the steering wheel with a force that jerked the car sideways. "Stop telling me how to drive." A demonic growl had entered her voice.

What was with Sophie's sudden change of personality, and why were they so condescending toward me?

What I'd learned from Gina's kind attempt at an explanation confused more than explained things, so had Mama's call.

The mother I knew never ventured beyond the grocery store in the north and the pharmacy in the south, the liquor store on the east and the pot shop on the west. Her agoraphobic life was so small, it could fit into five square feet in Westwood. Now she was driving, about to arrive in Sedona, and with someone else in the car? Who was with her, and when did she get over her fear of open spaces?

If I accepted Gina's claim that some head injury had caused my amnesia—a hackneyed plot point in fiction, but let's suspend disbelief—if that was true, had my mother caused the accident that injured me? Had guilt made her take care of me? Camille sounded like she actually gave a shit, which meant that my life had slipped into fantasy. Yet even fantasy had its strict rules. A character had to stick to character. I was lost.

Absurd. I didn't, couldn't, believe them.

If I was reading this in a novel, I'd have by now looked a few chapters ahead to see how the mess clears up later. As a captive audience, I had to actually read each word and wait for the hook.

I tried a new vein. "Where are my books?" I asked.

Gina asked, "What books?"

"The book I was going to read."

"Your things are in the trunk if that's what you mean."

The racing mind inside my achy head was in such turmoil, Gina's cold touch on my knee startled me.

"In a nutshell," she said, "you keep forgetting and we keep reminding you, but that's okay. Now we're going to Earthlings."

"Right." I felt a smidge of relief. Finally she mentioned the bookstore. "This weekend is my time to celebrate."

"Of course it is." The patronizing tone remained in her voice. "This is your first time away from home since the injury, so please take it in. I promise, it'll make sense eventually."

Last night on Rose Avenue, Gina had suggested we leave Sophie home with Max, but I insisted on taking her to the cemetery to solve some problem that wasn't a problem anymore.

"I should have listened to you," I muttered.

Gina, now engrossed in a heated argument, didn't hear me.

"I told you we shouldn't bring her," Sophie said.

"*Take* her," I corrected.

"Don't start." Gina threw a back glance at me, then to Sophie. "She needed to get out." Her voice softened. "Calm down now, honey."

Honey again.

Out of control *honeys* kept firing full-power rifle cartridges and hitting the wrong targets.

Then in a gentle gesture that burned the eyeballs out of my tortured skull, Gina rested a hand on Sophie's thigh. Sophie put her own manicured hand on Gina's and squeezed it.

"Hell," I cried out. My feet pushed the floor down and my head nearly dented the ceiling of the SUV.

"What's wrong with you now?" Sophie glared at me through the rearview mirror while not letting go of Gina's hand.

"Everything's wrong," I said in raw anger. "When did you ever paint your fingernails and what's . . . what's going on between you two?"

"Stop it, Ellie," Gina said.

This kind of hand holding, this desperate squeeze, meant only one thing. Whatever else was going on, my wife and my best friend couldn't wait to get rid of me and be alone.

25. Triple Cruelty

W hen writing fantasy fiction, you should let your characters teach you the bizarre rules of their universe. In my confusion, I switched into writer's mode, moved out of the characters' way and let them tell me their story. As I sat back, observing this version of my life as a sci-fi horror story, my eyes burned from what I was seeing. My body was in agony from some injury or accident, and I couldn't make sense of the characters' behavior.

That morning, standing with Sophie on the side of the road, I'd witnessed the first hints of her madness. My mentally unstable friend was lost to me, but why was my loving wife going along? People cheated on each other all the time, and obviously these two were cheating on me, but this cruelty? Why not tell me the truth before showing me? I was asking them legitimate questions, and their answers confused more than explained. Was that part of their vicious plan?

Sometime in the last twenty-four hours, a shift had happened in the world I'd inhabited for the last thirty years. No one I trusted before that shift could be trusted now.

Virgil had warned me in the road. What exactly had he said when he pointed at his countdown watch?

There's still time, he had said. *A new transition will soon take place, and you should be home if you want to keep that home.*

I should have listened to him.

Sophie's impostor made the turn onto the highway and lurched the Explorer forward, leaving my internal organs behind. Gina kept her worshipping gaze on Sophie, who occasionally, and too often, glanced sideways at her.

"Keep your eyes on the road or you'll kill us," I spoke my thoughts.

It seemed, some creature inside my skull had eaten my brain filters to make room for itself. I could imagine it stretched out in a rocking chair, set to the rhythm of my pumping heart, growing by the moment and making me blurt my thoughts out loud.

Sophie drove like a maniac. In the back seat of the Explorer, I ran fingers over my scalp again and met the prickly pear buzz that had replaced the familiar softness. I'd always been Ellie, with the mane of a mythological heroine. Who was I without it?

Since nothing made sense, I rested my aching head on the soft leather seat I had chosen when I bought the car for Sophie. Awake and vigilant, I watched them through half-closed eyelids.

I recounted a blow-by-blow account of what happened so far today.

Sophie and I had figured out a way to change the name on the headstone. Virgil warned me to stay home, but I thought he was crazier than usual. Red lightning painted the sky, then my forty winks turned to forty years. When I woke up, my emaciated body was broken, and a humanoid in a rocking chair moved into my skull.

The red lightning played a part in the changes, either causing them or being caused by them. Virgil wasn't crazy at all, but rather a prophet, or my guardian angel, who tried to point me in the right direction. Multiple times, and I resisted him.

Even as I thought this, I knew that uttering my thoughts out loud would make me sound textbook delusional.

My beloved wife was another issue altogether. She was cheating on me, and I didn't mean like that time she pre-watched Jeopardy and watched it with me again, acing the questions way before the contestants. As unforgivable as that was, her prank hadn't killed me. Now she was cheating on me with poodle-murdering Cruella de Vil, and the two weren't even trying to hide their double treachery.

When did they have the chance to become lovers?

Aha . . . *The mistress.* That's what our other friends called Sophie, because that was true, and I was the last to know.

That stung like vinegar in my eyes.

How did Brainless Brian fit into this sickening picture? I hadn't met him, but I'd heard a lot about him. He had picked up the phone in my home, mine and Gina's, and answered *Venice house of pleasures*, as if the place was his, then Gina said he lived there with his wife and kid. Lived in *my* home.

Apparently, I'd suffered a head injury and subsequent amnesia, and my recollections of a perfect life proved to be but false memories that originated in an injured brain. Unbelievable.

How did I remember a totally different setup for the cemetery visit, if the injury had been so long ago? Why would I have made up a false cemetery scene, and other stuff that hadn't happened, a whole year after my injury?

I was *willing* to suspend disbelief. I'd read and watched enough stories based on selective amnesia. Yet whatever I'd forgotten, certain fundamental truths could not be changed, because those truths were as important as the sun rising in the east and setting in the west.

For instance, Gina and I loved each other.

For instance, Sophie was my best friend.

For instance, my mother could barely take care of herself, let alone take care of me or drive a car.

I couldn't escape the ugly conclusion that I'd lost an entire year. A year ago—shut up, disbelief, and let me work this out —while I was recovering from some injury I didn't remember, my wife had fallen in love with my best friend, rented out our little house and dumped me on my mother, who had no choice but to take care of me. What's more, I, who used to be a solid rock for everyone else, became an object of pity and contempt for those who used to look up to me.

What a knife in my heart. Was that possible? I scratched my temple. Could my vivid imagination stretch that far?

I checked my phone. It was five. Even a quick check-in at the Ritz would leave me no time for a shower, a change of clothes, or even makeup. Maybe reading out the words someone had paid me to publish would give me back a shred of myself. I was still the author of a novel titled...

What was the title of my novel?

That question was so basic, the fact the answer was a blank made me woozy. Sophie's sharp turn off the highway and onto Mission Street intensified the dizziness.

Gina said, "Honey, slow down. We're almost there."

Honey again.

These two were obviously cheating on me, and they'd involved my mother, who was normally too lazy to wipe her own ass but for some reason had agreed to become part of their plan to take me down a notch in my greatest triumph. Their triple cruelty worked as planned, and I felt like a slug inching along in the dirt.

I'd get the bitches back somehow. All three of them.

26. The Shindig

"We're late and it's packed and we should of been there to greet the guests," Sophie said.

"Should have," I corrected under my breath.

She was ranting while searching for a space in the full parking lot. The voice was hers but not its sharp and hateful tone. Even when stressed, Sophie was kind. Except this morning, when the serious change in her personality began and she dumped accusations on me.

Elegantly dressed people streamed into the bookstore. I didn't realize how many fancy fans I had, so that was a nice surprise. Now I had to appear before them looking like shit.

I touched my head and was again horrified by the spikes. How would I go on without my signature feature? My hair had given me courage and confidence. Without it, I felt naked, vulnerable and so cold, I kept shivering.

"Let's go to the hotel first," I said. "I want to shower and change at least this T-shirt you threw up on."

"You threw up on your own T-shirt." Sophie stopped in a screech of tires. "You two get out and start inside, and I'll park somewhere."

When I stepped out of the car, the pain in my foot made me drop to one knee. Right in front of Gina.

I lifted my head. "It's like that day I asked you to marry me." She'd found the ring I'd dropped into a glass of champagne and said *Yes, yes, yes.*

Now she helped me to my feet. "Let's go inside and sit you down."

Why wasn't she participating in the memory?

"When did I throw up?" I asked.

"You got sick at the store because of some cinnamon candles, so we had to buy fake candles for the headstone."

Cinnamon candles could be nauseating, but Sophie was the one who got sick.

"I still don't get it," I said. "Where's the spare tire of fat I always wear around my waist?"

"If that's what you want, with time, you'll get it back," she said, as if that answered my *where* questions.

"Actually, here's another question. Why did you pretend you don't know Dante?"

"I teach Greek mythology, but you keep forgetting."

Was this something different too? But even if I'd lost a year, she would have taught Dante not more than a year ago. "What about your night classes in medieval poetry?" I asked. "What about *La Vita Nuova* and *The Divine Comedy?*"

She chuckled. "I know *Beowulf,* and I may have read a little Dante at some point, but I don't know enough of it to teach a class."

"Don't do this, Gina," I begged. "You can talk Dante until the five rivers of hell dry up. You're the expert!"

She finger-brushed the long red hair away from her forehead in that sexy way I'd found endearing when her hair was short and golden. Now the little gesture made a scream of terror gather in the back of my throat and threaten to spew out of me.

She pretended not to know what I was talking about—or, hell, she really didn't know, and that would be so much worse

—so I tried a Hail Mary. "Remember Elviva Geronimo and *the love that moves the sun and the other stars?*"

"What or who is Elviva Geronimo?"

"One of your coming announcements." I clutched at the straw of familiarity as I dangled above an abyss. *Coming announcement* was our private—very personal—joke. It was Gina's own term, at least the Gina I knew.

Her stare remained blank. "Look, I'm sure what you're saying makes sense to you, but we're late. You know how she gets when she's angry."

Now I was the one sure that what *she* was saying made sense to her, but I didn't understand, and I couldn't cope. I had to distance myself from the madness and switch gears. I hadn't had anything to eat since the burger at Franco's on our beach walk, as my growling stomach reminded me.

"I'd kill for some food." I touched my head. "And a baseball cap."

Gina pointed straight ahead. "You'll find one there."

A long-haired old hippie minded the magazine stand on the corner of State and Victoria. Bandanas and beach flip-flops lined the sidewalk next to stacks of newspapers. Tie-dyed summer dresses swayed in the evening breeze.

"Don't linger," Gina said. "We'll be inside."

I limped up to the stand, where I immediately found a blue baseball cap with a white emblem of a unicorn on its rim. As I'd left my jacket in the car, I was cold. For another twenty bucks, I bought a button-down shirt to cover my pointillistic puke-splashed tee.

"Who is Paul Signac?" I mocked Gina's voice silently to myself, then changed my tone. "Right, the board is yours."

This need to entertain myself was a sad turn of events I blamed on Gina and Sophie, who'd stopped being any fun.

"Is there a place to get a quick bite?" I asked the old hippie.

"That coffeeshop has great sandwiches." He pointed across the street, a burning cigarette clutched between two yellowed fingers.

I followed his direction with a longing gaze. The coffeeshop was so near, yet my aching foot and the busy traffic made it seem too far. I tore myself away from the smell of roasting coffee beans and limped toward the bookstore. They'd promised me wine and cheese.

Insipid piano jazz improvisations emerged from inside. Why jazz, when I supplied them with my favorite opera recordings and clear instructions? Plowing my way through the crowd of fashionable people, I searched for someone in charge to give them a piece of my mind about the music.

A steady flow of guests streamed into the already packed space. In my baseball cap and tie-dyed shirt I certainly didn't feel like the star of the show.

Scanning the crowd for Gina, my gaze fell on a tall stylish woman in her fifties who wore her gray hair in a low chignon. A stooped man who walked with difficulty clung to her arm. The woman was an older version of Sophie and the man...

I gasped. I hadn't yet met Sophie's estranged parents despite being her bestie for years. Why were they here? Sophie had no business inviting them to my event.

She'd kept her home visits short, staying only until one of them called her by her dead sister's name. One time, she'd had to stay with them because her father was sick. Constant texts dinged my way, including *I can't take it, Ellie. Dad is better but I'm dying.* And *They call me Peggy and the nightmares started.* And *I can't eat a thing.*

That cursed visit turned her into a recluse for weeks. As she couldn't tolerate her sitters during that time, she used her wild imagination to produce jaw-dropping masterpieces. Either Gina or I had gone nightly to her door, pried her away from whatever persecution scene she was painting and forced her to eat with us.

Sophie—now poodled up in her ABBA-inspired coat and boots—rushed to greet her parents with kisses and hugs. She dragged over a chair for her dad and handed both of them drinks. It was good to see her being nice to someone, yet why would she fake her love and care in public, when in private, she wanted nothing to do with them?

I burned with anger at her charades, her downright betrayal. She invited her parents to *my* show—her dad barely walking—knowing that my own mother, who had nothing physically wrong with her, didn't want to come.

I caught a snippet of their conversation. "We're so, so proud of you, Peggy," Mrs. Sanders said, her husband echoing her.

Peggy. How could they not know their own daughter?

Sophie glowed, not at all upset at being called by her dead sister's name, going along with whatever made them proud. Why were they proud of *my* book? Not that there was anything wrong with the sexual contents, but if I were Sophie, I wouldn't want my parents anywhere near that salacious fantasy based on my life.

A man with a fluffy beehive do and a clipboard, who appeared to be one of the organizers, stopped to talk to Sophie. She raised her arms in angry exasperation and frowned, acting like a bridezilla at *my* event. I expected him to walk backwards and bow repeatedly.

I stopped him. "What was she so angry about?"

He ran a finger on his clipboard. "And who are you?"

"Elektra Brooke, the author who reads tonight. The music you're playing—"

"Ma'am, you're in the wrong place."

"I'm not," I said.

"Does this place look like a bookstore to you?" he asked. "Tonight's featured artist is quite wonderful. Look at the walls. Yes, sometimes we play music or schedule readings with up-and-rising *choice* authors—"

"That's what I am, an up-and-coming author of the novel—" A touch of hysteria sneaked into my voice. The title still eluded me.

"I don't have time," he said with impatience. "As you see, Ms. Sanders is quite agitated."

"Ms. Sanders has been agitated all day. She threw up on copies of..." My voice trailed away, but then I remembered. "I got it! My novel is called *Fucking My Way Through Life*."

"Look, ma'am. I have no time for pranks."

"This isn't a prank," I protested at the back of his head. I grabbed him by the shoulder. "Hey, don't walk away from me. Ravi, the *manager*, set up the evening for me."

"There's no Ravi here—you're in the wrong place." He dismissed me with a hand wave and sashayed away.

I reined in a sense of impending doom. My mouth was parched. I grabbed a flute of champagne from a passing tray and drank it straight down, like water. I replaced it on another floating tray and seized hold of a second flute, but from over my shoulder, someone snatched it away.

"You shouldn't have this," Gina said.

"This what?" I was angry.

"Your pills react with alcohol. I'll get you water."

"What pills, and why should you care, you best-friend fucker?" I asked, but Gina didn't hear me in the noise.

Tonight's featured artist is quite wonderful. Look at the walls.

This was the right place, Earthlings, on the corner of State and Victoria, but when I finally looked up from my confused misery, I saw the walls. Instead of bookcases, the walls were covered with huge paintings. Was some new artist scheduled to open the show for me like I was Lady Gaga? Either that, or their practical joke grew more cruel and extensive by the moment.

Gina shoved a cold, wet bottle of water into my hands and vanished again. The first sip went down the wrong way. As I gasped for air, choking on ocean waves of nausea, no one asked if I was okay. In fact, a clearing had formed around me, and people steered as far from me as the space allowed.

My coughing subsided and a loud burp—the kind that would have made my old Sophie proud—escaped my throat. I didn't care. They didn't see or hear me anyway. Gina stared at me from across the room, concern in her eyes, but she didn't come to check on me. The bitch would have let me drown in a mouthful of water. Among these people, I felt lonelier than I'd been back in that cold, dark cemetery.

"Fancy fuckers." I entertained myself. "Category, alliteration."

"One, two, three." A man tested the microphone. A shrill sound followed, then Sophie hopped behind the podium and smiled sweetly at the crowd like she didn't just bridezilla the shit out of the poor organizer. I saw in her face the brief ghost of my loving friend, but she still wore that strange, strange smile. I hated that smile.

Shushing sounds followed, then *Gling, gling, gling.*

I stepped forward with relief and adjusted the baseball cap on my head. At last, the nightmare was coming to its end. She'd introduce me, peel the animal carcass off her shoulders, and end this ghastly farce.

I pulled my cellphone from the back pocket of my jeans and quickly flipped some screens in search of the speech I'd prepared. I found nothing. No biggie. I could easily wing something short and sweet, starting with a joke about being properly inebriated. People liked a drunk joke.

27. The Gods

"Good evening ladies and gentlemen," Sophie started. I flinched at the sight of the thick stack of pages in her hands. "Thank you all for coming tonight. My parents being here gives me unparalyzed joy."

"Unparalleled," I silently corrected. "Dumbass," I added.

Sophie continued, "I give them credit for being the rock in my life."

"Rocks," I corrected again, this time louder. What did her parents have to do with my book?

"Mom and Dad, you gave me the good start that allowed me to be who I am today," Sophie continued in that bizarre vein. "If it wasn't for your affluence..."

I grunted. "If *not for your influence*."

What was this sudden closeness, when every visit with them started her nightmarish episodes of depression?

I was getting tired of correcting her. I was used to Sophie making the occasional mistake—wrong pronunciation, certain malapropisms—but never so many and every other word. This wasn't amusing anymore. This was painful. Why didn't she ask me to check her lengthy introduction? My head and foot were on fire, but the real torture was her stilted speech.

Hoping to take my mind off the agony, I scanned the art on the walls. The general theme seemed to be dark portraits against nightly landscapes illuminated by fluffy clouds.

Tonight's featured artist is quite wonderful, the man had said.

So who was this featured artist?

I carefully examined a large canvas depicting the gods of Greek mythology at what seemed like a family wedding. Athena was leaning against Artemis, who was posing with her bow and arrow next to Apollo with his lyre. The three looked like siblings bearing a ridiculous genetic resemblance. The palace of the gods and Mount Olympus loomed in incredible detail behind them. The painting had already sold for ten grand.

The signature at bottom right read…I choked back a cry.

Peggy Sanders.

Above the signature, two mirrored figures—one in red, one in blue—posed in ballet's arabesque, fingertips nearly touching. Sophie could never reach such mastery of proportions, but there it was.

I eyed Gina, who gazed up at Sophie with the pride and love that belonged to me.

I stepped closer to the wall. The pieces were priced in the thousands, and multiple red stickers declared that most of them had been sold. All were signed at the bottom right instead of Sophie's normal bottom left, and the signed name was Peggy Sanders.

What was her game?

I couldn't explain the sheer sophisticated talent of this disturbed version of Sophie. Why had she hidden those masterpieces from me but not from Gina, and why oh why did she give her sister credit?

I remembered a story she had told us by the fire pit on Rose Avenue. Once, she and Peggy had jointly created a magical painting of faeries, some in a ceremonial circle and some hanging from tree branches.

"It won first place in the school's art show," Sophie had said dreamily. "I painted their hair, their gauzy wings, the candle lights, you know, all the fun bits. You could see through those wings, and if you stared at it long enough, the lights flickered."

The teacher had praised ten-year-old Peggy, saying that she could already paint like the masters. The teacher also said that Peggy knew how to contrast her internal darkness with spots of light and fun.

That's mine, little Sophie had thought proudly, believing she'd be praised next. After all, both of them had signed the piece—Sophie at bottom left and Peggy at bottom right—but the teacher didn't mention Sophie at all. She handed the award to Peggy, who had taken the glory, loving every minute.

A tremor started in my hands. Why was Sophie letting Peggy take the credit again?

I glanced at my cellphone, as I'd done in the Explorer, and still it was the same Friday, same day, same year, same world. Or was it?

What happened at that gravesite? Nothing made sense since I'd left her there alone. My hair, my marriage, my life were ruined. I didn't know if I'd actually written a book or only believed I had, and Sophie herself was possessed. A head injury could explain the memory loss, the headache, the foot ache, even the buzz haircut, but not this art show.

As far as I remembered—which apparently wasn't much— Sophie Sanders had never had a one-woman show at a real gallery, not that she hadn't tried. The closest she'd ever come, was a booth at a street fair between a hotdog cart and a cotton candy stand, where she sold her powder-pink paintings to clueless shoppers in beach flip-flops who called to each other, "Look, Ernie. Isn't it cute?"

At the podium, Sophie continued reading page after page, but I wasn't listening.

Even if she had landed herself a show at the same place, same time as mine, and even if she had collected her paintings from the dark months to create a show in Peggy's honor, why did she sign her sister's name?

I searched for hints of Sophie's mock-religious Nouveau Kitsch, those funny paintings with the pinks and baby blues and the crosses made of big erections and Mount Sinai in the shape of huge tits. Nothing.

I thought I'd seen all her paintings, but never these. Yet despite their brilliance, these new pieces lacked color and depth. I was baffled by that. Sophie was an expert at depth, and if these were really her work, the *sfumato* effect—her great pride—would have made the gods seem three dimensional. She'd bragged that she had learned light and shade from Leonardo. I'd get annoyed with her fake Italian accent when she'd say, "It's called *chiaroscuro*" or "*impasto*" or "*pentimento*."

These paintings were as flat as a week-old pancake.

Rather than Bible stories, Greek mythology ruled these works. Zeus and Hera posed head to head, fluffy clouds in their background—the same cloud motif ruling Sophie's new public image. Dionysus and Hestia plucked grapes at the table, and in another painting, Poseidon raised his trident to fight a storm. In yet another, Aphrodite floated in her sea-foam, and Hermes hovered above her in his winged sandals.

Then I saw it.

Not siblings with a genetic resemblance, but rather only one person.

The portraits were all . . . What in Dante's hell was *this?* All the images were Gina. *All* of them. Even Zeus and Apollo were the male representations of Gina's face.

It was clear now.

Sophie was obsessed with my wife.

The first portrait of Gina that had so affected me, the one I'd seen leaning against the easel in her messy bedroom, should have been my earliest clue. Sophie had loved her even then.

Yet later, when I'd trusted her with my painful story, she'd been so supportive, my first true friend, encouraging me to take Gina on a date when she herself had been so in love with her... Were they both in on it even then, laughing behind my back while pretending to be my family? Gina going as far as marrying me...

Surely, this had lasted years right under my stupid nose, because it would have taken ages to create such a body of work. She could not have kept so many large pieces in her small studio apartment hidden from me, so she must have rented a storage unit with the money she borrowed from us and never paid back. She had built up her collection only to use *my* big night to showcase them.

And Gina had participated. Gina, whose love for me had clearly turned to hate. These two had been in love for years, and they'd chosen my happiest day to thrust their daggers into my heart.

28. The Smile

"This show is a celebration of my sister's short life," Sophie continued her endless monologue. "Today is the anniversary of her death and I wanted to honor her. I still miss her so much and this show is dedicated to Sophie as an apology for the things I did when we were kids." She choked on tears. "Me and my friends just visited Sophie's grave—"

Sophie's grave? We visited *Peggy's* grave.

I couldn't listen as Sophie spun her tale. From the walls, Poseidon rode an ocean wave and came at me, trident ready. Athena threw the cornucopia at me. Olympian Gods with Gina's face spun around me while the humanoid parasite in my head rocked its chair to the rhythm of my pulse and smoked a Cuban cigar.

"Sophie and I were both artists from a young age. We used to switch our clothes, and also our paintings. We had very different styles. Sophie painted happy art." She gestured at the walls. "Mine is totally depressing, as you see."

Laughter erupted in the room.

Why was she stealing my show? I couldn't stand the confusion much longer. I had to stop this madness.

I pushed my painful way toward the podium until I reached Gina's side. "Why is she pretending to be Peggy?"

"Not now, Ellie." Gina's adoring gaze rested on New Sophie. "I promise, we'll help you get better."

"Help me, Gina? We were both supposed to help Sophie."

"Sophie died years ago. Now we're supporting Peggy on her big show. You forget and that's okay."

"You've got it wrong." People began looking my way when I loud whispered, "Sophie's name is on the headstone, but it was supposed to be Peggy's because she's the one who actually died. That's why Sophie hated visiting her parents, yet now she's thanking them as if they have the closest relationship."

I took off my baseball cap and rubbed my shorn head in what was becoming a new and comforting motion. "Why are you allowing this madness, Gina? You're my wife." I choked on tears of frustration and fear. I took her arm for support, but she freed herself from my grasp and stepped closer to Sophie. That broke my heart all over again.

"What's wrong? Even if you stopped loving me, I don't deserve this."

"This is her moment," Gina whispered. "Let her enjoy it."

"Her moment?" My shaky voice was loud. "Here's a blank I need filling. Why are you fucking her?"

"You're getting excited."

"The wrong choice of words is *her* specialty." I pointed up at the speaking fraud. "I'm angry, not excited."

"She's still talking. It's her night, please keep quiet."

"No!"

A strange force I couldn't control propelled me toward the podium. I grabbed the mike from Sophie's right hand and pushed her aside, all the while asking myself a fundamental question.

Why would a lefty hold the mike in her right hand?

I said, "Tonight was supposed to belong to me."

The place buzzed with sudden confusion, then got very quiet. All eyes were on me, so I kept talking.

"My picaresque fantasy novel titled *Fucking My Way Through Life* is based on my friend's sultry experiences. This friend." I pointed at Fake Sophie. "My own celebration was scheduled for tonight, instead I find myself living a nightmare."

Infused with mysterious courage and power, I kept on. No one stopped me, and I wasn't about to stop myself, now I had an audience. An enraptured, maybe simply stunned, audience. We all want a good story, and mine, as crazy as it sounded even to me, was a hell of a lot more compelling than Sophie's rumblings.

"These two used to be my family." I pointed at both wide-eyed traitors. "Sophie, as gratitude for the stories you told me, you got the Explorer to help you schlep your canvases around. My dear wife, Gina, I'm the one who bought you the car of your dreams from my proceeds, that also paid off our mortgage."

"Stop her, stop her," Gina muttered, covering her mouth and pressing against Fake Sophie.

"My wife and my best friend conspired against me—with my mother's help, mind you—to turn my special evening into this depressing art show."

Sophie's righty frown disclosed her plan to murder me. Yet details other than her homicidal face nagged at me.

She frowned toward the *right*.

Well, fuck her for fucking my wife, and fuck the rest of them who participated in stealing my paradise and tossing me into this hell.

"Sophie, we both laughed when you said your art was Nouveau Kitsch that went out pink and brought in green, but that chocolate-boxy art had soul and whimsy. Your paintings were amusing and funny, and a sense of humor goes a long way. I could see coughing up greens for your mock religious tits, asses, and dicks, but not for this shit you suckers are paying five and ten grand for."

The commotion in the crowd got louder. I felt triumphant, having stunned them with the truth.

"And, Sophie?" I smiled sweetly. "When you talk about money, it's *proceeds*, not *precedes*." With that, I hurled the wireless mike at the wall and watched it hit a square of gloom that had cost someone a fortune.

A woman immediately commanded, "Take off that red sticker." Then more voices shouted out to each other, "I changed my mind, I don't want it," and mayhem spiraled the gallery into a bear market day on Wall Street.

I didn't stay to watch the full devastation of my words. I longed for a dark room and a warm blanket.

As I stomped toward the exit, one important fact about Sophie nagged at me.

Her smiles and frowns were supposed to twist left, an asymmetrical trait I'd so far found charming. She was supposed to hold the mike with her left, *dominant* hand.

The truth crashed into all the alarms, clangs, and bangs on the door inside my head. In this sci-fi nightmare of a life, New Sophie wasn't Sophie at all. My friend Sophie had been swallowed by the earth when the red lightning struck, and the poodle woman who considered the word *fuck* bad language, who signed her paintings at the bottom right and held the mike with her right hand, was her formerly dead sister, Peggy Sanders.

At that realization, the blood froze in my veins, the lights flickered, and the world died.

29. Abandon all hope

Two faces framed by Titian red hair glared down at me with the utmost revulsion. One belonged to the woman I loved and who used to love me back. The face imitating my Sophie was crying, and smears of black eyeliner *à la* Liza in *Cabaret* dripped down her cheeks. My tightening fists wanted to sock both faces in their lying mouths.

"Do you have any idea what you just did?" New Sophie's straight hair wavered around her head in ripples of seasickness. "You should of stayed home with a babysitter instead of ruining my evening and humiliating me on my big night and causing so much damage to me and the gallery." Her higher voice shot out the words at a supersonic speed. "People canceled their purchases because of what you said . . . You ruined me."

Fighting brain fog, I sat up in the soft bed and looked around a hotel room that definitely didn't belong to the Ritz, as decent as it was. A connecting door led to another room. How had they hauled me up here?

"Where you're at is my fault," Sophie's impostor continued, "but I can't stand the sight of you. Just had to have that drink and ruin my evening."

Her fault?

"*Where you're at* is barely literal." My voice was coarse from fatigue or some drug they pumped into me.

"Come on, honey," Gina begged her lover. "Let's call it a night."

"*Gaslight* is one of our favorite movies, Gina," I said. "I recognize a fuck-with job, and you guys are totally fucking with me. Why?"

"Calm down, Ellie," Gina said.

"Give me a few," said New Sophie, or *Peggy*. "I'll give her the pills and be right over."

"Sure you can handle her on your own?" Gina whispered.

"*Handle her?*" My thoughts kept turning into spoken words. "When did I become someone who needed a handler?"

"I told you we shouldn't of brung her," the impostor said.

"Taken her," I said.

"What?" she snapped.

"*We shouldn't have taken her* is the correct grammatical form."

"Go to hell."

"There already, listening to you." My head throbbed in quick, short bursts. "You should speak a different language, Sophie."

"It's Peggy, and I only speak English."

"You don't." My itch to correct her was a good sign I was on form.

"Don't be long." The door clicked shut behind Gina.

Now she was gone, I had a glimmer of hope that Sophie would drop the façade, take off the ridiculous wig, and say they didn't mean to hurt me. She'd tell me this long practical joke started as her very bad idea and it's gone too far. She was going to surprise me with her own show, and she thought I'd be happy for her and while yes, I caused damage to her budding career, that wasn't on me. She'd cry and say that my own reading would actually happen tomorrow.

My glimmer of hope died in its embryonic stage when Sophie opened her crossbody white fluffy messenger bag, shook pills out of a few bottles and handed them to me.

I said, "You used your right hand to shake the pills."

"I'm right-handed, genius," she said with venom.

"Since when?"

"Since birth."

I missed my gentle Sophie, my fragile friend who cussed every other word and called it poetry. This prissy version of her objected to foul language yet oozed poison.

"Say," I tried a new vein. "Do you have dissociative identity disorder, like that character on *Law and Order*? Are you Sophie one minute and Peggy the next?"

"Just take your meds and shut up," she said.

The pills rolled around my open palm. One red, two white, and a huge blue horse pill. "What's this shit you're giving me?"

"The doctor wants you to take them for pain and for sleep."

"If I need pills, I can take them myself."

"Go on. Get under the covers and take your pills like a good girl."

"I don't trust you," I said. "What if you want me dead?"

"I do," she said, "but death from pills is too good for you."

I wanted to observe her walk—Sophie stomped like no one else.

"I need water," I said.

She stomped to the bathroom—getting the heavy walk right, but hers was angry—filled a glass with tap water, stomped back, and slammed it on the night table as if she'd rather throw it in my face. She was eager to knock me out, then slip next door and be with my wife. I wasn't about to make it easy on them.

I quickly ran through the little I knew.

New Gina and the Sophie thing had promised my mother to take me off her hands for a few days, which meant I had become an obligation for the three of them. *Where I was at* was apparently Sophie's fault, and she felt guilty for it. I could squeeze that rotten lemon of guilt to its stinking, dripping pulp and at the same time, gather information.

"What'd you do with my Sophie?" I asked.

"Your Sophie? Sophie's dead and I'm Peggy."

I played with the pills in my hand. "I'm starting to believe you. Know why?" I got perverted joy from making her as angry as I was. "Sophie kills long words with malapropism, you kill grammar, your parents bury the wrong daughter and kill punctuation. Do you Sanders dudes do anything right?"

That did it. Her face contorted to the right and her fists clenched in fury, which made us somewhat even. "I do want to kill you sometimes."

Her makeup was melting off. Since I didn't believe she'd actually kill me, I drilled deeper for the nerve. "Your lipstick is smeared."

Her right hand instinctively went to her face. Her *right* hand. She wiped her mouth with the edge of her fluffy sleeve but only smeared it more. I felt strange pity for her.

"Tell me, Sophie." I called her *Sophie* one more time as a last attempt to hold on to a lost reality in which the vital elements of my life could fit snuggly into their boxes.

"For the last time, my name is—"

"Fine, Peggy," I said.

Gina had already clarified their version of what happened, but I wanted to hear how this one told a story. I'd heard her short sound bites, and those were too hateful for the real Sophie. In her lengthy, written speech, she messed up words and phrases the real Sophie got right. Now she'd verify her new identity for good with a mid-length ad-lib.

I asked, "If Brainless Brian lives on Rose Avenue in this twisted version of the world, where do I live? And where does Gina live, and how come she doesn't sleep in my bed with me? What car do I drive? And what happened to my foot, head, hair? Give me the skinny in a nutshell, you owe me that."

She bounced restlessly from boot to poodle boot, burning bright to be with *my* wife. Then she said, "Your toes like crushed in a mishap, and the surgeon had to put your foot back together. You also had like a head injury, and another surgeon had to shave off your hair for more surgeries. Can we like talk about it tomorrow?"

Like? Sophie never used the word *like* as a verbal crutch.

"Now, or I won't be able to sleep. What do you mean by a mishap, and what surgeries did I have?"

"You were badly hurt." She faked a yawn while delivering her quick version of my life story. "You had two brain surgeries, and you were out for like a long time. When you woke up from the coma, you had to learn to speak again, and you got better but your mouth and manners got worse than before the injury. Now you like fix my English left and right like you're better than me or something."

"The word *like* is a tick." Scratching my itch to correct her while pissing her off was a win-win.

"See? That's what I mean. You have no right to lecture me," she said. "Go on now, take your pills and get into bed."

"I'm going to bathe first."

"Not without supervision you aren't."

Not without...

"I can wipe my own ass, thank you. I'm the one who takes care of you, my mother, Gina, the dog, the house. I even wrote a book about your sexy stories."

She waved both arms in that bridezilla manner. "You keep talking about this book you want to write, but you have problems with your eyes. Once and for all, you live with your mother in Westwood and she has to take care of you, like she took care of your dad when he was dying of cancer—"

"My *dad?*" I tossed the pills from hand to hand. "That sperm donor left when I was a baby and had nothing to do with me or Mama since."

"That's crazy talk." She sounded exasperated. "He named you Elektra and you and him were very close. Look, I'm tired, and I can't do this now. Anyway, your mom called and asked if we could take you for the weekend because she wanted to drive to Sedona to hang with some friends. See? Even she's sick of you. Gina promised to take care of you, but you're making her so uncomfortable with the *wife* thing, I ended up being stuck with you."

"Gina *is* my wife," I said.

"That." She shook a long manicured fingernail at me.

Even that pink fingernail should have told me the truth, that she wasn't Sophie. My sweet friend had hardworking hands with paint embedded in the creases from using her fingertips to paint. This one probably painted with rubber gloves on.

"This fantasy of yours is like the book thing," she continued. "You so want it but it isn't true and Gina doesn't feel that way about you. You always had the hots for her, and since you woke up from your coma you can't hide it because your emotions are on the surface. The doctor said it will get better, but you're very inappropriate, so if you want us to continue to be your friends you'd better stop embarrassing yourself and all of us—"

"Take a breath, Peggy," I said, finally convinced that's who she was. "Gina *is* my wife, and Max is our dog. You're the one who gave him to us."

"I've *nothing* to do with dogs and you know it," she said through her perfectly straight, paper-white teeth.

Another thing. Sophie's teeth were natural ivory with a slight charming overbite. Peggy seemed to have had her teeth straightened and whitened into military uniformity.

"Now take the pills and go to sleep," she said.

I couldn't stand another moment of her voice, teeth, nails, melting makeup. I wanted her out of my face. I popped the pills under my tongue, then pretended to sip some water.

At that she left, and I felt somewhat accomplished. I'd achieved my goal of maybe ruining whatever sexy mood she still had in her.

As soon as she slammed the connecting door, I spat the pills onto the night table, but the nauseating taste shriveled my tongue. In the bathroom, I rinsed my mouth a few times. When I caught a glimpse of my reflection, I recoiled from the skeletal face I didn't recognize as my own. The chopped-off mousy drab on my scalp bore no resemblance, not even in color, to the former glory of my hair. A long scar ran diagonally across my forehead.

I'd have to give up on mirrors.

Back in the room, I searched for toothpaste in the blue backpack I didn't recall packing and found toiletries among clean clothes I didn't recognize. The wintergreen toothpaste didn't erase the sour taste of the pills. Mama must have packed for me.

In a side pocket, I found a white cube and a phone cord. I plugged in my phone and sat down for some initial exploration. I clicked Facebook. The profile picture I had chosen was a shot of my own cascading red hair.

"That's who I used to be," I said in that new tendency to blurt out loud whatever popped into my head. "That red mop everyone adored was my identity."

My Facebook account didn't show much recent activity, but a few smiling shots of a long-haired girl I recognized as myself populated my home page. In one, I was with a man I assumed to be the now-deceased Roger Brooke, who, in this life, had been quite an attentive father. I expected to feel a pang of love, maybe a touch of sadness at the image. I felt nothing.

No entries from the last year.

I moved on to Amazon. I typed in *Fucking My Way Through Life*. The book didn't exist. I clicked my saved files on the phone. The drafts of my published book were gone in the same brutal transformation that had torn me from my life.

Back to Facebook. I searched, but none of my friends were very active on social media. My mother was always yacking away inanities on Facebook, yet I couldn't even find an account under her name.

Lilly Green. She'd surely have an account and a whiny presence. Lilly was the student who had complained to Gina about having to study Dante. In turn, Gina had given her an hour-long answer, the gist being that if not for Dante, Italy wouldn't have become the country it was today, and we wouldn't have had this or that invention, and what a terrible world it would be.

Lilly had done very well for herself. Hers was one of the nonfiction manuscripts I'd recently edited and formatted. When *Root Canals and Other Pleasures* was accepted by a prominent publishing house, a group of us celebrated her success. Afterwards she had posted photos from that evening and changed her profile picture to a blurred shot of her smiling face behind a cocktail glass larger than her head.

Lilly posted daily on social media. Every praise she enjoyed prompted a long new tearful post of how we should never stop believing in miracles. Her success wasn't a miracle, but the result of her hard work and a tiny bit of my help.

That was then.

Now, in this world, I found nothing on her page about her publishing success. Her profile pic was a childhood photo of herself with pigtails. Her cheery daily posts were gone, and her last post complained about the heartlessness of publishers and agents who didn't get her.

Back to Amazon. Lilly Green, it seemed, was never published; a fact I strangely mourned.

I quickly plugged in names of other clients—Jason Brack, Una Marx, Evangela Ross. Each one was present on social media, but when I searched Amazon for their books, I found zilch. The lump in my throat expanded. None of them were published authors.

Abandon all hope, ye who enter here, was inscribed on Dante's gate of Hell.

My glimmer of hope turned to dark despair. All the manuscripts I'd helped publish, including mine, didn't exist. My hard work had come to nothing. I was nothing.

30. Aphrodite's Tits

With so many questions in my head, I had to talk to someone, anyone, but those friends who were on a call-anytime-even-at-midnight basis with me were either dead or cheating on me in the next room.

Pickup truck George. What about him? I quickly checked my friends list on facebook and he was there, caveman beard in his profile photo and next to him, a petite woman cradling a sweet baby boy. Among the "likes" was one of mine, but that was it. No further interaction between us. Did we ever date? Did one of us break the other's heart? Did he know anything about me in this version of my life, or was he just a casual acquaintance gracing my friends' list? George was out.

Mama. From what I'd heard so far about this version of my saintly mother, it seemed she'd be my best source for information. In my last life, she'd call me in the middle of all middles, including once to deal with a beeping smoke alarm while I was having the best sex with Gina, who now fucked the bitch who was supposed to be dead.

Anyway, I'd rescued Mama so many times, it was her turn to rescue me. I dialed her number.

A sleepy voice answered, "It's you." She sighed. "God, what time is it?"

"After midnight."

"Ellie, Ellie, Ellie," she said, exasperated. "Why aren't you asleep?"

Like Gina in my lost life, she'd always called me Elektra.

"I'm scared, Mama. Please tell me again what happened to me. They won't tell me the truth."

She said, "I'm too dead tired to tell you that long story again."

"Mama, please."

"Did you spit out your pills again?" So I'd done it before. "Where are Peggy and Gina?" she asked, actually sounding concerned. I could see her in my mind's eye, sitting up and lighting a cigarette or even a joint. Her wig, also made from my stolen hair, rested askew on her sleepy head.

Abort. Mama was in on it with both traitors. For her, I was the post-accident fuckup who required pills and caretakers. I had to keep her from alerting Peggy that I was up and exploring.

"They're sleeping." I steadied my shaky voice. "I'm okay. I just needed to hear your voice and to thank you for packing my backpack so well."

"You're welcome," Mama said. "Did you have a good time last night?"

"Great time. Hey, what happened to your Facebook page? I can't find it."

"Facebook?" Her laugh turned into a smoker's cough. "Who has time for such nonsense? Between taking care of you, fixing the car and the broken plumbing, even that one tile on the roof last week, I barely have time to rest. Now let me sleep."

"Good night, Mama."

"I'm here for you, sweetheart," she said, and her last word proved beyond doubt that Camille Brooke was no one I knew.

I hung up. "Sweetheart, my fat ass."

So it was true. I did live with Mama, and my care kept her so busy, she couldn't go on social media or do anything else useless. Damn me.

What did she have to do for me anyway? I hoped to hell that she, or anyone else I knew, never had to wipe my ass at any point during my recovery, because that repulsive mental image made me feel so dirty and disgusting, I wanted to scrub my skin raw in boiling water. A bath was next.

I squeezed the entire lavender contents of a small soap bottle into the gleaming white tub and started running the hot water.

Back in the room, I stripped off slowly, paying attention to each item I removed.

That Friday morning before my trip, I wore my blinding-white T-shirt and my skinny jeans, and those had been too tight around my waist.

Now, late at night on the same Friday but in a different world, I peeled off the tie-dyed shirt I bought from the street vendor and my puke-garnished T-shirt. When I got to my skinny jeans—now belted and even so, loose around my hips —I noticed that my boots were wrong.

That morning in Venice Beach before the drive, I pulled on my lucky black boots. The left one bore bite marks, souvenirs from Max's first month with us. Sophie had the same style in brown, and we practically lived in them. Those boots could be kicked off easily.

Not the pair I was supposed to take off in this foreign universe.

These eyesores were a cross between orthopedic braces and some S&M hardware Gina and I once saw in a porn movie but couldn't figure out their use. I had to click quite a few buckles, and when I slid my left foot out of its monstrous enclosure, it screamed, "Fuck!" in my own voice.

On the other side of the wall, Gina and Peggy were arguing. I couldn't call her Sophie anymore, as the only traits she shared with my real friend were purely physical.

"She talks about her house," Peggy said. "And about some damned dog and the book she wrote when she can't write the grocery list."

"Give her a break," Gina said. "Her impulses are raw."

Naked as I was, I hobbled to the connecting door and put my ear against it.

"You're downright mean to her," Gina scolded. "I heard what you said and it was uncalled for."

"That's bullshit," said the other traitor. "Even before the accident she had the hots for you, and you encouraged it. Go next door and fuck her brains out, but be careful not to dislodge that thing."

What *thing* would be dislodged? And now she called what had happened *an accident*.

"You can be a complete cunt." Gina was sobbing.

Complete cunt. My sweetheart was still fond of alliterative insults.

I couldn't stand her crying. How dare that bitch hurt the love of my life? My on-the-surface impulses prompted me to burst in and give that monster a piece of my mind and—once and for all—claim Gina as my wife.

I started to turn the doorknob, but right before I burst into their room, I looked down and noticed my skinny pathetic nakedness. As I reached for my crumpled clothes, Peggy started consoling Gina. In no time, they went from enemies to lovers.

I stood naked and angry, confused and insulted, yet also strangely aroused by the sounds of passion from the next room. I slipped my hand between my thighs and into my own wetness. As I had the right to make love to my wife, I went along with them, imagining Gina's passionate face above me, then under me. My hand became hers. I joined their rhythm, allowing various thoughts and images to crisscross my head as I was going at myself against the connecting door.

My mind conjured an image of a new lesbian couple devouring each other in bed. Soon, I imagined, they'd introduce their dogs and cats to each other, pack up the U-Haul, and combine their books into one glorious library with wall-to-wall sliding shelves. But this relationship wasn't new, and Peggy hated dogs, cats and probably books.

As always, Gina and I finished at almost the same time. At the moment she was supposed to cry out some orgasmic exclamation known only to her lovers, I whispered, "Elviva Geronimo!"

Only she didn't call out *Elviva Geronimo* or anything familiar to me.

What Gina cried out was, "Aphrodite's tits."

I gasped and collapsed into their room, naked and with my hand between my legs. I closed the door quickly before they noticed me, but not before I glimpsed Peggy's bony ass up in the air.

I fell to the damp carpet, laughing and repeating "Aphrodite's tits." My laughing morphed into crying and complete despair. Nothing is lonelier than having just fucked yourself to the sound of others having sex. What made the carpet so wet?

Was it true? Was my head injury the reason I falsely remembered a paradise I wanted as mine? What, I'd made it up somewhere along the way to replace my real memories? Maybe I'd dreamed it all when I was in a coma. The loss of Gina ripped at my soul, and my other losses…

What about the rest? What was I supposed to do about the rest?

"We should keep it down," Gina said. "She'll hear us."

"She's out from the pills."

"She forgets all the time." Gina again, sounding sleepy and sexy. "She probably isn't long for the world, what with that head thing."

What head thing? Not long for the world?

I sat up. I must have fallen asleep or passed out on the damned wet carpet. Why was it wet?

"Shit." I hobbled on soaking, squishy carpet to turn off the faucet. At least my backpack on the bed remained dry. "Yes, Gina, I forgot the bath."

I threw towels on the floor to soak up some of the flood from what had become an infinity edge bathtub with luke-warm water and exploding bubbles. I let some water drain out, then went back to listen at the door.

Gina continued in her husky voice, "I thought it would do her some good to get out and have fun with us. I thought—"

"You thought, you thought, and I'm stuck taking care of her."

A few more pieces of my private horror story fell into place as the two who considered me a burden unwittingly fed me information. Apparently some *thing* in my head was about to dislodge and kill me because of an accident I'd had a year ago.

I touched both sides of my head. What was in there? The monster rocking back and forth, was it holding the *thing*, the time bomb that would soon kill me?

"I'm uncomfortable being alone with her," Gina said, "what with the *wife* thing."

"Right," Peggy said in a voice that meant *wrong*. "It's your fault for encouraging her. I saw you taking care of her then and the way you look at her. You always had eyes for her. That red hair you admired... What's there to love about her now?"

"You're an *ass*." Gina's voice choked. "The accident was *your* fault."

Peggy accused Gina of looking at me?

"It was her fault for what she said to me," Peggy said.

Now she was accusing me of causing an accident that was her fault.

They continued to fight, and I learned more facts.

A year ago, I'd yelled something at Peggy while she was driving, causing her to crash. I was injured. Gina blamed Peggy. Peggy blamed me, but also herself, which was the reason she'd taken me with them this weekend.

The picture of my life was clearing up and it was no painted Madonna with pink tits.

I couldn't take more of their dizzying drama. I was too numb and miserable to deal with that *thing* in my head that would soon kill me. I wanted Gina's love and Sophie's quirks and fun stories. I missed...

What I missed didn't matter. I wiped away the stubborn tears.

Across a sluice of squishy carpet, a bath of tepid water waited for me. I stepped carefully into it. Soaking in the fragrant bubbles, I allowed myself a moment to relax, to calm my reactive anger, my bottomless sorrow.

I stuck my left foot out of the foamy water and the breath stopped in my throat. My foot was crisscrossed with red scars, just like that vision of doom I'd had last night—ten thousand years ago—on the beach with my little family. Gina and Max vanished, the sky turned black, the water ebbed and revealed my scarred and broken foot...

My nightmarish vision had been realized, and now I didn't have Gina by my side to calm me down with her sweet, loving words. *You'll be brilliant, and I'll be so proud of you.*

Enough self pity.

I counted five toes. In my heart, I thanked the surgeon who had put my foot back together in an anatomically correct way.

Banging started in the next room. They were at it again. This wasn't the Ritz for sure, because in a fancy hotel the bedsprings wouldn't squeal and the wooden headboard wouldn't so rhythmically hit the wall separating my room from theirs. How could Gina like this version of Sophie, let alone be her lover? It was so obvious they didn't get along, even hated each other, and their mutual hate fed their mutual lust.

Up until now, I'd managed to avoid the full-length mirror. Once I emerged from the water, I took a good look at my entire body for the first time. It wasn't a pretty sight.

Last night, when I stepped out of the shower on Rose Avenue, my head was held high and my skin was clear. I was confident and healthy, adored and happy, a published novelist about to launch her new book. I had a few extra pounds but I didn't care. I was a writer, not a runway model.

Now I scrutinized my reflection. If I'd seen this emaciated woman in the street, I would have bought her a happy meal at McDonald's, because anything larger than a child's portion would have killed her.

Last night, all the parts of my life fit together like a thousand-piece puzzle in glowing colors.

Tonight, a cyclone had blown in and scattered the pieces in a million directions. Some were under the table, chewed up by the dog into unrecognizable mush.

Last night in that dreamy world, Gina made love to me while reciting poetry. Tonight a strange man was sleeping in my bed—that was if New Gina rented the place furnished—or sitting with his family in my living room, below the ghost of a double nude painting featuring Gina and me, the same Gina who was now in the adjacent room fucking a dead woman who'd crept out of some hole in the ground and turned out to be alive and mean.

Last night, life felt too good to be true. Was *that* beautiful world only a fantastic dream and this, the ugly world of the accident, real and true?

As the death mask of my face slowly inched toward the mirror, another loss became apparent. The accident must have shortened my left leg, giving me a limp, costing me what Gina called *Elektra's dancer's walk.*

All my powers had been yanked away in this downward spiral into hell, even my walk. Peggy had summed it up: *What's there to love about her now?*

I turned away from my naked mirror situation—clear-minded despite the excruciating headache. My new alternative reality had preserved the elements of my life, like a full pack of cards, but reshuffled those cards into a different combination. Those around me knew only this hell, but I remembered paradise.

32. Soggy Carpet

In my backpack, I found a clean pair of jeans, some T-shirts, a sweatshirt, underwear, and a pair of blue canvas sneakers. My mother had done okay there. I pulled the sweatshirt over my head and dressed as quickly as the pain allowed. Then I sat cross-legged on the double bed in my lonely hotel room and rummaged in my backpack while my mind gathered the mental ingredients I'd need to make sense of my life. After a few minutes, I applied a pinch of imagination and a smidgen of suspension of disbelief, and baked a half-and-half shit cake I decided to call Reality One and Reality Two.

In an inside pocket of the backpack, I found a purse with money and a credit card with my name on it, but no driver's license or picture ID. Two paperbacks—neither the one I'd written—and a shiny laptop, a silver variation on the gold-plated Mac of Reality One.

To my utter delight, my laptop was fully charged. I nearly laughed out loud, because although I was dealt a bad hand, all the cards existed. Here I found an authentic piece of my reshuffled self, which meant I'd soon find the other cards.

The mere presence of a charged laptop in my otherwise dismal luggage gave me plenty of information. Some monstrous change had robbed me of everything I cared about, but not of my essence.

I could neglect the dishes, forget to open my mail, but gadgets were gods who had to be worshipped. Gina would tease me about my obsession to keep my gadgets ready for action. She'd say, *When the end of the world comes, you'll sit down to write about it.*

I may have lost Gina, but I found a genuine piece of what made me Elektra Brooke.

The answers were locked away in my laptop. When I typed a variety of passwords, none worked. I kissed the keyboard with reverence, closed the lid, then slipped it into its extra-padded protective cover.

Heavy breathing came through the thin wall—oh, fuck these two.

Despite the heartbreak and the injuries, a strong need to tell the story of this moment seized me. Words danced in my head, and my fingertips itched. Even in this glum version of myself, the tenacious affliction called *writer* saturated my insides.

Yes, yes, yes. I was still the same pain-in-the-ass me.

I picked up the four soggy pills I'd spat out earlier and bounced them like game marbles from hand to hand, weaving my updated theory of what had happened.

The weekend in R1 had started with *Sophie's* visit to the cemetery. The weekend in this R2 had started with Peggy's visit to the same cemetery

In R2, Sophie never got to be my friend, because she was the one who had died of pneumonia at age twelve. Now she had a six-foot hole in the ground, topped by her own engraved name and a unique grammatical error. Peggy lived and had met me, maybe in Gina's classes. Peggy and I became sort-of friends, although never as good as Sophie and I were.

Gina fell in love with Peggy—which made sense, because Gina adored depressing art—and her house on Rose Avenue was now rented to her ex and his family.

As I put together everything I knew about R2, the worst change was never having written a novel because Sophie Sanders and her stories didn't exist. The book's nonexistence was like discovering that a child you'd raised lovingly to be a decent human being had never been born.

This weekend's shindig was mine in R1, but in R2 it had turned into Peggy's art show with her fancy crowd.

Regarding my mother.

The roles were reversed, and she took care of me. For the independent me, the greatest cringe factor came from having turned into an invalid requiring care, yet if Peggy was the one who had caused my accident, why did my mother feel an obligation toward me?

Silence finally ruled behind the connecting door.

I was going to get my life back, even if that meant first severing connections with everyone I knew. If indeed somewhere in my head a *thing* was about to dislodge and kill me, time was short. I had to go before they woke up, and find the rest of my story by myself, because none of them told me the whole truth.

Careful not to slip on the wet carpet, I stole through the connecting door into the adjacent room, where the exhausted couple were now asleep. A short-haired Peggy snored on her right side, one arm covering her face and her back pressed tightly against Gina's back. Gina's head rested on her outstretched arm, and her hair was also short.

Where were those wigs made of *my* red hair?

Gina's pillow was tossed to the carpet. Nothing new. She hated strange pillows. Her open lips were slightly pursed, as if for a kiss. Was she dreaming of me? The hint in the air of her delicate Wild Rose was mixed with the sensual scent of their recent sex. I leaned over to kiss the side of her forehead, and only the sudden twinge in my foot made me stop before I actually did it.

In this reality, I wasn't Gina's wife, but rather a disturbed friend turned stalker.

A wave of red rage washed my vision and turned my fierce love into ugly hatred. I picked up the white pillow from the floor and stood over Gina's sleeping form, about to cover her face and press down hard until she stopped breathing...

Aghast, I dropped the pillow and scurried away. My face in my trembling hands, I was gasping for air. What was happening to me?

Her emotions are on the surface. Her impulses are raw.

They were right. I was just about to kill the woman I loved because she stopped loving me. Why were my emotions and impulses so raw and on the surface?

No time to ponder.

As my eyes adjusted to the darkness, I saw their wigs on a chair in the corner next to a thing with glow-in-the-dark poodle edges. Peggy's messenger bag.

Holding my breath, I grabbed both wigs and Peggy's bag and swiftly sneaked back into my own room, heart pounding in my ears.

I searched Peggy's bag. A Ziploc enclosed a few pill containers that came from a pharmacy in Westwood. And she called me a drug addict! But no, Elektra Brooke was the name on the labels, above my mother's address, also in Westwood. My name and my mother's address hadn't changed in this evil transformation. The bag contained an envelope and inside it, a page of instructions and my driver's license. I pressed the license to my bony chest and felt some of the tension seeping out. This little piece of plastic infused me with courage.

If indeed I'd become a drug addict, and they made sure to keep drugs out of my hands, why didn't I feel the physical or emotional need to take those drugs? Because I remained my same old self, I answered.

I wouldn't take the drugs. I kept my driver's license and replaced the Ziploc in Peggy's bag. A sudden stab of pain in my left foot made me reconsider. I pulled out the bottle of ibuprofen. It would come in handy also for headaches.

A fat prissy purse with fluffy edges was bursting with cash. I quickly counted three thousand dollars. Without hesitation, I shoved all the money into the side zipper of my backpack. It was mine fair and square and definitely a small price Peggy would pay for stealing her sister's life, my show, my wife. Now she'd either start me on a fresh new life or help me get back to my sane reality. If I found my way back home, she wouldn't need the cash anyway because she'd be as dead as she used to be.

I checked her driver's license. Peggy Sanders. Unless she carried a fake ID, I had to believe a state-provided document. Her registration, evidence of insurance, and credit cards were also assigned to Peggy Sanders.

I replaced her ID cards into their slots, then shoved the bag across the connecting door, where it skidded on the soggy carpet and toward the bed. Peggy and New Gina slept, exhausted from more sex in one night than I'd had the whole of last week. With the door cracked open a smidge, and for only a moment, I listened to Gina's light snoring, missing her terribly, yet wishing to poison them both.

33. God's Tesla

I left my ugly black boots like two roadkills in the room and closed the door behind me. The reek of wet carpet made me gag on my way down the hallway. Someone on the floor below was probably waking up to water dripping into their bed. As I waited for the elevator to schlep up, I kept looking over my shoulder, expecting either Peggy or Gina to storm out and stop me. When the doors slid open, I stepped in, pushed *L* for lobby and left the miserable fifth floor and its horrors.

I was lost in exile like Dante Alighieri, and the three beasts trying to keep me in place were Peggy, New Gina, and my frightening mother in her new angelic form. I'd have to find my way back home on my own.

I limped through the deserted lobby and out to the portico and the dark night. Dante had used a long-dead poet to guide him in his journey. Could I? I admired many dead authors—Woolf, Asimov, Bradbury. One of them could be my guide in this far-fetched depiction of *The Divine Comedy*. One of them could direct me down through hell and purgatory, then back up to my paradise.

A lone taxicab was parked by the curb. Its interior light was on, and the driver sat inside, waiting for night travelers.

I stuck my face in the window and squealed with delight. My guide through hell was curling smoke rings, reading a book.

I said, "You must be a CIA agent, the way you always find me."

"If I were, you wouldn't guess it," Virgil said with his usual calm demeanor, obviously not at all surprised to see me at this hour and in my terrible state. He was still impersonating the ancient poet. The white of his Roman toga dazzled against his olive skin, and the same disheveled laurel wreath perched atop his long curls. At least one of us had our hair.

The front passenger door raised open for me, like the lifting of an eagle's wing.

"A Tesla?" I asked. "I'll be taken through hell in a Tesla?"

"Assigned to me, not mine," he said.

"Does this mean you aren't homeless anymore?"

"I never *was* homeless," he said.

"So sorry, of course," I said, embarrassed at my assumption. This was a new reality for him as well as for me, and I was eager to ask him about it. Here and now he had a job, a home, a different life story.

He stepped out, opened the trunk, and reached for my backpack.

"Thanks, I'll keep it with me." Having lost everything, I desperately needed to keep what was left of me at my feet, however symbolic the action. I strapped on the seat belt.

"Where to?" he asked, back at the wheel.

"Home. Let's go before they find out I'm gone." I glanced back toward the entrance, expecting my two exes to run out, hysterical.

"I'll take you to your mother's," he said.

"Hell, no," I said. "Home to Venice, please."

"Are you sure that's where you want to go?"

"I want to get the book I buried under the Jacaranda."

He shot me a sideways glance and sighed in relief. "You do remember it. That's good."

"Why wouldn't I? Two days ago you told me to bury a copy of it and you gave me your *Dream Queen* in a brown bag. I wanted you to meet Gina and my friends, but you vanished and now . . ." My words drowned in my tears. "Take me back home."

"You'll need courage." His gaze was glued to the road stretching before us.

"Please," I begged.

He nodded. "You have a lot to tell me."

Virgil was the only one who consoled me when I'd lost Ms. Angie. Now, his was the first kindness since my world fell apart.

Street signs blurred into speeding neon when the car took off in a smoothness I could only describe as falling up through air.

I knew he'd believe me, so I opened my heart and told him everything as quickly as I could, stopping a few times to blow my nose—a flowery pack of tissues was conveniently mounted on the dashboard. What I said didn't make much sense because my crying got in the way, but he was there for me, a true friend who listened without as much as one exclamation of *no shit*, or *how could that be*.

I concluded, "Then my wife, who isn't my wife anymore, was fucking the Peggy-thing in the next room, not caring a hoot that I could hear them." I sniffed. "Even my hair is in a bag now," I pointed at my backpack. "Made into two ugly wigs."

Virgil remained silent for so long, I would have thought he had fallen asleep if it weren't for his smooth and straight driving. The car was air-gliding on a road I knew to be as bumpy and twisty as my story.

"It's a different world," he said at last. He reached back to the floor behind my seat and pulled out a brown paper bag, identical to the one he had given me the night of my party. "Have a smoke."

"I don't need a smoke." I tossed the bag aside. "You don't act surprised, and I need to know if you're in on some prank."

"No prank, Ellie." He did a stomach flipping U-turn.

"Last time I did such a U-turn, Sophie threw up on my books," I said.

"I know," he said.

"You know?"

"I was the one who turned your steering wheel for you."

"You . . . What?" My hands went to my chest. "How? What are you talking about?"

"I tried to save you from the approaching transition, but you insisted on taking the trip."

"Transition? You knew what was going to happen?"

"I did. If you remember, I told you to stay home with your loved ones if you wanted to keep your life. As it happened, you were exposed."

"Well, you didn't try hard enough, did you?"

"I really tried to—"

"You should have hit me over the head, knocked me unconscious, whatever." I sobbed. "What toxic substance was I exposed to and why?"

"You were exposed to the red lightning. Calm down and let me tell you everything you need to know. There isn't much time."

"Okay, okay." I pulled out another tissue and blew my nose. "I'm listening."

"I knew you were different from the rest of your friends when you could see me."

"When I . . . What do you mean *when I could see you?* Anyone would see you if they looked, right?" Okay, I'd never been sure whether people could see him or not, but I assumed . . . "They look away because you're so weird with your clicking sandals, and that whole *I'm the Roman poet* shit, and your muttering to yourself."

"Some claim they see us, but they see only movement and make up the rest. You, Ellie, can actually see and hear me. We communicate."

I didn't know where to start with my questions. I settled on "So who do they see now at the wheel of this Tesla?"

"Most living don't perceive me, the car, or even you while you're in it."

"Most living..." I glanced at his profile, his aquiline nose, his gleaming white toga, then focused on the distant gray horizon. "What do you mean by *us*? Who are these *us*?" I looked back at him. "Tell me again and make it clear: Who are you?"

"I lived in the first age of the Roman Empire, during the reign of Augustus. I died two thousand and forty years ago, at the age of fifty. My full name is Publius Vergilius Maro."

"**I** need to be stoned to make sense of this," I said. I retrieved the bag I'd earlier tossed aside, found the pot-packed cigar and lit it. I took one long hit, that familiarity opened the faucet and restarted my holy trinity of sobs, sniffles, snot.

A constant blur of lights blinked outside the window with our fast movement through the night. I pictured Virgil in his flowing white, cultivating marijuana behind his rented beach shack, marking the various strains with metal plant stakes— *Granddaddy Purple, God's Gift, Dream Queen, Blue Dragon.* He waved to curious neighbors who thought him eccentric but enjoyed his weed.

At last, a snort of laughter announced the kicking in of the best grass yet. The ride got even smoother, and the darkness beyond was brightened by exploding neon bubbles and ravishing fireworks.

"What's this hybrid?" I asked.

"*Skywalker.*"

"Sky—is this the new Elon Musk, like we need more entitled assholes on the road?"

"Not the car. You're smoking *Skywalker.*"

Another spell of hysterics hit me. "I assume you grow it in your heavenly little garden behind your little house?"

"My house isn't little, and my heavenly garden grows seventy strains of cannabis," he said without boasting.

My laughter twisted and morphed into loud crying, the sort that would draw chuckles from an audience of dark comedy. While I was falling apart, Virgil remained silent, allowing the truth to sink into place.

"I always thought you were hallucinating, fantasizing," I said when all my noises subsided and I could speak again, "but you've been telling the truth. You're a ghost."

"*Spirit* is our preferred term."

"But what do you want from me, and why are you always in my face, and how come you always find me when I lose my way?"

"I've been your guide for many years now, as I'd been Dante's."

"So are you actually…" I swallowed hard. "Dead?"

"I'm as dead as I was more than seven hundred years ago, when I took Dante through *Inferno* and *Purgatorio*. Just as dead as his beloved Beatrice was when she first asked me to be his guide, then took over from me at the good part."

I wasn't in the mood for his old grudge about *that pushy heavenly broad.*

"I hate to state the obvious," I said, "but Dante's work is fictional."

"Some fiction survived for so long it became as good as history," he said in that singular accent of a man with Latin as a native tongue. Now I believed him.

"Okay, let me understand. You came to my publication party and told me I needed to create a protective time capsule. Why?"

"Your novel deserved to survive. The ancient tree preceded and survived previous transitions, and it could protect a simple time capsule."

"Again, if you knew yesterday what would happen to me, why didn't you stop it? And what's a transition?"

"What happened didn't happen to you alone. A transition doesn't happen to a single person but rather to your reality. No one can stop it but the Big Kahuna. I could only warn you, which I did."

The Big Kahuna? Was he for real? But I could focus on only one outlandish detail at a time. "Donald Duck?" I pointed to the yellow countdown watch. "Let me see it. When's the next transition?"

"Nothing new is scheduled yet." He slipped the watch off his thin wrist and handed it to me. It was heavier than I expected. Donald Duck rested on his back, fast asleep and snoring.

"I tried to keep you home. I tried to U-turn you around."

"What about Gina, my mother, my house, my dog?"

"I couldn't warn your family and friends because, unlike you, they don't perceive me."

I asked, "Are you saying, if I stayed home with Gina, none of it would have happened to me? To us?"

"You would have noticed minor changes around you, some friends would have been lost, some gained, but your life wouldn't have been majorly affected." He briefly glanced my way, then back at the road. "You're so stubborn."

That, I did already know. "What happens to me now?"

"You adjust to the new reality, that's it. Sophie died, Gina is someone else's wife, Peggy lived and became a famous artist who sells artwork for thousands, whose art already changed the world, and you are Ellie—"

"The fuckup who ruined her show," I completed. "I'll talk to them and make them see the truth."

"Don't waste your energy. They know only this life."

"Let me see." I was thinking out loud, explaining to myself. "If Reality One was my true home, with Gina loving me and Sophie alive, then what about that first life I lived, with Ms. Angie in it?"

"For you, that first life was Reality Zero," he explained. "Your original reality, before the first transition."

"But is the problem the red storm itself? Did my exposure make me vulnerable?"

"The red storm was destructive for you and for your family."

He didn't really answer me. No one here in R2 ever did, but now he had me thinking. "Tell me, is there another me in a parallel reality?"

"There are no parallels. Your previous realities, zero and one, are lost forever."

"But am I the only one who remembers former realities? And if so, why? I'm not vain enough to think that the world —that any reality—revolves around me. Why?" I slapped the dashboard in my frustration. "Why don't I remember my present life and the accident? Why do I only remember my happy reality? Gina and Peggy apparently kept reminding me and I kept forgetting."

"Because in this life you've had an accident, and that complication caused amnesia and brain damage that makes you constantly forget."

I pulled another tissue out and dabbed at my weepy eyes. "When Angie Mead vanished, only the two of us remembered her. Was that…"

"You're catching on," he said. "That was a transition. You and Angie both stood under the sky, exposed to the red storm. She seemed to have vanished, but you retained your memories. The rest of the world, while remembering the red storm, would forget Angie Mead."

"But she didn't really vanish." I pointed at the black sky. "She came back to me years later as Gina Caldwell. I know, because Gina told me about the red storm on our first night together. She was exposed to it and her life changed, although not as much as mine."

"That's right," he said. "Nothing really disappears from the world due to the law of preservation. When a person is lost in a transition, another person appears elsewhere and with a new history. When I gave you Dante's poetry, I pointed you to the studies of medieval literature, where you found the love of your life again. In Reality Zero, you were a little girl, Angie had a loving family, and nothing would have happened between you two. As Gina, she could love you back. The transition actually worked for you."

"Until it didn't." My throat closed up as I choked on tears again. "What does a transition do?"

"In the House, we call it *once in a red storm*. The storm isn't the reason for a transition but its result. When a transition happens, the world changes, and those exposed to the red storm change with it. Some people are erased from ever existing, new people appear in their place, with new memories and new life stories. People like you, with faulty wiring, don't change. Your memories of previous realities never get erased."

"What happens to others with faulty wiring, those like me who don't forget?" The question burst out of me in a sudden need to protect *my kind*.

"Mental hospitals are full of patients who believe they're someone else."

"Does anyone... Do any of you help them?"

"It's too late once you've been captured by the system," he said.

"*Abandon all hope, ye who enter here*," I muttered.

I imagined myself tied up in a straitjacket, screaming my throat raw in some padded room. I had to avoid *the system* at any price.

Virgil's gaze was glued to the road. What was he not telling me?

"Those transitions..." I didn't quite know how to phrase this. "Are they reversible? I mean, could I be transitioned back to my happy reality?" A whine sneaked into my voice.

"You'll never go back to exactly the same coordinates. A transition changes your entire history including minor details along the way, like fashion. An artifact from the first century may sneak its way back in, like my toga or this." Virgil pointed at his laurel wreath.

I said, "You're the only one wearing those things."

"Good point, but you'll soon realize other changes around you. New items will appear, long lost items will reappear."

"Felt tip pens?" I recalled Angie's school projects.

"Those will have to be reinvented, maybe by you, but the Swiss Army knife was brought back."

"I have a Victorinox," I said, confused. "What do you mean by *brought back?*"

"That knife is a smuggle job from a much earlier reality, before your time, when Switzerland was quite the feisty little warmonger with an effective military. That reality was nixed, but the Swiss Army knife had been rescued in time."

"Who smuggles, why, how?" I asked.

"I can't, shouldn't, talk about it at all."

"Tell me anyway," I said.

"Ask anything else," he said.

"Is *The House* like the mob, and somehow I got entangled—wrong time, wrong place?"

"Good analogy," he said. "Only with spirits."

"Who do you report to?" I asked.

"The Big Kahuna, the owner of this Tesla."

"God?"

He winced. "Actually, BK is the last one you see."

"The angel of Death," I said.

He nodded. "Just Death."

"Here's another question. Why aren't my published friends and clients published anymore?"

"Because in this life, you didn't shape their manuscripts into publishable works. Here, you were always a little useless, and you could never support yourself."

We turned right onto Rose Avenue, toward the ocean. He stopped so smoothly on the side of the street, I didn't lurch forward as much as an inch. First light cracked through the mountains in the east, and the briny fragrance of the surf drifted from the west.

I'm home, I'm home, my happy heart sang.

The house, the gate, and the garden's wall were intact. The red roof was visible in the morning light, completely bare of foliage and debris.

My smile froze.

Where were the purple blooms that only yesterday spilled from the eaves?

I asked in dread, "What happened to my Jacaranda?"

35. Gaggle

I remained seated, shaking at the horrible sight of the bare house. Gina and I got married under the canopy of the ever-blooming magical tree, and the loss of it was the last link in a choke chain of losses.

Wiping the tears off my face, I toughened my voice. "I'm going to dig up my package."

I limped across the street and stopped at the low wooden gate. It was bleached by the sun and chipped around the corners, just as it had always been. I'd meant to freshen it up with a coat of white paint but never got to it. The same uneven red bricks stuck out of the garden wall, and green moss grew in the same cracks. All was as I'd left it except for the emptiness of the missing tree.

When I peeked over the gate, another loss hit me. The beautiful garden I'd nurtured on hands and knees had become a child's playground. The vegetables and the perennials had been yanked out and replaced with cheap plastic slides and a red swing set.

A skinny blonde in a tracksuit and a ponytail stepped out of the house, a buff cocker spaniel strutting by her side. My boy.

"Max," I called out.

The dog barked and snarled as if I were a stranger.

"Quiet, Buddy," the woman scolded.

Buddy?

She smiled with uncertainty. "May I help you?"

"I live in this house," I said, immediately correcting that to, "I used to live here in another life. I passed by and wanted to see it."

The dog kept barking. She silenced it.

People opened up when you talked about their dogs. "My Max was also a buff cocker," I said. "How old is Buddy?"

"We think two," she said. "But he's a rescue. Gina, our land-lady, found him roaming the streets, and they couldn't have dogs, so we adopted him."

The same cards are reshuffled in a different combination.

"Your landlady . . ." I choked on that. "I laid the bamboo floor with my own hands," I muttered.

"The floor creaked," the woman said. "We replaced it with oak. Come in and see."

I flinched with pain. That screechy floor board by the stove, the spot Gina and I had ordained as a shrine to our love, was gone.

"What happened to the tree with the purple flowers?"

"My husband Brian had to chainsaw it because the invasive roots ruined the pipes and the driveway." She pointed at the cracked concrete behind me. Gina and I considered the dam-age a small price to pay for owning such a magnificent tree. "Besides, my son is allergic to the flowers. He has asthma."

The control I hardly maintained evaporated. "Brainless Brian cut down my tree because of the fucking driveway?" I yelled.

The woman's big frightened eyes focused on me.

Would it be possible to grow such a majestic tree back once it was chopped down? I touched my shorn hair. It never grew back the same way.

"Did you repurpose it as fire logs?" I kept yelling, devastat-ed. "Where does the owl sit at night?"

Buddy kept barking and growling.

"Stop." She grabbed him by the collar.

"Don't pull him like that," I said in anger.

Her emotions are on the surface. Her reactions are extreme.

"I'm calling the police." She was on her phone.

I couldn't blame her. As far as she was concerned, I was some limping junky.

I swallowed my anger. "Forgive me." Then I made up a story. "My grandpa planted that tree forty years ago, and it's hard to see it gone." Stepping back, I tripped on the root extensions of the felled tree. "Hey, I guess it'd be moot to ask permission to dig up a package I buried in the garden?"

The woman thrust her lower jaw forward and raised her phone. "The police will be here any minute. If you're still littering around here, you'll be arrested."

"No need for that." I raised my hands in surrender. "And the word you want is *loitering*."

Back in the car, I said, "Let's go. She called the police."

"No worries," Virgil said. "We're invisible in the car. Even you."

"I'm homeless," I lamented. "My beautiful tree is gone."

He relit the joint, inhaled and passed it to me. Blinded by the rising sun, I fumbled inside my backpack for my stylish sunglasses, but what I found in a large eyeglass case made me gape in horror. The futuristic item could only be described as a narrow wraparound cyclops mirrored lens.

"What's this?" I dangled the abomination by its earpiece.

"The present fashion of protective eyewear," Virgil said.

The strange item actually hugged the bridge of my nose and blocked the light well enough.

A police cruiser arrived and two men in uniform stepped out of it, both wearing the cyclops sunglasses. The woman used wide gestures, pointing at the street, then spreading her arms —*I don't know where she is.* The cops scanned the street, not seeing us.

"Go inside," said one of them. "Stay safe."

The blonde slammed the door behind her—the very door I'd painted red with Sophie's wide bristle brush while Sophie told me her stories. If I got close enough, I was sure I'd find one stray hair from that brush stuck above the peephole and another below the doorknob.

My lost paradise gleamed in the morning sun, and no one went in or out its wooden gate or its red door. I'd poured my heart and soul into my home and garden, and both were ripped away from me. I tore my gaze from the house that wasn't mine anymore.

"Let's go somewhere. Anywhere," I said.

The car took off in its dreamy float, and my stomach met my throat. The scenery of houses, shops, and people on the beach blurred into blinking neon colors that throbbed along with the humanoid rocking inside my head.

My phone dinged twice. One message came from Gina and one from Peggy, who probably just woke up and realized I was gone.

New Gina texted, *Come on, Ellie. I don't know what's wrong, but you can tell me where you are and we'll come get you.*

And from Peggy, *We'll have to pay for the carpet damage you caused. Come back right now with the money you stole or you will be comprehended.*

"It's apprehended, asshole," I said.

"I'm taking you back to your friends," Virgil said. "Or would you rather go to your mother's house? They know your care, and your doctors—"

"My mother who let me raise myself can go to hell."

"Camille may have once been passive and dependent, but in this reality she's your rock. She deserves some credit."

"No credit." Tight fists dug my nails into my palms, but my throbbing headache canceled that pain. "I took care of her all my life, so now she has to suck it up a little. That doesn't make her an angel. I need to be as far as possible from those three toxic bitches. Start driving."

"Where, Ellie?"

"Can I stay with you?"

He shook his head *no*. "I know a safe place, where you can figure things out for a while."

"Take me there."

Restless messages kept dinging on my phone.

Virgil said, "Calm them down or they won't leave you alone."

"Five thousand messages, all about her money." I showed him the phone screen. "She'll never stop searching for me."

"Answer one of them."

I texted my mother, thanking her for everything she had done for me. *I've become a burden, but I'm going to find my own way to health. I'll let you know where I am soon.*

I texted Peggy. *Don't look for me. I apologize for everything. Your art is actually brilliant. The money I took is only a loan I'll pay back with interest once I get on my feet.*

I clicked on Gina's texts. Our daily communication— *Walk the dog*, or *what's for dinner*, or *Elviva Geronimo was great last night*—those trivial love treasures I'd never deleted were now gone. My loss was immense. I wasn't going to text her back. In this world, I owed her nothing.

In films and novels, the protagonist flings her phone far out of a moving car. As I'd already lost enough, I kept my fully charged gadgets with me.

My phone—which had somehow transitioned along with me and with the inner pocket of my leather jacket—could be traced in airplane mode, but not if I turned it off altogether, so that's what I did.

Virgil slowed down enough for me to see road signs advertising nearby hotels and waterparks.

One big sign announced a Santa Barbara art show of the incomparable Peggy Sanders. Her larger-than-life airbrushed image was adorned with poodle edges.

"Up yours, Peggy." I raised my middle finger when I noticed the typo. "It says, gaggle Peggy Sanders dot com for more info. A typo?"

"No typo," he said. "In this reality, it isn't Google."

"*Gaggle*," I repeated, tasting the new word on my tongue. My ears perked up. Hypnotic music came from the sound system, my sort of relaxing music, but I didn't recognize it.

"What's this piece you're playing?" I asked.

"The composer was a pioneer in her field. She was lost, but we saved her music."

"Why was she lost?"

Virgil flinched. "For the same reason you are."

I lunged forward in reaction and was immediately fixed in place by the snapping seat belt. "I'm not lost, my reality is. What was her name?"

"She was known by a single name," he said. "Whimsy."

I took another healthy hit from *God's Gift* and exhaled, relaxing enough to ask my next question. "If Whimsy was lost, how come you have her music?"

"Enough questions," he snapped, but I knew him well enough to realize he was dying to tell.

I repeated. "How come?"

He briefly glanced sideways at me, then back at the blurred mountain road. "I see your mouth moving, about to ask more questions. I'm not supposed to talk about our system, and if my colleagues find out, they'll do to me what my people did to that Jewish guy from Nazareth not too many years after I died."

"Go on. Tell."

"What I told you earlier about smuggling... Well, we have a bootleg retrieval network. Couriers."

And there it was. I lived for weird tales, and finally, I was about to get the meat of the story.

36. Couriers

"Couriers," I said.

"More like smugglers," he said.

"Explain."

"Ellie, once I drop you off, we may never meet again, so listen carefully. Each transition loses important items, like your Victorinox, also masterpieces along with their creators—books, music, paintings, movies. However, if we're quick enough, we can illegally get our hands on a piece of art despite the loss of its creator. For instance, this music you're enjoying."

"What do you do with those artworks?"

"They go into the Cosmic Library—"

"The *what*?"

"The Cosmic Library is a shrine to those who stopped existing due to a transition. Their important art is unavailable to the living, but the dead enjoy it. We brought in—"

"We . . . Are you one of them, those smugglers?"

"I actually train fresh recruits for that career," he said, a proud sing-song in his voice.

My anger mounted. "What does your Big Kahuna say about those *illegal* activities?"

"How do you think he gets his beloved Italian sambuca?"

"Don't give me that. Sambuca is available in any liquor store."

"Not in this reality."

"What happened to Whimsy?"

"A transition eliminated her from existence."

"You steal the art and eliminate the creator." I rubbed my prickly head with hands that wanted to punch him. "How dare you?"

"Don't see it that way, Ellie. It's a great honor to have your name on a shelf in the library and your art saved for posterity. We each have our favorites, naturally, so there's a lot of banter, lively repartee, and—"

"What utter bullshit," I said. As angry as I was, an idea came to me. "If you can smuggle art or wine from one reality to another, you surely can smuggle me back into mine. I'm not that big."

"Your reality doesn't exist, Ellie. Besides, our skillful couriers transport only artifacts."

"You aren't that skillful then, are you?" Ahead, I saw the colorful stripes of a 7-Eleven. "Do you mind stopping at that gas station?"

"I drive a Tesla," he said.

"I don't know about you or your dead buddies, but we mortals sometimes need to eat or use the toilet."

"Of course." He pulled in.

I peed and splashed cold water on my face, then frowned at my reflection. I washed down two ibuprofens, then ran my hand through my shorn hair before covering it—hiding it— with the baseball cap. I bought a hotdog from the sleepy night clerk and inhaled it on the spot without tasting it.

Refreshing Diet Coke sizzled down my throat. It was perfect, until a syrupy aftertaste coated my tongue. I spewed soda all over the floor. This cursed reality had dripped some revolting alien sweetness into my favorite drink, and I had yet another reason to hate it. I drank down a bottle of cold water to get rid of the cloying new flavor.

"Diet Coke is way too sweet," I said as I dropped into the Tesla. "How'd you guys screw that up?" I flounced around till I was comfortable and laid my head back. The pain was somewhat dulled by the pills. "Your mob are just dead humans, except for the Big Kahuna, who is Death, is that right?"

"We're not the mob," he said. "And yes."

I had so many questions for him. How many of you are there? Where do you meet? What do you do when you're not smuggling? I started with one, "What do you all actually do?"

"We aim to improve human life by targeting an artifact from history. We send two smugglers—one dead, one living—back in time to remove it. The Big Kahuna pushes a button on his game pad to bring back the artifact, and the living see a red thunderstorm—"

"Wait, I don't get it," I said. "If the smugglers remove an artifact and bring it back with them to the present, the change would automatically happen, wouldn't it?" The questions were forming on my tongue as I spoke, and I barely knew what I was asking. "Why do you need BK and his thunderstorm to help them bring back the artifact?"

"Because when history changes, the dead smuggler or the living one—or both—may cease to exist altogether."

A chill ran through me with the echo of Gina's words long ago. *If it weren't for Dante, none of us would be here in our present form.*

"Can you repeat that?" I asked.

"All changes in history will affect the future from that point, you see?" His long vowels lengthened even more as he spoke calmly. "BK has to catch the artifact mid mission, because—"

"Because the change in history will be so massive, it would prevent the birth of both smugglers," I said, looking at him with accusation. "The change would erase them altogether." I was trembling with anger. "And you, you who trains those recruits will send them to face certain oblivion while you, who lived and died before Christ was born, will remain unaffected."

He nodded. "You got it."

"Why mess with history in the first place?" I insisted.

"You have to understand, Ellie." He hesitated—embarrassed? "We get a bit bored, more bored than you down here, and we look for some amusement. I mean, how many centuries can you spend on the up and up? After a transition we have game nights."

"Go on." I suppressed those *on the surface* emotions and my strong need to slug him. If I wanted to make it back home, certain things were crucial for me to know.

"The House members get together, eat, drink, and bet on the unintended consequences. Anything could happen as a result of a transition. Some things appear, some disappear from existence."

"Some people." I opened my eyes in disbelief. "It's a game to you."

"Pretty much." He chuckled. "You should see the risky version of Transitions, when the high rollers eliminate an influential work of fiction in some reality just to see what would be missing from the future of the world. For instance—"

"The whole concept of your game is immoral, unethical. How dare you play us like chess pieces?"

"Why do powerful people play with others' lives? Because they can, and it's fun for them. The living are left with a new world, and that's what they know. Let's face it, for some, the new is an improvement on the old. Look how you found Gina. We entertain ourselves at no one's expense."

"Changing realities and erasing people's memories is robbing them of who they are," I said. "Without our happy and sad moments, without our good and bad times, we're nothing." I reined in my flailing hands, afraid of what I might do with them. "What about the memory of a beloved teacher in the minds of the children who enjoyed her classes, her roses, her kindness?"

"For them, she never was," Virgil said. "So what's the damage?"

"Look at me and see the damage." I couldn't draw in enough air. He didn't understand how utterly malevolent they were. How heartless, coldblooded, evil. "This is the second time I became the only one who remembers a different life."

He said, "That fault in your wiring makes you hold on to the old reality with a tenacity our system can't control."

"The fault is in your system, not in my wiring. You don't know the misery of my childhood." I pulled one tissue from the pack but more tissues followed and flew about me like a flock of peace doves when I had war on my mind.

He kept his eyes on the road but slightly lowered his head. Ashamed? Not likely. "I'm sorry for the pain we've caused you, Ellie. I wish I could take it away."

"You only wish you could erase my mind," I said.

"On the contrary," he said. "You need to remember everything, as my new living smuggler."

"I'm not going on time travel missions for you!" I attacked him, but my fists bounced back from a cool and slimy membranous substance. "Yuck." I wiped my hand on my sweatshirt. "What's this shit?"

He shrugged. "I move in my own space."

"And I want to move in mine," I said, wiping between my fingers with the edge of my sweatshirt. I didn't want whatever I touched on me. "I'm not your smuggler or your courier. Fucking do it yourself."

"I can't. As I said, the specific time and place requires two smugglers, one living and one dead. The dead one spots the artifact but only the living can take it. It's the only way. You'll go back in time—"

"Not interested," I said.

"Just hear me out, Ellie," he said. "You'll prevent much pain and suffering if you go back to Venice, Italy, 1554—"

"The time and place *The Comedy* was published... Why?" I growled at him in anger. "Why would I go back there?"

"You'll prevent the poem's wide publication by stealing it from its editor on the way to the press."

"Are you insane?" I asked, appalled. "Why would we want to lose a great literary masterpiece? And what does Dante think about your plan?"

"He's too busy for the games, admiring his own influence on the world, teaching history classes and his poetry to the unwashed dead masses as a way of bragging about it." Virgil briefly glanced at me, as if to make sure I was buying it, then back at the road.

"I guess the best of us could be corrupted by endless boredom," I said. "But he'd honored you by writing you into his masterpiece. Wouldn't he get mad when he finds out?"

"He may, but I assume he wouldn't mind, because, you see, the poem won't be lost."

"How so?"

"You'll bring the unpublished manuscript to the Cosmic Library, where it will be preserved for all eternity and, mind you, read by more eyes. Let's face it, more readers are dead than alive."

I clenched my hands when I wanted to slug him again. "You can't predict the consequences of artifact removal so far back in time, but if you could, I'd probably win your stupid consequences bet." I recalled Gina's long-ago lecture. "No light bulbs, no espresso, no football, no Renaissance, no ice cream, no pizza. Imagine life without pizza, Virgil."

He raised a hand in dismissal. "No cholesterol-related diseases, no need for triple bypass sur—"

"But how sad and boring life would be," I said.

"No fascism." He raised a finger.

"You don't know that," I said. "What if you end the world altogether?"

"Not likely."

I shook my head in disbelief. "What a coward you are," I said. "I dare you ... say, go further back from your own time, remove a rock from the temple in Jerusalem and make King Solomon trip and die before writing his *Song of Songs*. Would that prevent you from writing the *Aeneid* or even from existing altogether?"

"You have a point, but I don't make those decisions," he said. "I can only take you this far."

I hadn't noticed till then, but we'd stopped next to a two-story apartment building. A vacancy sign flashed *Paradise Point Apartments.*

"Are you abandoning me in this nothingness?"

"Rent an apartment. Figure out how to live your new life."

"I'm going home, with or without your help."

"That's not possible." He was suddenly aloof, probably on his way to break the bad news to some other poor sucker with a glitch in their memory. "Goodbye, Ellie."

"I'll find my way home by myself."

He turned to face me. "Look, I'm really sorry for what happened to you," he said. "If you ever need me, whisper my name in any public place."

"I'll never say your name, you fake friend." My fists were so tight in my wish to hit him, my palms hurt. "Go burn forever in the ninth circle of hell."

"That circle is freezing cold," he said.

"Good for the circle." I counted out three hundred dollars from Peggy's stash. "Hope this pays for the gas."

"It's a Tesla." He handed me back the money.

I threw the notes back at him and they flew about before joining the tissue mess on the floor, console, dashboard. "Fuck you and your Tesla and your Big Kahuna."

My bad foot slowed down my theatrics as I stormed from the car. I couldn't even slam the door because it hovered above me and then closed with the most silent *whoosh.* In my anger, I stuck both middle fingers in the air, probably seeming quite mad to any onlooker.

When I blinked, the car was gone.

Far ahead in the mountains, a huge Ferris wheel with flickering lights turned, dominating the skyline and mocking the stars.

Purgatory

. . . go back now while you still can see your shores;
do not attempt the deep: it well could be
that losing me, you would be lost yourselves.

The Divine Comedy, Dante Alighieri

37. Virgil

He pushed a button on the dashboard and a calm voice answered, "Paradise Point, good morning." "I dropped her off," he said.

"I'm here," she said.

38. The Wheel

I lowered my gaze from the slow-moving Ferris wheel to the sign announcing *Welcome to Paradise Point*. Dante's nine spheres of Heaven came to mind, and I could almost hear Gina's low voice, reciting the very last lines of *Paradiso:* "*As in a wheel whose motion nothing jars, by the love that moves the sun and the other stars.*"

Dante's wheel of paradise, I thought.

The street was alive with activity. Some kind of street fair was in progress, with carnival-like attractions. People in costumes came in and out of colorful little shops, some waited in a long line for a fortune teller's booth. Tinny music came from a merry-go-round, and cheerful lights flashed from store signs—Paradise Point Yoga, Paradise Point Swims, Paradise Point Gifts. What were they celebrating?

The jolly picture seemed lost in time, blurred, flat, unreal. I had a feeling that if I tried to blend into this cheerfulness, I'd fail, and the scene would prove to be but a sequence of images screened on a huge wall.

The vacancy sign flashed. The apartment building seemed decent enough, despite the red graffiti on the wall announcing *L'Inferno* in blood drippy spooky font.

I smiled—surprised I could still manage to do it—at the thought of a small-town gangbanger with butt-crack pants and a can of red spray paint, making sure to get the right font and the correct Italian spelling. Then I was saddened by the long ago memory of Gina claiming half in jest, that if not for Italy and frescoes, we wouldn't have graffiti. That Gina had been about to fall in love with me. New Gina never would.

The delicious aromas of mozzarella and basil made my stomach churn with hunger. The vacancy sign could wait while I grabbed myself a quick bite.

Paradise Point Pizza was the sort of little hole-in-the-wall one could find in any Florentine alley. I was immediately at home hearing a familiar scratchy recording of Rosa Ponselle in my favorite aria from *La Gioconda*. When Sophie, no lover of opera, was my roommate, she'd come to my bedroom and listen to that one piece in humble silence.

I sat at a table covered with a checkered red and white tablecloth. A young waiter in his twenties immediately served me ice water and garlic focaccia. I ordered spaghetti without looking at the menu. Then I checked the photos on the wall. This hidden gem hadn't been so hidden in the past, as was evident from the rich gallery of Italian celebrities, their framed photos all autographed.

Waiting for my order, I sipped ice water and read through the colorful menu. One item made me gasp out loud: a fried bologna sandwich named *the Peggy Sanders.*

Peggy apparently knew this out-of-the-way place, had been here at least once, but would she know to look for me here?

I was getting used to the constant barrage of Peggy-related reminders in this new and hostile world. I could easily imagine her name engraved on a brass plaque she herself designed and affixed to her childhood home in nearby Oxnard. *Here lived the great artistic phenomenon Peggy Sanders*, the plaque would say, a comma tucked in at some randomly chosen place.

Well, I'd had enough of Peggy.

A bowl piled high with spaghetti marinara arrived, and I attacked it to the sound of Callas in "*Addio del Passato.*" Sophie used to laugh out loud when I wore a dramatic expression and mimed the last words of the dying Violetta.

Five bites and I was full. A few spoonfuls of vanilla gelato were enough to seal the deal, and when Anna Moffo sang Puccini, my daily fix was complete. This little gem of a place was my new Jerusalem.

My waiter brought me the check.

"You've been here long?" I asked.

"From the very beginning," he said with pride. "It's a family business."

"You're way too young for that." I laughed and pointed to the theatrical release poster of *La Strada* on the wall, one signed by the film's director. "If Fellini signed it, this place must have been open in the 1950s."

"He dines here often," the young man said.

"*Used to* dine, right?" I asked, a chill starting at the top of my scalp.

"That one's from last week," he said with a straight face.

He was too ignorant to know Fellini, I thought, or had a strange sense of humor. Yet the chill in my scalp skittered down my back like melting ice.

39. Miss Scarlett

I dragged my limping, tired self toward the vacancy sign, backpack and my full stomach weighing me down. The building's exterior wasn't promising, but once I entered the main gate, my second impression put my mind at rest. The place seemed well-maintained and clean, an oval-shaped dark blue pool took up most of the courtyard, and three women lounged in their bathing suits, all reading paperbacks and laughing as they turned pages.

Next to a pissing boy fountain, another sign invited: *Our office is always open, come in for cookies.*

Inside the shabby office, a hint of pachouli hung in the air. A worn couch was pushed against one wall. A large screen hung from the opposite wall, displaying flickering security images of shadowed corners, a staircase and the pool area.

Next to the screen, a Roman numeral wall clock was frozen at ten to two.

An oval conference table, scattered with dirty coffee mugs and leftovers, took up most of the space. Chairs were strewn about in disarray, as though a large and messy family had just had breakfast, then got up and left the cleanup to Mama.

Yet Mama—an ancient woman with wispy hair—sat at the reception desk, also engrossed in a fat paperback and in no rush to clean anything up.

She looked up from her reading. "How may I help you?" she asked in a sweet voice, her intense eyes measuring me.

"I'm Ellie Brooke," I introduced myself, immediately reciting my rehearsed cover story. "I've a deadline for my novel, and I need to work in peace and quiet, away from my noisy family."

"I'm Betty." Her winning smile made her seem younger than I'd first guessed. "You'll find this a perfect place for work. There's free Wi-Fi and my other tenants are very quiet."

"I don't have references," I said, "or whatever you people check."

"I trust my instincts," she said. "The only vacant unit is a studio on the second floor, but I could give you a special deal."

That was the second time life gave me a deal when I most needed one. I hoped I didn't have to sit for her in the nude.

"You're smiling," she said.

"You reminded me of an apartment in Westwood and the special deal a new friend made with me."

"Let's hope my deal is just as good." Betty stood up with difficulty and leaned on a thick cane. "Please help yourself to coffee and cookies."

"Thank you," I said. "I've just had a big meal."

Up the stairs, on the second floor we made a left in the open hallway and stopped at apartment 203. Betty fumbled with the key, dropping it twice. I picked it up and unlocked the door.

She clicked the switch on the wall and bright light filled the room. The place was furnished with a sofa bed, a round table, two chairs. The kitchenette had a fridge. The bathroom smelled of detergent and had a simple shower. It was very clean. Outside the window, *Paradise Point Apartments* flashed in a string of red lights.

Betty's expressive eyebrows gathered. The unearthly glint in her eyes could be just cataracts, but it gave me a chill. Her lips opened, hopefully not for questions I didn't want to answer. I was eager to go online to check out this new world, find out what had been added to it and what was missing. I longed to unlock my personal file and discover who I was in this reality. Did I keep a journal?

"I'll leave you to settle in today," she said. "Come anytime tomorrow and sign the contract. The coffee maker is simple drip and there's ground coffee in the cabinet, some dishes too. The grocery store is across the street." She leaned on her cane and slowly headed toward the door. "If you want to talk, come in. I don't sleep much."

"I may take you up on it," I said.

Before closing the door, she said, "Wi-Fi password is one word, lower case, *paradisepoint*."

When she was gone, I peed and washed my face. The shiny mirror reflected the gaunt cheeks and haunted eyes of a battered wife. No wonder Betty took pity on me. I ran a hand over my buzz cut in this new and liberating acquired habit. I had no desire to wear one of the wigs, but I was happy to have rescued my dead hair from my one-time friends.

There was much to explore, and if indeed I wasn't long for the world, very little time to do it. In this new sanctuary with the white walls and the minimalistic furniture, I felt protected and far removed from those who searched for me. I'd even made a new friend. Betty trusted me enough to rent me an apartment without references, and as the greeting card says, when you have at least one friend, you are home.

Outside, the red lights continued to blink, yet even as I watched, the vacancy sign went dark. My unit had indeed been the last one available. The light in the room was midday bright, but my eyes wanted to shut. I forced them to remain open, afraid of new disasters I'd have to face when I woke up.

The kitchen cabinet offered only a common brand of drip coffee. I brewed a pot, missing terribly my espresso machine abandoned to the house that wasn't mine anymore. I poured myself a cup, and not wasting any more time, opened my laptop.

Does espresso exist?

I google searched *espresso—gaggle* in this reality.

According to R1 Gina, the first prototype of the espresso machine was invented by some Italian dude in the late nineteenth century and was improved by another Italian named Gaggia sometime in mid twentieth century.

"Gaggle Gaggia," I said, amused.

Small mercies; espresso did exist in this R2.

Next, I was ready to discover what I could about that *thing* in my head that was going to dislodge and kill me.

My attempts at a password failed. In my former life, I used the last line from Dante's *Divine Comedy*, which also happened to be Gina's last line in the throes of passion.

I typed *thelovethatmovesthesunandtheotherstars* and pushed enter. *Boing.* No access. I typed *Elviva Geronimo*, with and without the exclamation mark, then with and without the space.

Boing, boing.

Both those phrases were related to Dante Alighieri. Here and now, Gina was into Greek mythology. I typed *Aphrodite's tits* in every possible form. *Hera's white arms, Poseidon's trident, Ariadne's thread, Hermes' winged sandals*...

I was running out of ideas, but nothing worked.

I had no way to break into my private files. Without a password I was a stick figure pinned with a cookie magnet to a kitchen refrigerator. I was lonely and tired. I wanted to be home with Max in my lap, Gina by my side, a bottle of tequila between us.

My life sucked sweaty balls, as Sophie would say.

Saliva gathered in my mouth in sudden nausea. I bolted to the bathroom and spent the next ten minutes on my knees in the fumes of chlorine bleach, hurling coffee, spaghetti, partially digested fragments of Gina's words, Peggy's mangled sentences, and Virgil's disclosures.

She's not long for the world. Barf. *Her emotions are on the surface.* Hurl. *Transitions is a game the dead play to amuse themselves.*

I rinsed my mouth. "Enough drama," I said to my reflection. "Work."

I couldn't get into my private files, but I had options.

Felt pen tips were gone forever from the world, Virgil had said, but the Swiss Army knife had been smuggled back in.

I used the guest screen of my laptop to explore.

My mental exclamations appeared in my head in italics. That typeface, as I remembered from Gina's long-ago improvised lecture, was designed by someone named Griffo in the early sixteenth century.

A gaggle search brought up a similar slanted typeface called Germanic, invented by a Dresden book publisher named Heyne.

I yawned. Damn, what would my password be? I really had to catch some Zs.

"I'll think about it tomorrow," I exclaimed with a Scarlett O'Hara pout.

I gaggled *Gone with the Wind* and was flooded with a mix of disappointment and relief. The history of slavery had not changed in this new reality and the novel had been written by Margaret Mitchell, although it was only six hundred pages long. In the film made by MGM, instead of Vivien Leigh, Bette Davis played the lead role and the Academy Awards poured like wine in an Italian wedding.

Gina loved Bette Davis. She'd be so thrilled to know this. I reached for my phone, about to say, *You won't believe it, but...*

My phone was off to avoid being tracked, and anyway, New Gina surely knew who played Miss Scarlett. She'd probably watched *Gone With the Wind* with her favorite actress fifty times.

I couldn't find anything about Vivien Leigh. I typed her real name, Vivian Mary Hartley. *The Broadway star was born on 5 November 1913 in British India* ... In this reality, she sang and danced in musicals.

I kept tossing questions at the search engine the natives named *gaggle*.

My eyes wanted to shut, but I forced them open. What was my password? In my delirium, images free-floated in my mind. The twisty roots of a felled tree. A red door I'd once painted with Sophie's help. A wooden gate I needed to paint. A snarling buff cocker spaniel who used to sleep in my arms.

My brain was nudging me in some direction, but where? The arms of a huge octopus undulated in a calm ocean. Did *octopus* mean anything to me in this reality? I didn't know, yet the image made me sit up straight.

Completely awake, I typed OCTOPUS in capitals. *Boing.*

I typed *theoctopus*, one word, lowercase.

I got in.

"Hooray," I cried out loud, then I laughed in joy, because when the desktop revealed itself in all its organized glory, three files floated in a vertical line on the left of a clean blue screen. This peculiarity, this super fussy geometrical arrangement of files in progress, was signature me. What Gina called *Vintage Elektra*.

"Gina, you wouldn't believe it."

I again reached for the phone to share the exciting news with her, but New Gina was in love with the poodle-murdering bitch.

Excitement was only exciting if you could share it with your loved ones, and I had no one. My emotions rose and welled in my throat, producing excessive laughter. How ridiculous it was. I laughed with snorts and squeaks, like I used to laugh with Gina and Sophie back in my other life, when things got funny and stupid.

Still, without my two sidekicks, I was a one-legged tripod. And just as quickly as I'd fallen into laughter, I deep plunged into the dark abyss of melancholy and cried the way I laughed, the way I vomited earlier—without control, shoulders shaking, nose and eyes dripping.

Here I was, teetering on the spectrum of extreme sensations—laughter and tears, despair and nausea—when I needed my wits to anchor me. I was swirling about helplessly in this second circle of Dante's hell, battered by violent winds and torrential rains and about to be washed into the ground like Ms. Angie Mead had long ago.

One of the pills I'd left behind in Peggy's bag was probably meant to even out the mood swings. Which meant I wasn't going to get evened out.

Deathly exhaustion eventually overpowered me. I curled up on the still folded sleeper sofa as it was, bare of linen. In the twilight before sleep, I promised myself to see Bette Davis as Miss Scarlett if it was the last thing I did before I died.

40. Before

Red lights were blinking in the dark when I woke up. Motionless in my half-sleep state, I let bitter truths descend full force. In the middle of my perfect life, I somehow took the wrong fork in the road, and like Dante Alighieri, found myself in a dark wood, unable to climb toward the receding lights of paradise. The path was blocked by terrifying shadows, and if I wanted to find my way back home, I had to travel the long, frightening way through even darker darkness.

Those who'd loved and respected me, now pitied me. My home had been invaded by strangers, and my beloved dog bared his teeth at me. The woman who promised to have and to hold me, in sickness and in health, was now in love with my best friend, and both considered me an obligation and a burden. Worst of all, I was dying.

It happened because of a red storm, and a game called Transitions, and because of a glitch in my ability to forget. To complicate things even more, an accident had fried my brain and made me forget even the little I had left. Lucky me, any way you mixed that Bloody Mary.

I touched my skeletal ribs again and recoiled in disgust.

But if my brain didn't have that glitch, I wouldn't remember Ms. Angie, or married life with Gina, or fun-loving

Sophie. I caught my breath. *No one* would have remembered Sophie.

I replayed some of Sophie's greatest moments and some of her dumb-assed moves, our hysterical laughs, and those margaritas she mixed from any fruit, including tangerines. No one but me held those memories.

I sat up, wide awake. How many *thousands* of others had been erased in that one recent transition and the one before it? Those monsters who played out of boredom were destroyers of lives and memories. Their games canceled those people so thoroughly, leaving no trace of them ever having lived.

"How long did I sleep?" I asked the white room. My voice bounced back at me from the bare walls.

I turned on my phone to see the time and a barrage of dinging messages bombarded me. They were searching for me, frantic, Peggy bemoaning her money. It was eight in the evening, which meant I'd slept for almost eight precious hours. Time was quickly draining away. I turned the phone off.

As Betty promised, the place was silent enough for uninterrupted hours of work or sweet sleep during the day.

I stood with some difficulty, aching from the long sleep. In the window, the bright lights of Dante's Ferris wheel dazzled against the sky and the stark silhouettes of the Santa Monica Mountains.

My open laptop gleamed on the round table. Life wasn't half bad when you had the password. My three files in progress were named *Before*, *After* and *The Octopus*.

I clicked open the last file.

A title page read *The Octopus*, a novel by Elektra Brooke.

I had a work in progress, which was obviously a secret, at least from Peggy, who had said, *She can't even write the grocery list.* I was looking forward to a read, but my first priority would be basic facts. I needed personal journal entries. How had I started my life in this reality, and what should I do to go back home?

I clicked open *Before*. It was a big file.

My first entries began when I was six, I guess as soon as I'd learned to read and write. I enjoyed listening to opera with my daddy, Roger. In both my previous realities, Mama and I called him the sperm donor.

My stomach growled in hunger. When I opened the fridge, its emptiness yawned back at me. The Italian restaurant would be open, so I decided to read there while munching on dinner.

I slipped on my leather jacket and stuck my laptop in its extra wide inner pocket, with a few bills from Peggy's confiscated money.

The sight of a dead animal inside my backpack startled me.

No, not an animal, but rather those hideous red wigs. I tried one on for laughs. My reflection mocked me. Unlike the shiny gorgeous hair I used to have, the wig was thin, dull and lifeless and it made me look like a TV actress in a show with the laziest hair and makeup department. I stuffed both wigs into the trash where they belonged, washed my face, and finger-brushed my short hair in a movement that reminded me of Gina.

Stop. *Stop.* Gina and her fingers want nothing to do with you.

I was off to dinner.

As I hobbled down the stairs, the neighbors sitting by the dark blue pool turned to me.

"Hi, Ellie," a man called.

I shuddered. Did his knowing my name mean that Peggy had found me?

"Hey, you're here," another voice said. "Come, take a load off."

A quick inspection showed no sign of Peggy or Gina. Apparently, my indiscreet landlady had already prattled about me and my business. I was too hungry to play friendly—I waved as

I hurried away—but I might stop to talk on my way back if only to ask a few questions to aid my quest.

The warm soprano of Maria Callas singing the mad scene from *Lucia* took me home again. A waiter in white asked, "Can I interest you in the house red?"

"Yes, please," I said, "and a large Florentine pizza."

He smiled. "Right away."

I opened my laptop. *Before*, *After*, and *The Octopus* popped up on the desktop. I began flipping through journal entries in the *Before* file.

My opera-crazed father had given me my name. He and my mother were married. Camille still loved her smokes and cocktails, but she was actually a productive adult and a loving parent who had allowed me to be a little girl. In one entry I wrote, *Mama never has to call the plumber or the electrician because she can fix everything in the house.*

The first sip of wine on an empty stomach made me lightheaded. I emptied the glass of ice water into myself and waited for the food.

A few hours ago, when I sat in the back of Peggy's banged-up SUV, she said, *Your mom is the most admirable and capable woman I know. She has to take care of you, like she took care of your dad when he was dying of cancer.*

Peggy's words, plus my journal entry, meant that in this reality I had two functional parental units for most of my life, and even so, by some miracle, I managed to become a total fuckup.

I skimmed through some childhood entries, meaning to explore those later. I was more interested in what had made Gina and Peggy the happy couple and me the outsider, the broke-on-her-ass friend. I read years of words, skipping over excessive descriptions and frivolous stream-of-consciousness reflections.

I mentioned a man I'd befriended who wore a white toga and noisy sandals, and did odd jobs for the school. He used to read my stories and encourage my writing. When I told my parents about Virgil, they both performed their parental duties and lectured me about staying away from grown men I didn't know. My father spoke to the principal, who claimed no one of that description worked there, which freaked my parents out completely. At home, I heard the two of them discussing what they called "Ellie's imaginary friend."

I ignored their warnings and secretly kept meeting him, until one day he wasn't there anymore.

My father died of a long illness, leaving Mama and me heartbroken.

At twenty, I became a student at UCLA. It wasn't easy for me to leave my loving mama's home, but I felt that moving out would be my only way of growing up, so I'd responded to a flashy ad with neon colors in the school cafeteria, intrigued by its strange phrasing and the special deal it offered. Like her sister Sophie in my home reality, Peggy lived on Wilshire in her aunt's eighth-floor apartment.

The Florentine pizza arrived, and I savored the sight and smell of it. A perfectly cooked egg topped silky spinach, tomato, and ham. My eyes and nose—the eyes and nose of another life—wanted to devour it in one bite. Tears of gluttony dripped down my cheeks, but my stomach—the stomach of now—disappointed me again. I was full after two slices.

As I sipped my wine and relaxed—for just a moment, I reminded myself—I studied the black and white photos of Italian greats on the walls. Marcello Mastroianni, Sophia Loren, Monica Vitti, Pier Paolo Pasolini, and next to him, an autographed smiling portrait of Monica Bellucci with short black hair.

Wait . . . I stood up, queasy, and examined the photo. My food again threatened to come up my throat because the image wasn't Monica Bellucci at all but . . . Could that be her?

"Who is next to Pasolini?" I asked a passing waiter, to make sure my eyes weren't taunting me.

"Our local great, Peggy Sanders," he confirmed my suspicion with pride of ownership. "We have some of her original art in the back if you want to see it."

"I've seen enough." I got up. "Please pack this up for me."

I shoved my laptop back into my inner pocket, paid, and grabbed the box of pizza. The fresh air outside made my stomach feel better, but not the monster in my head who banged his hammer in quick, short pulses. It was time for more pain killers.

The neighbors still sat by the pool. Weren't they tired of each other? Why weren't they in their rooms at this time of night, having dinner or watching shows, or in bed having sex or sleeping? To my relief, no one noticed me as I stole by. I wasn't in the mood for socializing.

Upstairs, I went back to reading the *Before* file.

When I'd walked into Peggy's apartment in Westwood, I was immediately impressed with the panoramic views and taken by the dark beauty of the paintings on the walls. Each canvas was some godly scene from Greek mythology.

"Your work?" I'd asked.

Peggy nodded. Her signature included a small emblem of two figures in an arabesque—one in red, one in blue—mirroring each other and almost touching hands. I'd asked her about it.

"This is a tribute to my mirror twin," Peggy said quietly. "Sophie died when we were little girls."

"I'm sorry to hear that," I had said.

One particular portrait of a strong-featured woman, her head held high in royal attitude, had made my heart go pitter-patter. A delicate tiara was cleverly concealed within her golden hair.

"Hera." I recognized the Greek goddess.

"Right." Peggy blushed and lowered her head. "She's the woman I love, my professor of Greek mythology."

Despite the art supplies and the paintings drying against the wall, the apartment was very clean. When I'd confessed that I might not be able to afford such a place, Peggy presented me with the special deal. She wanted me to keep the place in its pristine condition. In return, I'd pay only a tiny portion of the rent.

That sounded like a piece of cake. With a clean freak for a roommate, how hard would it be to keep up the already immaculate apartment? Without hesitation, I agreed to become a live-in housekeeper, hoping I wouldn't regret the deal.

As I sat there reading in my white-walled refuge, with the ever-turning Ferris wheel of paradise in the window and the sparkling pool below, I came face to face with my regrets.

41. The Faceless

The aroma of coffee drifted in through the open window with the night air. Good coffee for a change, when all my kitchen had to offer was a can of ashtray dust posing as coffee. A coffeeshop must be nearby. Again, I stuck my laptop inside my inner pocket and started down the stairs. The strange pool party was going strong, and people emerged from the blue depths of the water, their clothes dripping wet. Too modest for bathing suits?

I followed my nose out of the courtyard and to the street. I found an open door beneath the *L'Inferno* sign in its red spooky font. Relaxing music enveloped me like a warm blanket, inviting me to explore. Inside, Gustave Doré's illustrations for Dante's poem decorated the walls, and clips from Giuseppe de Liguoro's 1911 film *L'Inferno* jumped on big screens. Painted murals of climbing roses snaked through *Dia de los Muertos* skulls, and a pair of Roman caligae dangled from the ceiling.

I held my breath, overwhelmed by the immersive experience of Dante's poem.

A stooped man behind the counter wore a pleasant smile on his gaunt face. "What can I mix for you?" he asked.

"Double espresso would be great," I said.

I checked a selection of snacks, fruit, cookies. Small cupcakes were decorated with colorful chocolate chips. Tears filled my eyes, and I knew I'd finally lost it. Who cries at the sight of a cupcake? The man placed three on a plate and I made one of them disappear with one bite of bitter sweet chocolate, anise, and orange peel.

"These are to die for." I smiled through my tears.

"Thanks, Ellie," he said. "I pour my love into each of them."

"Wait, how do you know my name?" I asked.

"News travels fast here." His espresso machine hissed. "I'm Oscar."

"Oscar, I'm barely newsworthy," I said.

"Au contraire." He served my coffee in a demitasse. "You have a flawless memory and you write like an angel."

"How do you know what I write?" I asked, as puzzled as I was flattered. "And about my memory?"

"Don't expect to keep secrets in a town with one traffic light."

Right. Another person giving me a non-answer. When I wanted to pay, he raised a hand. "This one's on the house."

I sat down and let the first sip hit the spot. Who was I in this reality, and who were my friends? I clicked through pages in the *Before* file. The experiences I read about washed over me like someone else's life. My lost paradise was clear in my head, while this world felt alien.

Unlike Sophie, Peggy had been totally open about her twin sister's death, spoke of her often, painted the little girl she remembered, missed her out loud. Like her sister, Peggy would occasionally use my hair to get the exact color in her paintings.

At Peggy's pleas, I'd added Gina Caldwell's Greek mythology night classes to my list of humanities, primarily because my roommate didn't like to walk home alone after dark. During classes, she'd sketch Gina as the powerful Athena behind a round shield or as a full-figured, naked Aphrodite. Those sketches turned into masterful oil paintings that filled our apartment.

In between classes, I had to listen to Peggy obsessing about Gina, then I wrote about it in my journal. Since an obsession in itself isn't very interesting, I'd eventually get bored with Peggy's lovesick moaning and escape to the library to avoid her altogether.

One of those library nights, Gina Caldwell sat down next to me and said that her total turd, absolute asshole ex-boyfriend was moving out at that moment and she was giving him space.

I sipped my cold espresso, rubbed my spiky head and smiled. *Absolute asshole. Total turd.* Gina's alliterations. I stopped smiling when my gaze fell on one of Doré's illustrations—Dante and Virgil on a narrow mountain road, peering down a dark abyss.

Behind the bar, Oscar kept busy despite the fact I was his only customer.

An odor wafted into the air, the kind of muddy smell you notice when you sit in a well-watered garden. Strange, though, since we were in a dry room.

I turned back to reading my library scene. New Gina had asked what I was doing there so late. In my exhaustion, I'd blurted out the truth. "I'm avoiding my roommate, who is utterly obsessed with you and sticks your face into all her paintings."

New Gina opened big eyes and said, "Really?" She wanted to follow me home to see the paintings. On the way to our eighth-floor apartment, she waxed lyrical about "the gorgeous Peggy," asking, "Do I look okay? How's my hair?" as if I didn't have enough obsession to deal with already.

My twat of a roommate gushed excitement out of her eyeballs—those were the exact words I'd used in my entry—at having her idol in our apartment. She then made a big production of complaining about the mess, as if I hadn't scrubbed well enough. I watched Gina, interested in how she'd react to those paintings depicting her face.

"Would you like me to sit for you?" she asked the swooning Peggy. "In the nude," she added, eyebrows dancing up and down.

I wasn't invited into their conversation, as it wasn't particularly verbal. They were at each other pretty much as soon as they realized their mutual infatuation. I could hear them through two closed doors. At the moment of climax, I had to laugh because Gina cried out, "Aphrodite's tits." Five minutes later—like that old cliché—Peggy rented that lesbian U-Haul and moved in with Gina to Venice, leaving me no choice but to move back in with my mother.

Gina had activated some academic connections to help Peggy's career. Months later, with her first show in a Beverly Hills gallery, Peggy Sanders became an overnight success in the art world. From then on, her shows packed trendy galleries in New York and Beverly Hills, and the money poured in.

The Venice Canal Historic District was known for its man-made wetland canals that attempted to recreate the feel of Venice, Italy in coastal Los Angeles. With me as her confidant, Peggy secretly bought an old tear-down in that district. She turned it into Gina's idea of a dream house, meaning to present it to her as a wedding gift.

Peggy designed the place to create the illusion of living inside a diamond. She broke some walls and added a barely visible glass spiral staircase. She turned the ground floor into two interconnected open spaces—one served as her studio and the other as Gina's office, allowing them to work apart while still together. The kitchen and the dining room opened onto a gorgeous blooming garden overlooking the canal and the buoyant rowboat in it. Peggy painted the boat bright red.

For a moment, in this dark Dante bar, I recalled the red door Sophie and I had repainted together back then, giggling and silly all the way through the job.

I stopped reading. I sniffed the strong muddy smells engulfing me.

The upper mezzanine—the house had a freaking *mezzanine*—became a huge romantic bedroom with an adjoining mosaic-paved master bathroom. A shiny fire pole was installed between the two floors for extra fun: Gina's dream.

Yet part of the design was for Peggy herself, meant to satisfy her idea of perfection. For instance, none of the rooms had doors, including the guest room and the bathrooms, because Peggy wanted complete openness and no secrets.

Total bullshit. As their double confidant, I knew they lied to each other constantly.

The house was beautiful and weird.

I'd found the gleaming glass too cold and impersonal, but what scared me out of my mind was Peggy's special effects. The glass walls became prisms that broke the morning light into three-dimensional bubbles and those bubbles floated in the air, reflecting people's faces back at them. Literally coming face-to-face with yourself was creepy.

The earthy smell of mud intensified. A beehive buzz had me lifting my head from my reading. A long line of people—so long it snaked through the bar a few times and out the door—had appeared. They were so quiet, and I'd been so engrossed in my reading, I was surprised to see them in this dark space with its jumpy clips of horrors.

"What the hell?" I whispered.

I tore my gaze from them and forced myself to keep reading.

Both Gina and Peggy kept telling me of their mutual infatuation as it bloomed into love. So wrapped up in each other, they only used me as a sounding board and were never interested in my life. I, in turn, documented their unfolding drama as material for my work in progress.

I looked up from my laptop to the slowly moving line, then again tried to read, but reading about two obsessed, boring people was less intriguing than the here and now. People kept pouring in, as if the world had become a desert and only this place could satisfy their thirst. Some held babies or let their toddlers crawl on the floor and rummage through the display items with sticky fingers.

What was that earthy smell they brought in with them?

I assumed I'd become an unintended extra in some weird commercial or on a movie set. I peered out and searched the street for cameras and film equipment, but I didn't see any. The street was packed—not alive like Manhattan or any other busy city—just packed with silent people.

I remained still, afraid to move. As I suffocated on their smell, the breath sawed in and out of my lungs with difficulty.

I shoved my laptop into my jacket and stood to leave. With my I movement, the line swung around like a single entity, blocking my way, then one by one, they slowly turned to stare directly at me. I say *stare*, but they didn't have eyes or even faces, and even so, I knew they were focused on me. Despite their terrifying facelessness, they seemed just as frightened as I was.

Behind the counter, Oscar noticed my distress. "What's going on, Ellie?"

I asked, "Where did they come from?"

"We were always here." His teeth glowed bluish white in the cavernous darkness. "Now you can see us."

"We?" I squeaked in a loud whisper. "You're one of them?"

He nodded. "Dante described us as the souls who move together on our way to Paradise."

"He describes those souls in Purgatory," I whispered, "but this is hell."

I thought of Gina's words from long ago, when Sophie had asked her about the dead. They're around us here and now, she had said, but only some people can see them.

I looked down at the crumbs on my plate. My skin crawled at the thought of having eaten anything there.

Oscar gestured with his head, and the others all stiffened before parting like the Red Sea for Moses. As I hurried out, I saw that they weren't faceless at all. These souls had faces. Familiar faces.

My face.

An operatic scream gathered in my throat and poured out of me and into the night, clear, loud and wild, echoing across the Ferris wheel of my lost paradise and through the mountains to its final death.

42. Ginger Mistress

"Let's get you home," Betty said in her vibrant voice.

Fresh patchouli engulfed me within the turquoise of a rustling muumuu as she pulled me by the arm away from the bar crowd, then through the pissing boy fountain, up the stairs to my door.

"You need rest." She unlocked the door to my white-walled sanctuary.

I dropped into a chair. "What the fucking fuck?" I asked when I could speak past the shock and see through the headache that included my eyeballs. "How'd you move so quickly?"

"Pure adrenaline," she said, "when I heard the racket you made."

"Where's your cane?" I asked.

"My arthritis sometimes acts up, but I had a good day," she said.

"What's happening in this place?" I asked, still shaking, my skin hot. "Their faces…"

She pulled the sofa bed open in one swift motion. "Whose faces?"

"The people in the bar turned to look at me…" I was crying.

She opened the closet by the bathroom and pulled out blankets and very white linen—as white as Virgil's toga.

"Don't make the bed. I can't stay . . ." My voice squeaked. "Who were they? Why did they wear my face?"

"They must have mirrored your fear." Betty paused her steady motions of making my bed, her gaze calm, reassuring. She filled a glass from the kitchen faucet and set it on the table in front of me.

I sipped cold water from the glass hexagonal and thought of Peggy's reflective house on the Venice canals, with the creepy bubbles that followed you around in nasty little ghostly mirror reflections and made you shit your pants.

"Will I ever find my way back?" I murmured to myself.

"Get into bed," she commanded. "Sleep will do you good."

Betty was convinced I was losing my mind from exhaustion. *They mirrored your fear.* Right. She obviously didn't really look at them, and they weren't wearing *her* face. I wanted her to leave me alone to discover the rest of my story.

"I do need rest, thank you." I got into bed. "I'll stop tomorrow morning to sign those papers."

"Don't worry about the papers," she said, then the door clicked shut behind her.

The blanket was fragrant with her patchouli and so warm and soft, I gave in to sleep.

I dreamed of a dark recording studio in an auditorium full of dead people who were playing a cruel game with the living. It was up to me to stop them. Whitney Houston, Elvis Presley, Maria Callas, and Michael Jackson were the judges. They sat in the big swivel chairs from *The Voice* and listened to my singing of that dark aria from *La Gioconda*. One of them called out "transition!" and they all hit their buttons, and I died in a red storm.

I sat up, wide awake. I didn't have time to relax or to hide from a crowd of Ellie-faced lost souls. I was still a long way from my family, and I had to learn more about this cursed reality in which Peggy lived and Sophie died. What if another red storm hit and I moved even farther from my real life? I couldn't let that happen.

Back at my laptop, I went online to see if anyone had ever talked about *Transitions* as a game. Nothing helpful came up.

I gaggled *Peggy Sanders* and got her Wikipedia page. I quickly read through her early biography, most of which I already knew. Then I found what I wanted. *The artist Peggy Sanders is known not only for her clever depiction of Greek mythology but for her fashion designs that favor black, white, gray or red monochrome with feathery white edges*—I knew that. *She had popularized the diamond design in architecture.*

The page went on to list Peggy's shows and accomplishments. Boring, when my burning question was how to return home to a life that did not include her.

I tried to go back to my old journals, but the thought of those restless dead would not leave my mind. Those lost souls roaming about only a few feet away, looking for their paradise, just like me...

Music would help. I clicked the Pandora app on my laptop and was relieved the site had survived the last transition. I was already signed on. My choice of music was set to my familiar Middle Eastern rhythms, which I found soothing and inspiring when my dead divas were out of reach.

My aching foot and hammering head throbbed an Egyptian darbuka beat straight to my eardrums. I downed two Advils with tap water, then took a deep breath and plunged into the *Before* file, determined to fix my life.

After the wedding, the couple rented out Gina's cute little house—*our* house—to absolute asshole, perfect prick, total turd, brainless Brian and his family, including his dog—*my* dog—and moved to their diamond palace on the canals, where they lived in apparent happiness and prosperity. They used the fire pole as a shortcut from their bedroom to the ground floor, but mostly, the pole served as extra-sexy entertainment.

Gina's naked portrait—painted by Peggy during their first week together—was displayed above their fireplace. Gina secretly called it *The Picture of Dorian Gray.*

"What if I stay young and the painting ages," she once told me. "Peggy would insist on keeping it over the fireplace to make some point or another."

Peggy was sick of my joking about the dead poodles, but I couldn't help myself. The white, fuzzy cloud motif appeared in each of her paintings, in every piece of furniture she bought, in every article of clothing.

Unlike the Sophie of my lost reality, Peggy was very close to her parents. She'd made it a tradition to visit her sister's grave each year on the anniversary of her death.

Peggy and Gina had other best friends, now that they had money. I was their poor relation, the one who could never pay her bills on time. I continued working as a waitress while remaining the aspiring and constantly broke fiction writer who kept sending short stories to magazines and collecting rejection slips. I mooched money from my mother and from my friends, and in their generosity, they said nothing when I failed to pay it back.

"I'm such an ass," I cried out. "No wonder she's so livid about the money."

The music had stopped some time ago, and my exclamation echoed in the silent night. Peggy had more than one reason to be pissed at me for escaping with her money. Who knew how much I already owed her in this life?

Never mind. I'd soon be back home, Gina and Sophie by my side, and Peggy where she belonged, six feet under.

Peggy, who in the past had hired me as her maid, kept using me as her confidant and a flattering mirror. To her, I was never a real person with feelings, but I couldn't complain because I owed her that money.

I smiled when I read some of the tidbits they'd told me, for instance, Gina's confession that she had to have sex before important engagements. Just like good old Gina. Tears choked me, and I had to stop reading. I brewed a fresh pot of ashtray-flavored coffee. No matter how many scoops I used, the brew came out watered down. Tired of weak coffee, I poured it out and made tea.

A transition could lose artifacts, Virgil had said. For instance, good coffee. Indeed, when I searched online for my favorite brand, it didn't exist anywhere. The best coffee so far was in the dead bar down the alley, and I wasn't going back there. I'd rather live without coffee.

A few quick leg stretches, then back to *Before*.

When Peggy confided in me, I'd cringe at the intimate details, because I admired Gina and was secretly a bit in love with her. Just a little. Well, a lot. I actually crushed on her since that time she showed me a photo of herself as a sad kid with missing front teeth. She said the girls in school used to bully her for being overweight. For a split second, the sadness in the girl's face was reflected in Gina's eyes, and I was suddenly in love. No one knew how I felt, and I never dared to act on those feelings.

As I didn't have much of a life, I'd often plug a hole for Gina or Peggy, join one when the other wasn't available and mostly be a satellite to planet GinaPeg, as their glamorous friends dubbed them. Among those friends—mere acquaintances to me—I was known as the fifth wheel, the plug, the poor relation, the bridesmaid-never-the-bride. And the worst, *the ginger mistress*. "You know, that pretty girl with the long red hair."

Not that anyone suspected sexual interactions between me and either of them—GinaPeg was an example of the perfect couple. The three of us openly laughed about my nickname, but I loathed it because I was so in love with Gina.

All that time, I'd been diligently shaping the raw material of their confessions into a *roman à clef*, working title, *The Octopus*. I hadn't yet changed any identifying elements, such as names and physical attributes. As I'd written in my journal, I believed the story had the necessary ingredients for a gossipy read—money, fame, power, and the lifelong obsessive relationship between the famous artist Peggy Sanders and her wife, Gina.

I may have felt jealous of them, but I'd never dared express that jealousy, even to myself. After all, they were my best friends. Then one day, their life together stopped being perfect.

43. Inside the Diamond

That was exactly what I'd written in my journal about the perfect life that blew up. I sat up taller, eager to at last discover something meaningful, but pain stabbed from my lower back to the center of my head and back down again. I rolled my shoulders and stood slowly.

I rubbed my dry eyes as I watched the sky lighten and the sun climbing up from behind the Santa Monica Mountains. Time for food. I glared at the coffee maker, longing for my state-of-the-art espresso machine in my little house on Rose Avenue. The kitchen's window would stick from the humidity and wouldn't fully open nor fully shut, always letting in the fragrance of flowers, the sounds and smells of the breaking waves at night...

All that beauty, simplicity, joy would be mine again.

Standing in the kitchen, I gnawed on cold pizza and fantasized about a Sophie-style feast—a double omelet with cheddar cheese and a green salad to offset the cholesterol. I could almost see her—ravenous, entertaining, totally exhausting in her manic stage—sticking her hungry face into our fridge and asking if we had anything good to eat. And Gina filling up three shot glasses with tequila and prompting her to tell another story.

The kitchen always made Sophie talk, whether she cooked or mixed cocktails. "You won't believe this shit," she'd say while improvising a delicious meal as a way of thanking Gina and me for having saved her life yet again. She'd gesture left and right with the spatula and rain bits of scrambled egg on our gleaming kitchen floor.

Once she cried out, "Hey, your new bamboo floor creaks, right here." Then she moved side to side on that spot to demonstrate. The floor squeaked, and Gina and I exchanged meaningful glances and giggled, remembering that sexy day.

"What," Sophie had asked. "Did I say something foot-in-mouth wrong again?" When we laughed even louder, she pointed the spatula at us and said, "That's exactly what's missing from my life. This closeness of a couple. These secrets you won't share even with me."

I swallowed the last leathery bite of pizza and wiped away a tear. Nostalgia was death. Moving forward was life.

I sat again and read through the last entry in the first file. When I finished, I leaned back and sighed.

I now knew enough to assume that *Before* referred to the time before the accident, exactly a year ago.

Here's what happened.

I was having dinner with Peggy and Gina on Main Street, in one of those trendy restaurants that kept you hungry yet emptied your pockets, in this case Peggy's, the only one who could cough up that kind of money. I admired the way a minuscule steak and four mini potatoes were arranged on a square white plate.

Acutely aware of the tension between Peggy and Gina, I asked what was wrong.

Peggy said, "Tomorrow is my sister's anniversary and Gina got suckered into this school thing she can't get out of. Can you come with me to the cemetery?"

My only plan for the next morning was my highly involved hair ritual.

Peggy shrugged. "Wash it in our guest room tonight and we'll leave early tomorrow morning."

As I kept a change of clothes in my car, I agreed, lured by any change in the monotony of my life. I expected Peggy to use me as a mother confessor and talk at me rather than *with* me on the way to Oxnard. I didn't mind. I hoped for new material, so I'd returned with them to the diamond palace.

The house made me feel weird, what with not having doors in any rooms or bathrooms. Some mystery is a virtue.

Still, what their house lacked in doors, it made up for with showerheads. As I washed my hair with the special shampoo I kept at my friends' house, I marveled, as always, at the multiple nozzles and rain showers coming at me from unexpected directions, one cleverly designed to hit upward at a very specific angle. The rich got to fuck everyone and everything, including their showerheads.

I was horny anyway, acutely aware of Gina in the next room, but I couldn't get off on the totally diabolical little nozzle, what with no privacy and the glass shower and no doors and I hated this weird house to pieces.

When the water stopped running, I heard their voices raised in a heated argument. *Material.* I perked my ears while wrapping my head in my soft white towel. I'd once read that a hair towel had to be white to prevent damaging the pigment and soft enough not to break the hair shaft. Probably misinformation, but soft white towels couldn't hurt.

I kept to my hair ritual, toweling it gently top to bottom, then I dangled my head upside down to let the blood flow into the roots, massaging my entire scalp with argan oil. Yes, I was as obsessed with my hair maintenance as Peggy was with Gina.

"Who is she?" Peggy growled, sounding like an angry hound. "Or is it a man, because that would be the hugest insult."

I stood up so abruptly, my head banged against one of the nozzles. I was seeing stars, not only from the pain but... Trouble on planet GinaPeg?

Gina said, "I'm going for a walk."

"It's night and the homeless are scary—"

"The homeless are harmless," Gina said. "You're the scary one."

For the first time since I could remember, I didn't stick to my hair ceremony. I'd rolled it up in a sloppy knot when Gina burst into my room, which was a redundancy, as the room had no door.

"Put something on," she said, more beautiful than ever, with her eyes burning in anger and her hair wild. "We're going for a drink."

We left by the back door and walked through the canals to Penguins. My eccentric friend Virgil nodded at me from behind the bar, one of the three bartenders that night.

"Aha." At the mention of Virgil, I stopped reading and washed down another Advil with a glass of water. He'd been a constant in all my realities, appearing in various forms and always watching over me. I now regretted that our last encounter included throwing money at him and screaming *Fuck you and your Tesla.*

Gina had been silent on our hurried way to the bar, but as soon as she ordered shots of "the most expensive tequila you have" for both of us and swallowed hers in one quick go, she started talking. I let her.

"Peggy has this obsession with the house." She rolled her eyes as if she wanted to look anywhere but at me. "Doors don't belong in a house, dogs and cats don't belong in the house and I always wanted pets—"

"Peggy doesn't need pets," I muttered. "She has me."

"What?" Gina opened her eyes wide. "What do you mean?"

"Don't mind me." I corrected my error. My tongue had loosened, and I forgot to keep myself out of the story. If I wanted truth, I was supposed to remain mother confessor, satellite Ellie, the ginger mistress or whatever.

And here was finally a golden nugget, a dramatic development in a story that had lately gone stale.

"I'm stuck with her," Gina said. "You understand why."

Of course I understood. Peggy had talked about it ad nauseam, but I slowly sipped my twenty-dollar shot and cocked my head, feigning ignorance.

Gina said, "I'm her financial prisoner since she'd paid off my huge debt to the IRS. I owe her so much money, I have to live in this doorless cubic zirconia she calls *the diamond*, where I don't have a moment's privacy and the world is watching me even in the shower. Peggy's jealous behavior is the final straw."

"Why would she be jealous?" I asked.

Gina lit a joint and handed it to me. I refused. I wanted to remain clearheaded for this valuable new material.

"She says I'm having an affair."

"What do you say?" I asked.

"Absolutely not. God, you'd know it first." Gina drank down the whole second shot and motioned for another round, so animated and lovely in her anger. "But I'm this close to it." She gestured with the thumb and index finger of the beautiful hand I always wanted to hold. "I mean, she's going to accuse me, so would you blame me if I actually did?"

"I'd never blame you for anything." I continued to nurse my first shot, urging her to elaborate. "Why would she accuse you?"

"She needs to control everything when she should instead learn to control her own impulses."

"Meaning?" I encouraged, like a good therapist.

"That lack of control when she gets angry at other drivers, and yet, she always insists on driving. You should see her car insurance. She can pay it, but one day…"

She looked straight into my eyes, and I had to hold my breath at her intensity.

"I don't know where you get your strength, Ellie."

"My *strength*?" I felt so fragile, especially around the two of them. "Why, like Samson"—I displayed my nonexistent arm muscles—"I get my strength from my hair."

Gina remained serious. She took my face in her cool hands and lightly touched her lips to mine. She smelled of pot and of wildflowers.

"So sorry," she said. "I didn't mean to spring this on you."

Spring this? I'd burned for her since forever and here she was, using me to get back at Peggy, just because the one she cheated with wasn't available.

"What about that person you want to have an affair with?" I asked.

"What person?" Gina smiled. "Oh, *her*." Her smile widened. "It's you."

I pointed at myself in disbelief. "Me? I'm the butt of a mistress joke."

"Never a joke to me," she said.

She kissed me again, longer, deeper. I wanted to clear the bar of drinks with that one-arm sweep like in the movies and take her right there. Only Virgil and his watchful eyes stopped me.

"Get a room," a man slurred next to us.

"Good idea." Gina slapped a hundred-dollar bill on the counter, Peggy's money, and took my hand. "Where'd you park your car?"

"Far enough from the house," I said.

When we made it to my Chevy on Main Street, I was already good and wet, and so was Gina. It took us no time to lose our clothes and go at each other in the back seat like high school seniors at the prom.

When we came together, Gina cried out, "Aphrodite's tits," which I'd heard before, but this time she did it for me. I started laughing.

"This always kills," she said, which I found even funnier. I imagined her in a tight business suit, performing a sexy comedy routine.

She kissed me deeply again. "I'm over the moon, Ellie."

"Me too," I said.

"I so want to move back into my little house," she said, "and have you move in with me."

"If you really mean it, we'll make it happen. I'll find a real job and we'll pay her back every penny."

"Stay with me tomorrow," Gina begged. "Tell her you've had explosive diarrhea since dinner."

"As lovely as that sounds, what about the thing you have to do for school?"

"There's no school thing. I don't want to go with her because her driving scares me and you shouldn't go with her either." She held my face gently. "Do you really think we can do it?"

"I'll do anything for you."

"Shit, she's looking for us," she whispered. "Keep your head down."

Peggy was indeed walking in the direction of Penguins.

"Good," I said. "Let her catch us."

"Okay, let her." Gina's hands were all over me, and the prospect of getting caught made our next round even wilder and louder. I had to give Peggy credit for making sex feel so dirty, dangerous, insanely fabulous.

We helped each other dress in the back seat. The coast was clear, so Gina jumped out and started running home. I followed slowly behind, a big smile on my face. My dream lover was real after all! In the house, I sneaked upstairs and quickly got into bed with my laptop, where I'd sat up to record the bizarre and wonderful night. I was afraid that if I fell asleep, my happiness would prove to be a dream.

I wrote all night. In the morning, Peggy poked her face in the doorway and saw me writing away. She sat on my bed.

"Can you keep a secret?" she asked.

I nodded.

"I love her so much, but she's ungrateful. After everything I did for her, I think she's in love with someone else."

Yes, me. "What makes you say that?" I asked.

"If she leaves me, I'll destroy her financially."

I knew I'd slap her if she dared another word against Gina. In my head, I reconsidered the diarrhea excuse to get myself out of the trip.

"Hey, how come you're wearing Gina's T-shirt?"

Shit. We must have switched in the dark.

"I spilled food on myself," I said, "so I grabbed one off the top in your closet. I hope she won't mind."

Peggy the artist paid attention to the smallest visual detail. She narrowed her eyes, not buying my story. "We leave at seven sharp and I like punctuation."

"Punctuality?" I asked.

"You smart Alex," she said.

"Smart aleck," I corrected, annoying even myself.

Peggy didn't smile.

She knows, I thought. She knows.

Gina entered shortly afterward, coffee for me in one hand and my too-tight top stretched across her huge breasts.

"Did I dream it?" she asked with an uncertain smile.

"I know you didn't," I said, "because my T-shirt looks so sexy on you."

"I'll never take it off."

In the morning light, Peggy's prism effect sent up multiplied floating bubbles. For once, I didn't hate it, because one of the bubbles floated between us, reflecting sections of our faces like the shards of a shattered mirror. Gina and I both reached for it, and our hands met in the air. She kissed me lightly on the lips, and I couldn't trust myself anymore.

Footsteps came up the stairs. We quickly separated.

"I should get ready," I said. "She likes *punctuation*."

Gina smiled. "Don't let her drive like mad."

"No worries," I promised. "Only one more day and we'll be together."

"Please," she whispered. "Don't vanish like the happy dream you are, Elektra."

"What?" I yelled within my four white walls.

I reread those last words. Heart aching, I turned away from the laptop and its searing message, and covering my face, made the few paces to the kitchen, then back. Those had been Gina's exact words to me on Rose Avenue in my previous reality.

But that wasn't all. I'd ended the file by writing *The story of the ginger mistress is done and I'm turning over a new leaf.*

I inhaled a long, unsteady breath and ran shaky fingers through my shorn hair, smiling in perverse satisfaction. If only for five minutes, New Gina had wanted to leave Peggy and be with me. She loved me here and now, as she had loved me then and there, in my lost reality. Her love had always been mine. As soon as I thought that truth, I took what felt like the first natural breath in days.

"Don't worry, Gina," I said. "I'm going to find my way back home to you."

44. After

A stupid smile of irrelevant happiness remained pasted on my face—totally irrelevant, because New Gina would never leave Peggy for me. I clicked open the next file, *After*. I'd started it in a hospital bed about a year ago, following two surgeries—a craniotomy to evacuate blood from my brain and the orthopedic procedure to fix my broken left foot. I'd been coherent enough to record a detailed description of what had led to the accident, but most of it was a jumbled mess, filled with the madness of pain and semiconsciousness, drugs and bad news. The various surgical details, delivered in a professional manner by the medical staff, were followed by worried whispered conversations among my mother, Gina, and Peggy.

From all of the above, I also managed to put together my best guess of what happened during the last year of this cursed reality, until a few days ago, when I woke up confused at the cemetery.

The morning after New Gina had confessed her love for me, I accompanied Peggy on her drive up north. On the way, she rehashed Gina's offenses—how ungrateful she was, cheating and probably with a man, and who knows if it's only one man.

Once again, I should have stayed out of the story, but I was offended for Gina and suddenly bitter at Peggy for the years she'd made me play her servant.

I'd blurted out, "It isn't a man."

Peggy asked, "How do you know?"

"Gina loves only one person," I continued in my stupidity. "The ginger mistress, the plus one, the fifth wheel, the plug. She loves me, so shove it up your ass, Peggy Sanders."

At that, Peggy swerved off the 405 and we hit the barrier wall. She escaped without a scratch while I suffered head and foot injuries.

Splashes came from the pool.

I gazed out the window and down, toward the courtyard, where the pool party continued, apparently since the night before. The water stormed, as if hundreds of mice were swimming in it. Fully dressed people surfaced, dripping wet, and rested on the loungers to dry in the sun. The next moment, the dark blue water calmed.

Why did they swim with their clothes on? Why did they hang out at the pool nonstop? Did any of them, like me, see the dead?

I wanted to know but not really now. Back to the file.

While wondering when I'd be able to walk without crutches, I recorded in the *After* file what I was told and the little I remembered from the accident.

Then another blow landed.

My neurosurgeon, Dr. Rhonda Knochen-Hacker—I was fascinated with the complexity of her hyphenated name—visited unexpectedly. She held nothing back when she said with admirable honesty, "Due to a small hiccup in our otherwise trustworthy equipment, a new"—she gestured with thumb and finger and minimized her eyes—"tiny bleed had occurred, resulting in a blood clot. The clot is buried so deep inside your brain, it would be hard to operate."

In other words, Dr. Rhonda had botched the operation.

"Why...*how* did it happen?" my mother had asked.

"Some level of collateral damage is a common risk associated with this type of surgery, but without that surgery, your daughter would be dead." She turned to me. "We'll have to monitor you closely for changes in behavior or any loss of vital functions such as memory, thinking, or speech. Really, considering what the car looked like, it was a miracle you survived."

"No miracles," I said, my now-voice echoing within four white walls. "There's a reason for everything."

I raised my eyes from the screen and gazed toward the far mountains, the blue sky of noon and the ever-turning Ferris wheel of paradise. I wondered if it played a cloyingly sweet tune nonstop, driving those who heard it crazy.

I continued reading. A subsequent internet link in the same paragraph led to an article about craniotomy and its complications.

The surgical procedure involves the removal of a portion of the skull to allow access to brain tissue in order to excise a tumor or a blood clot.

My vision swam.

Shit, shit shit ... Why, oh why had she used craniotomy? Even I knew of a better procedure, a micro surgery that could have lowered the chance of damage to the surrounding tissue.

I froze in fear. Was that how I lost my memory?

I kept reading.

My prognosis wasn't good. The plan was to treat the clot with blood thinners in the hope it would disappear over time. However, if it got dislodged and blocked vital functions, I could die or become paralyzed.

If the clot wasn't yet dissolved, was I supposed to take blood thinners? Those must have been in one of the pill containers I'd left in Peggy's poodle bag, unless I used injectable thinners. I quickly checked my arms and legs for needle marks. Nothing.

Another internet link took me to another scientific article. *Dehydration thickens the blood, and the clot could grow as a result.*

When did I last drink anything but coffee?

I nearly tripped over my own feet on the way to the faucet, where I drank all the water my stomach could hold.

A time bomb ticked inside my head. Transporting myself back home wasn't only a matter of getting my wife, my friend, and my house back.

It was a matter of survival.

Enough. I couldn't read any more. I clicked out of the internet. I had to get away from this scariest part of my hidden history, or I'd end up smashing my coffee mug or my laptop against the wall, and I needed both.

My survival in that accident wasn't a miracle. My guardian angel was always there, meddling away, and I was sure he had a hand in saving my life. Now my life was in danger again, and he just had to take me back home.

He said I should speak his name in any public place.

I stuck a wad of money in the inner pocket of my leather jacket, and flew as fast as my bad foot allowed down the flight of stairs.

In the street, the snaking line of the dead and the faceless slithered slowly, waiting patiently for food and drink, or the fortune teller's booth. What did they want with a told fortune anyway?

The grocery store was a very public place, well lit and full of people.

45. The In-Between Reality

I snagged a cart and slipped into the cereal aisle, remembering how I'd once waltzed under the Cheerios to *The Blue Danube*, a smiling Gina in my arms in a tight suit and sexy stilettos. Here I was again, waltzing my way out of the River of Oblivion.

Shoppers pushed carts around me. A little girl with pigtails begged in a whine, "Candy, Mama."

My voice was breathless but firm when I said, "Virgil."

A whiff of weed preceded the clicking of sandals and the swish of a toga. Below the Fruit Loops, his unshaven face appeared, then the rest of him.

"How many times did my reality change?" I asked, not wasting words on idle greetings.

Smoke flurried out of his Roman nose. "Twice."

"You're lying." I held up three fingers.

"How do you figure?"

"The passenger's side of Peggy's SUV looked like it was in a demolition derby. They said it was a miracle I survived, but I know you and your games. I died in that accident, didn't I? And you kept me alive with one of your transitions—"

"Hush." He peered over his shoulder, a finger to his lips. "Eyes and ears everywhere."

"Spies?"

The little girl still whined for candy. The woman slowly pushed the cart with her daughter inside. Would the two exist after the next transition?

Virgil looked left and right. "Not spies but actual shoppers, unaware of us."

"Some alive, some dead?" I asked, knowing the answer before he nodded.

"We're everywhere, but very few see us. Remember?"

I raised my voice, "You're *all* supposed to be gone forever."

"Don't make a fuss. Pretend to shop." He walked by my side, his sandals booming as always.

I asked, "What's this metallic sound? And I don't mean the bronze hobnails."

"The echo of centuries," he said. "You hear it the way you perceive my mere existence, mine and my colleagues."

I pushed my cart forward, tossing in various toiletries and vaguely familiar food items. An anthropomorphic dog replaced Tony the Tiger on my Frosted Flakes box. Instead of saying *They're Gr-r-reat!* Rover the shaggy dog raised a cartoonish finger and said, *They're woof, woof wonderful.*

My brand of toothpaste had sprouted a disgusting purple-green version. I tossed white mint into my cart.

"There isn't much time, Ellie," he said. "Yes, you would have died on impact, and yes, I performed a simple time manipulation." He pointed at his yellow wrist watch. "I stopped time to prevent you from bleeding to death. I bought you a few precious moments."

"Thank you for that," I said.

"You can thank the emergency team who stopped the bleeding and pushed fluids into your veins. Thank the surgeons who did the rest." He looked down at his sandals.

"Why didn't you let me die?" I asked.

"Look, I should go. I was taken off your case."

"So I'm a *case* now?" I pointed at my chest. "What if I don't want you off my case?"

"Not up to us." He adjusted the crooked wreathe on his head. "They claim I got too involved with you. The same happened with Dante."

"Not so," I argued. "You couldn't cross to Paradise because you weren't a Christian."

"A total lie invented by religious fanatics. I guided him through the *Inferno* and most of *Purgatorio*, but that pushy Beatrice, who barely knew him, took over the best part."

I didn't care about his bitter old grudges.

"If you're powerful enough to stop time, you can transition me back home to the life I'm meant to live." I'd become a broken record, like the candy-whining girl.

"That life is impossible to retrieve," he said.

"I'm going home with or without your help, or I'll die trying."

Shoppers stared at me, and I couldn't tell the dead from the living. But then, I never could.

A mournful expression painted his face when he said, "It's time you made peace with this imperfect reality." Then he faded away.

An aisle packed with soft drinks blurred before my eyes. Coke cans, Pepsi, and Dr Pepper spun around me like a merry-go-round in a Hitchcock film.

"You new in town?" the cashier asked in a slow voice. Her name tag said Rita. Her smile said *Get me a dentist quick.*

"I rent across the street."

"Who do you rent from?" Rita laughed nervously, revealing the rest of her crooked, yellowing teeth. "You must be the only tenant."

"There are plenty of tenants, actually," I said, unsure of that. "They're kind of weird, but the manager, Betty, is a sweet old lady. She wears colorful muumuus and walks with a cane. You guys probably deliver her groceries."

Rita's red ponytail was a shade lighter than my hair, when I still had it, and it swayed left and right when she spoke. "That place is haunted," she whispered. "The neighborhood kids go there on Halloween and scare each other for kicks. They say it's disgusting inside and the pool has old stinky water and it's full of those disgusting water insects and rats and shit."

She was getting on my nerves with the word *disgusting*.

"The only stink—" I stopped before blurting out, *is your bad breath.*

Behind me, the line got longer. An annoyed man said, "Hey, you two should have a date later and let us get out of here."

"Say." Rita cocked her head. "Don't you look like her?"

She showed me a printed sheet of paper. The annoyed man snatched it and said, "Yeah, that's her."

A woman who looked like the Faerie Godmother took the paper and pointed at me. "It's you."

"What does it say?" I plucked it from her hand.

More shoppers came running, surrounding me, reading over my shoulder, pointing. People pulled out their cellphones.

"Yeah, that's you," someone shouted.

The ad featured a photo of a skeletal woman I recognized from the mirror. If that was how I looked, I should have let Dr. Rhonda butcher me.

Please help us locate this troubled female in her 30s who had an accident and lost her memory and now she is wandering about and presents a danger to herself and others.

"And others?" Now I was pissed off. "They present a danger to me with their awful syntax."

The grammar was Peggy's. Gina knew better than to use *wandering about and presents.*

A succession of three phone numbers repeated on paper slivers at the bottom of the ad—my mother's, Gina's, Peggy's.

A want ad came to mind—a flashier ad, dangling phone numbers on slivers of paper and a great deal for a student willing to become a servant to her roommate. And from another life, an ad seeking a roomie who wanted adventure and didn't mind posing nude for paintings of red-headed Madonnas.

I ripped the ad up and scattered the small pieces in the air.

The Faerie Godmother cocked her head at me. "You shouldn't have done it. Your friends are worried about you."

"Stay out of it," I said. "All of you. I want nothing to do with those prissy-assed bitches."

I quickly paid, packed my groceries, then ran out the sliding door, my crackly shopping bags dangling from one arm. Across the street, I paused to eye the dirty wall announcing *L'Inferno* in sprayed-on spooky font. Indeed, Paradise Point Apartments seemed abandoned from the outside, which made it the safest place for me to be.

46. The House

Echoes of Rita's slow voice chanted silently in my head as I hurried toward safety. *You must be the only tenant. That place is haunted. Disgusting inside. Stinky water. Disgusting water insects.*

Excitement filled the pool area. People sat around the deck, engrossed in conversations and fully clothed, it seemed, for a costume party with a period theme. Three women slept, their books turned upside down by their loungers and big hats covering their faces. If they had faces, that is, because lately, I wasn't sure about anyone.

The late morning light made the indigo water twinkle, so dark, I couldn't see the bottom, but clean. The cleanest pool I'd ever seen. The building was well maintained, fully occupied, *not* in ruins—stupid gossipy Rita with her broken teeth and her apocryphal stories.

She didn't know what she was talking about. People in general didn't pay attention, unless their own asses were involved. Still, the bug in my ear buzzed mad circles of new possibilities.

Two swimmers emerged from the water, fully clothed, and sat on loungers to dry in the sun. I had no desire to engage in conversation, but I *was* dying to see what identical cheap romance they were reading.

"Come in," Betty said from the office's door, like a work manager about to tell me that this time I really fucked up.

Had I waited too long to sign the papers and worn out my welcome? Maybe Peggy had found me and called to whine about the money I'd stolen, and now Betty had called the police...I'd be arrested...

It's too late once you've been captured by the system.

I couldn't let that happen. I should take off. Get out of here. I left my shopping bags where I stood and turned to flee.

"Stop," Betty commanded, as if reading my intention. "Get in."

I followed her inside, where no police was waiting to arrest me.

The office was still a mess. The oval table in its center was covered with dirty plates, bottles of beer, martini glasses, cartons of takeout. The big screen on the wall flickered constant images, and next to it, the Roman numeral wall clock was still frozen at ten to two.

I sniffed the air. Among the putrid smells of stale Chinese food was another, an incredible aroma. An espresso machine gleamed on the kitchenette's counter, like an object from outer space. My hands went to the prayer position, and if not for my excruciating headache, I would have dropped to my knees in front of it.

"I used to have one just like it back home," I whispered with reverence, my eyes on the shiny coffee goddess.

"I'll make you some," Betty said.

Good sign. She wouldn't offer me coffee if she was about to kick me out.

She took her time, maneuvering with apparent pain. Eventually, she served me coffee in a rose-patterned demitasse. The first sip filled my eyes with tears at the sheer surprise of bittersweet nostalgia. I was flooded with memories of my kitchen and its sticky windows with the purple flowers poking through the cracks, with me as *me*, the strong one who took care of everyone.

"Where did you find this coffee?" My voice cracked.

"The House," she said. "Here, have the rest of it."

I opened the bag and sniffed, then carefully sealed it and hugged it to me like it was a lost puppy. I glanced around the disordered room.

"Big party?" I asked, now eager to sign the papers and go upstairs to read the rest of my life story.

"First game night of the season," Betty said.

On the large screen, a quick montage of short video clips flickered with unrelated images—a stormy ocean, a lush meadow, a green oasis in a desert vista, a grassy soccer field, a glass building with prism reflections.

A ledger book, like those used for football bets, rested on the table.

"You bet on sports?" I asked.

"You could say that," she said. "Come, try your luck every night in the next week. You'll meet some of the most interesting people, including Chaos, our incredible game designer." Obvious pride was in her glinting eyes.

When I said, "I have a hard deadline," it wasn't a lie. The only game that interested me was the one she knew nothing about. Transitions, the game that could take me back home.

"They always leave such a mess," she said, "but yesterday I won the jackpot."

"Congratulations," I said. "And thanks for helping me last night."

"Did you get any rest after your little scare?"

"Yes, and I got some work done." I forced a smile. "On my book, that is."

"Of course." She shoved what I took to be a contract before me, and I signed it without reading a word. I paid cash for the month, which didn't leave me much, but I intended to be back home way before Peggy's money ran out. It was home or death.

If push came to shove, I could offer myself to Betty as a jack-of-all-trades, although my skin crawled at the thought of fixing a toilet or a kitchen sink in any of those weirdos' apartments.

Outside, I picked up my swishy shopping bags and—giving the outlandish ongoing pool party a wide berth—rushed up to my apartment to find some answers.

Standing over the kitchen sink, I devoured a full bowl of cereal with milk. Rover the shaggy dog mocked me from the box. *Woof, woof wonderful*, he said, pointing his paw. Some inorganic crunchy element had been added to my favorite cereal, and every bite of Frosted Flakes was a bomb exploding inside my ruined brain.

Back to work. No time to dawdle over my food disappointments. I needed to know my whole story before the clot killed me.

47. Delete

A few more normal entries followed Dr. Rhonda's bad news about the clot, but those soon stopped. Two months later, when I started again, I wrote childish entries like this one:

ouch Mama head hurts foot boil ouch Mama pain

"This illiterate shit was surely written by one of the Sanders asses," I muttered, still expecting my two sidekicks to respond and react to my comments and moods. My little quip fell flat.

I plowed through childish entries and scrambled sentences, hungry for the whole truth, as incoherently as I'd described it. What hell it must have been for someone like me, who so loves words. I skipped pages, reading forward for an explanation.

As Dr. Rhonda had warned, I was lucid for a while, then I'd slipped into a coma and had to undergo another surgery to drain yet another bleed. The old clot remained where it was, an irretrievable time bomb, buried deep in my brain near the vital functions.

My mother remained with me, and when she had to get away, either Peggy or Gina had replaced her at my bedside.

Such devotion from the three of them.

I turned on my phone. Multiple messages flashed from Gina, my mother, and Peggy, who was kvetching about her money and begging me to come to my senses and tell her where

I was. Their emotional, operatic pleas could match Maria Callas. I deleted them all. As an extra precaution, I tapped *clear history* and turned the phone off.

A captive audience in my semi-comatose state, I'd heard more stories from Peggy and Gina. They'd each told me intimate details, knowing, or not, about the other's confidence in me.

Through intensive physiotherapy, I'd eventually regained my ability to speak, walk, function. My journal entries improved in meaning and sophistication. As I knew already, I'd become addicted to prescription painkillers, and my mother was my main caretaker. That horrible reversal was hardest for me to take.

Virgil's potent weed would have come in handy to soothe my nerves as I read this, but Virgil had been taken off my case.

Focus.

I scrolled through more notes. Here was the bitter truth. My so-called friends took care of the injured me not for devotion, but to use me as a one-of-a-kind mother confessor, a dumb ear who'd never reveal their secrets. They had everything I wanted, yet they constantly dumped their complaints on me.

I, in turn, pretended to be too drowsy and senseless. I wanted them to talk away as much as possible and feed me their stories.

I kept expecting Gina to tell me again how much she loved me. I wanted her reassurance that we still had a chance together.

She finally mentioned our single tryst.

"That thing we'd had on the canals has to go into the vault," she'd said. "A big mistake."

Tears ran down the sides of my face and soaked the hospital pillow. I nearly died for what she now called a mistake. Had I stayed behind that day, I would have remained *the happy dream* I was for her. We'd be living together in our house on Rose Avenue, happy. In love.

Just as well. In this reality, Gina proved to be a self-serving piece of shit. When I became damaged goods, she stuck with Peggy for convenience. The two deserved each other.

"Please promise you won't tell her," Gina had begged. "Please nod if you understand."

Peggy already knew the truth because I'd blurted it out to her, but I took myself out of the story and nodded.

Nothing was wasted on me. This was good material, and my revenge was on. Even half dead, jilted and heartbroken, I'd let the drama of GinaPeg spice up my *roman à clef.*

When I was recovering at my mother's house and they started leaving me alone, I sat up and transcribed their words from memory. My writing of *The Octopus* began in earnest and with renewed energy, as I believed that my cognitive recovery depended on finishing that convoluted novel I'd been scratching at for years.

In total disgust, I clicked out of *After*, made a new pot of coffee and opened the *Octopus* file.

The book described Peggy's infatuation with her teacher, continued with their love affair, their marriage, their peculiar and expensive house, and the subsequent disintegration of their love.

I read every word at first, but soon I lost interest and skimmed those five or six hundred pages for key details. Peggy's career flourished, and her possessive love for Gina became more insane. Gina wanted to get away, yet was roped to Peggy with all the love financial ties could buy. Peggy suspected infidelity. Gina hated the house, its lack of privacy, its floating reflective bubbles. They loved and hated. They yelled and kissed. They craved each other's bodies and loathed each other with the same passion. They renewed their marriage vows in well-advertised celebrations that helped spike Peggy's career, then went on second, third, and fourth honeymoons in glossy locations featuring one sparkly body of water or another.

Their complicated lives dazed me. I was the one with the messed-up brain, but the confusion came from my so-called friends, whose stories mutated with meandering versions and more alternative realities than Virgil's game of Transitions. Their feverish plot lines wiggled like the tentacles of an octopus before it fell into the trap of a restaurant.

Why I wasted my precious life listening and writing about these two was beyond me.

My work-in-progress came to nothing. Its protagonists, those I envied for their good fortune, made whiny, boring characters. They had no true love in their hearts for me, for the world, for each other.

Their story went nowhere and was based on nothing of substance.

Fucking My Way Through Life had been loosely based on Sophie's life. It was written at her suggestion, with her approval, and her personal embellishments. I'd changed details, dropped or enhanced others, and we'd both had fun and laughs all the way to its publication. Sophie was beyond flattered that I'd found her lonely life interesting enough for a novel. Yet Sophie *was* interesting, and her stories died with her. Even if I tried, I'd never be able to rewrite that novel from memory.

I closed my eyes to shut out the life I didn't want and the stories of women I cared nothing for. My true home had Sophie in it and the loving version of Gina. Home was safety from a wandering cerebral blood clot.

I moved *The Octopus* into the trash and pressed *delete*.

Already, the air felt a little bit less polluted, and I could take a deep, cleansing breath.

I clicked on the file titled *After*.

I had only one more entry to read. This last chapter of my life had been written in Gina and Peggy's guest bedroom, exactly five days ago.

I paused to mull over the confusing situation.

November first of my home reality was clear in my mind. That night, I'd made love to Gina for the last time. We were the happiest and most loving couple, enjoying our jobs and our friends, living in our mortgage-free home. I had my health, my hair, my dog, my published book. Two days later, I messed up my life by taking Sophie to the cemetery.

The November first I was about to discover, happened after the transition, five days ago, in *this* cursed reality.

I took a sip of cold coffee and dove in.

Peggy's one-woman show in Santa Barbara coincided with the anniversary of Sophie's death. My mother had to drive to Arizona, and Gina and Peggy took pity on their injured, drug-addicted, supposedly half-witted friend. Instead of leaving me at home with a caretaker, they offered to take me on a weekend outing. They believed that spending time with them, revisiting the great times we'd shared before my accident, would do me good.

I'd found it hard to fall asleep in their guest room, what with the doorless doorways, and the two of them talking, arguing, or making love, so I spat out my pills and sat in bed, writing away.

They'd planned on pre-celebrating the opening of Peggy's show with a bottle of champagne at the cemetery. Peggy, who was driving, would have just a little, then they'd pour most of it over Sophie's headstone.

Peggy suggested that I be allowed half a glass of champagne. Gina argued against it, since my drugs would interact with alcohol.

"Come on," Peggy had said. "One drink won't kill her and she'll sleep in the car during the opening instead of me and you have to watch her. Just don't let her mother know about it."

Reading this particular entry in Peggy's typical phrasing—*me and you have to watch her*—I again got the terrible feeling that Peggy had intended to leave me wandering alone in a dark cemetery until I died of fright. If that was paranoia, I had a good reason for it. After all, I was Peggy's constant reminder of her loss of control and of Gina's cheating.

Did Gina ever find out what Peggy knew? I was trying to get that answer from further reading, but found no more illuminating revelations.

Let's assume I'd had that one teensy-weensy glass of champers on Sophie's grave. That glass had immediately interacted with my meds, but instead of making me sleepy, the potent combination shocked me—right there at the cemetery—into an awareness that I belonged in another life. For some reason, I'd been left alone until poodle-Peggy came to guide me back to the car. Later, at her show, I'd had another glass of champagne.

I smiled at the memory of grabbing the mike from Peggy and saying pure garbage that made a lot of sense to me, but not to anyone else.

They'd claimed I wasn't long for the world, but what about my clarity? Despite the broken body of this reality, I'd retained the memory of a better life, of a dear friend who used to make me laugh, of a wife who knew how to love.

In my lost reality, I'd read extensively about medical innovations and other subjects, so as to beat Gina in trivia games. I knew that any brain-related malfunction would scramble up my thinking way before it killed me. Yet, in Sophie's elegant words, I was as clear as a fuck in a whorehouse.

These journals, this whole worthless reality, were a big fat lie. A mistake that had nothing to do with me.

I dragged both *Before* and *After* into the trash and pressed *delete*.

48. Pink Impala

Exhausted, I slid between the sheets and slept without dreaming. My foot and head woke me, whacking their simultaneous performances of pain and suffering. It was early morning. Beyond the flashing red lights, the huge wheel kept up its slow turn against the dark mountains and the gray sky, promising me paradise.

It was time for more Advil and a pot of coffee from a store Betty called *The House.*

I briefly turned on my phone and checked the onslaught of messages from my mother, Gina, and mostly Peggy, who had gone batshit crazy over her three thousand bucks. They wanted to save me and protect me, but they didn't know the truth. I was the only one who could save myself.

I deleted two messages from my mother and three from Gina, both of whom wanted proof of life. Peggy threatened *legal procession* against me.

I muttered, "If you meant my funeral procession, there's a chance you'll soon enjoy it."

I was about to delete all when a new message flashed on the screen. It came from a medical lab in Westwood, reminding me of a scheduled follow-up MRI. Nope, imaging wasn't the answer. I deleted the messages and turned the phone off again.

I had to talk to someone. *Anyone.* The pool was lit deep dark blue from inside, and for once, no one was lounging around it.

The air outside was cool. I knocked on the door to my right, but no one answered. The door to my left. No answer. Something I wouldn't normally do, I tried the door. It opened. The apartment was empty, four white walls, no table or chairs, not even a refrigerator in the kitchenette.

I knocked on the next door, then opened it. That place was also empty. I walked in. The carpet hadn't been cleaned for a while, and a slow-moving, long insect crawled into the corner.

You must be the only tenant, Rita had said.

I couldn't inflate my tight chest for a single breath. What was this place? Was *everything* one big illusion? Virgil had said that my memory was indestructible. I retained the ability to remember my previous realities. But what if my home reality was only in my head, a remembered hallucination sparked by brain damage? What if Virgil himself was in my head?

I took the phone from my pocket, turned it on, and recovered the last deleted message. I was expected at the lab for a follow-up MRI tomorrow morning. Hallucinations weren't real, but the threat they posed was dead real. That appointment was important. I had to find a ride south to Los Angeles tonight if I wanted to make it. I wouldn't use my own phone, but Betty—Was she real?—could call me a cab.

Back in my apartment, my breath caught in my throat. The refrigerator was gone, so was the coffee machine. The green color was draining from the chair as I watched, and the sofa was tilted on two legs and melting away. Like a movie scene fading to black, the contents of the room were disappearing into white nothingness.

Dread saturated my T-shirt with cold sweat as I stuck my laptop in my backpack and backed away from the fading table. I pushed the door, but it was stuck. I had to get out before I also disappeared into whiteness, like the furniture and my next door neighbors.

The door's edges blurred, welding into its own frame. I held my breath. I'd soon be buried alive in the wall, like those Vestal virgins in ancient Rome, and no one would know to look for me...

Then I remembered it wasn't a push door. I pulled it open. Outside on the landing, a strong stench of decay hit me. Night replaced day, and all the lights were out, even the blue lights that came from the dark depths of the pool.

I was alone.

You must be the only tenant, Rita had insisted in her lazy voice, her red hair swaying in slow motion and her smile revealing broken, yellow teeth.

Bile rose from my heaving stomach.

As I started down, one of the stairs crumbled under my sneaker. I tripped but caught the banister. It was shaky and rickety in my hand. I suppressed a scream. More stairs disintegrated below me, like Rita's rotting teeth. I sat and slid my way down on rolling chunks of crumbling concrete.

The stench of urine and excrement wafted from the empty pool in the deserted courtyard. Rats scurried around piles of garbage and discarded condoms. The office was dark for the first time since I got here. My heart became an anxious alien, banging its violent way out of my chest. I was all alone...and now the walls were closing in on me, and the courtyard was shrinking. If the entryway disappeared, I'd be blocked inside this abandoned hellhole.

I blinked back my tears...

Suddenly, all was back to normal. It was daylight again, the stairs were whole and scrubbed clean, and the shimmering pool was full of swimmers laughing and socializing.

My brain or my eyes were constantly deceiving me, alternating first decay, then normal serenity. Which was truth? Which was fantasy?

"Come join us, Ellie," a woman called out.

"Tomorrow night," I promised, actually happy to see them. Not their fault the clot deep inside my brain was causing hallucinations.

I looked up toward my apartment, squinting in the morning sun. The door looked normal and the stuff inside was probably back in place.

I imagined the clot in my head growing by the moment, lengthening its wiggling, octopodian extensions and taking over my cognitive processes. If my hack of a neurologist could be believed, once it pressed on vital functions, I would die.

The light was on in Betty's office. I took a few deep breaths to calm myself before approaching her. She knew nothing about my situation, but she was my only anchor in this twisted reality.

"Would you know of anyone who could drive me to an appointment at UCLA, or lend me their car for a day? I'll pay for it."

I had my driver's license, which I'd confiscated from Peggy's poodle purse.

"I barely use my clunker," Betty said. "If you don't mind pink, you can borrow it."

I was touched. Betty was a real friend. First, she had trusted me enough to rent me an apartment, knowing nothing about me. Now she trusted me with her car.

And *ouch*, it was pink.

Pink pink.

My eyeballs were on fire. The Impala looked like another hallucination caused by my ailing brain, so retro in its ice cream cone sweetness and its fake wood dashboard. It was very clean and shiny, and so showy when I wanted anonymity. I toyed with the idea of mud camouflage.

It needed service and a wheel alignment. As my former life was clearer in my mind than the present fuckup, I itched to use my remembered skills, among which was tinkering with my mother's old jalopy.

"I know my Chevys," I said. "I'll work on it."

"You do that," Betty said.

When I drove it out of the parking lot, I expected admiring gawks, the same stares I used to get for my hair, my legs, or my long-gone dancer's walk. No one paid me any attention.

I drove south, once again thankful that the injured foot was my left. I meant to stop at Venice Beach, snoop around my neighborhood, maybe spy on Peggy and Gina. From my journals, I knew exactly where to find the diamond house.

My imagination soared with an unlikely fantasy. Gina would come out for a solitary night walk and see me. She'd sneak into the back seat of the pink Impala for some necking and a quick fuck, like that night before my accident, when she said I was the one. That night was not a hallucination. I knew it because I had documented events as they happened in my now-deleted files.

I turned the analog dial on the dashboard and let the news wash over me. It was all the same old shit.

"Forget the news."

I kept turning the dial, finally landing on the melancholic crying of a steel guitar. A sorrowful voice sang, "I've had everything a girl could want until my heart was torn out of my chest and eaten whole by the bear of betrayal and loneliness."

"Ditto, sister," I said.

Song after tearful song described my own pathetic situation. I never knew I could so identify with country music.

As I drove slowly down Rose Avenue, I braced myself for another heartbreak. The door of our house was still bright red, the roof still naked without its Jacaranda cover. I took the next left turn, south toward the canals, hoping for at least a glimpse of Gina and none of Peggy. It was Tuesday, early evening. Gina would be getting ready to teach—if she still gave night classes in this version of herself—and Peggy, if she were anything like her sister, would be playing loud music and painting away.

They were home, and I saw more than a glimpse of them through the stupid glass walls. I wiped tears away with my sleeve. Stalking my wife was as low as I'd ever sink. Or was she my ex?

Gina stepped out onto the terrace, a cigarette in her hand. She scanned the street the way she would an auditorium full of students. I expected her to click a slide and point with the burning cigarette. *And this is Dante's birth house.*

Her searching gaze passed over me without seeing me. She sniffed once, crying. I couldn't stand her pain. I got out of the Impala, crossed the little bridge over the canal and stood under the glass balcony.

"Gina," I said.

"Ellie?" She leaned forward, surprised. "What are you doing here?"

"Who're you talking to?" Peggy asked from inside.

"Come with me," I whispered. "We'll find a way to cross back to our happy reality."

"Ellie, get a grip," she begged. "Go back to your mother's. She's worried sick about you."

"And what about you? Are you worried about me? What about your promises and our dreams?"

"Go, please." Gina flicked the cigarette into the canal. "She'll call the police."

"Who is it?" Peggy insisted.

"No one." Gina turned and disappeared into the depths of the crystalline monstrosity. Her image broke and refracted through the transparent glass in prisms of light until only a ghost of motion remained.

I gathered a thick wad of spit in my mouth and let it fly out into the canal in the direction of her cigarette butt.

I clicked my phone on. Several messages waited for me from the usual three and another one from the MRI lab, requesting that I confirm my appointment for tomorrow. I clicked *yes*. Then I lingered over a new message from Gina and actually read it.

Please, please, please, Ellie, she texted. *Go back to your mother and forget about what happened between us. It was a mistake and one day you'll see that.*

"Go to hell." I deleted it.

49. The Salt in Lake Victoria

I didn't feel like checking into a hotel. I could stand a night of sleeping in the car. I quickly devoured the tray of tacos I bought at Abuelita's Street Food Truck. The business had changed hands in this transition, and the family who now owned it kept the name. The food was just as delicious.

As I crouched down to pee beside my car, I decided that from now on, my life would only go up.

A figure threw a long shadow under the streetlight.

I gasped. "Hey, can I piss in privacy?"

"It's just me." The man's hair was a mess of long curls.

I stood up and quickly zipped up my jeans.

"Here's coffee." He handed me a styrofoam cup.

"I thought you were off my case," I said.

"This is off the record."

"And whose case are you on now? Anyone I know?"

"I'm between jobs." He leaned against the Impala. "So pink. Barbie must be looking for her car."

"My landlady was nice enough to let me borrow it."

The coffee aroma made me swoon.

"The House," I said.

He nodded.

I leaned on the car next to him, took a sip and moaned in pleasure. "Coffee is one of the casualties in this world, but you and Betty manage to get this fabulous brand. Where's the House, and can we go there now?"

"It isn't quite your time yet," he said.

"Why?" Then I got it, and once I did, other facts started shuffling into place. "God, how stupid could I be? The House is the very same House, *that* House. The afterlife."

He nodded.

Overwhelming sadness descended on me. "Please, please, Virgil. Think of a way. I'm so homesick…" I was close to tears. "There must be a way to change it back."

"Impossible." He watched me with those ancient eyes. "I wish I could, but there's a process."

"Please, tell me again."

"The Big Kahuna approves a certain move that will trigger a transition. A team of smugglers is activated—one dead, one alive. They transfer an artifact from one point in history to another or eliminate it altogether. BK then pushes a button on his game pad. A red storm seals the deal, and everything changes from the point of artifact removal. That red storm will be the only event the world remembers."

"What artifact was transferred in my case?" I asked.

"Your case was actually a correction." He handed me a fat lit joint.

"What was corrected?" I took a hit.

"Sophie was supposed to die at twelve, not Peggy." He shrugged. "BK made a mistake."

Sadness changed into anger. "Let me see . . ." My hand holding the joint trembled. "Switching Sophie with her sister was a betting game for you and your thugs in the House."

"That switch would have happened sooner or later. As I said, Peggy's death was a mistake in the first place."

"Sophie was my friend and I loved her, and you're saying her life was a mistake?"

"Hey." He raised his hands in surrender. "Only the Big Kahuna has control of the game. I just bet on the results, like everyone else."

"Help me understand, because I'm thinking some nasty thoughts about you and your friends right now. Can I give you my take on it?"

"Go ahead," he said.

"Let's see . . . Murdering my best friend was the reason for the transition—"

"Not at all." He raised both hands. "The transition was already scheduled. Sophie's proximity to her dead sister was bad timing that had triggered their switch. Both of you should have stayed home."

I continued, "The minor casualties were bad coffee, an added crunch in my cereal, and the loss of the Swiss Army Knife, which you dead dudes smuggled back in. I'm a *minor* casualty, who became a liability because I can't forget, right? So *The House* goes a year back in time, puts me in a car with horrible driver Peggy Sanders, and adds a convenient accident that should have killed me." I crushed the joint under my sneaker. "Then you go, *no way, José,* and you show up with your countdown watch." I was running out of breath. "And your BK takes you off my case for meddling, right?"

"No, because we need you alive. Your accident was another *oops,* totally unplanned." He touched the face of his watch. "So I paused time."

"You lost control of your consequences, but you needed me alive, so you fixed it. How dare you call it *an oops?*"

He was pacing, losing patience with my line of questioning. "I told you, you should see the *major* historical changes we get with some corrections. For instance, adding salt to Lake Victoria rendered the Sahara mostly uninhabitable and wiped its entire population in one fell swoop."

"The Sahara Desert *is* mostly uninhabit—"

"It wasn't always that way. I remember a vast and populated oasis." He added dreamily, "I won the jackpot on that one."

"You lie, because I know my geography." I pointed at his face. "Lake Victoria and the Sahara are a hell of a long distance apart."

"By definition, an unintended consequence of an event is tangentially related to the event itself. Guessing and betting on minor outcomes is the name of the game—"

"You bastard!" I threw my cup at him and watched the black drips disappear without staining the white of his toga. "I thought you were my friend, you and your bets, and your minor *oopsies*. You died two thousand years ago. Why couldn't you stay dead?"

He eyed me calmly, like a therapist used to outbursts. "I've always been your friend, Ellie, but maybe you'll prefer your new handler."

"A handler? I'm not a show horse," I snapped, recalling Peggy's words, *I can handle her.* "Is it Peggy?" I asked in suspicion.

He shook his head *no*.

"If I have a new handler they're not handling me very well."

He raised his wrist, and I caught the flash of his yellow countdown watch.

"What are you looking at?" I reached for the watch, but again he got away from me. I managed to see a cranky Donald Duck showing his teeth through his yellow-orange bill. The second hand on the dial moved rapidly counterclockwise.

"What time is the next one?" I asked.

"The exact time of your mission: tomorrow night at eight." He backed away and started fading.

"Don't you dare fade away like a coward, you great Roman poet, beloved throughout history." I pressed my lips together, so immense was my urge to spit on the great man. "Will your new transition take me back home or farther from it? Tell me the truth."

"The truth is greater than you or me," he said in a soft voice. "You have to remain alive, because you're the only one who can perform that certain world saving move. Remember the first time you saw Gina, and how you wanted to give up on your Dante class?"

"I'll never forget that," I said. A scene from the ladies' room at UCLA came back to me.

"What stopped you from dropping that class?"

"Bea from my yoga class. She wanted me to learn everything about Dante because I was supposed to work on her totally bad idea of a historical novel, but she lied."

"She lied about the book," he said. "But the truth was, you *had* to learn about Dante. Let me tell you about your mission."

"You told me already," I said. "I'm not interested."

As we stood directly under the street light, his lively hand gestures turned to the shadow of a powerful bird flying overhead. "You won't do it alone. You'll be transported to the Rialto district of Venice, Italy in 1554."

"You can't transport me against my will—"

"One of our dead smugglers will be waiting for you on the bridge to give you directions. You'll see editor Ludovico Dolce on his way to the printing press, carrying the one and only copy of the newly edited version of *The Divine Comedy.*"

"I'm not going, but even if I did, how would I tell Ludovico Dolce from any farmer carrying potatoes or chickens?"

"Your dead teammate will point him out to you. Then you'll seize the package from his hands."

"Seize . . . That's so rude. I've never before seized anything from anyone's hands, and I wouldn't know how to do it."

"And yet, you will." He nodded in confidence. "At that exact moment, we'll transport you back. Red lightning storms everywhere, and you return to a reality in which the poem was never published. You see? World history from that point on would change for the better."

"I took the class," I said, remembering Lilly Green's question and Gina's impromptu lecture. "Without Dante's poem, none of the world will be the same."

"The decision has already been made. Don't fight it. Tomorrow night before eight, you'll be well on your mission." He opened the door to the back seat of the Impala. "Get in, Ellie. You have struggles ahead, so get some sleep."

An oversized shaggy coat was thrown in the back seat. I wore it. It was scented with motor oil.

"I don't want to save the world," I cried. "Leave the door open." The clot was probably pushing on the limbic system in the back of my brain, making me sob when the appropriate response would have been anger. "Your great powers are shit if you can't take me back. I miss my little family. I want Sophie alive, Max not to bark at me, Gina not to be a bitch, my Jacaranda to be blooming. I want those fucking tree killers with the asthmatic kid out of my home." I rested my head on the seat. "I'm so broken."

"You are perfect," he said. "*The more a thing is perfect, the more it feels of pleasure and of pain.*"

That made me sob even louder. Gina used to whisper those words when we made love.

"*The double grief of a lost bliss,*" he continued in the peaceful voice from across the centuries, "*is to recall its happy hour in pain.*"

"Dante, again. Why don't you quote your own work?" I tightened the shaggy coat around me and tilted my head back so I could see him. "Here, I'll start. *If I can't get to heaven, I'm going to raise hell.*"

"Very good," he said. "Let's give it a try." He closed his eyes. "Forgive the misquote. *Wars and a woman I sing—an exile driven on by fate. Let's see ... Yet many blows she took on land and sea from the gods above. Tell me, muse, how it all began.*"

He continued to recite from the *Aeneid* in a whisper, and I was engulfed in peace, a child calming to an ancient lullaby in the back seat of a bright pink Impala. His words and voice could soothe my aching more than anyone's, even as dead as he was.

"Sweet dreams, Ellie."

"More poetry, please." I reached for his hand, but it faded away. With the door open, I heard the pounding echo of his sandals on the sidewalk.

A chattering group spilled out of an open bar, coming between us and robbing me of the last glimpse of my friend and protector. People passed through him as if he were air, scrambling his image with turbulence that billowed his toga until he vanished into a white cloud of fog.

50. Captured by the System

Virgil may have been a mere hallucination caused by my dying brain. Our entire intense conversation—the coffee, the poetry, the yellow watch, Lake Victoria— could be a symptom of my cognitive decline. Yet, I could still feel the ghost of his presence as sleep stole over me.

My cellphone's alarm woke me at 6 a.m. The nearest civilized bathroom was inside a restaurant that wouldn't open until lunch. Buzzing flies encircled my head like a ring of light in religious art, descending with me as I squatted once more behind the pink Impala. I wasn't the first one who had that idea. The stench of old urine on the sidewalk made me gag.

Gaggle Gaggia Gag Green Grass, ran through my mind as I barfed into an overflowing trash can. I promised myself again that this would be the lowest I'd ever sink.

The MRI tech, a thin man with a day-old beard, said with a yawn that I was his last case at the end of a double shift. He just wanted to finish my imaging and go home. He didn't ask personal questions, which meant he hadn't been alerted to my fugitive state.

Might he be my new handler? I furtively studied him, but then he yawned again and loudly. My handler, I decided, would have more refinement. Exhausted, and despite the noise, I fell asleep in the machine.

The potent smell of tuberose woke me.

"Don't move an inch, Ellie," a steady female voice said.

I was out of the scanner but still on the table, the white ceiling above me. A stooped woman in green scrubs and a white lab coat studied me, vertical worry lines etching her forehead. A blue mask dangled from one of her ears, and wisps of gray hair had slipped out from her flowery surgical cap. I didn't recognize her, although I knew I probably should.

Was she my handler?

"Why isn't your mother with you?" she asked. "Where are your friends?"

"Too busy looking for their own brains," I said.

She hypnotized me with the to-and-fro sway of the dangling surgical mask. "Is one of them waiting in the cafeteria?"

"I divorced them."

She aimed the beam from a flashlight into my left eye, then my right. "I'm getting a room ready for surgery and starting your prep."

Not for me, she wasn't.

"Is this some *Twilight Zone* nightmare?" I asked. "What's going on?"

Her name and title—Dr. Rhonda Knochen-Hacker, Chief of Neurosurgery—was embroidered on the lapel of her white coat. I'd seen that name in my now deleted journals. In my dread, I clutched for the straw of a lame joke.

"Why hyphenate a name that means bone hacker in German, when that's what you do for a living?"

"Spare me." She sighed. "I heard all the wisecracks already, more than enough from you."

I didn't recall wisecracking with her or ever seeing her, but what I recalled in this world meant bupkis.

"The tech called me to look at your images and there's no good way to break the news. The blood clot is growing. It should come out pronto."

"You feel like knocking me over the head again with your rubber mallet?" I asked, but that dumb quip also crumbled without as much as a smile from her. The lady meant business.

I struggled to sit up, my heart sending vibrations through my neck and straight to my throbbing head.

The hand she offered me was rough from endless scrubbing. "Let's get you out of this magnetic room and make a few phone calls."

In the control room, she sat me in a chair.

"Don't move," she commanded, then pointed at a set of images on the glowing screen.

I leaned forward in my creaky chair. "Wow, that baby octopus is trapped inside a big walnut."

"This is your cerebral blood circulation." She pointed with a silver pen. "That small interrupted area here is the growing clot. If it doesn't come out, you could lose vital functions, even your memory."

"My memory is indestructible. Virgil said so."

She cocked her head in question.

"He's the author of the *Eclogues,* the *Georgics,* and the *Aeneid.* His full name is complex, like yours. Publius Vergilius Maro."

I was bragging a little, demonstrating my perfect memory to her, but even as the words left my mouth and I watched the worry line deepen in her forehead, I realized how crazy that tangent of conversation must sound to a hardheaded pragmatist.

Dr. Rhonda could not be my new handler. She wouldn't perceive Virgil if he fell through the ceiling and landed in the splits on her expensive machinery.

I took a deep breath to calm my nerves. "You told me that another craniotomy could give me a stroke, seizures, paralysis, blindness, nerve damage, etcetera."

I'd read that nugget in my now-deleted files.

"I'm glad you remember that, but weighing your present risks, we have no choice. When did you last eat?"

"I had a breakfast this huge," I lied, gesturing *big fish* between my hands. "You have to wait."

"We can do a conscious surgery. It's an emergency."

The hairy little bitch of a brain filter guzzling homunculus rocked back and forth inside my head. Conscious. I'd be awake for her drill.

"Why craniotomy? Why can't you use that minimally invasive technique, you know the one where you guide a CT catheter through a tiny opening and inject stuff that shrinks the clot and..."

I explained, leaving out the sarcasm and jokes. To her credit, Dr. Rhonda Knochen-Hacker listened with scientific interest.

I continued, "This article I read back in Reality One, when I was helping my friend Nora prepare her PhD disserta—"

"*Reality one* must be one of your sci-fi magazines, right?" Dr. Rhonda asked, hopeful.

No handler of mine would ask such an ignorant question. *Reality One,* my true home reality, was when I'd read about that minimally invasive procedure, which I guessed wasn't available in this world.

"One day we'll have that technology, I'm sure," she said. "As of now, I'm limited to craniotomy. It gives you a chance of surviving."

I felt robbed. A chance of surviving was also a chance of becoming a vegetative life-form. An image from a long ago Halloween party flashed before my eyes: Sophie as Count Ugolino, munching on my brain with a wooden spoon.

"*Adios muchachos,* I'm the fuck out of here." I started to stand, but Dr. Rhonda rested a hand on my shoulder and kept me in the creaky chair.

"No way," I said. "Not another hack job on my brain. I won't let you use your hammer and anvil, or other Neanderthal hardware on my head, when a better and *successful* technique is available."

Dr. Rhonda grunted. "You've read an article about what will eventually be available, but it's only a theory now."

"It already exists," I argued in my excitement. "You won't even have to shave my hair."

"Your beautiful hair will grow back."

Oh God, she thought I was worried about my hair.

"Please calm down and let us take care of you." She smiled a set of perfect white teeth, and that toothy smile frightened me more than her urgency.

I calmed, at least my voice. "Google—sorry, gaggle—Johns Hopkins neurologists," I said to the bewildered woman who happened to be the chief of neurosurgery in one of the leading hospitals in the nation. "The robotic procedure is called Da Vinci—"

"Da Vinci?"

"—after the Renaissance man—"

"Renaissance? Ellie, please stop talking—"

"Renaissance in German translates to *Wiedergeburt*." My fascinated stare was glued to her embroidered name. "Come to think of it, you should hyphenate the German word into your already complex name, and make your patients read it back to you as a cognitive test. Here you go, Dr. Rhonda Knochen-Hacker-Wiedergeburt."

I started laughing.

She spoke quietly into her phone. "I need a gurney STAT. I'm ready to operate now . . . a stroke, yes. She's stroking out and losing coherence as we speak." To me she said, "Sit back."

"Thanks. I appreciate this. Look, all I need is a week to put my affairs in order."

"You don't have a week." She started dialing. "I'm calling your legal guardian for consent."

"Stop," I said and she paused.

"You are not to notify my mother." I sat up straight and made my voice as rational as possible. "Please respect my wishes."

Dr. Rhonda hesitated, then dropped the phone into her pocket.

The clock on the wall was at straight-up twelve, and my stupid mouth added, "It's eight hours to a new transition according to Donald Duck."

"Donald Duck . . ." That did it. Out came the phone. "I need a witness for a consent," she called out.

One of the MRI techs left his post and came to listen.

"Mrs. Brooke, please," Dr. Rhonda said firmly into the phone. She repeated the information to my mother, explaining the procedure and its risks. My mother asked questions— sounding curiously like a responsible person one could rely on —and Dr. Rhonda answered at length.

I lost interest in their back and forth speaker sounds when —like any writer stuck on a complex plot issue—I switched to a whole new vein.

Betty and Virgil.

She had recently won some jackpot, and he won the Lake Victoria bet. Were those bets and jackpots related to the same game? Both Betty and Virgil got their great coffee at a place called *The House*—another name for the afterlife.

Dr. Rhonda was listing for my mother the same extremely unattractive risks she had listed for me. "Yes, memory loss, seizures, unilateral paralysis, incontinence."

As my mother grilled her, I continued a separate Q&A in my own fragmented mind about recent events.

After each transition, Virgil had said, the House met nightly in headquarters to eat, drink, place bets on possible outcomes. Tonight was to be yet another one of Betty's game nights.

Conclusion: Betty's office was headquarters.

The coffee, the bets, even the weird neighbors and their empty apartments all made sense.

The place is disgusting, Rita had said, checking out my groceries.

Rita wasn't wrong. Honest Rita, who I'd ignored. Paradise Point was HQ, where the powerful dead placed their bets. The living were frightened by the building, therefore the powerful and bored dead were free to use the property for their post-transition betting tournaments.

It was no coincidence that Virgil had dropped me off exactly there. But why? I closed my eyes to remember. He'd said, *You are no good to us dead. What if you are the only one who could save the world by something you do?*

The truth was as obvious as my nausea and my blinding headache. My way home had always been under my nose.

"*Eureka!*" I said, and *my* hysterical laughter started again, this time in relief.

Dr. Rhonda eyed me with that sober professional concern I so hated, and said into the phone, "Your daughter is becoming incoherent as we speak. Mrs. Brooke, I believe it's an emergency procedure, so if you don't have more questions, do I have your consent to perform a craniotomy?"

Dr. Rhonda believed my histrionics to be a symptom of cognitive decline or stroke, but I was more coherent than ever.

I knew the game they played. I knew their headquarters. I even knew they got their good coffee in heaven. Betty had invited me to play, and if I wanted to go home, I had to take her up on the invitation. Game night would start soon. If I left now, I'd make it in time.

I had to get out of there before they sedated me and trapped me forever in this doomed reality of antiquated neurological procedures.

"Your mother wants to talk to you." Dr. Rhonda handed me the phone.

"I'm an hour away from the hospital," said the responsible, multitasking version of my mother, her face distorted on the screen, her nose huge. And no, she wasn't wearing a red wig made from my stolen hair. "I'll see you when you're safely out of surgery."

Safely. A flash of my white skeleton against an X-ray screen burned bright in my frightened mind. "Don't make me have another surgery, Mama, please don't." I begged, unable to engage my damaged brain filters, or simply shut up. "I just found the way back to Paradise."

"Oh my God, listen to your doctor," she said. "I love you, Ellie."

"I loved you more when you didn't give a shit." I disconnected.

What was the point? My mother, in her new form, was my well-intentioned and clueless legal guardian, who had given the just as clueless Dr. Rhonda permission to strap me to a gurney against my will. Soon I'd be sedated, then they'd drill into my hard skull without anesthesia, like in Virgil's time, with instructions straight from the *Corpus Hippocraticum.* I'd wake up dead, or paralyzed, or blind, with my mind blank and my memories of past realities erased forever.

I'd much rather die searching for my true life.

Abandon all hope, once captured by the system, Virgil had paraphrased Dante.

I had to get out and drive north to HQ, that place deep in the mountains near Oxnard.

The door burst open and two large guys in white scrubs pushed a gurney into the MRI control room. With Dr. Rhonda's calm assurances, and despite my struggles, they managed to strap me down.

Captured by the system, I did not abandon all hope.

51. Do-Gooders

"We are here to help you." Dr. Rhonda kept a hand on my shoulder as I struggled to sit up. Her tuberose perfume was mixed with a hint of sweat. I must have really stressed her out.

"No one can help me," I wailed. Tears ran down both sides of my head. "I'm the only one who can help myself and that means getting back to HQ."

The walls swayed around me as the gurney rolled left and right down various hallways. A digital clock on one wall displayed 13:00. In only a couple of hours, the games would start. I had to be there to meet the House members at play. I had to beg them to help me.

My emotions remained on the surface. I couldn't stop talking, appealing, *explaining* to Dr. Rhonda and the tall men in white, that Virgil needed me alive for a mission that would save the world.

Dr. Rhonda spoke clear and brisk instructions into her phone. "Prep room number one. Yes. Yes. Conscious sedation. STAT."

The closing whoosh of an elevator's door sealed my fate. I was surrounded by the natives of an alien planet, who planned to drill industrial hardware into the delicate matter of my one-of-a-kind brain.

Death by drill. Category, alliteration.

"Please listen, Dr. Rhonda," I said as we exited the elevator. "I don't need surgery. Really. I need to talk to the dead players. You see? They can send me back to my sane reality, where my brain doesn't have a clot in the first place."

This made great sense to me, but not to Dr. Rhonda Knochen-Hacker-Wiedergeburt, who kept to her brisk walk beside the gurney.

"Trust me," she said, holding my hand in what she believed to be a reassuring manner. "At the moment there's no better place for you than right here with us. I'll scrub while they prep you."

Nurses in blue and green hurried about the pre-op unit, tending to potential victims who, like me, faced hack jobs. I didn't struggle when the large orderlies transferred me to a bed. I focused on saving my energy and sizing my distance to the closest exit.

As soon as they left me alone, I stood up.

The walls wavered and darkened. When I came to, I was wearing nothing but a thin hospital gown. Shit. They took everything off me including my underwear.

A young nurse, barely out of diapers, measured my blood pressure. A pink headband decorated her forehead, her hips swayed, and her feet boogied to the rhythm of dance music only she could hear through her white earbuds. Her name tag said *Dede* in flowery font.

"How're you feeling?" Her annoying chirp cracked my dental enamel—definitely not my handler.

"Fine. Where are my clothes?"

"You'll get your stuff after your operation." She checked the infrared thermometer. "I'll be right back with your sedation."

Wanna bet? I asked quietly behind closed lips, struggling not to express every incriminating comment in spoken words. The nurse pulled the green privacy curtain around the bed and left me alone.

A stout woman in green scrubs and a bouffant cap entered next and introduced herself as "Dr. Rockhart, your anesthesiologist."

"I was hoping you'd be my new handler," I said, half joking, but she was all business and not amused.

I answered her questions calmly. Elektra Brooke. Thirty years old this May, blah, blah. Born in Los Angeles two or three realities ago.

She looked up from her notes, one eyebrow raised. Oops. She didn't like that last bit. All the while, I was eyeing the exit, preparing to run for it the moment I was alone again. My clothes were gone, but my blue sneakers remained on the floor, forgotten and ready for my feet.

When Dr. Rockhart was gone, I carefully stood again, still unsteady, but this time I didn't black out. I slipped my feet into the sneakers, wincing at the pain in my left foot. I gave the pre-op unit a once-over through the green curtain. Nurses rushed to and fro among sedated patients, someone cried in pain. The child-nurse faced a cart against the wall and was preparing syringes, her back to me, her feet dancing in place.

My annoying limp kept my movements slow. Still, I was quicker than Dancing Dede, who started turning just as I grabbed one of the lab coats hanging on a hook by the wide-open door. In the hallway, I slipped my arms through the sleeves and immediately gagged on the ripe stench of tuberose and sweat. Abandon all fucking hope, indeed. I would have barfed if I actually had anything in my stomach.

In the elevator, I pressed street level and nodded a greeting at a nurse and her patient, a woman in a wheelchair.

A quick glance at the ID badge clipped to the lab coat sent a quiver through me. *Dr. Rhonda Knochen-Hacker.*

"Wiedergeburt," I added in a whisper.

The mad laughter ebbed in my throat at the mental image of Dr. Rhonda who, while scrubbing for an emergency craniotomy, managed to lose her lab coat, her badge, her patient.

The gagging, gasping, laughing combo, plus the hospital gown peeking from under the lab coat, apparently made me look suspicious. Both the woman in the wheelchair and her nurse eyed me with fear.

"Private joke," I explained, hoping they'd go back to their own problems.

I limped into the busy reception area and out again, heading toward the visitors' parking lot, discarding Dr. Rhonda's smelly lab coat along the way. I stopped and tried to recall what floor I parked on that morning, when a magical pink glow led me to the Impala.

Two huge orderlies in white, maybe those who had earlier wrestled me onto the gurney, seemed to be searching the parking deck, most likely for me. I expected them to easily spot the Impala—not exactly the optimal getaway car—and block the parking lot exit with their beefy bodies.

They didn't move out of my way. But of course, like Virgil's Tesla, Betty's pink eyesore was probably invisible to the living.

The worn engine groaned, and tires squealed on dry asphalt as I stepped on it and headed straight for the barrier and the bulky bodies blocking my way. The air turbulence pushed them aside. When the barrier broke, I drove through.

I maneuvered frantically, avoiding visitors, patients, hospital workers, then I was out on the street and on my way to the 405 freeway.

I laughed in the fake baritone of an opera villain, finally safe from clueless do-gooders who wanted to fry my brains.

I headed north on the path that would take me home.

An hour or so later, I parked the Impala in front of Paradise Point Pizza. As I pulled my backpack from the back seat, its bottom ripped open, spilling all my earthly possessions onto the sidewalk. The remaining cash rolled along the street and some flew away in a sudden gust of wind. And my laptop…

"Shit." I stared at the carcass of my precious laptop that had never left my side, now crushed and shattered, its fragments strewn about like the amputated limbs of an insect.

Gina's words from long ago came to me now. *When the end of the world comes, you'll sit down to write about it.*

Gina knew nothing. The end of the world was coming. I was facing death, and all I wanted was life. I cared nothing about money, writing books, or even about Gina.

I grabbed the shaggy coat from the back seat, then left the door of the parked Impala wide open, keys inside, engine running. None of it mattered to me anymore.

My way home was ahead, through the dilapidated building with the red gang graffiti on its outer wall, announcing *L'Inferno* in blood dripping spooky font.

52. The pool of Life and Death

I tightened the fuzzy coat over my flimsy hospital gown and limped into the courtyard, past the pissing fountain. Right away, I was taken aback by the higher than usual activity level. Golden ripples dazzled bright in the gleaming celestial blue water. People stepped out of it, brushing wet stardust off their clothes.

Players from the other side.

"What's all that glitter?" I asked no one in particular.

"Celebration," explained a female British voice. "A big night."

"What's with this pool anyway?" I looked around for her.

"The pool is our way of traveling back and forth," she said.

"Where do you travel from?" I asked.

"The afterlife, of course." The pleasant voice came from a face somewhere below curls coifed in the shape of a heart. The woman's black dress and white ruff collar seemed to be stuck in Elizabethan England. "This hollow-bottomed pool is double-sided. This side opens to life and the other to death."

I recognized her from the flap of a book I used to have.

"Ms. Sidney," I whispered, starstruck. "Are you really the Countess of Pembroke?"

She smiled in mock humility, settling into a lounge chair. "Call me Mary."

"I had your poetry collection, in my last reality that is." In the presence of my cross-centuries' idol, I became self-conscious of my poor appearance.

"It'll take at least an hour in the cold sun to dry up this heavy brocade." She spread her black dress on the plastic lounger. "I'm going to have a little slumber."

Next, a man stepped out of the pool, his white hair long and dribbling water. A wide smile was on his face, like in his famous photographs.

"I read *The Martian Chronicles* about a million times," I said. "And your other works."

He shook his head like a wet dog. "Thank you."

"You may know this as a sci-fi master, Mr. Bradbury," I said. "Why do certain things stay the same despite transitions?"

He wet-plopped into a lounge chair and squinted at the blue sky. "Rephrase your question for clarity."

"Why did my reality change, but I'm still me?"

He rearranged himself on the plastic surface, and his soaked suit made an embarrassing sucking sound. "Oops." He smiled an apology.

I tightened the coat over my hospital gown. The wind was cold, but I had to know his take on this immoral game they were playing.

"A new reality changes our circumstances, but never our essence," he said, and I remembered Virgil saying something similar. "A new transition gives you a new set of data and endless possible combinations. Yet in your case, I'll bet on one certain thing. You'll always be a writer. You may be wearing a bear coat over a hospital gown, Yves Saint Laurent in Paris, a colorful kimono in Tokyo, or you may be writing in Bengali about the slums of Calcutta from an insider's POV, but a writer you'll be. And judging from your one novel, you'll write humorous contemporary fiction."

"My novel?" I cried out. "How do you know my novel?"

He closed his eyes and giggled. "I just loved that scene where she finds herself on Wilshire, dressed in nothing but flakes of dried-up red paint." In seconds, he was snoring.

"What fresh hell is this place?" a woman asked, passing me on the way to Betty's office, a cigarette dangling from the side of her mouth. She trailed smoke behind her and the fumes of Scotch whiskey.

"Dorothy Parker," I said in awe, but she spotted her old friend Lillian Hellman and marched to her side.

More famous faces emerged from the pool, most not bothering to dry themselves. I recognized Charlotte Brontë, Isaac Asimov, and Mary Shelley.

Brain out of commission or not, I noticed a certain pattern. All these newcomers had one thing in common. Their works—dust jackets intact with pictures of their faces—packed my bookshelves in my home reality.

"Why?" I asked myself in that new uninhibited way of blurting out my internal monologues. "Why are my favorite authors gathering in the shittiest possible location on the planet?" Then I replied, my teeth chattering from the cold and the tension, "The dazzle of clout is supposed to lure me into that unethical mission, that manuscript-seizing mission in the sixteenth century. I won't fall for it, because their attempts to change history are misguided."

"Stream of consciousness as a narrative device, belongs in writing, not in speech," said a patrician English voice. It came from the gaunt, slightly stooped silhouette of Virginia Woolf as she passed me. Her wet fuzzy coat was a darker version of mine.

I followed her in the direction of Betty's office, careful not to slip on the little pools of footsteps she was leaving behind.

Divine aromas of mozzarella and basil welcomed me as soon as I walked in. The famous dead sat around the conference table, eating, drinking, speaking in hushed tones, and mostly immersed in reading dog-eared books with curled-up covers. Pizza boxes were piled up on the table.

A big man, as tall as he was wide, grabbed the last two slices in an open box and made them disappear into his hungry mouth, then washed the food down with something clear and bubbly, maybe Prosecco. I recognized him from Virgil's description as the Big Kahuna, BK, or simply Death. With his Hawaiian shirt, and those kind eyes beneath a whale-patterned blue bandana, he was nothing like the classic depiction of the Grim Reaper. This image of Death would have no argument from the dying.

A new box was immediately opened by greedy hands. I marveled at my glossy idols eating and drinking as if starved in their eternal death.

As for me, I nearly passed out at the sight of the perfect Neapolitan pizza. The thin, soft crust was charred in spots, still bubbling, and topped with tomato sauce, mozzarella, and fresh basil: a combination I could never resist. The digital clock on the monitor said 16:00, four hours before the new transition and twenty hours since those tacos from Abuelita's. Without an invitation, I grabbed a slice. Tears of gluttony ran down my cheeks with the first bite of what could be my last meal.

Someone pushed a chair toward me and a huge Styrofoam cup. I sipped through a straw, but immediately spat it out. Flat Pepsi. I pointed at what the big man was drinking, and he poured me a glass of the same bubbly.

My eyes could have easily made the entire pizza disappear in no time, but my stomach felt queasy after two slices.

"Is this from down the street?" I asked.

"Read the box," said a woman with 1920's hair.

Luigi Trattoria, the inscription read. Via Scarlatti, Napoli.

"Italy?" I asked, amazed.

She pointed at The Big Kahuna. "He just traveled back from Italy. Quiet. Let me read."

They were all reading, and frequent chuckles came from around the table.

"I thought this was one of your game nights," I said. "Did I accidentally walk into a book club meeting?"

"The game is usually first on the agenda," said the woman from the twenties. "But tonight the author of this novel will discuss her work."

Having my own burning agenda, I cared nothing about their scheduled author, but my natural curiosity got the better of me. I just had to sneak a tiny peek at the popular paperback.

As I reached for one of the books, the woman stood up, cleared her throat and started vocalizing riffs and runs in a familiar dramatic soprano. My reaching hand froze midmotion and pointed at her in recognition.

"Which one of the Ponselle sisters are you?" I asked in awe.

"I'll give you a hint." She sang the first few notes from "*Suicidio!*" in a glorious voice.

I knew immediately. "*Gioconda*, the Met, 1921. You are Rosa."

"I also performed it in Covent Garden, 1929," she said with pride.

"Yes, great triumph. How did you keep your voice, what with being so dead for almost forty years?"

She put her manicured hands together in prayer, like her famous Desdemona. "They play their game. As one of the greatest sopranos of the twentieth century, I play mine. I'm here just to meet you, Elektra Brooke, one of the very few alive who still play my records."

"How do you know my name?"

She slapped the battered paperback on the table before me. "Aren't you the author of this?" she asked with a beatific smile.

With shaky hands, I picked up the book. The gold title was worn, but I could easily read *Fucking My Way Through Life* by Elektra Brooke.

My world darkened. I was about to pass out in front of dead people. I leafed through it. This was my book all right, but the cover was so curled and scratched, I could barely see Sophie's artwork.

Murmurs came from around the table. "Good book, good book."

"How?" An ugly choking croak started at the bottoms of my sneakers and slithered up to my belly and out through my mouth in the voice of Linda Blair from *The Exorcist.*

I looked up at Rosa Ponselle. "How and why does this copy exist when the rest of what I used to be is gone?"

Rosa remained silent while I leafed through the book backward and forward with disbelief. It was mine, my formatting, but...

I stood and waved the worn paperback over my head. "How and where did you... *Why* did you..."

Rosa eyed me with theatrical sadness and wilted a little where she stood, like Tosca before she leaps to her death.

I turned to the Big Kahuna and asked in begging hope, "Did you already transition me back home? Is this why my novel exists?"

"A smuggler brought a few copies to our Cosmic Library, and we're so enjoying the read," he said. "That sexy moment in front of the great masterpiece was so hilarious, I laughed out loud—"

"How did the smuggler... I don't get it."

He cleared his throat. "The books were strewn about in a cornfield."

"Yuck, they're covered with Sophie's puke," I said. "I'm going to republish it."

"You can't." He swallowed another mouthful of Prosecco. "It's time to prep you for your mission."

"Not doing missions for you. I'm going home."

He pointed his fat thumb at a closed door behind him. "Talk to her."

53. The Transformation

I knocked twice on the closed door, then entered without waiting for an answer. I'd been polite long enough. A table with a vase of flowers was pushed against the wall. An upright wooden chair and a narrow bed made a near replica of Van Gogh's yellow painting. Betty sat stooped on the edge of the bed, her sun-spotted hands resting on her wooden cane.

I should have known right away, but I missed the clues because Dante's lost love and guide into Paradise, Beatrice Portinari, was a beautiful young maiden. Betty was about two hundred years old, and that's why the truth didn't hit me until now.

I took a deep breath in, then released a long one out to steady myself. "Betty is short for Beatrice, right?"

She nodded, her wizened face stoic.

"My surgeon was ready to operate on my head, but I came here instead."

"You've made the right decision," she said with gentle sweetness.

"Good decision? What do you know about me or my decisions?"

"I know everything about you. Even details better left to the imagination, which you kids call TMI." She tightened the grip on her cane. "I know you live for a good story, but if you don't calm down, you'll be dead before finding out the rest of what you're starting to understand."

"Virgil said I'd have a new handler. If you are it, why did you let me go on with my cover story?"

"You had to be ready for us, and we for you."

"I get it—I'm your scheduled author. I'm supposed to talk about my work and answer questions. So here's the first question of the evening. Am I going back to paradise?"

"That depends on the meaning of paradise."

"Paradise means my home with my dog and the purple flowers and the sticky windows and Gina and my published novel." I waved the worn paperback over her loofah hair.

"That reality is lost forever." Her face sank a little, as if the skin was melting off her bones.

I stepped away from her in revulsion.

"Next question." I tossed the tattered paperback to the carpet at her feet. "I know that a smuggler found the books strewn in a cornfield in the previous reality." I pointed at the book on the floor. "I know how you have my books, but why do you need them?"

"We had to study your mind and learn the best way to send you on your mission to—"

"To Venice 1554 to steal Dante's manuscript from its editor," I completed. "Not going on missions for you, especially not this one, and if I had a way, I'd be telling *him*."

She flinched. "Dante?"

"I know you keep the meetings and the games from him."

The gathering in the adjacent room grew rowdy, as more dead players arrived and greeted each other in a variety of languages. On top of that racket, Rosa Ponselle continued practicing her vocal riffs.

"We need to lighten up in the afterlife," Betty said. "Which means a funny book like yours will find wide readership in the Cosmic Library. More people died than ever lived—"

The self-control I meant to project was fraying. I recalled the incredible music from Virgil's sound system and his words: *The composer, Whimsy, was a pioneer in her field. She was lost but not her music.*

"I'm not lost." Through the window, the Paradise Point Apartments sign blinked against the evening sky. "I made it to the new transition."

I was starting to understand even more.

She kept leaning forward on her cane, trying to stand. "Once we've discussed your book and asked you the necessary questions, you'll go on your mission. If you're lost—"

"Do you intend to lose me on that mission?" I asked, already knowing the answer.

"—your book will enjoy a place of honor besides another one-book wonder, Lloyd Brookberg."

"Who the hell is Lloyd Brookberg?"

"He was lost in a previous transition, but his *Green Flamingo* deserved to live. It made us all cry."

"Why was he lost if you so loved his book?"

"He couldn't produce more literature. Like you, he suffered from a hopeless case of sophomore slump and—"

"Excuse me very much," I argued, boiling mad, "but you don't *produce* literature. The emotional process of writing a novel is delicate labor...I'm actually hard at work on *The Octopus*."

"That one was no good. You deleted it."

"Transition me back home and I'll write more."

A series of audible creaks and cracks accompanied her attempt to stand. I watched her painful movements, and for once, didn't rush to give her a hand. Something about her effort didn't seem real to me.

"I have to change for game night. If you want to keep talking, you can stay here—"

I shuddered. "No thanks." I had no desire to watch the wrinkly bare ass of a two-hundred-year-old when my own young body in its present form disgusted me enough.

Betty/Beatrice swayed on her old feet, as if balancing against a seismic aftershock. She cracked her knuckles, twisted her shoulders, and stretched both arms back—a yogi preparing for a complex yoga pose? She was on my shit list, but I didn't want to laugh.

Next, before my fascinated eyes, she flung the cane aside and straightened to an impressive height. She then reached for both sides of her face, and to my growing horror, pulled her skin down and off and dropped the bulk of it to the toxic-spill-green carpet. She grabbed a handful of her loofah hair, slipped it off, and tossed it atop the pile.

Shiny midnight hair fell to her shoulders, fragrant with patchouli, and almost as long as my hair used to be. When she raised her eyes to me, she wasn't an old woman anymore, but a stunning beauty in her twenties with smooth dark skin, red lips, and brown eyes with thick black lashes.

In a dramatic final move, she ripped off the yellow muumuu. A tight white tank top and black yoga pants stretched across a perfect athletic figure.

"Bea," I whispered. "From WildWest yoga…"

"And from Gina's Dante class," she said.

A sharp headache knocked me for a literal loop, where I was at eye level with the heap formed by her dropped costume. Did I really just witness Betty's incredible transformation from a muumuu-clad old lady to a gorgeous young woman?

"I wanted to write a historical novel about Beatrice, but you said she was a peripheral character."

I whispered the only sensible words that came to my mind, "What the fucking fuck?"

"Not so peripheral now, am I?" she asked in a bitchy tone.

54. Fake

"Just like my fake friend Virgil," I said in mounting anger. "Fake." Awash with nausea, I blinked up at Beatrice. "He pretended to be my protector, but he only wanted me alive for his smuggling mission. And where's he in this?"

"Tonight he's instructing a group of the freshly dead, new recruits for the smuggling team. We're shorthanded and the realities breeze by. How fortunate we are to have found a living talent with solid memory, like yourself, to fetch us Dante's manuscript."

"I'm not running errands for you."

"You're the only one who ticks all the boxes for the mission. First of all, you're alive," she chirped from her proud mountain pose. "You should see it as your contribution to humanity."

"Don't you spew yoga positivities at me," I said. "You were always fake, like this whole little town. *Paradise Point*, for God's sake. Fake like the sparkling pool and the cane you were pretending to need."

I picked the cane up from the carpet. It was too heavy for the old lady she never was. "Do the walls even exist here?"

"The walls exist," she said.

"Beatrice Portinari." I sighed. "Why disguise yourself as an old lady when you look like that Rossetti of yours?"

She gestured at the window, where the Paradise Point Apartments sign relentlessly flashed red. "Would you have believed I managed this hellhole if I looked like this?" She turned her flawless profile to me. "Is it a wonder Dante fell so madly in love with me? This face, this hair, this body inspired two major classic literary masterpieces."

"One of which you plan to eliminate," I said. "Why prevent the publication of a masterpiece he wrote for you?"

"He wrote *La Vita Nuova* for me. *The Divine Comedy* is more for everyone else. His love for me may have set him on his journey, but my appearance as his guide was a metaphor for a higher love. The love—"

"—that moves the sun and the other stars."

"The poem won't be lost, only transported—"

"To the Cosmic Library. Why did you lie to me?"

She walked, posed, twirled a few times, modeling her narrow waist, her perky boobs, her perfectly round butt in the stretchy black pants. "Do I look like I belong here minding this shithole?"

"Hey, I don't exactly belong here either." I gestured to myself in imitation. "If you remember me from back then, my hair is like yours, only red, and I'm really quite a babe. *I* inspired quite a few religious paintings of naked Madonnas with big tits. Maybe not exactly great masterpieces..." My eyes started dripping when self-pity struck. "No one would believe me because all those paintings and my photographs are trapped out of reach."

"I saw you then," she said with a sad smile of sympathy. "And I remember how beautiful you used to be. I even remember Lilly Green." She mocked, "*Why do we study Dante anyway?*"

I laughed in spite of myself and added my own mocking. "*Why is such an overrated and misogynistic work considered so important more than seven hundred years after it was written?*"

Two fine parentheses appeared at the sides of Bea's perfect pink lips when she smiled. "Gina Caldwell did well with that answer, and you...You were so in love with her."

"I still love her," I said. "And I lost her because of your games. I *hate* you."

"Hate me all you want, but I took notes." She smiled her pearly whites. "No espresso, no opera, no pizza, no football as we know it, etcetera. After your mission and the subsequent transition, we'll play the game of unintended consequences." She put her hand on her hip in coquettish defiance. "I'll win the jackpot again."

"Gotcha," I said. "Gina faked that whole lecture, to make a point."

"But it made total sense," she argued, biting her lower lip.

"Hold your bets." I pointed at my head. "I'll be dead way before your mission, which I keep refusing, in case you weren't taking notes on that."

Even if the entire exchange was a long hallucination due to a growing clot, this nightmare of a conversation wasn't the weirdest thing that had happened to me since I'd lost a whole reality in the blink of false eyelashes.

"Hey, Bea," a voice called from the next room. "What's taking you two so long?"

"Hurry up, Bea. This is not your Florentine wedding!"

"Let's start already, I'm not getting any deader."

Gales of laughter followed each smart-assed comment.

"Patience, I'm not done," she called out to them. She sat cross-legged on the edge of the bed. "Please, sit and listen," she said.

I could use a rest. I chose the wooden Van Gogh chair.

"I used to be Virgil's teammate. On his team of smugglers, that is. When we search for living talent like yourself, we watch kids in school playgrounds. You'd be surprised how much potential can be revealed during play. We perform menial jobs and observe kids without being noticed."

"That sounds creepy."

"It isn't." Her face glowed in the colors of the sunset. "Virgil worked in your elementary school, where Ms. Angie was a teacher. He'd spotted your talent when you saw him and no one else could, and his delight was complete when you realized the change of reality. While Virgil befriended you, I worked as a teacher's aide at another school."

"I thought you were invisible to the living."

"We're like a magic trick, visible only when we allow it. Well, except for you." She pushed her hair off her face. "In that particular assignment, I didn't spot new talent, but I got to know mirror identical twins. Sophie was an angel."

My ears perked up at the mention of my friend's name.

"Peggy . . ." Beatrice shook her head and silky strands floated around her in the slow motion of a shampoo commercial. "Peggy," she repeated. "I hated that little girl from the moment I set my ancient eyes on her. My life was short, but in all seven hundred plus years of my death I have not seen such an evil little *pezzo di merda* . . ."

"Peggy is a piece of shit," I said, delighted. "And when she died, her parents made a terrible mistake."

"It wasn't their mistake, or a mistake per se," Bea said. "What happened was intentional. I suffered for it, but I didn't regret it."

"What did you do?" I wasn't sure I wanted to know.

"Sophie was much sicker, and she was the one scheduled to die. I stole into Death's office and changed the name on the form. As a result, Peggy died and Sophie lived." Beatrice dropped her gaze to the nauseating carpet. "When you two visited the cemetery, the scheduled transition and Sophie's proximity to the headstone triggered a spontaneous correction."

"But how could that happen?" I asked.

"No clue," she said, shaking her hair like a contemporary girl. "Totally scary . . . Virgil then contacted me to tell me that his protege, you, had found herself in a whole new reality, memories intact—"

"What?" I snapped. "That man . . ."

"You needed protection and guidance. He said he'd prep you before transferring you here to Paradise Point. So I came here to wait for you." She narrowed her eyes. "Nothing bores me more than waiting."

"Who gives a shit about your boredom?" I was so livid, a stream of words poured out with my tears. "Those mindless parents give a funeral to the wrong daughter. I didn't even know them back then, so how did *I* end up losing everything in a new transition? I mean, how could anyone with eyes and ears mistake one sister for the other? Those parents are idiots."

"In their defense, even Death was fooled," she said. "Those girls were truly physically identical, and it wasn't like they didn't have fun with it, switching clothes and beds. Well, the mistake confused the parents, and we had a big mess of unintended consequences on our hands. I was demoted and taken off the smuggle team. For a long time, they only sent me on minor spying gigs, like cooking for rich people and scrubbing toilets. I was on probation for the longest—"

"Probation?" Insane laughter bubbled in my throat.

"Yes." Her eyes widened in reaction to my laugh. "We get probation for malpractice."

"Great news." I kept laughing. "I always thought that once you died, you could rest, but the afterlife is just a workplace with malpractice, assignments, probation, toilets—"

"The House *is* merely a workplace. Those who run it have no clue what's going on until someone like me screws up." She seemed irritated. "What's so funny about that?"

"Nothing. My brain injury caused what my hack of a neurologist calls emotional incontinence and Peggy calls . . ." I was laughing in waves while describing my cerebral disaster. "Peggy calls it *emotions on the surface.* Basically, a growing blood clot keeps tickling my emotional center, making me act insane before it will kill me."

I pulled myself together and dried my eyes. "Just let me go home to my sane reality."

"I wouldn't know how to do that," she said. "Let's see if the House has ideas."

"This is why I came back," I said, following Bea into the conference room.

55. Not Exactly Dante

The dead clapped and cheered, "The author, the author!"

A ghost of a memory flashed before my eyes: my friends roasting marshmallows and saluting me before I asked them to help me bury a book. How different that scene was from this one.

The Roman numeral wall clock was running counter-clockwise. Two hours to the next transition. Only two hours to convince these powerful dead people to send me back home. They already claimed many times they couldn't do it, but weren't they the wisest souls who ever lived? They may pity me, and together, figure something out.

More than twenty of them from various eras in history sat around the oblong conference table. A huge woman in full Viking regalia—the breastplate, the battle-axe, the horned helmet, the works—picked her brown teeth with filthy fingernails, her dirty bare feet on the table. What was she doing here? I tried to recall if my bookcase held one of her books.

"Game over," I said. "Transition me back where I belong, and stop messing with history."

"She remembers," someone said. And, "She's good." And the Viking woman in a very deep voice, "She has moxie."

"Sign my copy," someone begged, handing me a pen and a tattered book, opened at the title page. This copy was particularly dirty and covered in coffee and food stains. I was so touched, tears filled my eyes as I wrote down my planned phrase from long ago:

May you find your paradise and the love that moves the sun and the other stars, Elektra Brooke via Dante Alighieri.

Another person handed me a book, but I changed my mind. "I'm not signing library copies," I said.

"She's funny," said the Viking.

The Big Kahuna cleared his throat and the room silenced. He wiped his mouth with a paper napkin. "Let's sum up the plot of *Fucking My Way Through Life*," he said in a booming voice. When he stood, his big belly disturbed the table, toppling stem glasses and spilling drinks all over the pizza boxes.

Drops of red wine dribbled from the edge onto the bilious carpet as BK continued. "An artist goes into her fresh paintings and has quickie sex with her oil-painted images. If she fails to leave before the paint dries, she gets trapped in ridiculous situations. Who wants to speak first?"

Arms were raised, the Viking banged a fist on the table, and Rosa Ponselle stood up and seized the stage. "*Fucking My Way* is both poignant and warm-blooded," she said. "Like my 1930 London debut of *Traviata*." She then burst into cheerful torrents of "*Sempre Libera*" in joyful cascades of coloratura.

BK raised five sausage fingers to stop her. "This isn't about you, Rosa," he said. "You had quite a few fiascos."

Rosa flounced back into her chair, visibly deflated and upset.

Virginia Woolf emptied her glass of red and turned to me. "Your experimental work is the reason we've gathered together here. The Bloomsbury Group is active in the afterlife. Come join us when you die."

"Best offer I've had in a while." I said, then my stupid mouth kept going without me. "Isn't *gathered together* a redundancy?"

"Oh, bite me." Woolf raised an eyebrow. "Cattle gather. People with a common purpose gather together."

That was rich of me, correcting Virginia Woolf.

A famous silhouette darkened the doorway. The new arrival cast a formidable shadow on the wall as he slowly and noisily dragged a chair to the table and poured himself a shot of Sambuca.

When I was done gagging on anise fumes, I said, "I'm your greatest fan, Mr. Hitchcock. I loved *Rebecca* and *Notorious*. Less so *The Birds*, what with the pecking of faces. My life story could have been one of your films."

"In my story, you'd be the MacGuffin," he said in his oily voice. "A mere plot device."

"Please," I said. "Can you tell me how to get back home?"

"There's a way," he said without emotion. "But first you'll have to . . ." The master of suspense calmly sipped his drink, and I knew I'd get nothing else from him.

"Your imagination is a plus," Bradbury offered. "But some of your sexual positions seem improbable."

"It's fantasy." I tightened my coat over the hospital gown.

"Even fantasy requires a few geographical peaks and troughs—who's on top, etcetera. All in all, I'll drink to your talent." He raised his glass and utters of "word" and "well spoken" sounded around the table.

Most of them read my book more than once—I was strangely flattered—and they had a lot to say.

"This is my favorite scene." BK leafed through his copy until he found the page. He stuffed his moon face with a whole cannoli, chewed, swallowed, washed it down with some bubbly, then started reading out loud. I became hypnotized by the multitudes of his trembling chins.

Here's the scene he read in a nutshell: My Sophie-like protagonist has a quickie with the painted image of a beautiful woman. The quickie turns into an all-nighter and then into a properly lesbian all-weeker. By the time she comes up for air, the paint has long since dried, and she finds herself wandering Wilshire Boulevard with flecks of red decorating her naked body.

As BK read, the House members laughed in the right places, and I recalled how I laughed through writing that chapter.

"Ms. Brooke." The Big Kahuna turned to me when he was done reading. "You should be proud for making us laugh. We need to take ourselves less seriously in the afterlife."

Murmurs of agreement came from around the table.

If this was a long and beautiful hallucination, I didn't want it to end. I was flattered by the sudden attention showered on me. At this lowest point in my life, I welcomed praise, any praise from anyone. Peggy had stolen my Santa Barbara show and here I was, getting some of the glory back, and from literary, cinematic, and musical giants. My head and eyes tennis-jumped left, right, and over the net, trying to keep up with the accolades.

Beatrice sat cross-legged. "The book transcends time and place. The settings and the characters are engaging—"

"Okay." I interrupted her gushing.

Now they'd expressed their opinions, they may be more inclined to take my side and help me on my quest, or kindly point me in the right direction. Up on the wall, the Roman numeral clock was speeding backwards.

"If you so value my one book," I said. "Please allow me to go back to my home reality, where I was about to start an even sexier and funnier fictional account of my life with Gina. If I stay here, I'll die from a growing brain clot. Wouldn't you want to enjoy an actual body of work?"

Complete silence fell in the room. A moment later, the crunching of crusty bread between a set of jaws broke the silence. Someone said, "We should move on to other items on the agenda," and a harmonious gush of murmurs concurred.

"What?" I asked. "Did I fuck up my only chance?"

"You can never go back," BK said. "Even if theoretically we could send you to your sane and healthy reality, your ability to remember all realities, including this very conversation, has turned you into an inconvenience, and with you being an author... Well, you shouldn't survive to tell."

"Come on." I jumped up, self-conscious in my hospital gown and my big ugly coat. "I write fantasy, and what, five people will read it. Why is the House so worried about a nobody like me?"

"You tell truth by means of fantasy. Like Dante and Shakespeare, you'll write about it in the common vernacular and you'll be widely read." He chuckled. "Although, let's face it. You are neither of those geniuses."

All the slights I'd felt each time a story of mine had been rejected rose to the surface with this greatest insult yet. I felt the hopeless need to defend my nonexistent literary career.

"Who wants to write like a Florentine who lived more than seven hundred years ago?" I asked "Or... or like an Englishman from the sixteenth century?"

They laughed.

"I'll give you that, you're funny," Bradbury said.

A grunt came from the corner. "And gutsy," the Viking said.

"I'm not joking," I said. "You asses are the reason I lost everything. I'd appreciate it if you made an effort to put back together my broken little pieces."

"I can actually see a great career for Ellie," Beatrice said, surprising me. "I read *Fucking My Way* three times, and with each reading, I found new and amusing details. That book makes me laugh more than I laughed in my entire life or death."

"You'll become popular," BK said, "which is exactly the problem."

"Is there another version of me in a parallel reality?" I asked. "Say, the one in which Ms. Angie didn't stop existing?"

Virgil had tried to explain the way things worked, but here was my chance to get an answer from the one who actually pushed the button.

"There aren't multiple versions of you or your life," he said. "Only one at a time. A transition eliminates the old reality forever. In yet another variant, your father could admire Puccini and name you Mimi."

I shrugged. "If it were up to my mother, she'd name me Mary Juana."

BK raised an eyebrow, amused only for a moment. "It's impossible to replicate the exact same coordinates. Even Dante admits in *Paradiso* thirty-three that he couldn't square a circle."

"Yes, yes. That's just him waxing poetic about geometry." I stood, arms akimbo. "Let me square your circle. Gina Caldwell loves me, and she teaches poetry of the Middle Ages. We both live on Rose Avenue in Venice Beach, California. Our cocker's name is Max, our best friend Sophie Sanders is alive, and her bitch sister smells the flowers from below. Now, replicate those consequences and"—I shook my fist at him—"push correction or transition and make the sky red."

"That isn't how we play," the Viking complained in her big voice.

"Corrections are meant to improve human history," Virginia Woolf said in her aristocratic lecturing voice. "A living smuggler and a dead one go back in time and remove an artifact from the past. A great deal happens as a result."

Isaac Asimov puffed on his pipe. "You can't play a game by predicting its unintended consequences," he argued.

"Exactly." Dorothy Parker sipped from her glass of red. "If you think you're in hell now, try playing the game backwards."

"Tell me again," I said, "why we need a dead smuggler and a living one."

"Naturally," Bradbury said, "when a dead smuggler goes back in time, they lose their physical presence, and a spirit can't whisk away an actual object, can it?"

Aware of the passing time, I listened with my typical tendency to lap up weird stories. They were all storytellers, eager to be clever and butt into each other's words.

Like Ms. Angie, I said, "Now, children, one at a time."

I learned further that game nights had started small, but the game became so popular, they needed a larger venue for it. They might hold the next one in the courtyard, under the sky. Lately, more bored dead people had been sneaking out, emerging on the side of life soaking wet from the pool. They enjoyed earthly food and drinks unavailable in the afterlife— last week was curry night. The betting was illegal and unethical, but it kept the dead from rotting in boredom. When the Big Kahuna joined, like tonight, he brought with him goodies from across the world and the centuries.

The monitor on the wall was not a security camera for the premises, as I first believed, but rather the very game board meant to reveal the results of each transition in various spots around the world. On game nights, the House members placed bets, and the one who got the most correct predictions won the jackpot.

"May I ask, what are those jackpots?"

"Money," BK said. "Naturally."

"I don't get it," I said. "They say you can't take it with you."

"We have our own coin." Asimov jumped in. "*Cold cash.*"

They laughed out loud.

"Cold cash," I repeated. "But, really, post mortem currency?"

"Ever heard of *mort*-gage?" Bradbury raised his glass of bubbly.

Cheers, clapping. Their eyes burned, their faces glowed in excitement. Money was still desirable after death.

"Sometimes we call it *heaven cents*," someone said. "It depends."

"*Dead presidents*," someone said. "*Blood money*," from someone else.

It was chaos. They whistled and toasted, banged on the table and turned downright rude and unruly. I didn't care anymore. My head was spinning from their explanations. Now I'd heard their stories, it was time to turn their attention to mine.

"Your game played me out of two good realities and trapped me in this hell. Why play in the first place when you can ruin so much with the unpredictable? Please," I begged in a whisper. "You are all so powerful here."

"You are the powerful one," BK said. "Virgil groomed you across three realities. You are the one who brings peace to the world by going to back to 1554."

"What are we waiting for?" Bradbury urged. "Let's send her already."

They gathered around me, chanting, "Send her, send her, send her." My senses sharpened with the crescendo of their chanting voices. The lights swayed with their movements when they joined hands in a circle around me. Now I was frightened. They were actually going to send me back against my will.

Only Mr. Hitchcock remained unmoved. He was calmly eating and drinking, like a cameo appearance in one of his own films.

I was done begging for my life. I had no intention of letting them kick me five hundred years back in time to assault an innocent man and seize a masterpiece. The only thing I'd seize would be my old life, or die trying, in the process, breaking their evil game for good.

I leaned against the table and gawked at the chanting and swaying circle of my dead idols. They were so humanly mindless and oblivious to what was really happening. My vision was darkening from a slow trickling of blood inside my brain, still I could see what none of them could. I was going to tell them.

I raised both my arms like a prophet of doom and said, "Death made you all stupid."

56. Squaring the Circle

I felt powerful despite being practically naked beneath my thin hospital gown and drab coat. I stretched to my full height and held my head high, the way I used to back when my hair was beautiful, and both my pride and my dreams intact.

All at once, the chanting and swaying stopped.

"Sit down and listen," I demanded in a voice that had become robust and full-bodied.

They took their chairs at the table while gaping at me like we kids used to look at Ms. Angie in her rose garden.

"Death killed your imaginations and scraped your minds empty," I said. "There's more to the afterlife than food and drink and your stupid jackpots. Don't you see what would happen if that mission was a success? Once I seized the manuscript, once I prevented its publication, nothing in the world would be the same. We'd all become a paradox. All of you and your works would cease to exist."

"Why? What do you mean? How'd you come up with that?" Voices called out from the length of the table and from the doorway, as more of the dead spilled into the room, dripping wet. The intense decay they brought with them had the noxious effect of perfume sprayed by a pampered lady inside an airplane.

"History builds on itself, right?" I asked.

"Right," came the responses. "Right on."

"Don't you see?" I asked in frustration, because if these were kids I was supposed to teach, they weren't the brightest. "Losing Dante's manuscript may prevent wars and famine in the name of religion, it may even stop the rise of fascism, but you'd hate the unintended consequences. I'll tell you some—"

"No, no," they begged. "Don't."

A whiny voice asked, "What's the fun if you spoil the ending?"

"I'll tell you anyway," I said. "If Dante's work doesn't get published, the world doesn't get a unified Italy. We lose the Renaissance—art *and* medical. Pizza? No." I swiped my hand across the table and the remaining pizza boxes tumbled to the carpet. "Sambuca? No." I grabbed the bottle by its neck and smashed it hard against the wall.

BK cried out, "That brand took special smuggling!" Beads of perspiration broke out on his forehead, above and below the whale-patterned bandana.

The reek of decay and spilled anise intensified, and my overactive gag reflex threatened to bring up my two slices of Neapolitan heaven.

I banged on the table, making glasses rattle against each other. "You don't impress me with your big names and voices. You are all dead and I'm still alive."

"Alive only until eight, which is soon," Bradbury said. "Once you're done with your mission, you'll come back to the House a hero. Dead, but a hero, with a glorious new career in the afterlife."

"That's a big lie, Mr. Bradbury," I said, staring him down. "No *Fahrenheit 451*." I pointed at Woolf. "No *Lighthouse, Orlando*, or *Mrs. Dalloway*." I pointed at Asimov. "No *Robotics*. Hitchcock, no *Psycho* or *Rebecca*."

At the mention of their names and works, each gave an audible gasp. "You and you and you"—I pointed at each of my dead idols—"would cease to exist, and your work will have been nothing." I couldn't tell if they were getting the message, so I added, "All this potential wasted. All the effort invested to change the world, to touch someone, to use your voice to advance mankind, meaningless. Everything you gave up for your writing, every hour away from family, gone."

Silence ruled in the cramped room, even as more of them came in, trickling pool water and stinking of death.

"Rosa." I turned to the opera singer who still sulked into her glass of red wine, her face pinched in a tragic expression, since BK reminded her of past fiascos. "No Italian opera as we know it. No *Gioconda*, no *Traviata*, and no you to interpret the music with your immense gift. You know why not? Because you won't have existed."

I wasn't even sure I was using the right tenses or grammar, because that concept of nonexistence was unprecedented.

The chock-full crowded room was like the setting of a horror film, as more glamorous dead pushed in. I didn't recognize most new faces, and those who were completely faceless made my skin crawl. My vision blurred. I could barely move or breathe in the thick air and the overwhelming stench of decomposition.

Grocery-store Rita had told me that the pool was full of grimy water and decay. Rita and the kids in town who refused to play around the property already knew what I was only now figuring out.

The pool would drown life, not with its water, but with the dead players arriving in their multitudes and taking over. They needed a bigger venue, because more of them planned to join the games and because more people had died than were currently living. Like gangrene that started in one toe and took over the foot, the leg, and the entire body, the dead would take over the world.

It was up to me to stop them coming. Up to me to destroy this place they called headquarters and smash everything in it before the rot spread to the rest of the world.

One living person, even as broken as me, had more importance and power than a thousand famous dead game players.

I took a deep breath in the suffocating air and even that little bit of oxygen cleared my mind. My broken body filled with the energy and power of the last hurrah.

"You had your chance," I said with new vigor. "Now stay dead and gone."

I reached over and grabbed the battle-axe from the sleeping Viking. Then I started smashing everything within reach.

57. Headquarters

I took a hard swing at the wall monitor, but only its corner broke off. The rest remained intact.

"The game board is too sturdy for a simple axe," Asimov said. "It's made from an indestructible element they found on Mercury in the last expedition."

A second swing kept the monitor intact. "No one landed on Mercury," I said. "You're lying."

"A new technology in this reality helped research in optics and enabled that landing," he said.

"Is this too sturdy?" I asked, hitting his game pad, which looked like a smartphone. It broke, and its small pieces soared around the room and landed on the carpet amid food scraps and spilled drinks.

"Hey, you shouldn't have done that," Asimov said.

I expected the dead players to show some gumption, to get up and fight me, but to my utter amazement, some started for the exit, leaving their game pads behind. I smashed another, then another, my satisfaction rising with each broken gadget. I felt liberated, infused with power.

Loud splashes came from the pool as, I assumed, they jumped back in. Those who remained in the conference room lost depth and flattened into cardboard figures, then folded into themselves and disintegrated to ash, like paper in a fireplace.

Rosa Ponselle was the last one standing. Her face wore tragedy as she lamented her defecting comrades with "*Nessun Dorma*," the most depressing opera aria ever. Then she also lost depth, withered like an autumn leaf and vanished.

I squinted. My sight was going, but I could still see the horrifying scene.

I kept swinging the axe left and right, not exactly seeing what I was smashing away, not caring what I hit, but determined to destroy headquarters in its entirety, along with their games.

Someone had joined me, swinging Betty's heavy cane like a pendulum, hitting bottles and sending food flying against the walls and ceiling. Was this another hallucination, or was this really her?

Sophie.

My dear old friend in her leather jacket and brown boots was mad and beautiful, and hungrily stuffing her face with slices of pizza she somehow saved from our demolition.

I rubbed my eyes in disbelief. "Are you alive?"

"I'm pretty dead, and I hate where I'm at," she said between chews and hits. "With this bunch of incompetent deadbeats and the monotony foods."

"Death didn't improve your grammar or hurt your appetite." I laughed despite the nausea and my darkening vision. It was like old times again because Sophie was by my side the way she was when we painted together the red door of the little house on Rose Avenue.

She dropped Betty's cane and fell on my neck, covering my face with kisses.

I choked up. "Sophie…" Nothing else mattered, if only for that moment.

She held me at arm's length, narrowing her eyes with concern. Water dripped from her long hair down her frightened face and onto her jacket. "When'd you die?"

I kissed both her hands, definitely Sophie's strong and industrious hands, with the green and blue paint embedded in the fissures. "I'm not dead yet."

"Oh good," she said. "I need you alive."

"Why does everyone need me alive?" I complained. "I'm not going on that stupid mission—"

"We're going home, Ellie." She gestured at the destruction with one hand. "Look what you've done. It's over." That was her voice all right, warm and full of life. "You look like shit. Where'd you get this woolly monstrosity and this hospital gown, and hey, where's your hair?"

"A casualty of this reality. I kind of got used to the buzz cut." I didn't tell her how cold I felt without it. "Why'd you leave me with your bitch sister?"

"Long story," she said. "I know how to take us home."

"They said it's impossible to smuggle a person back," I said. "Because you can't square a circle, or get the exact coordinates, or base a transition on its unintended consequences."

"Forget their excuses," Sophie said. "It's art, not science. Remember *sfumato* and *chiaroscuro*?"

"How could I forget the twins of special effects?"

Even the paint was peeling off the walls as the room disintegrated and melted in on itself. The place was deserted except for the two of us and the Viking woman, who was still asleep. She'd slept through the commotion and didn't hear a word, and I guessed, when you have no clue what's going on around you, you remain unaffected.

The monitor's screen continued to display images of green mountains, blue oceans, and sprawling fields of wild flowers. I prepared to take one last swing at it, but Sophie seized my arm.

"Look how the colors are more brilliant as they get closer to the eye." She pointed at the screen. "Look here at how the front image sharpens and the details blur as the objects recede. Da Vinci called it *sfumato*. The French called it *grisaille* and broadened the meaning to cover all strong contrasts in illumination between light and dark areas—"

"What's your point?" I snapped. "I'm dying and you're lecturing me on art techniques."

"*That's* my point. Triggering a transition and getting home to the right coordinates is no more than achieving the right color or perspective."

"Not following." My vision blurred as I tried to focus on the picture.

"Okay. You're alive and I'm dead. You're the light and I'm the shadow. We go back to our starting point, the situation that fucked us up in the first place. Our intention was to change the name on the headstone to Peggy's. That would either correct the coordinates and we'll find ourselves back home, or you know…"

"We cease to exist altogether," I completed. "You make it sound so easy. How come all those experts said it was impossible?"

"They're clueless," she said. "Those dead greats you so admire were put together to dazzle you. Writers and musicians. You see? Not a single visual artist who can paint a picture."

"Hitchcock knows his light and shadows."

"Did he help?"

"No," I said. "He called me the MacGuffin."

"Right. Hitch is the master of mind fuck and suspense." She flicked food crumbs off her jacket. "You got a ride?"

"I do." I grabbed the battle-axe. "One more thing."

I swung the weapon one last time, aiming at the center of the monitor. This time, it smashed to pieces. Headquarters was no more.

58. Decay

"Look, the pool is broken," Sophie said. "Even if I wanted to go back, I'm stuck here." Decomposition wafted from the water. In the moonlight, swarms of rats devoured unidentifiable debris.

"You're not going back." I lost my footing, and Sophie tightened her grip on my arm. "Supported by a dead woman," I muttered. "Way to go."

"What's wrong with you anyway?" she asked.

I quickly told her about the growing clot inside my head, about not being long for the world if I remained in the current reality. "We move forward with your plan," I said.

"Do you understand what happens if we get it wrong?" she asked.

"We cease from ever existing," I said, swinging the axe as I walked. "We've nothing to lose."

"I'm so sorry about everything, Ellie. You and Gina took such good care of me, and I was nothing but trouble. Miserable and jealous of you guys for having each other, but my life wasn't bad. Now look at the mess I made."

"It wasn't your fault," I said, deliberately aligning one foot in front of the other, careful not to stumble again. "Virgil warned me to stay sheltered from the red storm. He gave me quite a few chances to save us, still I insisted on doing my own thing."

I exhaled in relief when we were finally out on the sidewalk. The night bustled with energetic, living people who were enjoying the fun rides in the busy carnival. Kids were skateboarding up and down the street, licking ice cream on their way to ride the ever-turning Ferris wheel of paradise.

Behind us, Paradise Point Apartments was but a dark and fading blob. I couldn't tell whether or not it was still there.

A banged-up SUV slammed to a stop by the sidewalk. Peggy Sanders stepped out of it and grimaced at the red sign that used to flash but had gone dark.

"Your sister found me," I said. "Can she see you?"

"I'm not invisible," Sophie whispered from behind a fat tree. "What poor creature died for that coat?"

"Stay hidden," I said. "Jump into the car when I pass you."

Gina came out of the passenger's side and joined Peggy in front of the ruined building. I thought if they turned their heads they'd see me. And then they did.

"Here you are, Ellie." Peggy started slowly toward me, as if goading a wild animal onto a trap. "We've been looking for you all over the place. Your doctor is very worried about you."

"Leave me alone."

"It was silly of you to escape," Gina said in that husky voice that could still make me swoon. "Let's take you back for your surgery."

"Stay away." I raised the battle-axe. "I don't need your help."

While the distance was shrinking between me and the two determined to haul me back to the hospital, the pink Impala remained too far away where I'd left it, door open, engine running, keys inside. No one had stolen it, because no one could see it.

I put on some speed, feeling the carcass of my laptop crunch like bugs under my sneakers. Just as Peggy reached out her manicured hand to grab me, I tumbled into the car and slammed the door.

I backed up, nearly dragging her along, as she couldn't see me or the car. Peggy looked around, perplexed at my disappearance. As I neared the tree, Sophie came out from behind it and jumped into the passenger seat.

"My parents' home in Oxnard first," she said. "I have supplies from a sculpting class I took when we were ten. I hid them deep in the closet, where I hid the stuff I didn't want my sister to find."

"It's possible you never took that class in this reality," I reminded her.

"Then we'll find an open art store," she said.

"How do we actually do it?" I kept rubbing my eyes. The road ahead got darker with my shrinking field of vision, but I kept driving.

"We fill up the grooves of my engraved name with sculpting cement," she said, "wait for it to dry, then chisel Peggy's name instead."

"You should take over driving," I said.

"Stop at the curb," she said. "We're here."

Her parents' place was a little yellow house, or pink. It was hard to tell with only the dim streetlight glow and my dying eyes. Sophie pointed up at the second-floor window. "I used to sit up there and paint the mountains and the city."

"Your mom will kick me out," I said. I quickly told her about the fiasco I'd caused in Peggy's show and how I insulted her and her art.

Sophie laughed out loud. How I'd missed that sound.

"Make nice with my mom because she won't see me. Tell her Peggy sent you to get a few things from her room. She'll let you go up on your own because she hates it up there. We'll get my sculpting supplies and something for you to wear, then we'll be off."

My failing eyesight could be the reason, but Mrs. Sanders looked nothing like the well-dressed woman who attended Peggy's show. In a stained house dress, hair in disarray and without her makeup, she seemed like an old woman who had endured a hard life. The snoring from deep inside the house, I assumed, belonged to Mr. Sanders.

"You!" She glared coldly, not seeing Sophie next to me. "What are you doing here?"

I said, "I apologized to Peggy for my awful behavior, and she sent me here to fetch one of her old paintings to add to the show."

"Her stuff is in her room, but I can't climb those stairs. Get what she wants, then lock the door behind you." She gave me a grim appraisal, obviously in disbelief at her daughter's bad taste in friends. "I'm off to bed."

As soon as she was gone, Sophie attacked the refrigerator, eating straight from containers.

"Want some?" she asked between bites.

The sight of her making a pig of herself made me sick to my already queasy stomach. "She'll think I ate the food."

"It won't matter, will it?" Sophie kept stuffing her face. "We'll either be dead or alive in another reality."

"Come on, we don't have time," I begged.

As Virgil had promised, our essence remained the same. Even dead, here was Sophie, eating away. I kept searching for signs of madness or deceit in her, finding none in the gravy-covered face, nothing but my dear old friend scarfing her way through what may be the last moments of both her dead and living existence. I smiled despite my approaching demise.

"Heaven isn't a culinary experience," she explained between bites and swallows. "The vending machines are crap."

"Vending machines?"

"You use those fake plastic coins that drop into the wrong holes, and whatever falls out tastes like cardboard. They love those game nights because they get to eat real food."

She wiped mashed potatoes from her face and left the empty containers in the sink.

The walls swam around me like breathing rubber as I followed her, lightheaded, down a dark hallway and up a steep narrow stairway into the attic.

The little room was a shrine to the twins. Two side by side beds were draped with colorful bedcovers. Sophie slid open the closet door, exposing painted canvases, crammed against one another. She pulled them out, one at a time, and threw them on the beds. They were Peggy's work, dark and serious with occasional angelic fluff.

I let the coat and the hospital gown slide to the floor and wore a huge T-shirt and a pair of jeans I assumed belonged to Peggy.

A notebook flew at me. "My diary." Sophie glanced back. "Want to correct my spelling?"

Despite my growing headache, a smile of new hope twisted my lips. "I missed you."

I leafed through pages covered in childish writing, but I couldn't discern the words. I left it on the bed. Wherever we ended up, Sophie would have no use for old diaries.

"It's all here." She held up a plastic shopping bag. "Let's go."

We left the room in a shambles and descended the staircase, crept through the darkened house—now reverberating with two sets of snoring—and hurried to the pink Impala.

"Drive, please." I sat in the passenger seat, my head back.

Time was running out. Once I joined Sophie in death, we'd lose our advantage of an operation requiring one human from death and one from life. We didn't have BK to push that certain function on his game pad and cause a red storm, but... What was this? A zigzag painted the sky such bright red, I could see it. The red storm already started.

"Quickly," I whispered. "Step on it."

"Don't you dare die on me," Sophie said. "We're almost home."

"Almost home," I echoed.

"How fragile we are," Sophie said. "In a few hours we could be anywhere in the world. We may not know each other."

I said, "What exactly happened to you back in the cemetery?"

"I saw my name on the headstone for the first time and I totally lost my shit. When I fell face down on the grass and cried, a hand grabbed mine and when I opened my eyes, you were gone and everything changed. I thought you were playing a dirty trick on me, taking revenge for the nasty things I said—"

"I thought the same about you." I could barely hear my voice.

She said, "I was moving like I do when I smoke too much weed or when I dream and people and words and colors from my waking hours creep in and rearrange themselves in totally twisted ways."

"Like that Halloween we dressed up as Ugolino and Ruggieri, and you were eating my brain?" I was floating with the sway of the Impala.

"Not creepy like that. Like…"

I opened my aching eyes enough to see her right hand painting forms and movements in the air between us.

"More like regular scary, which is scarier than creepy scary. I did nothing, maybe blinked and there was West Hollywood on an ordinary night with the gay couples holding hands and kissing and it was totally normal, like the music from the bars on Santa Monica was loud, but I knew I was dead because suddenly I'm seeing David Bowie through the window at McDonald's eating French fries, like he was alive. No one was bothering him. What the fuck, you know?"

"David Bowie, wow," I said. She was acting out her story, as usual, and I couldn't get enough of her.

"And Tina Turner humming to herself right there in the store that sells the hoodoo voodoo crystals where Little Frida's used to be. It was unreal how you could talk to celebrities and see how they die just like us. It was exciting at first. In life we make them into gods…"

"Death is the great equalizer," I muttered.

"I'm not ready, Ellie, for all that space of being dead. I so miss those nights with Gina and you."

"I missed you too, Soph. You can't imagine how much." I couldn't help smiling.

"Why are you smiling?"

"For a moment, you reminded me of that night we had tequila shots and you were going on about that sitter of yours, Aphrodite."

"She was incredible," she said. "But my best work was *Love in Titian Red*. I turned your beautiful hair into the background." She rubbed my head. "Sorry about your hair. What I wouldn't do to get back to that night and *not* go to the cemetery."

"Let's just fix things." A glimpse in the rear view mirror made me shudder. A black SUV with a loose front bumper followed us. "They're on our tail," I said.

"Can they suddenly see us?"

"I don't know," I said.

The gravel crackled under the Impala, then we stopped.

"Can you walk?" She offered me a helping hand.

The smell of freshly mowed grass filled my nostrils. Around us, helium balloons floated above headstones and bumped into each other like butting heads.

Sophie asked, "What idiot decorates a headstone with floating balloons?"

The world was dark, and I was moving in thick water, fighting the sucking swirls of undercurrents.

Sophie chuckled. "You won't need the axe."

I looked down. Yes, to my surprise, I was holding it.

I let her lead. I could barely feel my feet as we made our way through tall headstones and dead dreams. My own life was seeping away, but I had to remain alive for the mission to succeed. Sophie couldn't do it alone. One from death, one from life would trigger our old reality back into existence.

She pointed at a cluster of red tendrils in the sky. "Here's our once-in-a-red-lightning chance."

I could barely see, but I felt the blood-red in the suffocating air. Then we were at the headstone.

Lying beside the grave, the grass cool and soft beneath me, I watched as Sophie filled in her name with wet cement. She wiped her hands on her jeans and turned to me.

"Quick," I said, but I couldn't hear myself.

Sophie sat by my side and held my hand. "It should dry before I chisel in Peggy's name."

"Paint it on," I said. "Please make it work."

Sophie dipped a thin paintbrush in black oil paint and scribbled *Peggy* where her own name used to be.

"What now, Ellie? I should do something with more oomph." She pumped her fist. "What am I doing wrong?"

My head shuddered with jackhammers and loud explosions. I raised myself on a shaky elbow and blinked to clear my vision. Peggy's painted name was right, but the inscription was wrong. What was wrong with it?

Here rest's, Peggy Sanders our little angel gone too soon.

"Tell me how to fix it." Her voice clashed with the drill inside my skull. "Please, stay with me."

I could see it.

"Don't you dare die on me." Sophie's eyes were round with fear.

"One spelling, one grammar," I said.

Red tendrils of lightning broke through ocean waves of nausea.

All was lost.

"Drop the apostrophe." My voice rasped out. "And that comma."

"I can't hear you," Sophie said.

The fragrance of Wild Rose overwhelmed me. A second face joined Sophie's in my field of vision, a face from my long ago childhood, pure, beautiful, loving.

Angie Mead coming to say, *I told you so.*

The end of civilization, Ms. Angie, comes down to a punctuation mark or two.

I couldn't let it be the end. Not yet.

In a wild Hail Mary move and with that burst of energy sometimes given to the dying, I lifted up the battle-axe and slammed it down with all my might on the headstone. Once, then a second time, until it toppled.

The sky lit bright crimson.

The new face came closer and she wasn't Ms. Angie at all, but Gina. My beloved Gina.

"Three-legged tripod again," I said. "Take me home."

And Gina took me to home to paradise with that gravelly voice I had so longed to hear. "I love you, Elektra," she said. "Always and forever."

Nothing hurt.

My path toward the light was made of fading memories. The jackhammers gave way to the gentle sounds of ocean waves on a hot summer morning.

He waited for me, as wide as he was tall, all beachy in his flip-flops and his colorful Hawaiian shirt. The blue bandana around his forehead featured greenish whales. His smile was sunshine and when his huge, warm hand wrapped around mine, I wasn't afraid.

"Am I dead?" I asked.

"We'll see," he said. "How do you feel?"

"A tiny bit disappointed," I said. "I never got to see Bette Davis as Miss Scarlett."

His round face contorted in disgust. "It was awful. You missed nothing."

I asked, "Do they really call you the Big Kahuna?"

"It ain't what they call you, it's what you answer to."

"Who is W. C. Fields?" I replied, Jeopardy-style.

"Correct, the board is yours, Elektra," he said.

We bantered back and forth, until magical rainbows, painted in Sophie's pastels, appeared all around us. We floated above a shimmering blue ocean sprinkled with lush tropical islands of palm trees and ever-blooming purple Jacarandas.

All the while, the gravelly low voice spoke words that clung to my consciousness with the claws of life, "It's you, always and forever."

60. Silver Shoes

Beatrice Portinari—dead for more than seven centuries but still excited by new challenges—flipped her shiny hair left and right and smiled at her own reflection. No wonder he'd written two great masterpieces for me, she thought. No wonder artists repeatedly painted this face and this figure. Dressed fashionably in a Prada pantsuit and stilettos by the same designer, she was ready for her new career of managing IsolaVista, a high-end resort hotel in a picturesque locale.

She wheeled her packed suitcase out of the back room and surveyed the destruction in headquarters with the detached amusement of one who didn't have to clean up.

Ellie was nowhere in sight. All the house members were gone except the Viking woman who snored away, feet on the table.

Rats and insects swarmed the oval table and the littered carpet, eating pizza crumbs and lapping up spilled cocktails. They had food to sustain them for weeks.

The Viking emitted a loud snort and opened her eyes, but did not see Beatrice standing there. She mumbled in her ancient language, "Crazy living people," or something to that extent and stood to leave. On her way out, she stepped on a still-functional game pad with her big dirty foot. Soon afterward, the heavy splash of a jump announced her return to the pool of life and death.

Beatrice stared at the stepped-on game pad. It was larger than the others and sturdy enough to have survived both the great demolition and the recent massive foot. That particular game pad belonged to the Big Kahuna, and it had enormous battery power. Its sensitive buttons were meant to be pushed gently and only once, to enable or disable transitions.

Now one of those buttons was lit and stuck down with the glue of sticky food and syrupy drinks. What should she do?

As she hesitated, a drunk rat swayed on its wobbly feet and vomited on the game pad. She recoiled in revulsion. The rat dropped on top of the gadget, asleep or dead from the poison of alcohol. About to kick it off the game pad, Beatrice paused to admire her perfect small foot in the glittering silver shoe. The Big Kahuna be damned. In the near millennium she'd been around, fashion was her one true god, and she could not bring herself to touch a puke-smeared dead rat with her new Pradas.

What would happen next was anyone's guess.

Virgil resented her for her role in *The Divine Comedy*. He'd been robbed of Paradise, or so he claimed for centuries. He was quite capable of taking Dante all the way home without her involvement. Let's see him complain again when he and his new recruits have to troubleshoot what comes next.

She was done manipulating human history.

Beatrice was giddy as she closed the door on the mess and rolled her suitcase behind her.

"To hell with control games," she said out loud. "Let's have some surprises."

About to jump into the pool, she pinched her nose in disgust. The moonlight shone bright on the putrid, muddy water of a mode of transportation that had lost its functionality. No wonder, with all the extra recent activity.

She dialed for a ride to her new destination as she turned and sauntered out to the street. The glittering lights of the ongoing carnival illuminated her silver shoes and made them glow like hundreds of stars.

Maybe Paradise

From those holiest waters I returned
to her reborn, a tree renewed, in bloom
with newborn foliage, immaculate,

Eager to rise, now ready for the Stars.

The Divine Comedy, Dante Alighieri

6i. Rebirth

"It's you, always and forever," whispered the gravelly voice in the dream.

Ella Brooke opened her eyes in the sunny bedroom of her new house on the cliffs of Palos Verdes, high above the ocean. Morning light filled the room and glittered on Max's fur. His front paws on her chest, he thoroughly licked the right side of her face. Indie, black as soot, was licking her left ear.

"Are you two trying to drown me?" She sat up in bed and pulled both cocker spaniels into a hug. "Geez, what a nightmare. I died in my dream." She stuck her nose in Indie's fur. "But it was just a dream."

The dogs tilted their heads and lifted their heavy ears.

Today was special. Why was it special? Because tonight, she'd return to her alma mater as a celebrity and read from *My Death and Rebirth* to a group of UCLA students and their guests.

"I hope my audience will give me as much loving attention," she said to the dogs.

The vivid nightmare gnawed at her, clinging to her consciousness like the memory of real events. In the dream, she had been visiting Santa Barbara with three close friends to celebrate the publication of her first novel. Two of the women were identical twins. The first was a bully, the second was dead, and the third woman was her true love. In the dream, she'd had a miserable headache, but she was free of it now.

Her vivid dreams sometimes turned to stories. There must be a story in that last one.

Why did a dream about a group of friends feel like a memory when she'd never actually been part of such a group? Her mother was her only friend. Her social skills were nil, because she'd buried herself in books during her formative years. In high school and college, when her classmates had sex, drugs and rock 'n' roll, Ella studied, read, and fiddled with writing fiction.

She'd observe families or groups of friends—celebrating birthdays and holidays together, frolicking on the beach, playing in the park—and she'd feel like an outsider looking in. During the holidays, she'd have a quick dinner with her mother, then take solitary walks in the streets. She'd stop to stare at big, light-filled houses with people celebrating inside and kids playing ball in the garden. She always wanted to be part of a loud family, part of others' lives, but she had chosen the solitude of a writer, and loneliness came with the territory.

Her efforts finally paid off. She had a published book, money, and even some fame. Still, she was lonely.

The question remained: Why did the dream feel like a memory of friendship when she had no such memories?

She couldn't turn on her side and linger in that strange dreamland, because the dogs wanted their kibble and a walk. When she stood, both jumped to the floor—Indie heavy with puppies.

A worn-out paperback rested on her nightstand. Her mother must have left it for her last night. She leafed through it. It was smudged with food and drink stains. What slob had pre-owned it? She chuckled at the title: *Fucking My Way Through Life*. It sounded promising, but Max was pulling at her pajama leg. *Take me for a walk, Mommy.*

She dropped the book back on her nightstand, cleaned herself up, and pulled on her yoga pants and a T-shirt. She walked the dogs on the beach trail by the lighthouse. Wild mustard weeds grew taller than her head in a landscape turned green by recent rains.

Tall weeds were in her dream.

She stood still, the dogs following suit, as slivers of the dream nagged at her. At one point, she'd been visiting a little house with just such tall weeds in its garden. A beautiful woman she loved waited for her at the open red door. Who was the woman?

Back in the house, the mouth-watering aroma of baking wafted from her mother's kitchen. Camille had again made the heavenly chocolate chip cookies she'd recently learned to bake in a cooking class at IsolaVista, the nearby resort hotel. She'd befriended Beatrice, the elegant hotel manager, and the two of them would curl smoke rings, shoot the breeze, and exchange recipes.

Beatrice had read Ella's book and said she was looking forward to her next novel, but people said such things without meaning them.

Ella sipped coffee with her mother by the gleaming pool.

"Did you leave a book on my nightstand?" she asked.

"What book?" Camille asked.

"I guess not. I wonder where it came from."

Pregnant Indie plopped down next to them, and they talked excitedly about the black noses, needle teeth, and puppy breath that would soon reduce them to baby talk. They planned to keep all the puppies.

Ella ran fingers through her recently chopped hair. Even that simple motion reminded her of the woman she'd loved in her dream, and of the book on her nightstand with the dog-eared pages. The book, the dream, and the woman were connected. Why or how?

Far off in the turquoise ocean, the sleeping dragon of Catalina Island rested in its eternal slumber. Ella imagined it opening its yellow eyes, spreading its wings, and flying along the majestic California coastline. Hmm. That might make a good story.

She'd bought the house from the advance on her first literary success and moved her mother into her own apartment on the ground floor. Camille tended the garden with expertise and planned to eventually make a good living selling marijuana to friends and neighbors.

This home she'd created for Camille and herself was heaven, but her real paradise was inside her, in finally being allowed to write without the anxiety of having to make a living.

Today, however, there wasn't much time to enjoy the view. She finished her coffee and headed up to her study, an oasis at the top of the spiral staircase. Indie waddled behind her with proud papa-to-be Max at her side. No one knew for sure whether or not Max was the biological puppy daddy, but the two were inseparable at the shelter, and Max never left Indie's side. Ella adopted them both.

Up in the study, the dogs curled up by her side and into each other. She scratched their ears. *My Death and Rebirth* had been a breeze, its writing guided by a divine hand. The second book wasn't as easy. The clock was ticking on a looming deadline and Ella, too busy admiring herself for her recent success, barely had the first draft.

That worn paperback with the curious title—where did it come from, and who was its author? Yeah, another distraction, but she had to know.

"Stay," she told the dogs who'd gotten up to follow her. "I'll be right back."

She hopped down to her bedroom, then ran back up the spiral staircase, book in hand. She sat on the floor between the sleeping dogs and opened the book to the title page:

Fucking My Way Through Life by Elektra Brooke.

Chills. The author's name was so close to hers . . . How could that be?

A dedication read:

For Gina and Sophie, my pillars of strength, who were the reason I could write in the first place. And to Virgil.

Below the dedication, an inscription puzzled her even more. It was strange and, what's more, *in her own handwriting.*

May you find your paradise and the love that moves the sun and the other stars, Elektra Brooke via Dante Alighieri.

She smoked the occasional joint from her mother's crops, liked a glass of red wine with her dinner, but she'd never suffered alcoholic blackouts, so what was that about? How could she explain this? The autograph and the vaguely familiar handwritten inscription, echoed that vivid dream with the lingering effect. The dream flowed and ebbed, died away and came back like a memory of a former life. She didn't exactly believe in reincarnation, although she'd written about it in her first, now published book.

She read and re-read the inscription, reading herself into a trance-like state. She leafed through the book, yet kept returning to the author's name. Elektra, with her own last name. What was the connection between this book and the tenacious dream?

Ella didn't have friends close enough to play practical jokes on her, which would have been the only logical explanation.

She'd promised herself to finish the first draft of the second book today, but the mystery was killing her. She grabbed a cushion from the couch, made herself comfortable, and began reading.

Fucking My Way Through Life captured her full attention from the first line. It was a guilty-pleasure page-turner she could not put down. It was also familiar. She laughed out loud at the witty narrative and the zingy, risqué dialogue. She recited a few lines, after barely glancing at them, then further lines came back to her, ones she hadn't read yet. Now she was freaking out for real.

She melted with sudden sorrow at the story of a magical tree, and nights in a little house with a red door and sticky windows, and a beloved woman whispering poetry by the fireplace. She remembered a dear friend telling stories while waving a spatula over her head and raining bits of food on a kitchen floor that had one creaky bamboo board. Kernels of those stories had seeded this novel she was now reading.

But how? There was only one of her, and she hadn't lived that life.

Two hours later, she read the last line and closed the book, satisfied, as if having read her own work, finding it brilliant. She wanted to have written that novel.

What if she had? Somehow, somewhere, hypothetically, she could have written the novel, couldn't she? If she poked that idea with a stick, even her name, Ella, could be derived from Elektra.

The copyright verso page with the publisher's info was so worn out and smudged with coffee and food stains, she couldn't read a word.

She checked the internet for the book. Spell check kept changing the word *fucking* to *falling* and *feeding*. The book didn't exist in any published form—print, electronic, or out-of-print hardback. It had never been published, so how did she have a paperback?

As she was in the habit of emailing herself every new draft of her work, she looked for answers in her email accounts. She opened the mail app and clicked *search mail* at the top. Just for laughs she typed, *Fucking My Way Through Life.*

To her utter astonishment, a single email, sent from her, appeared in the search results. It contained an attached file—FMWTL. The file opened without a password.

She ran eager eyes over the manuscript. The fonts . . . the overly organized table of contents . . . those formatting peculiarities could only be hers. Who else made fussy footnotes in red Arial Narrow and called them *notes to self*? Who else wrote *missed opportunities, get real, gratuitous sex,* and *enough with the word* flabbergasted *already*?

So the book had *not* been published and—she couldn't believe what she was thinking—it was hers to publish even though she didn't remember having written it. Would that be theft? Theft from whom? That question was like the one about a bear shitting in the woods.

"Not another me," she concluded, her imagination running wild. "Rather, another reality altogether."

She *had* written this book in some parallel world, and the universe was handing her the beautiful gift along with that peculiar dream.

In case the kind universe changed its mind, she printed a hard copy of the manuscript, stuck it in a manila envelope and slipped it into her desk drawer. If the manuscript was still there in the morning, it was hers to publish. She'd wait a month or two to make it seem legit, then submit it to her publisher as her second of the two-book deal.

A question remained. Who had left the book on her nightstand?

62. Beatrice

B eatrice Portinari sat next to Camille Brooke, her new best friend. Folding white chairs were arranged in wide rows in front of the podium, and the library quickly filled up for the event honoring UCLA alum Ella Brooke, who was scheduled to read from her madly successful coming-of-age novel *My Death and Rebirth*.

Beatrice scanned the growing crowd and waited for the star of the show to appear in her new fusion of existence.

She recalled the last postmortem.

The Big Kahuna had stormed into the boardroom. Without his usual jokes and travel stories, he poured himself a hefty shot of Sambuca and drank it straight down.

"My machine is lost," he said, furious. "No more game nights."

Beatrice didn't want to open a can of worms by pointing out the obvious. Why didn't BK the almighty think of going back to the ruins of old HQ to search for his precious game pad? Had he already commissioned game genius Chaos to build him a similar, new one?

They still needed to find a new headquarters, inconspicuous, yet large enough for their growing numbers, and it had to have an adaptable swimming pool.

She had barely suppressed a deviant little smile. She hadn't said anything about having seen headquarters destroyed, the big foot stepping on the master game pad and gunking it up with the glue of rat puke and syrupy drinks. Unless she said something, that pad would never be found, and without it, they couldn't play Transitions or place bets.

In her new gig, chosen by her, Beatrice became the manager of IsolaVista, the luxury beach resort in scenic Palos Verdes. At that last meeting, she'd claimed to be checking the option of converting the resort's pool for the purpose of renewing the stalled games. She had deceived them all, BK, the House...

In truth, she only meant to remain close to her favorite author by befriending her mother. She and Ellie hadn't started on the best of terms, but Beatrice was impressed by Ellie's courage and decency even at the worst of times. Ellie always did the right thing. Now she, Beatrice, would do the same.

"Without the games, we've only movies and books to pass the great eternity," BK had said.

"No, no." The House members moaned and some shed tears.

Beatrice had kept silent. She recounted her crimes against the House, among them, leaving the scene of a demolition, concealing information, creating a paradox.

She'd done it all for the sake of Ellie—Ella in this transition—who now made her appearance in the library at UCLA, dressed smartly in the blue business suit of a political candidate and low heel pumps in a matching hue. Ella lowered her head, accepting applause, smiled and gave her short blond bob a sexy shake. This hairstyle suited her better than the very long version of her home reality or the buzz cut of the last one.

"My dear mother, Camille Brooke," she said. "I would not be standing here without your support or your homegrown weed."

Camille, a willowy old hippie wearing a big cloud of white hair and a flowing flowery dress, stood and waved to her daughter's crowd, enjoying a round of applause.

Beatrice leaned back in her uncomfortable chair. Ellie, now Ella, had fought to near-death for her paradise and got very close to it. By destroying headquarters, Ellie, now Ella, had single-handedly stopped the practice of Transitions, while remaining oblivious to her triumph.

Or was she oblivious? Were her memories of past lives wiped clean? Beatrice wasn't sure, and it didn't matter. Now she'd do what she could to lead Ella all the way home.

Last night, she had stood over Ella's sleeping form—it wasn't easy, what with both dogs guarding her—and weaved a long and tenacious dream that would linger in her mind all day long. Had she opened the door to a reality that was better forgotten?

She then placed the one inscribed copy of *Fucking My Way Through Life* on the nightstand. She hoped that Ella would read it, somehow recognize her own brilliance and have it re-published in this reality. Far-fetched, she knew. Ella would more likely toss the book aside and forget about it. No damage there, as it already enjoyed its place of honor in the Cosmic Library.

Ella read in a firm and intimate voice the chapter depicting the moment she had realized her losses. Beatrice, who knew that part by heart, silently recited along word for word. She so enjoyed Ella's fresh interpretation of the afterlife, images drawn simply from dreams. It was all there, down to the symbolic jump into a pool as a way of transport from death to life and back. The long swim to the other side was an extended metaphor for the depths of boredom in idle eternity.

"Sounds like my marriage," a smart-assed woman deadpanned. Voices chanted their agreement.

In the Q&A, the audience asked the usual questions. "Where do you get your stories?" and, "Is your book autobiographical?" etcetera. Once you'd published, people believed you had the answers, and maybe you did, because the questions kept coming, and Ella's answers were kind and thoughtful.

"Most of my stories come from dreams," she said.

"Are dreams important?" asked a man in a baseball cap.

"Embrace the lingering dream because it may be a prophecy," Ella said and heads nodded in agreement. Beatrice grinned. Ella really had a knack for the whole author song and dance. "A vivid dream that scrambles the elements of our lives into different combinations is the universe's way of handing us the gift of endless possibilities."

"What about alternate realities?" another reader asked.

"Various realities may exist." Ella took a dainty sip of water. "But in essence, we remain who we are from one reality to another."

Did Ella make it up or actually believe she's lived another reality? Beatrice didn't know.

"Can you give us an example?" the woman asked.

"Of course," Ella said. "You may be attracted to your friend's wife or husband. That attraction may mean that somewhere, sometime in another life, you used to be together and love each other."

"But what's the purpose of it all?" another asked.

Ella smiled. "I like to imagine a tribune of bored angels who play games with the living for entertainment, while gorging themselves on earthly food and drink."

The crowd laughed, but not Beatrice. This Q&A was getting ridiculous, with Ella laying it on thick, talking too much and enjoying the sound of her own voice.

"What's the truth about heaven?" a woman in a miniskirt asked.

"Heaven is what we make of it," Ella said. "For most of us, heaven is purgatory at best."

Enough. Beatrice stood up. "Ms. Brooke," she said. Now that all eyes were on her, she jutted out her hip like a runway model. In her favorite Armani, her hair down, she felt particularly attractive. "Ms. Brooke, I loved your first book. What about your second?"

"Funny you should ask, Bea," Ella said, smiling. "An old project of mine is tucked away in my drawer, and I'm about to start rewrites. It's an"—she leaned toward the crowd to confide in a loud whisper—"an erotic, picaresque novel I started long ago."

"Yes, yes, you should publish it," eager voices called out.

Beatrice relaxed into her uncomfortable chair, having managed to get Ella off the dangerous subjects of bored angels and alternate realities. Her plan was working. Ella had read the book and she'd promised her readers; therefore, *Fucking My Way* would have to be republished.

No, Beatrice concluded. Ella didn't remember her past lives or having written that book. Yet, she recognized her work the way a mother would know her long-lost child, even grown up.

"*My Death and Rebirth* is like the story of my life." The gravelly voice came from the direction of a woman in a tight white business suit. "Ms. Brooke, your journey is mine."

Eight hundred years of fashion sensibilities screamed in Beatrice's head, *Too tight, too white, but what a sexy sight.*

Suddenly serious, Ella said, "I'd like to hear about your journey."

"I'll buy you a drink later," the woman said, and the crowd exploded in laughter.

Beatrice laughed along, but Ella remained serious and held her breath—trying to place the woman? Recognizing her?

"What's your name?" Ella asked.

"Gina Caldwell. I teach medieval poetry two nights a week. You're welcome to sit in on my class."

"I may do that," Ella said, breathless.

A string-bean tall California blonde in shorts jumped up, towering over the crowd. "Gina, you're fan-girling again," she said in a perky voice.

"I am," Gina said.

"How can she write the next novel if she wastes time on your Dante class?" the string-bean asked. "Hi, I'm Sophie Sanders."

"Are you also a teacher, Sophie?" Ella asked.

"Life drawing," Sophie said. "I won't make you take my class," she mocked good-heartedly. Gina raised a middle finger at her. "But I can help her buy you that drink at *L'Inferno.*"

"I'll be there," Ella said.

Then the Q&A was over. A line formed, and Ella signed copy after copy of *My Death and Rebirth.*

Beatrice watched from afar, satisfied. Her mission was complete, as Ella was finally pointed in the right direction. Home.

Red storms and transitions were disabled forever. From now on, history would unfold as it may. No more jackpots, no game nights, no unintended consequences. No longer would new variables be introduced into history. Only the untouchable past would inform the future. Big arguments would often lead to wars, but also to medical innovations, to quirky surprises, and to those whimsical delights that made life worth the trouble.

63. L'Inferno

Ella signed books, the entire time thinking of the secret manuscript in her drawer. Would it still be there tonight? She smiled up at strangers. "Please make it to Mindy." "To Sandra." Some didn't even say please.

"Hi, again." Gina Caldwell offered her hand for a shake. The tiny smile in her eyes, that one uneven tooth, that delicate scent of wild roses . . . Ella had a brief flash of memory, and what she remembered made her so weak at the knees, she thanked the chair beneath her.

She swallowed hard. "Hi again to you."

The blonde string bean popped her head out from behind Gina's raised white collar. "Hey, there." Her rough hand was creased with blue and green.

Ella wanted to find out more about these two. Gina and Sophie—their voices and vibes—bridged the way into that ever-gnawing world of the dream. She wanted them to not be a couple.

Gina said, "You promised to join us at *L'Inferno*."

"Gina owns the bar," Sophie bragged. "And it's making her tons of money."

"That's crass, honey," Gina scolded her.

The endearment confused Ella. Was that a love *honey* or a friend *honey*?

Ella signed another copy. "I'll see you there when I'm done," she said.

"It's walking distance," Sophie said. "You can't miss the graffiti sign." She bragged, "I painted it."

Forty-five minutes later, she signed the last book, then she was on her way to meet her new friends.

Indeed, who could miss that sign? Ella marveled at the huge *L'Inferno* painted on the side of the building in red blood dripping font and below it, *Lasciate ogne speranza, voi ch'intrate.*

"Abandon all hope, ye who enter here," she translated out loud, shuddering.

With urgency, she hurried in. Once inside, she recalled another rippling nugget from that prophetic dream in which she'd been lost in an alien universe. Not only that painted wall outside, but also inside ... those jumping movie clips, Doré's illustrations for the *Commedia*, skulls and roses, even that dangling pair of Roman caligae. Virgil's sandals...

Ella had another flash. That mysterious tattered book she didn't remember writing was dedicated to three people.

Gina, Sophie and Virgil.

In the dream, the dead had formed a long line, resting on their exhausting journey through purgatory. Ella's breath fluttered in fear as she looked around, searching for faceless, slow moving travelers.

Not in this place. This place was alive, noisy, animated.

An arm linked with hers. "Cool, isn't it?" Sophie asked, as if they'd known each other for ages. "Nouveau Kitsch."

"A bit heavy-handed on the Divine Comedy motif," Ella said.

"I know, right?" Sophie said with pride. "I decorated. I'd like to teach my classes here, but the place isn't large enough for all my students."

"Where's Gina?" Ella asked, searching.

"Working the room," Sophie said. "Let's wait for her at the bar."

Gina glowed in the dark like a white angel as she chatted at a corner booth with hippie Camille and the elegant Bea.

"Come meet my mother and her new bestie," Ella said. Sophie followed.

Camille's face lit up, no doubt happy to see her daughter, the recluse, socializing like a normal person.

"Stay as long as you want," Bea said. "I'll drive your mom home."

"Thanks," Ella said. "Mama, call me if Indie has her puppies and I'll be there."

The big bartender—his name tag said BK—wore a whale-patterned blue bandana and an Hawaiian shirt. He looked like the Death character from her dream. Just another coincidence in a day full of those.

"Hey, boss." He handed Gina a bottle. "The good stuff."

At a corner table, Gina poured three glasses and lit a joint Ella recognized as her mother's product.

"How did you two meet?" Ella pointed at Sophie, then at Gina.

"Sophie took my class," Gina said, then she laughed. "No, no, no. We're just good friends."

Sophie giggled. "You're not that far off, though. Gina and my bitch sister just broke up."

Ella gasped. "You have a bitch sister?"

"My twin," Sophie said.

Just like in her dream!

Gina, so beautiful with her shining eyes, said, "In fact, at this very moment Peggy the dog hater is packing up to move out and I'm giving her space. I mean, how can you live with a person who doesn't do baby talk when she sees a puppy? She doesn't and I can't, so I replaced her."

"Replaced her with Sophie?" Ella wanted to make sure.

"No," Gina said. "With Brady, a golden retriever rescue."

"I'll soon have a bucketful of puppies at home," Ella said. "You're both invited to baby-talk to them."

"Puppies melt me," Gina said.

The three toasted their new friendship.

"Please join us tomorrow," Sophie said. "We're going to Santa Barbara to drop off some of my paintings at a group show." Sophie gestured as she spoke, reminding Ella of the unnamed protagonist in that mysterious paperback she had somehow written.

Ella recoiled in sudden dread. A trip to Santa Barbara would be too much like that lingering dream. She couldn't, wouldn't, mess with fate.

She smiled at her new friends. "Thanks, but I have a prior engagement."

In the dark space with its jumpy clips of horrors, she felt like she'd known the two since childhood.

Gina's eyes burned in the semi-sweet chocolate darkness. "What you said before in the Q&A, about people having known each other in another life . . . I feel that way about the two of us. Like we used to know each other, you and I."

Gina's full lips were slightly open. Ella's heart quickened in response and she made a move toward the coming kiss.

Time slowed, and she knew, the dream hadn't been a dream at all, but a memory of real events. She had lived another life, and in it, she'd written that picaresque novel now hidden in her drawer. Sophie had been her best friend and Gina, the love of her life. The memory of warm lights flickered in her mind and the sort of love that could move the universe and stop the stars.

The End

What If?

An Alternative Ending

64. Transition

Shouts came from the street. "The sky is red! Come look!"

Thunder rumbled and shook the floor, the ceiling and the painted walls with the jumping film clips.

The room darkened with her vision, people and objects turned fuzzy around the edges and faded away.

65. The Bridge

It was twilight on a hot day, and the noisy city was alive with the hawking of street merchants, the clucking of chickens, the singing of the gondoliers on the Grand Canal below.

An old man walked slowly toward her, huffing and puffing from the weight of the precious package.

"Take it from him," a voice said behind her.

Her anger boiled. She'd refused the mission, and they'd sent her anyway.

As she turned to give the dead smuggler a piece of her mind, the man carrying the manuscript tripped on her foot, the precious bundle fell from his hands and its wrapper tore open. The pages scattered aside and away from him.

The man's cries of despair were drowned by the hollering street vendors. Carefully, lovingly illustrated pages became crumples under rushing heavy boots and the squeaky wheels of a passing carriage. Some pages flew up and away with the afternoon breeze, some slowly landed among debris and garbage and were soon swallowed by the dirty water of the canal, lost forever.

66. Virgil

His airborne Tesla was packed with new recruits—three freshly deceased, wide-eyed and eager to discover their postmortem talents. The fourth was Chaos, a long-dead, computer-savvy girl, who in life had been a hacker and in death, had developed the original game of Transitions by finding a way to hop back in time.

The ride was smooth, but Virgil remembered a reality in which Tesla was nicknamed Asshole Wheels. He couldn't remember why.

The five were on their way from the rubble of old HQ, where they'd found the live game pad underneath the skeleton of a dead rat, renewable battery going strong. A sensitive function was stuck down on that fated, last programmed transition. Virgil had immediately removed the battery, but it was too late.

Dr. Gina Caldwell, the love of Ellie's life, once spoke of what would happen to a world without Dante. Before her, Ms. Angie Mead had told her little students that the wrong word could end civilizations. Ellie believed them both, and they were right. As it happened, cities crumbled to dust, and the end of civilization came because of one drunk rat.

Ellie had been sent against her will back in time to Venice, Italy, 1554. She resisted, a glitch happened, and as a result, Dante's masterpiece was lost to both the living and the dead.

The present reality was a fiasco. Nothing worth living for remained in the world. No pizza, no ice cream, no football, no

Renaissance, no wars, and therefore, very few medical innovations. Without penicillin, people died from simple dental infections.

The magnificent creature named Beatrice Portinari had died at childbirth, as she had before, but without Dante's works, she'd lived her short life and died in total anonymity.

Virgil navigated the flying Tesla with his usual ease to a certain spot in the Northwestern Quarter-Sphere, the former Venice, California.

Venice to Venice, he thought, and that symmetry somehow comforted him in his sorrow.

He started his descent as soon as the purple-violet blooms were visible from the air. A Jacaranda tree grew wild in majestic loneliness in a green meadow that stretched north, south, and east for miles, stopped in the west only by the blue Pacific Ocean.

They landed next to the ancient tree. Four doors opened upward, making the vehicle look like a four-winged eagle. The new recruits poured out.

Virgil smoothed down his toga and surveyed his group of trainees. They would help him acquire a certain artifact for his private collection.

He gestured at the green field, the huge purple canopy of the tree, the blue ocean. "Exactly in this spot, in a little house with a red door, lived Elektra, Gina, and their dog Max. Their best friend Sophie had lost her twin sister Peggy. Or maybe Peggy lost Sophie."

Virgil couldn't remember exactly who lived and who died in any particular reality. Those small details were drowned by the great eternity.

He pulled out a rolled-up cigar. Immediately, Chaos jumped up and offered him a lighter.

Virgil took a deep inhale and thought of his long-ago friend. She would have loved this new strain he had named *Willful Elektra*.

He pointed at the Jacaranda. "This magical tree conceals within its roots a protected bubble." He gestured an approximation with his hands. "It's yea big."

They searched until Chaos came upon a sharp plastic edge. She used a pickaxe to loosen up the hardened earth around the flowering tree. She dug deeper, pulled on the thing, and wiggled it until a bag finally slid out of the earth.

The bag—called Ziploc in that long-ago reality—was the obsolete kind that sealed hermetically. When Virgil unzipped it, another, similar bag was inside. The book *Fucking My Way Through Life* slid out, mostly undamaged except for the bite marks in one corner.

"We have so many copies of it already," Chaos said.

"This one is signed and inscribed by the author, and look at this corner." He chuckled sadly. "Chewed up by Max."

He opened the book to its title page.

The inscription read: *Nothing would ever be perfect, not even heaven, and for most of us, paradise is purgatory at best. Yet my paradise is the love that moves the sun and the other stars. Elektra Brooke via Dante Alighieri.*

In the current reality, Dante had never been published and Elektra never existed.

"I need a moment alone," he said. "Go look around."

As he riffled through the pages, a photograph fell out, and slowly, like a leaf, landed on a carpet of purple-violet flowers. The faces of Elektra, Gina, Sophie, and Max smiled up at him when he picked it up.

Here, on this carpet of flowers, they got married, he thought, wiping away a tear.

"What's this picture?" Chaos asked.

"This was paradise." Virgil slipped the photo into his toga, close to his heart. "This was home."

Night was falling. Above him, far off in the dark sky, glittered a blanket of stars.

End #2

For Claire

My writing teacher, my beloved Aussie guru, my wickedly-witty friend and mentor, thank you for that look that said, "Stop whinging and write the ending first." Thank you for teaching me how to walk into fiction. Thank you for telling me that brevity is god and that nothing, even sadness, is wasted on a novelist. Every budding writer should have a Claire like you. How lucky I was to make it in time to give you my first published novel! You will forever be part of me, in all that I am, in every word I write, in every life experience.

About the Author

Award winning author Victoria Avilan was born in Israel in 1957, where she learned art from her mother, and cared for sick NICU babies as a military nurse. She studied creative writing at UCLA with Australian author Claire McNab. When she isn't scribbling away or twisting herself into complex yoga poses, Victoria still saves lives as a Neonatal Intensive Care Nurse. She lives in Southern California with her wife Tracey and their Cocker Spaniels.

Made in the USA
Columbia, SC
27 July 2024

1b3b9ab4-372c-4d26-aaf6-9e11f0456520R01